"The tales in *A Plague of Shadows* are captivating and entertaining. Put simply, they are amazing. Without doubt, this collection of ghost stories is the best anthology I've read in years."

— Tony Tremblay, author of *The Moore House* and *The Seeds of Nightmare*

"This collection of 20 stories will leave you wondering what lurks in the gloom behind that half-open closet door or in the mists that shroud the streets in the wee hours of the morning. ... Would send shivers up M.R. James' back and have Poe reaching for extra lamps. I recommend it highly!"

— JG Faherty, author of *The Cure*, *The Burning Time*, and *Carnival of Fear*

"*A Plague of Shadows* is this year's 'don't-miss' anthology. Some of the stories creep up on you, while others come at you full force. In the end, all of them will lurk in the back of your mind, just waiting for the lights to be turned off."

— Shaun Meeks, author of *Shutdown* and *At the Gates of Madness*

"This is the kind of book writers and readers need. Writers need it because it showcases their work and readers because it offers fresh perspectives on complex subjects."

— Paul Dale Anderson, author of *The Instruments of Death* series

"Gloriously dark and gripping, the stories and poems in *A Plague of Shadows* will burrow under your skin and make themselves at home. Highly recommended!"

— Christina Sng, Bram Stoker Award winning author of *A Collection of Nightmares*

"Shadows take many forms: from past mistakes to uncertain futures, from unresolved relationships to unanswered questions. The shadows in the pages of this anthology are guaranteed to prey on your psyche and leave you gasping for breath."

— Suzie Wargo Lockhart, Executive Editor at Digital Fiction Publishing Corp.

"All the speculative fiction stories—whether they concern ghosts, engineering malfunctions, post-apocalyptic, cultural beliefs, and crime sprees—are exciting and compelling to read. Each story should be read in one sitting to appreciate the twists, turns, and surprise endings."

— Frank Hopkins, author of *Abandoned Houses: Vietnam Revenge Murders*

A Written Remains Anthology

Praise for the previous Written Remains anthology
SOMEONE WICKED

"This is a perfect example of a top-notch collection of mostly spectacular stories from a wide array of authors."

"I particularly enjoy the diversity of writing styles that are showcased in this anthology ... the authors lend a distinct voice to their stories, an almost trademark for their individual talent. ... SOMEONE WICKED is a huge win for me."

"It is one of the best anthologies I have read in recent years."

"There is a dark tone, but there is also some real humor and some fairy tales in the mix. And the best part is, they all flow so well together. There is not a story to miss in this one."

"The introduction described the anthology like an all you can eat seafood restaurant where readers can pick and choose based on their tastes. But it would be difficult to find a story in the collection that isn't worth a second helping."

A PLAGUE OF SHADOWS

A Written Remains Anthology

Edited by JM Reinbold & Weldon Burge

Smart Rhino Publications
www.smartrhino.com

CONTENTS

ACKNOWLEDGMENTS

Thanks go to Tomoki Hayasaka for his amazing cover illustration, to Ju Kim for designing the cover, and to Terri Gillespie and Gail Husch for their excellent proofreading skills.

Thanks also to the Written Remains Writers Guild for their marvelous contributions to this collection of stories. It would not have been possible without them!

STARVING TIME, JAMESTOWN 1609

BY JANE MILLER

My seed rattled in the bowl
of my wife, begging.

No more ribbed beef
with sagging hides. Nor cats,
nor mice. No shoes for winter.
Eaten. Starvation took the dog.
No frogs drumming. No
songbirds. No stopping
the crickets' parched song.

In this drought, nothing
rose to sun but my hand lifting
a stone. I panted at the labor,

tossed the shriveled unborn,
a negative of us light would never see
in the dirty swirl of the James.

Her blood was warm. I nursed,
readied the fire and gave her thanks
until men came at the smell of meat.

They noose my thumbs and leave me
to hang heavy where weak.

I remember her ankles,
her bare feet. Mine swing weighted
in this savage place. I feel my wife and child
pull on me. What held them last,
breaking.

I confess. I will burn in winter
for what I salted and I ate.

They do not believe a wife's duty is to feed.

BARK OF THE DOG-FACED GIRL

BY MARIA MASINGTON

The gestation period for a walrus is 465 days. A black rhinoceros fetus takes 450 days to develop. But they've got nothing on me. I brewed for 10 years from the crisp morning of my conception until my violent birth a decade later, when I emerged fully developed, fully formed, and excellent at my job. Family rumor has it the porcelain-skinned toddler was a happy, singing, dancing chatterbox who smiled easily and had an awesome imagination, until the day I found my way into the womb of her tiny soul and began to gestate, and learn.

Her blonde mother's name was Betty, and the dog was Jughead. So, when the couple's black-haired infant girl was born, they thought it Archie Comics destiny, and named her Veronica. I arrived in embryo form one October morning when Veronica was three years old, in their Halloween-decorated house that had pumpkins on the front porch and a princess costume hanging in a closet. But Veronica had changed her mind and now wanted to be a bride for Halloween. She was supposed to be napping when she snuck into her parents' bedroom and began her costume design. She hummed "The Wedding March" as she put a plastic tiara on her head, and rifled through Betty's lingerie drawer until she found the perfect gown: a white, nylon half-slip, the kind that all proper women owned in the '60s.

Veronica slipped it over her head and admired herself in her mother's full-length mirror. Then the little fool stood at the top of the stairs and started singing, "Here comes the bride, all dressed in white." Unable to hang onto the railing, arms pinned at her sides in the makeshift gown, her pink-socked feet slipped on the polished wood of the step. It was impossible to break the fall.

She tumbled, arms and legs encased in the slip, step after step, her face taking the brunt of the fall. In that split second, when the sharp edge of the bottom step cracked into her nose and mouth and cheekbones, before Betty got there to provide comfort, before Jughead started barking in distress, even before Veronica began to cry, a piece of the beautiful child died, and a wisp of me swept in and took seed.

Facial wounds are the best. The tiniest cut causes a lot of bleeding. So, as the blood gushed from her nose and mouth, I slipped in through the void where a front baby tooth had been and began a parasitic relationship with her tiny body. With one misstep, this young soul went from joyous to broken, adorable to distorted, and that is when evil ghosts like me know when to make our move and find our homes. Ghosts are born of opportunity—we enter the picture when someone dies, a house is abandoned, a body is laid to rest, but I am special and I needed a special host.

Veronica's body was the perfect chamber for ghoulish growth, and I germinated inside her tiny being for 10 years. I was well-nourished on her insecurities, quenched my thirst with her incessant tears, and learned well. Eventually, I would become a full-fledged haunting machine. They say beauty is skin-deep, but let me tell you the truth that I learned as I grew inside this damaged child. Beauty may be skin-deep, but ugly goes to the pit of your being, every molecule of your make up. People place value on the packaging, and anyone who denies it is a liar.

Betty and her husband did everything to make it better. Veronica had smocked dresses from exclusive boutiques, hairbands, diamond-stud earrings, professional haircuts, and ballet lessons, with the requisite pink tutus and rhinestone tiaras. But, as she heard one of the fathers joke after a recital, "You can put lipstick on a pig, but it's still a pig." Oink, oink! I delighted in that!

They lied and told her that if you were smart enough, funny enough, or charming enough, looks did not matter. But she and I knew the truth. The beautiful baby in the portrait over the mantel was now a hatchet-faced little girl, and she would be mine to haunt and torture. No one likes ugly people, and I took notes as I grew in the uterus of her subconscious on how others treated her.

I watched a little girl hand out birthday invitations on the playground. She teasingly handed one to a longing Veronica, then pulled it away and said, "You can't come, my mother says you're ugly." On Valentine's Day, while other children had dozens of heart-shaped greetings, Veronica only got a few cards from the compliant children of nice mothers who made them give a card to everyone in the class. A tougher soul would have started plotting a Carrie-esque revenge, but Veronica was a kind, sensitive girl who, fortunately for me, interpreted that she was not just ugly but unlovable. Every mean jab, every stare was like an iron supplement that made me stronger, built my haunting muscle, and made me scarier than hell.

My best ghost training started in St. Monica's sixth grade where, in the 1970s, bullying was not only allowed, but the motto should have been *salvos aptissimum*—survival of the fittest. It was obvious that even the teachers liked the pretty, athletic kids the best, much more than they liked the smart kids or the kids whose parents donated a lot of money. Even in my embryonic "mean-ghost" state, I could tell the teachers, too, wanted to be popular, wanted to make up for sitting home playing Monopoly with their parents on prom night or being stuffed into a locker after their 1964 high school gym class.

St. Monica's was my finishing school, where I learned the simple tricks to become more vicious than I had ever hoped. The hallowed grounds, with statues of saints on pedestals, crucifixes above the doorways, and girls in baby-poop brown kilts and boys with Kelly-green blazers. The nuns wore full habits and lay teachers donned cheap polyester suits and shoddy McCall's patterns skirts that they'd sewn themselves. While my ghost colleagues learned to say "Boo" and rattle chains, I learned the real scary stuff. I learned that you can tell an 11-year-old girl she is pretty a thousand times, and she won't believe you. But tell her she is ugly, just once, and you have succeeded in haunting her for the rest of her life. Almost too easy, too good to be true. The stairwells were the best, with their stale smell, sticky handrails, and calligraphied *Our Fathers* in frames—places adults tried to avoid and where meanness blossomed.

First it was quacking. Pairs of girls would walk behind Veronica and quack and giggle. It did not take her long to catch on, quacking at the ugly duckling. How easy the lessons I learned in these stairwells. Two quacks and she dissolved into tears! One particularly mean girl named Leigh Ann made it even better. Leigh Ann boasted that she had no ugly, fat, stupid, or poor friends, so she was one of my heroes. She turned it into a little ditty, "Quack, quack, you ugly duck, no boy would want to fuck." If Veronica was the mother womb in which I grew, Leigh Ann was the father figure who fertilized the ghoulish egg, bulked up my mean-ghost muscle, made sure I would be the scariest ghost around when I was finally born a few years later.

The boys were also helpful, usually boys interested in Leigh Ann. Like cats bringing mice home for their masters, they, too, taught me stairwell lessons. Pushing in front of Veronica, they'd race past her, stand on the steps above her, look down and bark in her face, "Woof, woof, woof." Ahhhh ... easy as pie. Even better, once I saw a mousy teacher, Miss Miller, standing at the top of the steps when it happened, and I noticed the tiniest hint of an evil smile, which taught me an important lesson. We ghosts need to work extra hard to evoke terror, because human beings are scary enough on their own.

After growing inside Veronica for a decade, I came to life on the day they fixed her face. I was born on Tuesday, June 7th, 1977 at 10:20 a.m. in an operating room. I prepared to emerge as IV medication knocked her ugly mug out for the count. I waited while the first incisions were made, precise scalpel lines that opened her flesh and then emerged during the exciting, violent crescendo they call "reshaping." Reshaping is the most dramatic part of the surgery and includes wonderfully horrific-sounding tools and noises—forceps, bone rasps, retractors, and a metal mallet called the "bone crusher." While they snipped and crunched and cracked, I journeyed through Veronica's left Eustachian tube, into the auditory canal, and drew my first ghostly breath hovering in her outer ear—my permanent home, perched on an invisible halo of self-doubt.

I emerged in the presence of a masked surgeon, two nurses, the reek of antiseptic, and the rusty-nail smell of Veronica's blood. And then I heard the first noise I'd ever heard on the outside, coming from a transistor radio, a smooth voice singing, "Ain't gonna bump no more with no big fat woman." That's when I gave myself the moniker of Joe Tex. Admit it, that's a good ghost name! Joe Tex had entered the world and it would not be long until my life's work began.

Ghosts take many forms, from vaporous, misty figures floating down hallways to banal white-sheet types. But, again, I would be unique. I was born invisible, but with a deep baritone voice, audible only to Veronica. Just an hour later, Veronica's father came into the recovery room with flowers and said, "Hi, Doll Face." Too easy! I used my new voice, and whispered in her ear, *Dog Face*. I saw it register in her eyes.

"What did you say?" she asked her father.

"Hi, Doll Face." *Dog Face*, I whispered simultaneously. The magic slipper fit. This is what I was born to do, and I was good at it. Everything she would hear, I would reframe and repeat. She would never trust the mirror, her loved ones, or herself. No surgeon can undo ugly when Joe Tex is on the scene!

When they gave her a mirror, I had to use my imagination a little bit. *You'll never get rid of those dark circles under your eyes.* When she read the note that came with flowers aloud, "For pretty Veronica," I said, *God knows what you look like under those bandages.* When she could not get the aluminum-foil taste out of her throat, I said, *Everyone can probably smell it. You probably smell like a cat carcass.*

The good part about being a ghost is that I do not require sleep or food or vacation—24/7 I would be here to remind her. For weeks I wormed around in Veronica's head, wondering what she would look like when the bandages came off. At the unveiling ceremony, I saw the bruising was significant but the result was obvious. She looked normal. Average and nothing to write home about, but for Veronica it was like the gates of hell swung wide open. My job would be to keep the flames licking at her heels.

The opportunity came swiftly as the doctor used the skinny clamp to pull packing out of her nose, extracting it from inside her face, feet and feet of it. The doctor kept pulling, and piling the soiled bandages on the exam table. *It looks like afterbirth,* I whispered into her ear. *It reeks like rotting flesh.*

My job got harder in ways I could not predict. Everyone was nicer to her because she looked better. People who always had loved her now loved her more. People who were mean to her were now tolerant. Joe Tex, here, had to up his game. For the first time, other kids were saying "Hi" to Veronica in the hallways, which made her so happy. I had to stop it. At least once a day, when one of the more popular kids acknowledged her with, "Hi, Veronica," I'd jump in and say, *That was a pity hello, Hatchet Face,* just to keep her in line.

The better she felt about herself, the harder I had to work. How many different ways are there to call someone ugly? It became a game as I stewed amid the canopy bed, shag carpet, and the reek of Love's Baby Soft. I thought of a different word each day to remind her who she was: grisly, grotesque, hideous, unsightly, foul, repugnant, revolting, repulsive. What I said was gospel, and Halloween was especially fun. *You don't need a mask! They can rent you out to haunt houses.* I even got a shout-out when she attended her first dance. While the surgeon-sculpted wallflower stood around in her gypsy costume, the DJ played my theme song, Joe Tex, singing "Ain't gonna bump no more."

Then came what would become my biggest challenge, when boys started to notice her. When The Snowflake Dance rolled around, Veronica had integrated enough with the other kids that a hormonal 13-year-old boy, who smelled like a goat and had the IQ of a rock, asked her to be his date. When he stopped her in the cafeteria and asked her to the dance, I growled in her ear, *It's a trick! Who would ask you to a dance? He's going to make a fool out of you!* So effective was yours truly that Veronica did not even answer, but broke into tears and ran to the nurse's office. But, alas, a ghost's work is never done, and that night my plan was ruined. The walking hormone's mother called Betty to say that her son was upset and he wanted to take Veronica to the dance. Meddling bitches! The next thing I knew, she's calling him from the Princess phone in her Pepto-Bismol pink room, apologizing, and telling him she would love to go with him, and the nightmare had begun.

The problem with Veronica was all the work she'd done before her plastic surgery. It's one thing to haunt a dummy, but this girl had been working on her personality and intellect for years. She spoke three languages, played three instruments, and was on the path to graduate a year early. We'd move out of the pink prison bedroom into a dorm room with another loser Vassar wannabe feminist, but she would always be an ugly duck and I knew the buttons to push.

Boys and beauty were Veronica's buttons, fear that no one would love her and, for her, what seemed even worse, that no man would ever "want" her. It was so big, this fear of being undesirable, that it was child's play. When she began going to coed parties, I had a field day. As she stood in the shower with her new bottle of Gee, Your Hair Smells Terrific, I snarled, *Gee, your hair smells like shit!* When she'd open her makeup case, stocked with dozens of powders and creams, I said, *Jeez, no one's that freaking ugly!* She would cry, real tears, every single time!

When she thought, "I wonder what I should wear?" I yelled *A bag over your head!* This boy-girl party thing was so much fun!

I knew it was going to happen soon, some desperate blowhard kid was going to make a move on her. She was going to melt like ice cream in his hands, so I practiced many ways to ruin it for her. Fall 1979, my prediction came true at the Homecoming dance. Gold disco dress right out of *Saturday Night Fever*, Candies "fuck-me shoes," and a rutting moose named Patrick who came from Fighting Irish Stock. His many impressive talents included imitating Donald Duck and opening beer bottles with his teeth. God forbid she should be attractive to someone higher up on the food chain! Figures, she settled for the first male appendage that pointed in her direction.

They missed the first half of the dance. After he picked her up and Betty took the obligatory photos with that disgusting dog Jughead sitting between Ugly and the Irish kid on the couch, they left in his old man's 1974 Grand Torino. Right away he starts complimenting her, how smart she is, how nice to everyone, how beautiful. *I'm going to vomit!* I hissed into her ear. "I want to make love to you, Veronica," he said. This kid "making love" was about as likely as him dancing *Swan Lake*, but it was the moment she longed for. She didn't care about Vassar. She just didn't want to die a virgin.

We parked in the back of St. Monica's lot, behind the dumpsters. While they drank Boone's Farm Tickle Pink and kissed, I worked fast, as I figured this blockhead had the staying power of a two-minute egg, and that was being generous. With one Candies on the floor and the other against the rear window, her dress bunched around her neck, he mumbled nice things as I screamed into her thick head, *He should throw a flag over your head and do it for glory! The last time Patrick had to stare at a face that ugly, he fed it a banana. No Patrick, it's Veronica's face, not a baboon ass.*

When it was over, I knew I had gotten into her head good, even while the hard-on was getting into her pants. So desperate was this pathetic creature that she was happy, even with all my one-liners, that she would not die a virgin. Of course, the girl was so sure that no one would ever want her that she was not prepared, and stupid Patrick thought you could not get pregnant the first time, and by Christmas our little non-virgin was two months gone with an Irish-Italian train wreck.

The popped cherry on top of this surgically altered sundae was that Veronica was proud of being knocked up. She had no regret for spreading her legs for the first numbskull who gave her a second glance. No one was barking at her now. Of course, they were calling her a slut, but she didn't care, she was proud for the world to know someone had wanted her.

Within 24 hours of the crying and gnashing of teeth that went on at the house on learning the bad news, Veronica's father had brokered a private adoption with one of his aging partners who had married a young chick and for some reason could not hit the mark. It was all worked out. The accident would make its grand appearance in June, after graduation; would be adopted by the cradle-robbing partner; and then, by mid-August, Veronica and I would be off to Vassar.

Lucky for me, there were pregnancy symptoms that were wonderful: weight gain, stretch marks, varicose veins. The fat factor was particularly fun! As she carefully Noxzemaed her face at night, I'd say, *Don't worry, Veronica, your face is becoming— becoming even fatter and uglier.* When she'd undress in front of the full-length mirror, I'd wait until she'd look up and see her full face, stretching breasts, and big maternity underwear in the mirror and yell, *Beast!* And like magic, her puffy eyes would swell with tears.

And then, like a gift from the ghost gods, Veronica got what the doctor called "pregnancy mask," in the form of *brown patches* on her forehead and cheeks! As she tearfully inspected them in the mirror and tried to cover them with makeup, I'd tell her matter-of-factly, *Every girl has the right to be ugly, but you've abused the privilege.*

When she was weeks away from delivery, and all her friends were off smoking pot and making out with boys—like during prom and senior week—Veronica was stuck home sitting on the couch with Jughead and Betty watching *Fantasy*

Island. It was not enough that her friends were in ball gowns and bikinis, or that she was suffering from hemorrhoids and swollen ankles, but I was always present, *You're so ugly now, the garbage collectors won't even pick you up. There's only one problem with your face, Veronica—it shows!*

Graduation Day was a weird day, even for yours truly. It was Veronica's 18th birthday and it was the day she gave birth, but those were not the weirdest parts. Back at the hospital where I was born, back to the smells of bleach and disinfectant, silver metal tables, paper-thin sheets and gowns, and a delivery process spiked with my weapon of choice, horrible, scary-sounding words like "ruptured membranes," "episiotomy," "afterbirth." Thirteen hours after it started, Veronica reproduced.

But after the offspring had sprung, it happened. Perhaps something was wrong with my hearing, or maybe it was all the commotion in the room, but then I heard it a second time and I knew something was really out of whack. When the nurse brought the product of Veronica and Patrick's seven seconds in heaven over to her to see, I said, *Woof! Woof!*

Congratulations, the dog had a puppy! This was the first time I thought I heard it.

As she stared at the baby, who the adoptive parents named Mary, Veronica leaned down and kissed it. Right then, I whispered, *Scary Mary! Here's another one who will need the plastic surgeon.* And that's when I was sure. She said it a second time, with her lips right against the baby's cheek—but this time I was positive I'd heard correctly.

She told me to go fuck myself.

I had to think. Something was horribly wrong with this picture. I acted quickly. I left Veronica's body and brain for the first time in 15 years, and floated down the hallways to the same operating room where I had been born. There she was, young Genevieve, having a large wine-stain birthmark removed from her forehead. I entered through the open flesh, and started to think of *scarred face* and *marred face* comments. I sang to myself, "Ain't gonna bump no more with no big fat women," until my new host awoke from the anesthesia.

THE STORIES THAT WE TELL

BY BILLIE SUE MOSIMAN

I don't know what sins I've committed that sent me to the frigid wasteland of northern Alaska—and during the Cold War at that. Brian, the radar tech, and I have often sat mulling—over steaming cups of the blackest coffee we could make—to figure out how we came to be stationed in this freezing hell. Being a government employee means taking a risk on where in the world you might wind up, but two years' duty in desolate Alaska seems the cruelest punishment. And for my friend Brian, the deadliest.

He has done something unforgivable, and they have sent a Corps team to check us out. Tomorrow the plane should land and they will take Brian away. If I had the strength to argue, I'd beg them to take me, too.

It's the isolation that either makes you mad or kills you. They tell me a few years ago another recruit went insane and had to be locked up in a supply room for months before they could ship him out. If he'd been allowed to run amok, they feared he would have murdered everyone at the base. Another time at a Chinese research base in this region, two men argued over a sandwich and one buried an ax in the other man's head.

If only we had locked Brian away ...

It began with stories. The days and nights are interminable here. Once our stations are secure and all the work complete, the hours stretch out before us like years until the next day can begin. Brian came from Alabama. He had a soft drawl and a sunny smile. At least he did back in the beginning. We had struck up a friendship early on. He had been in Alaska for two years already when I shipped in. Since I was a replacement in Brian's sector and new and raw, he took me under his wing. The first year of my exile, we played games to pass the time. Cards, dominoes, chess, darts. Brian nearly always won. He was quick-witted and able to recognize patterns inside patterns, giving him the edge in most competitions. After a while, when it appeared I'd never improve and he would always be the victor, he suggested that I might like to hear some of the old tales he had heard or experienced as a boy in the rural South.

"Sure," I said, happy to be freed of the role of loser. "I'd love to hear some stories."

During those first few months of storytelling, after work we'd take our mugs over to the heating vent in the corner of the radar room where it was quiet and warm. Brian told me about watching his grandfather pick cotton on the farm; the ice cream socials on warm summer evenings; many hunting and fishing stories involving detailed descriptions of rifles, shotguns, frog gigs, 'coons run up trees, the proper way to tan hides; and the best bait for catching bass and catfish in country fishing holes. Being from Chicago, a city boy all my life, these stories were of great interest. Picking cotton? The boles with their spiny covers that made the fingers bleed? Gigging frogs with a trident, taking them home to fry the legs for dinner? It was like an entirely new and strange world, and Brian made it vivid and real for me so that I could hear the whippoorwills calling in the woods, I could see flocks of yellow butterflies hovering over a field of high green grass, I could smell the scent of wild meat frying in a big, black skillet.

"Damn, you tell good stories," I told Brian. "Makes me wish I had grown up in the South."

"Oh, the South has dark days, too," he said cryptically. "Dark and ugly days." Then he left it at that.

The stories passed the time—the long, empty time that began to weigh like a row-long sack of cotton on the mind. It was time that was the enemy of all of us in this Alaskan station. Men on the base used obsessions to get them through the hours. I knew guys who kept mice (shipped to them through the mail from a supplier in South Dakota), catalogued music, put together endless model car kits, wrote daily letters home, or watched old movies until they knew all the dialogue. It was like prison at the radar station, each man to himself, trying to pass the days. Telling stories was just one more way to beat down the loneliness.

I noticed after several months of swapping stories— because I told a few myself—that, just as in playing games, Brian was the better storyteller. I had to admit that coming from Chicago, raised by a single mother and having no extended family, my stories were dull and mostly uneventful. Just to stay alive, my mom and I had to work hard. It's all I remember either of us doing, working and working. Who had time for family stories?

Then one week a couple of months ago, Brian said, "I could tell you strange tales you might not believe."

"Strange? Like having a watermelon eat-off using no hands isn't strange? Like tracking a bobcat that ends up ripping apart your uncle so he's scarred for life is a tale that isn't strange?" I laughed and slapped my knee the way I thought old people in Alabama might behave when tickled pink. "How strange a story can you get up to anyway, Brian?" I just couldn't stop grinning. He knew I wasn't making fun of him and where he was from. I'd already let him know how I admired him and his background for being so colorful and amazing. Whereas I had been a kid growing up in the streets and alleys, frequenting little corner stores and pool halls, Brian had woods and forests, lakes and creeks, wilderness and people who were comfortable with all that Nature-in-the-Wildwood.

Brian cleared his throat. "Well, I know some ghost stories and I know about a few odd murders that happened back then. But the best of all is the night Betsy Ann and I were out parking and making out when this man ..."

"What man?" Even Brian's tone of voice was different from when he told other stories to me. This one was much more serious.

"He had been around our little village ever since I could remember. No one had anything to do with him. They said he'd been to Korea and lost his arm and it made him crazy. He was always carrying on to anyone who would listen, how they sawed off his arm at the elbow in the POW camp to try to break him."

"Well, shit." I hunched forward in my chair, listening hard now.

Brian shrugged. "I don't know if it's true. He might have lost it in a fire fight, shrapnel or something, who knows. Most people thought he was so damn nuts that anything he claimed couldn't be true. I used to go to sleep at night and have nightmares about someone sawing off the guy's arm. His name was Folcum. I don't know his first name, I don't know if anyone knew it. He lived alone in a cabin in the woods that had once belonged to his folks—who were dead and gone by then—and he didn't have a lot to do with anybody. They all just called him Folcum as in, 'Here comes that crazy Folcum again.'"

"So he had just one arm?"

"No, he had two. I mean, he had one and then he had a hook for the other. They'd fixed his missing limb with one of those mechanized things that had two metal finger-like appendages on the end of it. He could open and close them to pick up things. The two contraptions curved when they were closed so they looked like a hook. He'd wave that at the kids around the country store to scare them."

"So what happened when you were out parking with your girl?" This sounded more and more like an urban legend to me. I'd heard the story about the man with the hook and the parked lovers. I couldn't quite bring myself to disbelieve Brian's story, though. It hadn't seemed to me he'd ever told me lies before, so why would he tell me one now?

"Well, I was 16 and Betsy Ann was just 15. Her folks wouldn't let her go on dates yet, but they let me drive her to church on Sunday nights. I'd come early and say we were going to stop for an RC at the store before church. We never did, of course. Instead, we took that extra half hour or so to turn down a little-used road that led to the old baseball diamond, park under the pines, and make out like bandits. By the time we got to church we'd be so flushed and horny, we'd have to keep our heads down like we were being so pious and hope the high color in our cheeks would go away before anyone noticed and suspected what we'd been up to.

"One Sunday night in late winter, we had the windows rolled up against the cool evening, and we're sitting in the front seat with our tongues in one another's mouths and I had Russian hands and roving fingers, as we used to say. I was all over that girl. Betsy Ann was a hot babe with very large tits for such a young girl and I was hoping eventually she'd let me have her, totally, you know?

"Anyway, we both hear the scrape of metal against metal and it came from the back driver's side door handle. I was driving my Dad's old Chevy Bel Air.

"It's real dark under the pines, can't even see the stars and there was no moonrise yet that night. We stop in the middle of a kiss, our lips frozen fast as Popsicles to each other, and when Betsy Ann pulled away, we heard it again.

"'What's that?' she said, and for the life of me I couldn't imagine. All I knew was suddenly I was too afraid to turn around in the seat to look back there. 'It's nothing,' I said, trying to believe it myself.

"Betsy Ann was looking back now, so I forced myself. I couldn't be a wuss, could I? I didn't see anything, but it occurred to me the sound we'd heard could have been made by Folcum's weird-ass, metal-hooked hand grabbing hold of the door handle. I put the thought right out of my head as fast as I thought it. It scared the hell out of me.

"I told Betsy Ann she could see for herself it was nothing. Time was running out for us to be at church, so I pulled her over to me for one more kiss, had just gotten my hand on her breast when the sound, louder, came again. I flinched, jerked around in the seat to look back, and saw ... nothing."

"That's damn creepy," I told Brian. "Was it Folcum, you think?"

"It sure was. I don't know what he was trying to do, scare us, play a trick, or get in the car with us, but I started up the car quick and took off. I saw his silhouette behind us in the rearview. Him and his awful arm."

"So what happened then?" I was perched all the way to the edge of my chair. Brian had me now. Brian had me in the clutches of his storytelling so hard that I wasn't even in Alaska anymore, freezing my ass off in a cavernous radar room, drinking mud coffee. I was in an Alabama night with a strange, deformed man stalking a pair of young lovers. I believed every single word of it.

Brian hung his head and contemplated his coffee mug, swirling the liquid there, watching the small well of darkness slosh. He had aged in the dim light. He looked to be struggling with bad memories and might be about to change the subject when he quietly said, "When spring came, Folcum killed little Betsy Ann."

Shocked, I sat back in my chair with a thud. "He didn't. He didn't really."

Brian looked up from his cup. I saw the truth written in his eyes. His girl, Betsy Ann, had been murdered. *It was true.* All of it was true. This was a story Brian never wanted to tell and, because it haunted him, because it rose like a creature of the night in his dreams, he had let it out and he had told someone. Now I carried the story as if it was a bucket and the handle was welded to my hand. I owned the story the same as Brian did. Betsy Ann was my girl, too, and I grieved for her as if she had been a real girl in my own life.

Brian continued, "Folcum caught her walking home from a girlfriend's house one late afternoon toward the end of May. School had just ended and summer stretched before us like a dream. He dragged her into the woods at the edge of the road and ... and ..."

My imagination was way ahead of the story. I knew what Folcum had done and what life had been lost. I resisted the urge to stand up abruptly and leave the radar room before he could say any more.

"They found her three days later. She'd been strangled and mutilated. She'd managed to tear off a snippet of the shirt Folcum had been wearing. Her hand clutched it. When they went to pick him up, they found him without his mechanical arm. He always wore that thing, so they went searching for it in the house and found it had been bent all to hell. It wouldn't work anymore. And there was some of Betsy Ann's blond hair caught in the pincers like he'd tried to hold her head down by her hair."

"Jesus, that's awful, Brian. It must have shocked your whole community."

Brian looked up and a sly, ferret look came into his dark eyes. "While Folcum was out on bail, he disappeared." Brian smiled and a shiver of apprehension ran up my spine.

"He left the state or something?" Brian just stared at me. "You don't mean ... you're not saying ..."

"No, he didn't leave the state, he left the planet. I caught him out behind his house and dragged the bastard down to the creek and held his head under until he stopped fighting. He only had one arm. He couldn't fight me off. I threw his stupid metal hook arm into the deepest part of a fishing hole and I guess it's still there today."

"You killed him?" I whispered.

Brian stood up and stretched. "Bedtime," he announced. "I've told enough stories for tonight."

I couldn't sleep for thinking about Brian being a killer. I understood the grief and pain his girlfriend's death must have cost him, but he took the law into his own hands. Is that what they always did in the South? Was that idyllic picture I had of it as twisted as a corkscrew? What Brian had confessed to was one cold business.

But then he called all these tales "stories," and maybe he just made them up.

It wasn't until he really lost it and went berserk at the outpost that I truly believed he was capable of murder and had probably killed Folcum, just as he claimed.

* * *

It was weeks after he'd told me about the man with the hooked arm and the death of Betsy Ann that Brian started acting weird. He stopped telling me stories and clammed up tight. He didn't want to play cards or watch videos or throw darts. He started keeping to himself in his quarters and, when I went to see about him, he was gruff and unfriendly. I asked him, "What's gotten into you? What's wrong?"

He claimed to have headaches, they were killing him. The station medic wouldn't prescribe anything stronger than aspirin. Radar techs have to be careful about what medications they take. No one wanted them seeing flying saucers or incoming missiles on the screens.

I left him alone and started reading an Edgar Allan Poe collection of stories I found in the station library. I worried about Brian, but if he didn't want my company, I was not about to force it on him.

The shift radar techs started coming to me and asking if I knew what was wrong with Brian. I was his friend, I should know what was up. He'd been saying he heard things and couldn't keep his mind on the radar blips. Couldn't they *hear it*, he asked them over and over, that terrible scraping sound like someone outside the hut dragging something metallic along the corrugated metal sides?

They couldn't hear anything, they claimed. They were afraid Brian was losing it and might have to be shipped out on the next available transport. "See about him," they said. "Do something."

I stood in the rec room, staring at the coffeepot, thinking whether I wanted to pour a cup or not. It looked like black poison. I decided not. I went to the nearest window and stared outside into the dark. Security lights spread a white light over white snow; the world was white and silent and so empty. I knew the guys were probably right—Brian was in real big trouble. He shouldn't have talked about Folcum and that May night of murder. He shouldn't have told me about the creek and the drowning. It was hard on me keeping that kind of secret. You shouldn't have to know about a murder—no matter how deserved—and care so much for the murderer.

Snow began to fall, the light winking and speckling outside the ice-rimmed window, the night drawing nearer as if slithering softly toward the compound, the emptiness beyond the night growing into galactic proportions.

I hurried to face Brian in his quarters. If I was chosen to save him from himself, then I would do the best I could. The entire base was constructed of Quonset huts made of corrugated metal and fully insulated on the inside. Nevertheless, you could still hear the rising of the wind wailing out there and once in a while the creak of shifting ice or the thunder of a far-off avalanche falling into the Sound, but I knew that's not what Brian thought he was hearing. He'd become obsessed with a mechanical hooked arm.

"Brian, the other guys in radar are threatening to go to the C.O. about you. It's serious. We have to do something."

He looked up at me from where he lay on his bunk and said, "They don't hear it, or they pretend they don't. Did they admit to you they heard it?"

"It's that story you told me, Brian. About Betsy Ann. It's like you let it take over your mind or something. You're imagining those sounds."

He jerked up in bed, sitting rigid, his head cocked to one side. He glanced over at the small square of dark window. "You heard that, right? Didn't you?! Don't lie about it."

I shook my head slowly. "Wind, that's all it is. It's snowing and the north wind is up. It's the damn *wind*, Brian."

"Wind can't thunk against the side of the building and then rumble down the side, slapping those corrugated valleys. You're lying, just like the others. You hear it, you know he's there, but you just won't admit it."

I walked over and took him by the shoulders and shook him hard. "Snap out of it! You've been here in Alaska too damn long, that's all. Your mind is starting to play tricks on you, it happens to a lot of guys. Folcum's dead. You told me so yourself, you killed him, he's *dead*."

Brian wrenched free and pushed me back. "Get out of my room. I want to be alone. You never were my friend, you prick."

I gave up in defeat. I'd have to go to the C.O. myself, explain how this came about. I wouldn't tell them the story about Folcum, but I'd plead for Brian's relocation before his obsession spread any further. Sometimes a superstition or an idea that gets loose in such close confines has a way of spreading like a contagion in the air. It can infect everyone.

* * *

Brian's first victim was an office clerk sent by the C.O. to summon Brian for an interview. Somewhere Brian had found a lead pipe and, after he invited the private to enter his room, he cold-cocked him right in the head. They say the man was dead before he dropped, his skull cracked right down the center of his forehead.

When the body was discovered, Brian was gone and not to be found. A massive search was put on, the entire base under emergency alert. We had an escaped killer on our hands. We had a man driven by the searing cold, the isolation, and old bad memories, who was on a rampage. It wasn't as if it hadn't happened before, but this time it was my friend, it was someone I thought I'd known well. I knew he had to be stopped for our sakes and for his own. I just didn't want him to suffer any more than he had to and I didn't want anyone to have to hurt him.

They say in regions like northern Alaska, a man comes to know his real self. Mannerisms are exaggerated over the passage of time, habits grow into obsessive behavior, and a man's mettle is tested in myriad ways. I came to understand I didn't know as much about the human heart as I had once thought. I didn't really know human nature or where the limits were. I only knew Brian had been my best friend, and he was haunted now by a man with a mechanical arm. Folcum was as real and present to him as any of the rest of us who shared the base compound— maybe Folcum was *more* real.

Last night they found one of the radar techs who had worked with Brian bludgeoned to death in his bed. This morning the Corps police arrives and the search intensifies. Where could Brian be hiding? What nightmare is he living through now?

* * *

I had just sat down on my bunk and opened the Poe to where I'd saved my place. All day long the special Corps force team questioned me about Brian. I was bone-weary, and the wind rattling around the small wooden window frame unnerved me. It often *did* sound like someone was out there. I scooted my back against the wall and lifted my legs onto the blanket. That's the moment Brian chose to speak.

"Hello, traitor," he said quietly.

He was under my bed! I leaped up and leaned down to see him. He pushed from beneath the bunk. I didn't like the grim grin that rode his lips. I didn't like the cant of his shoulders or the dark gleam in his eyes. He looked like a man having a bullet removed, grinning and bearing it. "Brian! They're looking for you."

"I know. I'll let them find me soon. But first I have work to finish."

"What work?" I didn't mean to let the trembling reach my hands, which hung at my sides. I gripped them together behind my back so he wouldn't see. Brian was no longer the game-player and storyteller. He was insane as a drunk camel and he was dangerous.

"What work? Why, your disposal, of course," he said. "You turned me in. You went to the C.O. You've wanted to get me out of here for months now. It's so petty, you know? I beat you at games, I tell better stories, and you can't forgive me for that, can you?"

"Look, you know that's not it. You know you're my friend and I care about you ..."

"You've done other things, too, haven't you?" he asked, interrupting. "Dark things. Dirty, dark, deadly things."

He withdrew the pipe from behind his back. He had done something to it. He had welded pieces to it. Two or three pieces of pipe, some object on the end of it with two ... pincers ...

"Oh my God, Brian!"

"I need to send you to hell, my one-armed friend," he said, advancing.

Out of pure instinct, I raised both my arms and waved them around. "Christ, I'm not Folcum! Look at me!"

As he advanced, I backpedaled, and then when he swung, I ducked. I was yelling, out of my head with fear. "Listen to me! I didn't do anything to Betsy Ann! I don't have a missing arm! Brian look at me, just look at me!"

He began to laugh, a wheezing, crazy laugh that filled my room and hurt my ears. "You really believed my stories, didn't you? Don't you know that's an old story people have been telling for years? About the man with the hook? You didn't think he was real, did you? DID YOU?"

Then he raised the pipe-arm above his head. I was pinned against the wall, the door too distant to reach. My head was filled with his questions and questions of my own. If death was impending, it was coming slow, slow enough I could puzzle this all out if I had a few more seconds of time.

Brian's arm stayed raised, and now he hesitated. His head swiveled on his neck so he was staring at the window. "Look. *There*, see him? He was never real until I told you about him, making up that stupid story. Now he's come to get revenge. He doesn't like his story told, not by anyone. People think it was just a legend, all made up to frighten teenagers and kids, but it must have really happened somewhere, sometime. He must have once been real because he walks now. He walks outside, dragging his arm along the walls, waiting to get inside."

My gaze was drawn with his to the window, the dark square with the snowstorm blowing outside. For a brief second or two I saw what Brian was seeing. A wizened face pressed to the icy glass, the eyes mad and senseless with rage. And there, next to that face, the mechanical hand clenched so that the two pincers were curved, gleaming, pressed together into a hook.

Startled, I gasped. But then the apparition vanished and nothing but snowflakes gusted past the windowpanes.

I turned my attention back to Brian and saw he was still mesmerized, lost in that dark dream. It was my chance to make a move. I rushed forward and grabbed the weapon in his hand

and, twisting, wrestled it from his grasp. I hurried to the door to call for help and heard footsteps ringing in the hall, some of the other men coming to see what the shouting was about.

* * *

Now that they've taken Brian away, I wonder if the story he told was true or not. Or had he been the one who murdered Betsy Ann? Had there even been a Betsy Ann? It was maddening not to know the truth. Had he told me it was a lie, an urban legend, just to throw me off? And what had that been at the window, that madman with the hook? Had we shared a psychosis and a vision together, Brian and I?

I'm beginning to have real trouble deciphering between the real and the unreal. I hope Brian's madness wasn't catching. I've put in for a transfer. I told them I didn't care where they sent me, just as long as it was out of northern Alaska. They said it might take a while. Finding replacements was hell. I told them it was imperative. I'm not sure they're listening.

As I sit here in my bunk, keeping to myself, I hear the arctic wind, and it never ceases. It rattles across the corrugated walls like ... like a metal arm dragging past the window searching for the next victim. Waiting until the time is ripe for murder, taking all the time in the world for the next move—like a chess player who is patient, methodical, like a player who never loses.

The guys tell me I need to get more rest. It was a shock, what I went through when attacked by my friend, they say. They've heard the story about the winter night near the baseball diamond and the scraping sound at the car door. I had to tell them, something made me tell them the whole thing. I've broken down and told them about poor Betsy Ann, who was snatched from the road and dragged into the woods. I finally even admitted I took Folcum for a little walk to the creek and held his head under the water until he drowned. I can recall the chill of the flowing water, a bird singing wildly in a nearby tree, the muscles bunching in the back of Folcum's neck. I can taste revenge like it is a penny on my tongue. I can feel the man losing his battle, his body going limp to fall halfway into the water, ripples rolling over his motionless head and shoulders like he's a rock, just a centuries-old rock obstructing the water's flow.

I told them what happens then, how he comes back, sometimes years later. *He always comes back.*

No one believes a word I say. I just can't tell a story like Brian could. If I was a better storyteller, they would probably see what I see when I look out the windows, when I go outside to check the equipment, when I glance around in the dark shadows that squat in the corners like malevolent creatures. One man, Jimmy Datsuoto, says he believes me. He thinks maybe he can see something out of the corner of his eye sometimes, and it creeps him out. Jimmy's become my friend. He beats me at chess. Everyone beats me at games.

I will have to make a weapon to defend myself the way Brian had to do. That's what I tell Jimmy, and he agrees. He said he needs to make one, too.

We need protection from the demon who stalks this Alaskan wasteland.

I don't know about Jimmy—he's on his own, and I told him so—but I'm not going to let Folcum take me alive.

It's been two months since Brian was taken away, and I miss him. Jimmy's sitting across the table from me in the radar room, and it's his move. I'm about to block his queen from taking my bishop, if he doesn't move it.

"DID YOU HEAR THAT? WAS IT THE WIND?" Jimmy's shouting. I tell him to shut the hell up.

I reach for my welded pipes and Jimmy reaches for his.

We're ready. We know exactly what to do.

FOR NUMBER 11

BY CARSON BUCKINGHAM

FOR NUMBER 11—TO BE OPENED

IN THE EVENT OF MY DEATH

Charles Evans Hughes, Sr., turned the tightly wrapped, strangely labeled package over in his hands. "What manner of nonsense is this?" he demanded of the courier. "In the event of *whose* death?"

The messenger stood at attention, staring straight ahead.

Former military, Hughes snorted mentally. "I ask again: In the event of *whose* death?"

"I don't know, sir."

"Oh, very well. Off with you, then." He waved the young man away as one would a troublesome flying insect and, after the door closed, went to his desk in search of scissors.

Clearly, whatever the missive, it had to do with his position on the Supreme Court of the United States. That was the only way he could be associated with the number 11, since he was the 11th Chief Justice.

"I simply despise gratuitous mystery and drama," he muttered. As irritated as he was, Hughes sheared open the swaddled communication in the carefully deliberate manner in which he approached all things in his life, both personal and professional.

Envelope open now, he slid the contents out onto his desk.

It was a book.

Hughes picked it up. A black cover of what felt like expensive kidskin. No title. It was a slim volume. He flipped through it. It appeared to be a cookbook.

He checked the envelope again, in search of some explanatory note, and was rewarded with a clipped sheaf of papers that had apparently been wrapped around the book. Their bulk had prevented their easy exit.

Hughes carefully withdrew the manuscript. He started when he read the message affixed to the first page.

For Your Eyes Only

He glanced at the calendar. March 9, 1930.

William Howard Taft, 27th President of the United States of America, had gone to The Creator only yesterday. He wasn't even in the ground yet. The nation, and Hughes himself, was in deep mourning. What was this unseemly intrigue now? A tasteless prank? He thought not. He recognized his old friend's signature.

He sat behind his desk, removed Taft's note, and began to read.

My dear Hughes,

If you are reading this, then I am dead. Do not grieve for me, my friend. I had everything and more that life had to offer. I achieved my dream of sitting on our esteemed Court as its Chief Justice, and that is as much as I ever could have hoped for professionally. Personally, I was blessed with an exemplary domestic life, full of the love and laughter of my family and friends. I wanted for nothing. I have led a life well-lived, and I wish the same for you.

I am grateful that this missive has come to you, who knows me, and not to some stranger who would, I am certain, dismiss what you are about to read as the ravings of a deranged mind.

I will tell you now how I happened to come into possession of the black volume that lies on your desk. It is a bit of a long story, and I would ask only that you read it in private, in a single sitting, and in a place where you will not be disturbed.

Afterward, I beg of you to burn this letter.

Hughes' forehead creased with bewilderment and alarm. What could William Howard Taft—that beloved, fun-loving statesman and friend—have to say that would merit destruction of his words? He had been the 27th President of the United States. His written words are a part of history and should be preserved, not dispatched to a meaningless pile of ashes.

He rose from his desk, crossed the room in five long strides, leaned out the door, and informed his clerk that he would be unavailable to anyone for the balance of the afternoon. He locked the door. Back at his desk, he took the receiver of his telephone off the hook, placed the entire mechanism in the deepest drawer of his desk, and closed it.

Now nothing could disturb him.

He picked up the manuscript and smiled ruefully, knowing what it cost Taft in time and patience to block print this message. His cursive was nearly illegible, and with what he represented as the sensitive nature of the document, he certainly couldn't dictate it to be typed by a third party. Hughes wondered if Taft even knew how to type. Well, he'd never know now. He sat down and began to read.

As you know, following the Philippine-American war, I spent three years in the capacity of Civilian Governor of the Philippines, the administration of which kept me from my lifelong desire of joining the Supreme Court for a number of years. I do not blame anyone for this—it was my decision. The Filipinos were not yet ready for self-government, and so I had a moral imperative to remain until they were. I declined Roosevelt's offers with no slight regret, but took heart in knowing that I was doing the right thing—the only thing—for our brown brothers who were depending on me for guidance and help, and because they loved me and I loved them. I thank Helen every day for persuading me to take this post—I was initially reluctant to make such a drastic change in our daily lives. But now, looking back, I find that the three years I spent as Governor of the Philippines were among the happiest and most rewarding of my life. They are certainly reflective of the accomplishments of which I am most proud.

During that time, representing the United States, I negotiated the purchase of these islands from Pope Leo XIII and the Catholic Church for the extortionate sum of $7 million. We then sold the islands back to the natives at reasonable terms, much to their delight. The land was turned from papal concerns back to the farming that would do the people the most good. I labored long to provide and improve educational opportunities for those who wished them. There was even talk of making me King amongst the more giddy souls. However, it was more than compensatory for me that they, unlike many of my fellow American colleagues (and you know those to whom I refer), appreciated my dedication to the job at hand with little regard for self-interest. I suppose, though that may make me an acceptable person, it most assuredly makes me a poor politician.

My one and only clash during my civilian administration of the Philippines was with our American Military Governor of the Philippines, Arthur MacArthur, over his harsh treatment of these impoverished people, and this is where my story about the black book really begins.

A scant week before my time as Civilian Governor drew to a close, I happened to find myself on the island province of Siquijor—a tiny speck of a place, 30 or so nautical miles off the closest coasts of the much larger islands of Negros, Cebu, and Bohol. On a map, it appears that these islands seem to keep their distance from Siquijor; and it is in this case that geography reflects the truth among the populace of those places.

Siquijor is a reputed island of black magic, home to a number of Mambabarangs. These denizens are practicing black magic priests who follow a path similar to voodoo, I believe. It was difficult to get any coherent information from the obviously terrified natives whenever the subject was broached. But the basics, my dear Hughes, are these. There are two sects. "Kulam" is a sect whose practice is indifferent to the intent of the practitioner, since this magic draws its power from the spirit world and is at the mercy of the caprices of such entities and the ways in which they choose to execute the requested magic as to whether it shall be regarded as good or evil in the final analysis. This idea frightened me. This loss of predictability over one's request is shudder inducing, so I steered my intellectual curiosity clear of exploring the beliefs of Kulam and its clergy.

However, I found Mambabarang witchcraft more interesting, as the dark side of this belief is about revenge and cursing, but is under control of the Mambabarang and not the interpretive whims of fickle spirits. Do not misunderstand. I do not admire this practice, but it seemed to me at least more honest and assured that the petitioner would receive exactly what he requested. Intrigued, I visited this island to learn more, but despaired of anyone in a position of power there supplying me with much detail.

On my arrival in Siquijor, I was met by a local who, to my delight, turned out to be a Mambabarang whose family, by virtue of the policies I had worked so hard to write into law, I had benefitted. After they initially lost their farm during the uprising and subsequent bloody defeat (a blot that that bastard MacArthur will have a hard time explaining come Judgment), it was restored to them, in full, due to my new laws.

I cannot tell you his true Philippine name. I was sworn to secrecy and I do not break vows, as you know. For the purposes of brevity ...

"Oh, too late for that, old friend," Hughes chuckled.

... I shall refer to him as Juan. He was to be my tour guide of Siquijor during my stay.

I apologized to Juan (through my interpreter) for my tardiness in visiting his domain, pleading paperwork and meetings. Truthfully, I had been strenuously warned off the place due to its unsavory reputation, real or imagined, by the natives on the other islands. I had spent time on every island in the archipelago, save Siquijor, because of this. But now, with my reputation favorably cemented with the Filipinos, I suspected that I had little to fear during my stop on this fascinating and mysterious island, and I was correct.

"It is not for you to apologize to me, my sir. It is of no matter. You are a very important man," he said in perfect English.

I was delighted and dismissed my interpreter with a generous gratuity. He seemed pleased to take his leave.

Juan couldn't do enough for me. He was as endearing as a puppy, wishing only to please. But the islanders regarded him with fear in their eyes and gave us a wide berth. He remained outside the door of my lodgings whenever I was within, ever on guard. I doubt if he slept the entire time I was on the island.

Not only was he grateful for the return of his birthright, but also for the termination of papal rule. He and the other Mambabarangs could now resume the observation of their "religion" without fear of retribution.

As day became evening, I understood why the conquering Spaniards called Siquijor *Isla del Fuego* or "Island of Fire." The entire island gives off an eerie glow as the night descends. It's quite a spectacle, Hughes, and you ought to make it your business to witness it for yourself.

This glow that, in part, gave Siquijor no small measure of its frightening reputation is nothing more sinister than enormous swarms of fireflies living in the molave trees, which are everywhere one turns. But until I knew the cause, the effect was rather disquieting.

I must tell you, though, that even a natural phenomenon of this magnitude paled when compared to what I beheld in the village of Maria two days later.

Maria is a twisting, turning, nearly 20-mile drive through the mountains from the port of Larena. The entire island is riddled with abandoned churches and unexplored caves. But in Maria, they seemed particularly plentiful—no little help in maintaining the island's uncanny atmosphere. But we were bound for one particular abandoned church.

Once we arrived at our destination, Juan hurried me inside, past the altar and to the chancel.

There, I faced something blasphemous in the extreme. A statue so horrifying that I will never forget it, much as I have tried.

I gazed on Saint Rita of Cascia ... also known as "Black Magic Mary."

This was not a run-of-the-mill church, Hughes.

The figure was attired in a nun's habit of black and white, instantly calling to mind the vestments of the Holy Mother Mary—but the *face* on the thing! I knew it would (and did) cause me night terrors for months thence. It was oval in shape, and the clay was painted to resemble a flesh tone, but the visage was so pale as to appear cadaverous. The eyes were far too large and less human than feline, complete with vertical slits. The corneas were deep red, not white. The nose, human, was too long on the face but too small in the nostrils. The closed mouth, scarcely an inch wide, was thin and drawn down at the corners, with red painted lips.

In her exposed hands she held two ghastly items: in the right hand, a human skull; in her left, an inverted crucifix.

As I gazed on the hideous profanity, Juan was prostrate at its feet, murmuring some language I had never before heard. I surmised that he was *praying* to the thing!

When he finally rose, I had many questions for him, of course. But, when he looked on Saint Rita's countenance, he paled—and as brown as he was, I wouldn't have thought that possible. His skin took on an ashy hue that made me fear for his life.

"We must leave now!" he cried, eyes wide with horror.

"But ..."

"*Now*, my sir!" He swept me from the edifice and into our transport—no mean feat with my girth—applied whip to horses, and sped us away, leaving a thick trail of dust in our wake.

When he finally slowed, an explanation followed.

"We fled because it is getting dark, my sir. It is very dangerous to be near that church after the sun falls. Saint Rita is a nightwalker—or so it is said."

I'd have laughed if Juan hadn't been so clearly terrified. This Mambabarang, who was as feared and respected as any American gangster you'd care to name, was afraid of a statue! Religion is a powerful thing, Hughes—and the black magic of the Mambabarang is no different, as I was soon to discover.

We returned to my lodgings in Larena, where I retrieved my belongings and made ready to depart by boat for the island of Negros, where I had a dinner engagement with an island official.

As I walked to the docks, Juan was at my side. I turned to clasp his hand in friendship and gratitude—a gesture he returned warmly. He refused my offered gratuity and, instead, handed me a small, tightly wrapped parcel.

"This is to help you in your good works for people here, people everywhere, who are many but are not heard. I give my blood to you, and I do not do this lightly. What I give you is powerful, and there is a cost that travels with its use. The spirits demand tribute, you see, my sir. But it can be a small cost if it is used for the good of others. The cost can be great if used for the self or for vengeance. But you are a wise, kind, and learned man and will use this great gift to help many— this I know."

Then he bowed deeply, favored me with a rare smile, turned, and walked into the night without a backward glance.

I tore open the package once settled belowdecks, and it contained the book before you. I settled back to read.

At first blush, it seemed a collection of recipes—and that is what it was.

But not recipes for food preparation.

These were spells, Hughes. Spells for making things happen ... compiled by a feared Mambabarang! What a souvenir of my time in this lovely, enigmatic country. What a rare collectible with which to be entrusted. I tucked it carefully into my briefcase and shifted my thoughts to the dinner meeting for which I was presently bound.

I hadn't, at the time, noticed the two spots of dried blood on the inside front cover.

~ ~ ~

Now, we move from the islands back to the USA, as I did a few uneventful days later.

On my return home in 1904, I was bombarded with the news of more of MacArthur's deviltry directed at the poor populace I had just left. I sat at my desk, in my study, deliberating about what to do, and while thus occupied, was delivered a tray of sliced fruit and a pot of the tea so favored by my Filipino friends. (I had returned home with several cases of it.) On the fruit plate were mango and atis, the latter being a marvelous fruit from the Philippines (I brought those back with me, as well) that has a sweet, custard-like consistency. Atis also contains hard, ebony-colored seeds, all of which had been removed save one. I picked it out and propelled it through the open French doors right into a puddle of standing water outside (it had rained the previous evening).

As I consumed my repast, I remembered the book that Juan gave me and extracted it from my ever-present briefcase at my feet. I held it in my left hand against my chest and out of harm's way of the snack I was just finishing. I had just swallowed the last of my tea when the object of my morning deliberation reasserted himself and I muttered, "MacArthur must be relieved of his command. But how?"

I summoned the maid to remove my tray and, once it was gone, I set the book in its place. It fell open to a Spell to Disempower. My Mambabarang friend had graciously provided marginal translations, so it read thusly:

Combine:

Leaves, twig, bark of male Bignay tree

Leaves of the wild Guyabano tree

Mature leaves of Banaba tree

Kalamungay leaves

Yacon leaves

Seed from Atis

Brew dried leaves. Drink hot while considering he who must lose his power. Drop Atis seed into fresh water. Hold spell book above your heart and ask the spirits.

It was exactly what I had just done. Without intending to, I'd cast a spell.

But that's not the strangest part.

Later that day, I was summoned to Roosevelt's office and offered the position of Secretary of War, which I accepted, though I was hoping the purpose of the meeting was to discuss a position on the Supreme Court.

My new position had an interesting and immediate advantage, however.

I was now in the unique position of being that pissant MacArthur's "boss." I now had the means at my disposal to keep him from perpetuating his horrifying treatment of my island friends and others like them.

There were many small ways I kept him in check over the next two years, but the *coup de gras*, as it were, was in 1906, when the Army Chief of Staff position became available and he was then the highest-ranking army officer (to whom this plum usually goes). To avenge the blood of those gentle people spilled by MacArthur, I passed over him to award the position to Lt. Gen. John C. Bates, and three months later, on Bates' retirement, to Major General J. Franklin Bell. MacArthur never did realize his dream of commanding the entire army. I have no doubt the number of people I saved from a bloody and needless death by this course of action would number well into the tens of thousands. I felt a great deal of personal satisfaction in knowing that I had deprived him of the achievement of his longtime ambition and repaid him in full and more for all the trouble he'd been to me over the years.

I am normally not a vindictive person, Hughes, and perhaps you are surprised at my alacrity in springing to revenge. If you knew MacArthur, you would, no doubt, understand. My hope is that history will not be kind to him. But my belief is that it will probably be kinder to him than he deserves.

It was after Bell's appointment that two things happened.

The first was that I gained a bit of weight. I know you are smirking over that last remark, Hughes; but my college graduation weight was 243 pounds, and I had managed to maintain a weight of 270 or so until I assumed the post of Secretary of War. Over those two years, I had gained approximately 50 pounds. You know my appetite, of course, but while in the Philippines, I had fallen into the habit of a diet consisting of mostly fruits, vegetables, and fish—a proclivity I continued on returning to home soil.

As you may imagine, on this discovery, I became most alarmed, as my diet could not be the supporting reason for the gain. I barely slept, fearing some horrible disease; but when a battery of tests was run by a battery of doctors, the results were that I was in the pink, though they urged the loss of the new weight to ease the stress on my heart. How I was supposed to lose this weight was anyone's guess, since I had done nothing to gain it.

The baffled medical team knew of a physician who was said to work wonders in this area, and so I placed myself in the hands of Dr. N. E. Yorke-Davies, and the games began. I won't bore you with the details.

I did mention that a second thing happened, and that was that I saw Saint Rita of Cascia.

It was dusk when I looked up from a brief and found her standing in the garden outside the open French doors of my study. She stood, like the statue she was during the daylight hours, among Helen's lovingly planted and tended flower beds. It was early July, and though the parade of spring iris, jonquils, and tulips had passed by, sweet-smelling petunias, roses, and geraniums had marched in behind them.

But not for long.

As I stared in horror, beneath her downward gaze healthy flowers shriveled and bright green leaves yellowed and fell from their parent plants. It was a creeping death that traveled from the hem of her profane habit outward and did not cease until the entire garden was nothing more than a brown expanse.

She looked up at me then, raised her right hand that held the skull, and extended a skeletal index finger in my direction.

Then she did something even worse.

She opened her mouth ... and smiled.

The tiny slit of a mouth opened into a grin that was just ... impossibly wide. It literally stretched from ear to ear, displaying a huge mouthful of teeth—oh, God, Hughes, there were teeth everywhere—row upon row, like a lamprey.

At that moment, a gray squirrel tried to cross the blighted garden. The poor creature keeled over almost instantly on stepping foot into the surrounding death.

The thing that was Saint Rita picked it up, already stiff, and crammed it, whole, into her tooth-filled maw, chewed it twice, and swallowed. The huge bulge in her throat as the animal descended caused my gorge to rise, and I looked away to vomit into the nearest receptacle.

When I looked up, she was gone.

The next day, when Helen saw what Saint Rita had wrought, she was devastated. And who could blame her? I feared for her life when she spoke of replanting that very morning; but when I saw a bird light on the ground unharmed, I kept my counsel.

No matter how many times that area was replanted, however, the earth itself was poisoned, and nothing would grow in that blighted circle. At last, Helen gave up on it and created a "garden room" using potted plants, trellises, arbors, pergolas, and so forth. As long as she kept the pots raised above the ground, on pedestals and such, all was well.

The lesson I took from Saint Rita's visitation was that she was extremely powerful and informing me that the consequences of her wrath were permanent.

I was worried enough by all this to relocate the black volume from its home in my briefcase to a safe for which I was the only one with the combination.

In focusing on Dr. Yorke-Davies' weight-management program and with the creative restoration of the garden area outside my door, the book slipped from my mind for many months. Over the next year and a half, I succeeded in trimming my weight by 70 pounds, putting me at 250 pounds and garnering notice from everyone.

My story now jumps ahead to 1921 and my unrequited desire for an appointment to the Supreme Court as Chief Justice—my lifelong dream. It seemed that, as they say, that ship had sailed. But one afternoon, when I opened my safe, there was my answer.

The black book.

Now, I know you think this would be committing the same bad wish as before. But I knew that I could do much good for many people in that post, and it was with this pledge of using that appointment for the benefit of many that I took the book in hand and used it as intended. I surmised that Saint Rita would leave me alone provided I didn't use the book selfishly or vengefully.

I was sorry to become Chief Justice as a result of White's death, and more than once I asked myself if my request hadn't caused it perhaps sooner than it would have naturally occurred.

The book now resided in my briefcase once again.

And you know the rest, Hughes.

"But that won't prevent your telling me anyway," he muttered.

I accomplished much during my stay on the Court. I traveled to Great Britain to observe procedural structure of its court system and to learn how they were able to deal with such a large caseload as quickly as they do. The result of that trip was the introduction and passage (with the help of the black book) of the Judiciary Act of 1925, which allowed us carefully to review appeals with the option of granting or refusing them. It also allowed us to give preference to cases of national importance. Our efficiency increased tenfold or more.

I won't go into the many details of my other decisions and opinions that have made the Court what it is today ...

"Thank God."

... but suffice it to say that I used the book to ensure passage and incorporation of each and every one of them. Everything I did was for the betterment of the country, and so Saint Rita remained in whatever demon-infested hell she normally inhabited.

Things proceeded well until late 1929 when I argued in favor of construction of the first separate and spacious Untied States Supreme Court Building, so that we could cease hearing cases in the Old Senate Chamber or the Capitol Building. None of us had private chambers in either place, and we were relegated to holding our conferences in the basement of the Capitol Building, as though we were some secret embarrassment to those in higher places.

We deserved better.

And, quite frankly, I deserved better.

It was passed and construction began.

By this time—I should also note that though I had been maintaining my 250 pounds for many months, always following Dr. Yorke-Davis' regimen—I had gained weight. I was still weighing myself daily, and watched my weight creep up to 340 pounds—the most I've ever weighed.

But I knew why this time.

I had been keeping careful track of my daily weight for years, and I noticed that after each time I used the book, my weight increased the next morning by exactly two pounds. By 1929, I had used the book 45 times and gained 90 pounds as a result—the apparent "cost" that the Mambabarang had mentioned.

But when I used it the 46th time to get the new Supreme Court Building passed, the scale still read 340 the next morning. No two-pound gain.

I was perplexed, old friend. But I shrugged my shoulders and carried on with my day and our holiday preparations.

The Thanksgiving weather had turned suddenly warm and brought with it one of those rare late-autumn electric storms. That evening, rain poured down in a wall, pelting the dining room windows as we ate and tried to converse above the racket. About halfway through the meal, we abandoned all hope of making ourselves heard and applied ourselves to our meal in our little dry oasis surrounded by the *sturm und drang* of the raging weather outside.

I happened to glance up at one point, just in time for a lightning flash to reveal a figure standing outside at the window.

A second flash revealed the identity.

It was Saint Rita.

Before, she had just corrupted the flowerbeds to warn me. Now I feared for my family.

My fork clattered to my plate and I rose so quickly that my chair crashed over backward, startling everyone at the table.

"I must go out for a moment. I believe I heard someone cry out—they may need help."

It was difficult to get Robert and Charles to remain where they were and not accompany me. It didn't matter how long this convincing took—I knew Saint Rita would wait. At last, I prevailed, donned foul weather gear, and outside and around the corner of the house I went.

She was there, of course. She'd stepped back into the shadows and away from the windows. As I approached her, she moved farther back into the trees.

Watching her move was unnerving, as well—as if there could be even more to be unnerved about. She didn't float or glide, as one might expect. Rather, she moved in what appeared to be a barely controlled fashion—jerky, spasmodically, and *very* quickly. She was first in one place, then there would be a twitching blur, and she would move five feet or so in another direction. She finally stopped in a stand of hemlock some 50 yards from the house.

She turned to me, then, her eyes glowing red and malignant. She opened her mouth to speak, but the conduit of her voice was my mind rather than my ears. Her lips did not move.

"I warned you before about using the book selfishly. But you have chosen to ignore it and build a structure for self-aggrandizement."

"Not for self-aggrandizement!" I cried. "For the use of the entire court!"

"And how does this building benefit anyone but you and a few elite others? How does it benefit those whose voices you swore you'd hear and aid? Can you not do your work as you have been and use those funds to better, more helpful purposes?"

I stared at the sodden ground, ashamed.

"Self-aggrandizement, then," she concluded in her whipsaw voice.

"Yes. You are right," I said.

"There will be consequences ..."

"Please don't hurt my family," I pleaded.

Where she stood, the air abruptly blackened deeper than the night and spun like a miniature tornado and stank of the grave. Hemlock branches slashed at my face.

"You *dare* to ask for *anything* now? Consequences are not determined by you!" she shrieked in my brain.

Then she was gone. I trudged back to the house, humiliated and terrified.

Back at the table once again, I halfheartedly took up my fork to finish my interrupted meal, only to find my plate filled, not with turkey, potatoes, and gravy, but with worms, maggots, and spiders. When I looked up from my plate, my family was eating the same.

I may have screamed, I really don't remember. I do know that I lost consciousness.

The doctor was summoned. I was examined and confined to my bed for a fortnight, after which I resumed my duties on the court.

I quickly realized that no one else could see food as I now did, and sighed with relief that this was to be my punishment, and no one I loved would be harmed. After all, it was my amercement, not theirs.

Over the next few months the only way I could eat anything was to close my eyes; because to open them was to see my food covered in all manner of filthy bugs and vermin, rendering appetite impossible.

As you may imagine, I began to lose weight at an astounding pace—far too rapidly to be healthful. I looked drawn, parchment pale, and I was ravenous, but unable to eat. I subsisted mostly on meat broths and soft foods that I could swallow quickly without chewing.

By February 1, I couldn't eat a mouthful, even with my eyes closed. Once anything touched my tongue, I could feel spindly insect legs and slimy bodies of worms crawling through my mouth.

On February 8, down to 244 pounds—96 pounds lost over just a few months—I retired from the court, a shadow of my former self.

I see Saint Rita daily now, and I know she will be coming to collect me soon, so I will close this letter, which I fervently hope you will use as the cautionary tale it is meant to be when you take up the book and use what is contained within. I know you will, and you know you will. I simply want you to do it with eyes wide open and with benefit from my hard-learned lessons. Be wise, my friend, be wise. The book can do much good.

And frankly, Hughes, you can stand the extra weight.

Yr. Obedient Servant,

Bill

BOTTOM OF THE HOUR

BY PHIL GIUNTA

For the lucky ones, death carries them away as gently as a dandelion pappus on a spring breeze, while others suffer in prolonged agony before drawing that final, wheezing breath.

Regardless of how the Grim Reaper went about its macabre business, Victor Orologio could always hear it coming—just as he did one early summer day traveling aboard a crowded bus from Manhattan to Bethlehem, Pennsylvania.

As it had since Victor was 10, death announced its arrival with an incessant two-tone chime and a throbbing in his left temple. It was a sound much like the simple, repetitive alarm of a car's dashboard signaling an unbuckled seat belt. In Victor's case, it was a dulcet death knell for someone in close proximity and only ceased when the victim did.

And I was having such a good day. In his window seat near the back of the bus, Victor massaged the side of his head while surreptitiously glancing at the other passengers around him. *So which one of you will it be ... and when? God, please let me get out of here before it happens.*

Abruptly, the bus stopped, and murmuring from the front drew Victor's attention to the window. As the bus inched toward the right, state police cars, fire rescue, and an ambulance came into view in the left lane—followed by the smashed, twisted remains of a minivan.

Finally, Victor noticed the woman atop the stretcher—and he knew. *Shit.* As the pinging and pain intensified in his head, Victor watched the EMTs load her into the ambulance. *I'm sorry. I'm so sorry.* He wondered if anyone else had been in the van. Husband? Children? He would find out later when he searched online. *At least I won't need to save the obituaries this time.*

✷ ✷ ✷

Outside the bus terminal in Bethlehem, Victor donned his sunglasses and surveyed the parking lot. It didn't take long to spot his best friend's 1971 Ford Maverick. It wasn't a car you see every day, and if one happened to cross your path, it usually stood out, especially with a dual color scheme of mustard and Bondo.

Victor opened the passenger door and climbed inside. The vinyl seat was cool to the touch. "You got the air working."

"Feels good, right?" In the driver's seat, Antonio "Toni" Herrera adjusted a set of levers to the left of the steering wheel. Cold air blasted from the vents. "Replaced the compressor this morning after I dropped you off. Wanted to get it done before this heat wave hits tomorrow."

Victor buckled in and leaned his head back with a sigh.

"You all right, man?" Toni asked as he pulled out of the parking space.

"Headache."

"Normal headache or oh-shit-it-happened-again headache?"

"Accident on 78," Victor muttered. "I heard the chime just before I saw one of the victims loaded into an ambulance. She's probably long gone by now."

They rode in morose silence for a few minutes before Toni spoke up again. "So how did the sale go?"

Victor patted the check in his shirt pocket. "Perfectly." Earlier that morning, Victor had traveled by bus and subway to Brooklyn to close on the sale of his late grandmother's house. The windfall left him with more than enough to assuage his financial worries for the next few years. "Maybe now I can finally buy a place out in the country." He waved a hand toward his ear. "It's maddening to be surrounded by so many people here, waking up every day wondering if this damn death detector is going to start ringing in my head."

"You do realize you'll need a car if you move out to the sticks, right?" Toni said. "You won't be able to take the bus everywhere like you do now, and I ain't drivin' all the way out there every time you need a ride."

"I'm not looking to move *that* far out. Just enough to give me some peace."

"Do you even have a current driver's license?"

"Of course I do."

"How? You've never had a car since I've known you."

"When it comes time to renew it, I take the bus to the photo center."

Toni laughed as he merged onto the freeway toward Allentown. "You take the bus to renew your driver's license. You realize how funny that sounds? So, at one point, you learned how to drive."

"In my grandfather's Mustang, yes. I know how to drive. I just ... *prefer* not to. No car payments, no insurance premiums, no maintenance, none of that shit."

"Yeah, but now you got money. You can afford all that shit."

Victor merely stared at the passing landscape.

"So what kind of car you thinkin' about?" Toni prodded.

"I don't know. Something nice, something with style ... something I can buy in cash."

"I got just what you need, man. I know a guy sellin' a slightly used but pristine Camaro with—"

Victor rolled his eyes. "No used cars, man. I'm not buying someone else's problems. When I said something nice, I meant *new*."

Toni held up a hand. "Hear me out, bro. This car I'm talkin' about is perfect. It's a 2010 Imperial Blue Camaro LT with 300 horsepower and only 42,000 miles. Garage-kept. I worked on this car personally, so I can vouch for its condition."

"And who owns it now?"

"An old dude named Hal Marx. We used to fix police cars together in Bethlehem. I'm tellin' you, man, this Camaro is badass."

"How much?"

"Only 15 grand."

"If it's so badass, why's he selling it so cheap?"

Toni shrugged. "Hal's almost 70, gonna retire next year. He don't have kids to inherit the car when he kicks, so he had to make a decision. It's a great deal. Come on, man, ain't no harm in lookin' at it, right?

* * *

TING-ting-TING-ting-TING-ting ...

Mom had mentioned black ice before they left the house ... or was it Dad? Victor couldn't remember. All he knew was that his parents weren't speaking anymore—nor were they moving. Blood smeared the side of his mother's head. More on the front passenger window. From his vantage point, Victor couldn't see his father behind the wheel.

TING-ting-TING-ting-TING-ting ...

Somehow, Victor was lying above the backseat. *Above it? No, below it.* The backseat was on top. He was at the bottom. The dome light was a few inches to his left. Outside, sleet pelted the van, tapping on glass, pinging off metal. Ignoring the throbbing in the left side of his head, Victor craned his neck to peer through the windshield. The world was upside down. He remembered now. They had hit ice on a sharp curve and Dad lost control. The van had slid sideways off the road before tumbling down a hill.

In the distance, sirens and air horns grew louder, yet couldn't drown out the persistent electronic chime from the dashboard.

TING-ting-TING-ting-TING-ting ...

"Mom?" Victor croaked. He rolled over onto his side, gripped her shoulder, tugged on her coat. She didn't respond. Panic finally took hold as Victor crawled between the front seats and shook his father's arm. "Dad? Dad, *please!*"

TING-ting-TING-ting-TING-ting ...

Crying now, Victor slumped between the seats as the dimming gray sky flashed red and blue. Voices shouted. They came in through the rear passenger door. Hands gently tugged Victor from the car, placed him on a stretcher. Someone spoke to him, but Victor wasn't paying attention. All he could hear was the damn dashboard alarm, no matter how far they carried him from the wreckage.

TING-ting-TING-ting-TING-ting ...

With a jolt, Victor sat up on his sofa and squinted at the TV. The main menu of a Blu-ray disc flashed a repeating loop of scenes from the movie he'd been watching when he dozed off. It was the only source of light in the otherwise dark apartment. With a sigh, he slid his hand along the cushion beside him until he found the remote and turned off the Blu-ray player and TV.

Victor rubbed his temples, tried to push the memory from his mind. Yet the damn chime persisted. It was accompanied now by other noises—heavy-booted footsteps and scraping metal. Through the fading fog of sleep, Victor realized it was coming from the parking lot. He shot out of his seat and dashed to the sliding doors that opened to the balcony. He shoved aside the vertical blinds, followed by the glass and screen doors.

In the parking space directly below, the driver's side door of the Camaro was wide open. Since Victor had backed the car into the space, he could clearly distinguish a leg protruding from the driver's seat.

"Hey, get the hell out of my car, asshole!"

The leg shifted and a tall, bald black man climbed out. Victor raised an eyebrow. *Jeans and a leather coat in this weather?* The would-be thief made his way toward the rear of the Camaro and stood under the pale orange glow of a nearby lamppost. Victor leaned forward to get a better look at his face, now drenched in blood from what looked like a bullet hole in the middle of his forehead.

Victor pushed away from the railing as the dude raised a chrome-plated semi-automatic pistol. "That ain't your car, white boy!"

"Shit!" Victor dove back into his apartment, knees smacking the edge of the screen door, dislodging it from its tracks and sending it crashing to the deck.

But there was no gunfire, and the death knell faded into silence. After a moment, Victor sat up and peered through the spindles of the balcony railing. He could see the Camaro. All of its doors were closed. There was no sign of the bloody car thief. *So why did I hear the chime?*

Victor crept back outside. The parking lot was devoid of life. Roused by the commotion, a few neighbors along the front of the building emerged, but Victor ignored them as he lifted the screen door and leaned it against the side railing.

He ducked back into his apartment and snatched his phone from the coffee table. It was just after 1:30 in the morning. Victor drew a long, deep breath as his thoughts raced to catch up with the events of the past five minutes. *Why did I let Toni talk me into a Camaro? He was right. The car's flawless, but now it's a target. Should have bought a house with a garage first. Only had this car two days and some douchebag tries to boost it. And why didn't the friggin' alarm go off?*

After walking out to inspect the Camaro, Victor brought in a chair from the balcony. He closed the sliding door, but left the vertical blinds open and sat in the dark. By the time he nodded off, it was nearly dawn. After all, he didn't dare fall asleep while a car thief was still out there, lurking in the night.

* * *

The following day, Victor winced as he rolled his shopping cart out of the air-conditioned supermarket and into the sweltering soup of the summer's first heat wave. *And it's only 10 a.m.* Ahead of him, a plump, rubescent elderly woman in a sleeveless, flowered muumuu pulled four bulging tote bags out of her cart and started toward the parking lot. The moment he saw her, the chime began ringing in his head. *Damn it, not again.* He started after the woman, fearing she might give up the ghost any second.

She'd barely waddled three steps when the handle on one of her bags snapped. "Oh, hell."

As Victor approached, she set her burdens down on the pavement, struggling to find the best way to deal with the problem.

"Ma'am, can I help you get your bags to your car?" Victor offered.

"Oh, thank you, no." The woman smiled, despite the streams of sweat streaking her ruddy face. "I'm actually going to the bus stop. It should be here in the next hour or so."

"In this heat? Ma'am, it's got to be over 95 degrees."

"I can manage. It wouldn't be the first time."

"How about I give you a ride home? I promise I'm not a crazy person out to hurt anybody. I would just feel terrible letting you wait in this heat. I know the buses don't run often on Sundays."

"Well, I don't want to be any trouble ..."

"It's no trouble, ma'am." *Maybe this time I can finally save one of you.* He extended a hand. "My name's Victor."

"I'm Annette. My friends call me Netty. Thank you so much for your help. I normally don't go grocery shopping on a Sunday, but my son is coming home this week. He's been away for a while, and I want to cook him a nice meal."

Victor pushed his bags to the back of his cart. Once Netty's were loaded, they made their way across the parking lot to the Camaro.

"Oh, my, look at this car," Netty said. "My son would love something like this."

"Thank you." Victor opened the passenger door for her. After loading the groceries in the trunk and returning the cart, he climbed into the driver's seat and cranked up the air. Netty had already buckled herself in.

"It's just as immaculate on the inside," she marveled. "Although your time is off by a few hours."

Victor frowned as he looked at the radio in the center console. Sure enough, the clock displayed 1:30. "Huh, didn't even notice that. Well, I'll fix it later. If that's the worst problem with this car, I can definitely live with it."

* * *

He found it four days later. From his laptop screen, a picture of Annette Terro smiled back at him. "I'm so sorry," he whispered before sending her obituary to the printer. She had died the morning after he'd brought her home. He should have known. The chime had continued until well after he'd dropped her off and only faded after he'd pulled away. Still, he'd held out hope.

Victor stood and pulled a three-inch ring binder from the top shelf of the bookcase. He opened it and stared for a moment at the first page. *Ten days already?* Craig Breyer had been a coworker in the receiving department. Victor had heard the chime while working with him and about eight other people sorting shipments on the loading dock. By the end of that week, Victor had silently apologized to Craig's closed coffin.

He pulled Annette's obituary from the printer and read it over one last time. "Survived by her son, Geoff," he muttered. *My son is coming home this week. He's been away for a while and I want to cook him a nice meal ...*

"Sorry, Geoff. I tried to save her." Victor slipped the page into the electric three-hole punch before adding it to his collection. He flipped through the pages, the years, the faces, recalling the first time he showed the binder to Toni shortly after he'd revealed his ability.

"That binder looks heavy, bro."

Victor snapped the rings shut after adding the latest entry.

"You have no idea."

"It's like the Grim Reaper's scrapbook."

"But I'm not the Grim Reaper."

"Then why do you save their obituaries?"

"Because I couldn't save them," Victor replied. *"Sometimes, I hear the chime in a crowd of people and I don't even know who it's for. Sometimes I hear it when it's too late to do anything. But there are other*

times when I know who it's going to be and I try to save the person ... but nothing I do ever matters. Those are the ones I keep in this binder."

"I don't know how you stay sane with that ability."

Victor shrugged. *"To be honest, I was already used to it when I got to high school."*

"How the hell do you get used to hearin' death? That shit would creep me out, man. Though not as creepy as savin' obituaries."

"I don't have a choice. Not like I can turn it off. Believe me, I've tried. Pills, therapy, booze, you name it."

"Well, if you hear it when my time comes, you will let me know, right? At least give me a fighting chance."

"What are friends for?"

Toni pointed to the binder. *"You know, their deaths weren't your fault. By keepin' that thing, you're only torturin' yourself, man. You need to let that shit go. It ain't healthy."*

Victor snapped the binder closed, bringing his focus back to the present. "I wish I could, amigo." He looked up at the clock on the wall. *Time for a swim.*

* * *

Another day of sweltering temperatures meant a few laps in the complex's indoor pool before work. The usual horde of screaming kids and self-absorbed parents congregated near the shallow end, leaving the deeper side to Victor and a raven-haired 20-something with a body that absolutely deserved to be flaunted in the two-piece, baby-blue bikini that matched the color of her eyes.

This was one of those occasions when Victor was grateful he'd kept himself in shape. He might never have six-pack abs, but his stomach was flat and his limbs toned thanks to his workout regimen and the fact that his warehouse job kept him on the move most of the day.

As she stepped out of the pool and started toward him, Victor realized that he had seen her before at one of the other buildings. As she passed, he smiled and aimed a thumb toward the opposite end of the pool. "If only I could put up a wall to block off that racket."

She rolled her eyes. "Tell me about it. Some of those kids are my neighbors. I can't get away from them."

"Wait, did you just move into Building A last week?"

She shifted her weight and looked away for a moment. "Uh, yeah. Why?"

"I thought you looked familiar, and now I remember seeing you on one of my runs. We almost collided while you were unloading stuff from a van."

Her eyes widened as she let out a short laugh. Victor felt something quiver deep in his chest. *Keep it cool, dude. Don't screw this up.*

"Oh, my God, that's right. I'm sorry. I didn't recognize you. That day was a blur of activity."

"Moving day usually is." He extended a hand. "I'm Victor."

She accepted the gesture with a tepid grip. "Erica. So, do you run every day?"

Victor nodded. "As long as the weather cooperates—which is why a swim seemed like a better idea today. When the temps climb above 90, I'm in the water. I work nights, so I usually run midmorning, between 9:00 and 10:00."

"Gotcha. Well, as it happens, I'm off from work this week and there's a storm coming tonight that's supposed to cool things down. So if you decide to run tomorrow and wouldn't mind a partner ..."

Victor nodded casually. *That's right, not too eager.* "Sure. That would be great."

"And if it doesn't cool off," she waved toward the pool, "maybe I'll see you back here."

Victor smiled. "Sounds like a plan."

"Where's your apartment?"

"Oh, uh, Building C, number six. Second floor."

"Great, well, you obviously know where I live. If you don't knock by 10:00, I'll swing by your place."

"Sounds ... like a plan." *You already said that, idiot!* By now, Victor knew he was grinning like a fool but didn't care.

"Speaking of running, I have to take care of some errands," she scooped up her towel and keys from a nearby chaise lounge, "but I'll see you tomorrow, Victor."

As he watched her leave, Victor realized that he was gawking like a teenager but still didn't care. *Did she just ask me out ... sort of? This summer just keeps getting hotter. Money, car, possible new girlfriend. All within a week! Is this happening or am I dreaming? One way to find out ...*

Taking a deep breath, Victor ran to the edge of the pool and jumped in.

* * *

On the final stretch of their morning run, they rounded the corner of Building C, separating to avoid a puddle in the middle of the parking lot from the previous night's storm.

"Hey." Victor slowed to a stop, sweat dripping from his nose and chin. He nodded toward his Camaro. "Check out ... my new wheels. Well ... new to me."

Erica leaned forward, hands on her knees. "That's yours?"

Victor nodded. "Camaro LT. Seven years old ... only 42,000 miles."

Erica stood and made her way over to the car. "My ex-husband ... would've loved to get his hands on this."

Victor wheezed out a laugh. "Funny ... I met an old lady at the ... supermarket a few days ago. She said the same thing ... about her son. So, uh, how long were you married, if you don't mind my asking?"

"Too long. It was three years of my life I'll never get back and would rather forget. He's the reason I moved here. Didn't want him to find me when he got out on parole."

"Parole?"

"Two days ago." Erica waved dismissively. "Don't worry, he's not a murderer or anything. He used to steal cars for parts. Hence my comment about how he'd love your Camaro. I didn't find out until the dumbass got arrested. Anyway, that's behind me now. I'm starting over. Congrats on the car. It's a beauty."

"Well, if you want to take a ride sometime, just let me know." Victor snapped his fingers. "Hey, what are you doing Saturday night?"

Erica thought for a moment. "I should be available after 7:00. I'm visiting my sister in the afternoon. What did you have in mind?"

* * *

After his fourth consecutive win at the Water Gun Shoot-Out, Victor eyed the top prizes as Erica nibbled on funnel cake beside him. It was the final night of the county fair. Victor had wanted to do something different from the standard dinner and movie date and had been thrilled when Erica cheerfully agreed. She pointed at a row of boxed toy cars, one of which was a dark blue Camaro. "You should get that."

He shrugged. "Meh. I already got the real thing."

"That ain't your car, white boy!"

Victor drew himself up sharply, as if someone had shoved an ice pack under his shirt. "Did you hear that?"

Erica swallowed a bit of funnel cake. "Hear what?"

"That voice ..."

"Which one? There's a bazillion people here."

"Hey, buddy." The carny running the game leaned over as new players began taking seats. "Make up your mind yet?"

"Uh, yeah. Sorry." Victor shot a sidelong glance at Erica. "You like pandas?"

"Love pandas."

Victor pointed toward the back corner. Erica laughed as the carny returned with a life-size, plush panda and handed it to Victor, who, in turn, passed it to Erica in exchange for the rest of the funnel cake. She wiped her hands on her denim shorts before throwing her arms around it. "How are we going to get this in your car?"

* * *

In the passenger seat, Erica was all but completely buried beneath the black-and-white behemoth in her lap. Victor checked the rearview mirror before flooring the accelerator along an empty stretch of highway. "Comfortable over there?"

Erica rested her head on the panda's back. "It's like having a massive, fuzzy air bag in your face. Although it's comfortable to snuggle with."

"Oh, I think I could give it a run for its money." Victor flashed a lopsided grin—which vanished the moment he glanced over at her. Erica and the panda were gone. Instead, a dark, bloody face stared back.

From the car's sound system, the death knell blared like a klaxon.

"Who the hell *are* you?" Victor demanded.

"Don't get too attached, white boy." The man raised his right hand, leveling a chrome-plated pistol at Victor. "She don't belong to you."

Victor slammed the brakes.

Tires screeched.

The gun fired.

And Victor awoke with a yelp. He found himself doubled over on his side facing his alarm clock. *One-thirty. Always 1:30.* Once the pain in his head subsided, he forced himself out of bed and stood at the window overlooking the parking lot. The Camaro was exactly where he'd parked it after dropping Erica off at her flat. Victor lowered himself to the floor and sat against the wall, cradling his head in his hands. *It's just new-car jitters. Gonna buy that house in the country and get out of here. Better times are ahead. Just breathe and think about Erica ... think about Erica ... think about Erica ...*

* * *

It was after 2:00 a.m. when Victor arrived home following another night of overtime. He opened the car door with a weary shove and climbed out just as a blur of motion caught his eye. In the gap between the buildings, flashing red and blue lights danced across pale brick walls. *Now what ...*

Victor walked around to the front lot for a better view. At the opposite end of the complex, an ambulance and two patrol cars were parked in front of Building A. Victor watched for a moment before turning back. *Probably one of the elderly residents. Wouldn't be the first time ...*

Still, it was Erica's building. Maybe she was awake through the commotion. As he made his way toward the scene, Victor wasn't surprised to see all the spectators out on their balconies and several more gathered on the sidewalk in front of the building. Yet Erica was not among them.

Instead, Victor found her lying on the concrete patio below her balcony, surrounded by the ambulance crew.

"Oh, Christ. Erica!" He sidestepped the onlookers, only to be intercepted by two cops.

The stout male officer stood directly in his path. "Need you to stay back, sir."

Victor held up both hands as words tumbled out. "I'm her boyfriend. I just got home from work. I live in Building C. What happened? Is she alive?"

"She's alive," the female officer assured him. "Can we see some ID, please?" Victor pulled out his wallet and handed over his driver's license. "She fell from the balcony about 30 minutes ago. Neighbors reported hearing a scream and sounds of a struggle, so they called it in."

"Does she have family in the area?" her partner asked.

Victor nodded absently, his gaze firmly fixed on Erica as the ambulance crew lifted her onto the stretcher. *Thirty minutes ago. That would be about 1:30* ... "She has a sister, but I don't know her number. You mentioned a struggle. Was there someone else in her apartment? She told me her ex-husband just got out on parole and—"

"We can't tell you that." The female officer finished jotting his information in her notepad and handed his license back. "We need to talk to her family first."

Victor sighed. "Can you at least tell me what hospital they're taking her to?"

"Saint Mark's."

* * *

She fell from the balcony about 30 minutes ago ...

In the waiting room at St. Mark's ER, Victor sat bouncing his fist lightly against his thigh. It was a nervous habit he'd picked up as a kid. Right now, it did little to soothe his anxiety. "One-thirty ... *again*." He pounded his leg. "I don't get it."

Victor peered through the window as a black car pulled into a space across the narrow lot. Beneath the streetlight, a slim woman in white shorts, flip-flops, and a dark tank top stepped out and hurried through the rain toward the double doors. Although she appeared slightly older, her resemblance to Erica was unmistakable. Still, Victor waited until she approached the front desk and introduced herself as Rhonda Daykin.

"My sister, Erica, was brought in here about 45 minutes ago."

"Okay, ma'am. Please have a seat in the waiting room and I'll get the nurse to come out and bring you back."

Victor stood and made his way over.

"Excuse me, Rhonda?" he extended a hand. "My name is Victor. I'm a friend of Erica's. I live in the same complex."

"Oh, right ... yeah, she talks about you all the time. What happened to her?"

Victor shook his head. "I don't know yet. I showed up after the ambulance was already there."

"Swear to God, if I find out it was her ex, I'll snap that little bastard's neck."

Four hours and numerous cups of coffee later, Rhonda and Victor followed the doctor out of the waiting room and into a small office. "I'll take you back to see your sister shortly," she began, "but I wanted to bring you up to speed on her condition. Erica had some minor brain swelling, so the doctor performed what's called an EVD, or an external ventricular drain, to relieve some of the pressure. We now have her on an IV of anti-inflammatories and antiseizure meds. The swelling and pressure have diminished. So we're moving in the right direction, but now we wait.

"The police said she fell off a balcony. We found no traces of alcohol or drugs in her system ..."

"You wouldn't," Rhonda and Victor said in unison.

"She lives a healthy lifestyle," Rhonda added.

"So, was this a freak accident, or did someone push her off the balcony?"

"Her ex-husband just got out on parole," Rhonda replied. "She moved to get away from him. I can't say for sure he was there. The police thought Erica was alone." She looked at Victor.

He shrugged. "I was on my way home from work at the time." *But she wasn't alone ...*

* * *

Victor bolted through the double doors of the hospital and began pacing along the sidewalk, cell phone pressed against the side of his head. The rain had diminished to a welcome cool drizzle. "Hey, Toni, it's Victor."

"What's going on, bro? How's that Camaro?"

"That's why I'm calling. I need your help. Do you think you can track down who owned it before your buddy Hal?"

"Maybe. Why?"

"Remember when I said I didn't want to buy someone else's problems?"

"What's wrong with the car?"

Victor stopped pacing and tilted his head back to work a knot out of his neck. "The car's fine, but I've been having some weird experiences since I got it."

"Like what?"

"I'll explain later. I can't even think straight right now. I just spent the night in the ER with Erica."

"She okay?"

Victor sighed. "She took a fall outside her apartment last night and hit her head. Now she's in a coma."

Toni paused. "Aw, damn, dude. I'm sorry. Anything I can do?"

"Find out who owned the Camaro before Hal. You're tight with the Bethlehem cops, right? You used to work on their cars. If I text you the VIN number, can you ask around? Maybe you'll come up with a name. This is serious, Toni."

"All right, bro. I'll see what I can do. Hang in there."

* * *

It took Toni three agonizing days to find the name—and much more. It was Friday night, and Victor had offered to buy pizza and beer on his way back from the hospital. They met at Victor's apartment.

"Turns out the Camaro used to belong to a gang member named Brian Gless," Toni began. "He lived out in Reading. One night about five years ago, he caught some dude trying to boost the car, so he pulled a gun, but the other guy must have drawn faster. He shot Gless in the head before running away. Bro was dead before the ambulance arrived.

"They never found his killer, but the cops did find meth stashed under the carpet in the trunk of the Camaro, so they impounded the car. Turns out Gless had been sellin' for a local dealer. Hal must have bought the car from a police auction or somethin'."

Victor slipped a slice of pizza out of the box. "Did you happen to find out what Gless looked like?"

"Yeah, they showed me a picture. Tall, bald, black dude with a goatee."

That's got to be the guy. Though Victor didn't recall the goatee. *Must have been concealed by all the blood.* "Last question. Did your source mention what time he died?"

"Accordin' to what I was told, it all went down around 1:30 in the mornin'. Now, you gonna tell me what's goin' on?"

Victor slumped back in his chair and rubbed his eyes. *That explains it. What the hell do I do now?* "You're not going to believe the shit that's been happening."

"Like what?"

Victor took a sip of beer and launched into the events of the past week leading up to Erica's injury.

After he was finished, Toni gaped at him, clearly struggling to find words. "Dayum, bro. Hal never said anything about this. So you think this dude's ghost is haunting his old car?"

Victor shrugged. "I have more questions than answers. If Gless's ghost has been attached to the Camaro this whole time, why wait until now to show himself? Why fuck up *my* life? I had nothing to do with his death."

"What about Erica?"

Victor shook his head. "No way, dude. Don't even go there."

"Then why would Gless attack her? That is, if we believe there really *is* a ghost behind all this."

"There's no way in hell Erica would've been involved in murder. It has to be someone else."

"Like who?"

* * *

It was nearly midnight on Saturday when he heard the chime. Victor stopped fumbling with his keys outside his apartment and leaned against the door. *Damn it, just stop.* He knew someone in the building wouldn't live long enough to see the sunrise. That narrowed it down to about 20 people. *I can never save any of them, so why should I worry about it? God, please just give me one decent night's sleep.*

Victor pushed away from the door, struck by the possibility that Gless was saving him for last and that this time, the death knell clanging in his head might be his own. Fully alert now, Victor unlocked the door and darted inside. *Maybe I should have stayed at the hospital until morning.* As the pinging grew louder, Victor flipped the light switch—and froze.

He saw the gun first, by the light that glinted off its chrome barrel. Across the room, half-hidden in shadow and straddling a dining room chair, the man merely stared at Victor. His trimmed, frizzy beard wrapped around his lean face like a black chinstrap attached to either end of his red baseball cap. He was dressed for the season in a gray T-shirt and cargo shorts. One thing was certain—the guy was too white and too short to be Brian Gless. So, the question was ...

"Who the hell are you?"

"Funny, I was going to ask you the same question." The guy waved his pistol toward the sofa. "Sit down."

"Whatever you want, just take it and get out of here."

"I want answers, asshole. Now sit down and we'll have a quiet chat. Hands out where I can see them and don't even think about reaching for your phone. What's your name?"

"Victor."

"Victor what?"

"Orologio."

The guy snickered. "What kind of fucked up name is that?"

"Italian."

"Oh, paisano, eh? You know who I am?"

The guy shook his head.

"No? Well, that's surprising since you've been dickin' around in my life for the past week. You see, Victor, I got out of prison last Wednesday, but the night before my parole hearing, my mother died of a heart attack. So, I'm at her funeral, and I hear that on the morning before she passed, this nice young man in a dark blue Camaro drove her home from the grocery store. Now, I didn't think much of it at the time.

"Then I came to this apartment complex a few days ago to see my ex-wife, Erica. Maybe you know her? I was hoping to reconcile—convince her to take me back and start our life over—until I find out that she's at the hospital in a coma. So I start asking around, and guess what I'm told. My ex started dating some guy two buildings over and he drives a dark blue Camaro, too. What are the odds?"

"You're Geoff Terro."

"I guess Erica told you about me."

"She said you were a car thief."

Terro leveled the gun at Victor. "And who are you, the fuckin' Grim Reaper? What the hell did you do to my mother and my ex-wife?"

Victor held up his hands. "Nothing, man, I swear to God. It's the car."

"What car?"

"The Camaro! Look, man, I bought it from an old guy last week and ever since then, I've been having dreams and visions that someone's trying to steal it. Same guy every time, a tall, black dude with a bullet hole in his head and blood running down his face. So I asked a friend to look up the original owner of the car. Turns out, he's exactly the guy I keep seeing in the dream. Five years ago, this guy named Brian Gless caught someone trying to steal his Camaro. He pulled a gun to scare him off, but the other guy shot him in the head."

"Gless." Terro's eyes glazed over as he flexed his fingers over the gun's grip.

Was that recognition that Victor detected in Terro's voice? "Yeah, he owned the Camaro before the old guy who sold it to me, and every time I've seen Gless, it's 1:30 in the morning— which was the time he died. Get this, man. Every time I start the Camaro, the clock on the dash resets to 1:30. I gave up trying to change it. I'm telling you, that car is haunted. Everyone who rides in it ends up dead or close to it."

"Bullshit." Terro snarled, but doubt seemed to erode his conviction. "One-thirty in the morning," he muttered. "That's when my mother died."

When Victor spoke again, he adopted a softer tone. "I'm sorry for your loss, man. That's also the time when Gless's ghost attacked Erica. I guarantee you, she didn't just fall off a balcony."

Terro nodded. "So, in these dreams, does Gless say anything?"

"Yeah. He says, 'That ain't your car, white boy.'"

At that, Terro leapt to his feet and began pacing the length of the living room, back and forth in front of Victor. "Shit, that's exactly what he said when ..."

"When what?" Victor pressed. "You starting to believe me now?" His eyes shot open as he shifted in his seat. "Oh shit, *you* killed Gless. That's the only way this makes sense. This all started around the time you got out of jail. *Your* mother, *your* ex—"

Terro's head snapped up. He moved toward the sofa, gun leveled at Victor's head. "Shut the fuck up. We're going for a ride, just you and me, paisano. You drive."

* * *

Twenty minutes later, they were well beyond the city limits. Dense woods and cornfields whipped past on both sides of the highway.

"Slow down." In the passenger seat, Terro waved his gun toward the right side of the road. "Pull into the open field just after these trees."

The throbbing in Victor's temples grew sharper now as he turned the Camaro off the road onto the edge of the field. The chime had become a strident, piercing clamor in his head, louder than he'd ever experienced before.

"Further in," Terro snapped.

Victor couldn't help but think he was driving to his own funeral. He risked a glance at his watch. Five minutes after one. For a moment, pain and exhaustion overcame fear as Victor stopped the car in the middle of the field. "Why the hell are we out here? We meeting someone?"

With a grin, the little bastard raised his pistol. "Maybe. Get out."

Both men climbed out of the Camaro into a dank shroud of darkness broken only by the stark glow of the full moon. Victor backed away from the car as Terro walked around and stood beside him.

Victor massaged a pressure point between his thumb and forefinger in an attempt to ease the pain in his head. Of course, that didn't silence the incessant pinging. "Now what?"

"Now we see if your ghost story is true." Terro pressed the muzzle of his piece into Victor's temple. "Give me the keys, and don't even think of running away." With a quivering hand, Victor dropped the keys into Terro's open palm. As he slipped them into the pocket of his cargo shorts, Terro stepped back and peered at the Camaro. "Hey, Gless! I'm sick of hearing your name. Sick of replaying that night in my head for the past five years. I wouldn't have shot you if you didn't draw first, asshole. You took my mother. You tried to kill my wife. Well, I'm standing right here, motherfucker!"

Victor held up a hand. "Dude, I don't think that's a good idea."

"Maybe you're right, paisano. Here's a better way to get his attention." Terro opened fire, shattering the driver's side window.

"What the hell are you doing?" Victor shouted.

"Come on, Gless! You love this car so much?" The maniac began circling the Camaro, blasting out every window as he went.

Victor threw his hands up, fingers curling into fists. "Stop!"

By now, Terro was standing on the passenger side, partially obscured from view. "How 'bout now, Gless? Is that enough? No? You want some more?"

"Stop shooting up my car!"

Victor's rage was drowned by a shot that struck the Camaro's frame. A spark flashed along the far edge of the roof, then ... silence.

As if from the Camaro itself, a gelid breeze tore through Victor, chilling the sweat on his forehead and carrying a voice barely louder than a whisper. "That ain't your car, white boy."

Victor suppressed a shiver. "Dude, you still over there?"

There was no response. Even the chime had ceased.

He pulled his cell phone from his belt holster and tapped the flashlight app as he made his way around the Camaro. He spotted the legs first. *Oh shit.* Victor moved the light along Terro's prone form until he saw the blood seeping from a bullet hole in his forehead. Something glinted in the light beside the body. Victor leaned over and snatched up his keys.

He aimed his phone at the car. *There's no way in hell a round could have ricocheted like that unless ...*

As if in response to his thought, the Camaro's lights flashed on and a DJ's voice blared from the radio. "It's 1:30 a.m., bottom of the hour on your Sunday morning. Five-day forecast on the way, brought to you by Trover Dodge on the Lehigh Street Auto Mile. If your old car is shot, consider trading it in at Trover ..."

* * *

I'm not saving that bastard's obituary. I can't believe Erica was married to that. It was nearly 4 o'clock when Victor trudged into his apartment, drenched in sweat after a two-hour walk home in unbearable humidity. After gently closing the door, Victor peeled off his work clothes on the way to the bathroom. Under a cool shower, he leaned against the wall and closed his eyes.

After a quick nap, he would call the cops and report his car as stolen. Oh, and the insurance company, too. For the next few days, he would take the bus to work. When the cops finally found the Camaro—and the little prick lying dead beside it— they'd consider the area a crime scene and probably impound the car again for who knows how long.

They can have it. My fingerprints won't be on the gun. I'm in the clear. Victor no longer cared. Only one person mattered now.

No sooner had he stepped out of the shower than he heard the muffled buzzing. Victor charged out of the room and yanked his phone from the pile of clothes on the living room floor. He glanced at the screen and took a deep breath before answering. "Hey, Rhonda ..."

* * *

Victor heard the chime the moment he stepped off the elevator. He hurried his pace down the corridor, weaving past nurses and patients until he bounded into Erica's room.

"Did you hear that bell?" Rhonda asked.

Lying in bed, Erica opened her eyes and grinned up at Victor. "Yeah, I did."

"Wait." Victor held up a hand. "You both heard that?"

"Of course, whenever a baby's born, the hospital plays a little jingle over the PA system." Rhonda rose from her seat. "I kept it warm for you. I'm going to catch a smoke and give you kids some alone time." She frowned at Victor. "You okay? You look like a deer in the headlights."

"Let's not talk about cars, please."

"Whatever you say. Back in a few."

Victor lowered himself into the chair beside Erica's bed. "Welcome back, gorgeous."

Erica smiled wanly. "To the land of the living. Sorry if I sound raspy. I don't have my voice back yet. My sister said you were here every day."

From his seat beside her hospital bed, Victor gently took her hand in his. "Where else would I be? I missed you. So did the panda. He wanted me to tell you."

"Panda? Oh, right." Erica chuckled and immediately winced. She turned her face to the ceiling. "Hurts to laugh, or turn my head for too long. They said I cracked my collarbone in addition to the bump on my brain. Could've been worse, right? Better than breaking my neck."

"You'll be up and running before you know it. Just take your time. I'll be with you every step of the way."

She squeezed his hand but remained silent. Victor shifted his gaze to the window, unsure of how to broach the unspoken topic that couldn't be avoided. Erica saved him the trouble.

"What the hell happened to me, Victor?" Her voice cracked as she struggled to maintain her composure. "I was sound asleep in bed until someone I couldn't see grabbed me by the hair and dragged me out to the living room." She paused to breathe as tears streaked down the side of her face, becoming lost in her matted hair. "I don't think I'll ever forget watching the sliding doors open by themselves before I was hurled out to the balcony like a rag doll. I remember slamming into the railing and just sitting there in a daze.

"Then it was like two giant, invisible hands around my throat lifting me up. I couldn't breathe. My feet were off the deck ... and I don't remember anything after that. But there was no one there. It wasn't a person, Victor. It was like something out of a ghost story. I don't know what I'm going to tell the cops when—"

"It *was* a ghost," he confirmed.

She turned slightly and glared at him. "Are you telling me those apartments are haunted?"

Victor shook his head. "No. It wasn't your apartment that was haunted. We need to talk about your ex-husband ..."

∗ ∗ ∗

Four months later

"Don't lift anything too heavy."

"Victor, I'm fine." Erica pulled the first box from the back of the pickup. "Where do you want this?"

"In the dining room. Anywhere you can find the space. Thanks."

No sooner had she disappeared into the rustic two-story stone home than the Maverick roared to a stop inches from the truck's bumper.

Victor folded his arms as Toni emerged. "You're late."

"Overslept."

"Is that code for hung over?"

"Man, why you gotta be like that?"

Victor shook his head and began rummaging through one of the boxes in the truck until he found what he was looking for.

"Okay, I'm sorry I wasn't at your apartment to help you move out, but at least I showed up here to help you move into this awesome house." Toni nodded toward the pickup. "New wheels?"

"*Brand* new ... as in no previous owners and a lot more practical for living out here. Nothing against the Camaro. It was a sweet ride, just wasn't meant to be. "

"Speaking of livin' out here, how's Erica takin' all this? You won't be able to see each other as often."

"She's fine with it. She loves the house. For the time being, we decided to trade off spending weekends at each other's places, and if everything works out, she'll move in with me when her lease expires."

Toni pointed to the binder in Victor's hands. "Does she know about that?"

Victor shook his head. "And she never will." He nodded toward the backyard and led Toni to a rusted metal barrel into which Victor dumped 20 years of obituaries. He picked up a plastic gas can beside the barrel and handed it to Toni. "Care to do the honors?"

"What are friends for?"

POWDER BURNS

BY J. GREGORY SMITH

Hagley Powder Mills, Wilmington, Delaware

Despite a rough start this morning, Stuart Talley thought his wife Janie looked perfect standing in the thick-walled, open room of the old gunpowder mill. The springtime, pale-green leaves on the trees reflected off the water of the Brandywine Creek. They cast a soft glow on her blond hair, which she'd pulled back in what he liked to call her "School Marm's Bun."

This building, one of many similar structures dotting the banks of the creek, was a three-walled room where the DuPont Company used heavy steel wheels to grind and mix the finest black powder in the world.

Stuart knew the flimsy, corrugated tin roof and the open space facing the creek were designed for safety rather than a charming view of the Brandywine. In the event of an explosion, any blast would be directed outward and upward. This made things safer for everyone, except the unfortunates caught inside.

The guide addressed Janie's fifth-grade class. He was an older gentleman named Dave, who claimed to be a descendant of a worker assigned to this particular mill during one of the most notorious accidents to take place in over 100 years of operation.

"If you think mixing explosives all day made for dangerous work, you'd be right. They were as careful as they could be. Even so, when the mill was active, we suffered 288 explosions, resulting in 228 deaths," Dave said. He was dressed in period-correct, turn-of-the-century coveralls and, with tousled white hair, looked to be in his seventies

Stuart hated to think how difficult a casualty rate like that would be to insure nowadays. As a corporate attorney, he was certain such an approach would never get the green light in today's environment. Funny, he'd never made it to the museum before in 10 years of working within a mile of the place. Today, he was glad he'd agreed to be a last-minute fill-in to chaperone the class trip.

He noticed Janie reach out to the wall for support and now her forehead was shiny with perspiration. She'd been a little under the weather this morning, but even now waved Stuart off with a shake of her head so as not to interrupt the speaker.

"One day, back in 1920, in this particular mill, my grandfather, Elmer McPhee, was working when they had the one explosion they *don't* think was an accident."

This got the kids' attention, but Stuart barely heard him. Janie had gone pale and, despite the wall, was beginning to sway on her feet. He tried to slip past the group in the cramped space but, just as he reached Janie, her eyes rolled back in her head and she collapsed.

The students closest to her began to scream and Stuart reached her side as the rest of the class joined in the chaos. Stuart held her and the guide ducked out to summon help.

The ambulance arrived less than 10 minutes later. Stuart stepped aside to let the paramedics try their best, but he knew she was already gone.

* * *

Three Months Later ...

Stuart leaned against the thick wall of the old gunpowder mill and glanced at his watch. The stone felt cool through his dress shirt. His charcoal-gray suit jacket remained slung over one arm, unneeded in the late-summer heat.

The next tour would come through in a few minutes. He'd heard the history of the mill countless times since fate had sent his entire world spinning off its axis. He had time for one more tour before he returned to the office to go through the motions.

Where others saw a historic landmark that was the source of much of the early wealth for the DuPont family, Stuart saw the six-foot-thick stone walls more like tombstones. So many accidents, rough men doing dangerous work, snuffed out in the blink of an eye.

At least they'd *known* about the risks. They'd made a choice to step inside these walls. It was a museum now. A safe place to learn history.

Stuart got his own history lesson that day. The doctors told him they suspected Janie had hypertension in her family history. She hadn't known. She'd been adopted and the parents who raised her were still going strong in their late eighties. Nothing besides mild, elevated blood pressure had shown up in her routine physicals. One day, fine. The next, a massive hemorrhagic cerebrovascular accident—and Janie Talley, loving wife, gone at age 45. *In lieu of flowers, please send ...*

Once the calls, cards, and well-wishers had faded, Stuart kept waiting for the anger, the crippling sorrow, and, he hoped, the long climb back. Though to what, he hadn't a clue.

Instead, he'd felt a suffocating numbness. It was like he was portraying himself in some surreal film. He'd tried drinking. That made him sleepy. He'd tried exercise. That made him sore and sleepy.

Finally, he followed this insistent pull back to where it all happened. The mill. For weeks, Stuart wanted to blame someone or something—himself, the doctors, her, even the museum—but nothing prevailed. Now he just felt a void.

Except here. The rest of his day felt drab and colorless. When he came here and stood inside the walls of this mill, everything sharpened and became vivid. Even the stones popped with color, gray rocks flecked with quartz. Blue patinas dressed with green moss and the slice of the Brandywine was like a living painting. The birds and chipmunks supplied a soundtrack to the endless performance.

And tour guide Dave. Dave and the tours comprised the soundtrack as well.

In the weeks following Janie's death, he'd returned and quietly paid the entrance fee only to spend his entire time inside the mill. Once the staff realized he wasn't dangerous, either to the tours or himself, they seemed to grant him a "griever's discount."

He could tell they whispered when he walked in, but nobody asked him for money. He was sure they all thought of him as "that guy with the dead wife."

Stuart supposed they were waiting for him to get past it. Maybe he was, too. But all he knew was that the only time he felt anything, even sadness, was in that stone room. It was like being in a prison with a key to leave anytime. But he couldn't.

Sometimes he'd sit all day inside the mill, waiting. Janie would have asked him what on earth he thought was going to happen, and he'd be forced to admit he had no idea. Maybe because it was the last time and place that anything mattered?

The next group shuffled in. Stuart didn't recognize the faces and nobody took much notice of him. There were always people wandering the grounds in addition to the organized tours.

Dave didn't even look at him. He cast his eyes down as if he were embarrassed and began his presentation.

Stuart let his mind wander until Dave reached the part about the mysterious explosion that wasn't an accident.

"Now the way my grandfather told me, he worked with a pair of fellows who were friends, but must have had a falling out," Dave said.

Maybe it was the way Dave's practiced delivery captured the room, but Stuart always felt a chill at this part.

"One of 'em was a wiry fellow named Jake Riley. The other was a big guy everybody called 'Smokey.' Anyone want to guess why?"

Audience members invariably deduced the man was a smoker.

"That he was. Treated himself to a big old Cyrano cigar to celebrate surviving another shift. Pop told me Smokey got the habit when he served in the Army during World War I."

Usually someone would ask about the rules in such an explosive area.

"Right. They were so strict, the supervisor would search all the workers at the gate before they could come down here to work. Matches, lighters, anything like that."

The way Dave told the story, Stuart could picture it in jarring detail. Each time the scenes grew more vivid, even including breadcrumbs on Smokey's shirt from his lunch that day.

"Smokey had this fancy Art Deco lighter that was top-of-the-line at the time. Real proud of it, he was. Every morning, the supervisor would put out his hand and Smokey would turn it over, tell it he'd 'see her later' like she was his girlfriend or something," Dave grinned. "One day, my Gramps ran late and, when he reached this very mill, he could hear the sound of a struggle."

The chill deepened and Stuart marveled that nobody else noticed it.

"When he got to the door, Gramps saw the two of them fighting and, clear as day, he saw Smokey holding that lighter over his head and Jake leaping and grabbing for it," Dave waved his arms around to illustrate. "Then Jake yelled, 'He's off the deep end, get some help!'" Dave affected a terrified expression. "Gramps didn't have to be told twice, not with the pile of powder they'd already mixed that morning."

Stuart half-heard, half-saw what Dave described.

"Gramps barely got to the hill, yelling all the way, when behind him ... BOOM!" A couple little kids jumped and shrieked at Dave's sudden shout.

Dave finished the story describing how the investigators at the time reached their conclusion. Based on the statement from Dave's grandfather Elmer, Smokey had swiped his lighter back from where the supervisor held items and that he'd used it to threaten Jake Riley. But, in the struggle, had lit it and set off the explosion. Nobody was sure why Smokey would have been angry with Jake.

Stuart stayed behind after the group had left. He leaned back against the wall and closed his eyes, lost in the moment. He could almost taste the gunpowder residue on his tongue. Then he smelled something that made him snap his eyes open. A delicate scent, like citrus and flowers. He knew it like his own name. Her perfume. He used to make fun of the snooty French name, Jardin De Printemps. It meant Springtime Garden, but he always teased her that it sounded like "Jar of Newsprint."

"Janie?" Stuart felt a cool waft of scented air brush his cheek and he dropped to his knees in the exact spot where she'd died on the dusty floor.

Stuart felt a jab of fear and all signs of perfume vanished. He waited a moment to see if it would return and whispered his wife's name again. Whatever it was had left, so he used the wall to steady himself and stand.

Immediately, he thought the room must be on fire as he choked on a colorless cloud of pungent smoke. He coughed and ducked his head in search of fresh air. If anything, it was worse.

Gotta get out of here.

He didn't understand how fumes could collect in such a concentration in a structure with a wide-open side. However it was happening, he needed to get out. He scurried out the door and stood once he was a good 10 feet away. It must have looked strange to anyone who saw him, but for the moment the immediate area was clear of visitors.

The air smelled better here and he dared to draw in a deep breath. His head swam and he felt unsteady on his feet. For a moment, he thought he might faint. He leaned over, resting his hands on his knees, trying to keep the gray curtains from closing in across his vision. He glanced at the mill again, wondering if it had caught fire. No smoke anywhere, just the open door and daylight peeking from the open side that faced the creek.

Then a shadow crossed the door, paused, and moved away.

Stuart felt a cold stab while the shadow darkened the door, but he forced himself to walk back toward the mill.

You imagined it.

Stuart reached the door and poked his head inside before he lost his nerve. The room was empty and, even stranger, the room had the same damp, mossy smell it always did. Not a whiff of smoke.

No, he *did* smell something and realized that his clothes reeked like he'd worn them wet into an all-night poker party. Tobacco smoke. No question about it. He sniffed again. Cigars. He stepped back and blinked in the early afternoon sun. He rubbed his eyes. No sign of shadows inside the mill.

Stupid. Maybe it was time to give the grief counselor a try again. Was this what a nervous breakdown felt like?

He made it back to the office and barely remembered reviewing his case files. He'd made up some excuse about someone smoking at lunch and asking a couple coworkers if his clothing stunk. He got some funny looks, but nobody seemed to smell anything.

Once they walked away, he'd give his shirt a sniff.

He reeked.

* * *

Hockessin, Delaware—Stuart's house

Stuart stared at the ceiling between long blinks and looked at his clock in 15-minute periods of time, wondering if he'd ever get to sleep. A long shower hadn't relaxed him, but did scrub the tobacco odor off his skin. His clothes tumbled in the dryer downstairs.

He must have finally drifted off because he found himself at Hagley, walking down the path that led to the Powder Mill. It was night, though he'd never been there after closing. He often thought it would be easy to sneak in and even toyed with the idea sometimes.

When he reached the mill, he saw that same shadow creep inside the building. There was a soft yellow light flickering inside. He felt no fear and even a thrill of hope the shape would be Janie. Now and then, he saw her in dreams. Waking was a torment on those mornings.

Here he stepped to the door, the stone walls rough against his palm, and peered inside.

"Janie?"

Strong hands reached from the room and pulled him inside. In the dim light, he saw a hazy bearded figure tower over him. The hands were scarred and gripped fistfuls of his shirt while the man scowled at him. It was hard to make out the facial features, but the eyes flashed crimson and bore into Stuart to the point of being painful, like hot coals stuck on his shirt.

Stuart tried to speak, but no sound came from his mouth. He wanted to struggle, but his body betrayed him and he was dragged toward the river-facing open wall of the mill.

Now he could see the moonlight shining on the creek and the trees looked gray in the reflected light. There was a thick mist drifting across the water. The moonlight made it appear self-illuminating.

Stuart watched the mist gather on the other side of the creek, then rise into a shape. He forgot about the iron grip the instant the hands released his shirt. He stared, fascinated while the shape assumed a human form.

"Janie?" Stuart managed to speak at last. It *was* her. Her face, the skin was so smooth and her hair as neat as ever. Better than any of the dreams over the months since her death.

But she looked so sad. She opened her arms, beckoning him to give her a hug. Stuart knew the creek wasn't deep. He walked forward with his feet feeling like they were thigh-deep in mud. He lurched forward, one lumbering step at a time. He didn't care what horror the phantom with the beard had in mind, he'd endure anything just to feel her satin cheek once more.

Stuart wanted to ask her to come back to him, but the only word he could utter was her name. He called out as loud as he could but she never answered, just stared at him with her sorrowful expression.

By the time Stuart had waded to the middle of the creek, Janie looked more distraught than ever. Tears glinted down her cheeks in the soft light. Though it felt like he'd already run a marathon, he doubled his efforts to reach her. He felt a wave of cold pass and a dark cloud crossed the water, trailing a stench of charred flesh and cigars.

Stuart saw the red points that had nearly stared a hole through his body perched within the noxious cloud. Only now they moved toward Janie.

He tried to scream, but now he couldn't even speak Janie's name aloud.

Each time the spirit gazed at Janie, its crimson glow was like water washing away her substance. Her form began to fade and she held her arms up to ward it off, to no avail. The last thing Stuart saw was her face and an expression of pain and terror.

Now Stuart noticed the creek must be deeper than he thought as he began to sink. The icy water was up to his chest and he no longer felt the creek's bottom.

Janie's spirit had scattered into mist and Stuart twisted toward the dark cloud that was now forming into the shape of his attacker. The beard looked like wisps of smoke.

When it stared at him this time, he didn't feel the pain. He also couldn't look away from the burning red gaze.

The figure moved a short way along the shore to the base of the largest tree along the shoreline. It pointed to where thick root structures jutted up and formed a v-shaped crotch. The figure pointed a sinuous finger at the spot and Stuart heard a single word inside his skull.

DIG.

Stuart didn't care what it wanted and if he couldn't speak his mind, he'd see if this thing couldn't read his.

Bring her back!

Stuart never got a chance to learn if it heard him. Icy water enveloped his head and the panic of a drowning man swallowed him.

* * *

Stuart awoke screaming. His sheets were soaked with sweat and wrapped all around him. He had to struggle to get free of them. He kicked the covers off and stumbled to the bathroom.

His heart was still pounding while he splashed water on his face and let his eyes adjust to the blinding lights from the vanity. "Holy crap."

He was glad nobody else lived here, as he'd have to explain himself.

What *had* happened, anyway?

A dream. Really intense, but was it all that surprising after the stress of the day?

It was hard to pull up daytime-logic rationales before sunrise, but he began to feel better.

Until he saw his bare chest in the mirror.

Stuart let out a scream and stared at the pair of bright-red circles on his upper chest just below his throat. He touched them, hoping they would vanish, a mere artifact of an intense dream.

The pain snapped him fully awake and he stared at the spots that looked (and felt) like he'd extinguished a lit cigar on his flesh.

The thought sent a cold shock though his body. He whirled around, half expecting to spot an intruder. He neither saw nor heard anyone and stepped back into the bedroom. He flicked on the light and saw his bedroom door was closed. He listened for the sound of breathing and sniffed for any scent of burnt flesh.

Nothing. And when he rechecked his skin, he saw the discoloration was strong as ever, but the surface of the skin wasn't seared or charred.

The pain was as real as ever. He reached into his closet for an aluminum bat, leftover from his brief, undistinguished career on the company softball team.

Stuart pulled on some pants and screwed up his courage enough to check the rest of the house.

All the doors and windows remained shut and locked from the inside.

Nobody but you here, Champ.

He went into the kitchen and grabbed a bottle of water.

Maybe he was sick. Sudden fever and night sweats? That'd cause some bad nightmares, right? The marks on his chest forced him to remember the way that phantasm had looked at him.

Then he thought about how real Janie had seemed. Not in the way she materialized in the mist, but because the intensity of her personality had been so genuine. Stuart treasured the times she appeared in dreams. But then, despite how often he yearned to see her, those "appearances" were fragmented and brief, more like gilded scraps of memory. This was more, it was a presence.

Like a ghost?

Stuart caught himself about to laugh at the stupidity, then stopped. Why not, for lack of a better term? Why does that damn mill hold such a draw anyway? *I was right there when she passed away. Maybe we're still connected. Is that so farfetched?*

Maybe you're having a nervous breakdown and you need an IV drip full of antipsychotics.

Twin flashes of pain struck his chest and he rushed to a mirror. The pain was still there but the marks were shrinking.

Spider bites? Ticks? Might want to get tested for Lyme disease while you are at it.

Stuart felt for bumps or any sign of broken skin. Nope. But maybe that was it. He didn't think he was allergic, but it was possible. In the end, he tried to get a couple hours of sleep before it was time to get up and go to the office.

* * *

In the morning, it felt like he'd blinked before the sun popped up. Stuart went into the bathroom to check on his bug bites (which was what they had to be.)

Nothing. He could barely see red smudges on his skin and realized those were probably just chafing from him rubbing his skin over and over to confirm the spots didn't hurt.

Later, he put in a solid day's work at the office despite the fatigue because he was trying so hard to avoid thinking about the mill. He wasn't entirely successful and thought of Janie often, as usual. He did resist the temptation to head over to the mill, and worked through his lunch hour.

In his car, on the way home, Stuart was sure he'd caught a whiff of cigar, but the odor vanished as suddenly as it occurred.

He'd decided earlier to stop setting the table for two. It was a dumb habit, but a shred of normalcy he'd kept up, not caring that it might have looked odd. Tonight, it was cold pizza for one.

Maybe this was the road back. He'd been looking all this time for an answer, some magic elixir to start healing from his grief. Maybe the recent strangeness was his body's way of telling him to just slow down and let the sadness run its course.

I don't remember reading about these stages. Shock, Denial, Bargaining, Raving Insanity, then Acceptance?

He tried to read a book before bed. The phone remained quiet, even the telemarketers and scammers were giving him space. He was a fast reader, always had been, which was handy in law school and in practice. But tonight he ripped through the pages and realized he didn't remember a damn thing about what he'd just read.

He turned off the lights and closed his eyes ready for whatever the dream gods had in mind. Not much, he guessed, as he tossed and turned for hours.

"Screw it." He turned on his bedside lamp and shuffled to the bathroom. He reached inside the medicine cabinet. The orange pill bottle sat right where he'd left it months ago. His doctor had prescribed the Ambien to break the insomnia that followed Janie's funeral.

It wasn't that they hadn't worked. The last time he took one, he slept so soundly he couldn't escape the nightmares. He'd come to with his body sluggish and mind racing.

His vigils inside the mill struck a compromise within himself that at least allowed him sleep and function. Some days he wondered for how long. Mostly he was content to feel nothing.

Maybe now, if the dreams were closer to the surface of his mind, the sedative would pull him deep enough to ride under them like a bodysurfer diving under a dangerous wave.

He swallowed the pill and tried to think about all the countries in which his latest client would need to file incorporation documents. Better than counting sheep. Usually.

* * *

Cold.

Stuart felt it creep up his legs starting at his feet and a chill spread across his back. He wanted to pull the blanket up, but there was something in his hands.

There wasn't a blanket anywhere near. He was in a field, who knew where, and now and then a cow would charge past, only she had dazzling bright eyes and mooed when she passed.

His feet hurt.

He looked down and saw why. He wasn't wearing shoes and the dirt was too hard and uniform ...

BEEEP! "Out of the road, asshole!"

Heavy layers of confusion slid off Stuart's mind and he realized the cows were cars and he'd been walking down the center lane.

Sonofabitch!

He scurried to the side and heard something metallic drag along with him. Reality slowly came into focus and he saw what was in his hands.

A shovel.

He heard a deep voice echo from far away. "Dig."

* * *

The next night, Stuart left the bottle of Ambien on the shelf. He hadn't needed the therapist's recommendation for that one. The side effects weren't worth the benefit, which had been dubious at best.

One thing she did say, that he wasn't as sure about, was that the intense dreams were a good sign. What had she called it? "The poisons hatching out."

He didn't know about all that. But he did know one way or another he couldn't live like a zombie the rest of his life or the insanity would be neither imaginary nor temporary.

"But you'll have to do all your hatching without mother's little helper," he said aloud. It still felt weird to have skipped going to the mill today. He wondered if the staff at Hagley would send out a search party.

"More likely they're hoping I never come back," he said to the empty room. He'd tried instead to bury himself in work. The partners had been understanding, but sooner or later they'd insist he begin to pull his weight again.

Strange day, but at least he hadn't ended as roadkill.

* * *

The crashing sound made Stuart think of a truck hitting a pothole. He tried to jump out the way, but of what? His heart pounded at the next crash and his eyes snapped open. His hand was wrapped around a cool piece of metal. A handle.

He clawed to full wakefulness and saw he was outside again. He looked around in panic. Familiar. He was in his backyard. His hand still clenched the door handle to his shed. He'd been tugging on it and only now remembered that he'd locked it and put the key somewhere different. He'd done that when he locked away the shovel.

The moment he thought of it, he felt a residual urge to get it anyway and ... dig.

* * *

Stuart had already decided not to share the previous evening's nocturnal adventure with his therapist. She might suggest another sleep aid or something worse. Whatever this was, he was going to conquer it on his own terms. He even sounded tough to his own ears during his commute home, yelling inside the safety of his Lexus at the odd compulsion he'd developed. It wasn't going to beat him.

While he yelled, he missed his turn.

"Damnit." Stuart put on the blinker for the store ahead so he could turn around in the parking lot.

The sign caught his eye: Hockessin Hardware.

His heart skipped a beat, but as the traffic cleared, he made the turn. Instead of pulling a U-turn, he slid the car into an open parking spot.

"You want to play? Let's play."

He got out and heard the chime on the door as he entered the shop. The owner nodded to him. Stuart had never been much of a handyman. But, after more than 20 years in this town, everybody looked at least a little familiar.

"Can I help you find something?" The bald guy in the blue denim shirt with the HH logo embossed on the front asked.

"I know where it is, thanks."

He walked past a row of long-handled tools, smiling to himself at the torment causing his compulsion to dig. Did recovering drunks go to bars to test themselves?

He picked a new rake. Fall was right around the corner. He was glad he'd thought of it.

He paid the man and placed his purchase in the trunk. He felt good. Better than he had all day and wasn't even sure why. Instead of going straight home, he swung by the liquor store.

Drinking hadn't dulled the pain for him earlier, but he felt more normal than maybe any day since Janie's death. He was curious if he could enjoy a couple beers like a regular person again.

"Good choice, sir." The guy at the store complimented his selection. Stuart figured he might as well get something decent while he was at it. "Will you need this?" He held up a bottle opener shaped like a lighter.

"I'm all set," Stuart said.

He drove carefully over the speed bumps so he wouldn't have six foam rockets waiting for him.

Back at his house, he got out of the car and reached to the floor behind the driver's seat.

"What the hell?" He stared. Instead of bottles he saw "Cohiba" in large red letters stenciled across a fancy wooden box.

He picked it up as if it was concealing the beer he'd just bought, but it was the only thing back there.

"That's impossible." He shook the box and heard only the soft rattle of carefully wrapped stogies, not the clink of glass. And he felt the strangest craving to try one, although, outside a couple bachelor parties he'd attended 30 years ago, he never smoked the things.

He went to the trunk, opened it, and screamed in frustration at the shovel that lay on the pristine gray felt.

Stuart slammed the trunk and dug through his pockets for the receipts. He knew what he'd bought. This had to be an elaborate prank.

He saw the printout. Both receipts showed what he had. A $200 box of premium cigars and one garden shovel.

"But the beer was 12 dollars ..." Stuart was having trouble picturing the price sticker or even the exact brand of beer. Then he glanced at his signature on both receipts. The first one was hard to read scrawl, but it was in his hand for sure and it said "Stuart Digger."

The second one, for the cigars, made his head dance with panic. "Stuart Burner?"

Just as he read it, he got a mental picture and saw himself sleepwalking to his kitchen and putting a pot of gasoline on the stove for some midnight high-octane soup.

Message received, bastard.

* * *

Parking lot, Near Hagley Powder Mills

"Fine, we'll try your way," Stuart felt like a fool, wearing old wading boots and carrying a backpack with a small spade, and a flashlight that he hoped he wouldn't need.

He glanced at his watch and knew he only had an hour of daylight left.

Left to do what? He knew better than to go through the gates of Hagley dressed like some half-assed grave robber.

Instead, he wore a floppy fishing hat and decided to take his chances tromping through the woods until he reached Brandywine Creek.

He hoped he'd be able to recognize the tree from his dream. It was visible from the mill side of the creek and the tree was real enough. As for what he was looking for, well "it" never said, did it?

Stuart wondered if having some idea would even matter or if it was all some manufactured notion.

Of course it was.

The rational part of his brain was still trying to talk him out of this ridiculous effort. The dog-tired part of his mind pushed him on willing at this point to try anything if he could just get a decent night of sleep without jogging on the highway or setting his house on fire.

The cool weather that would suppress the late summer bugs was still weeks away. Stuart pushed through the overgrown foliage trying to avoid the worst of the thorns and thriving poison ivy. Mosquitoes found every part of his uncovered skin and he cursed at them while swatting himself hard enough to leave welts.

Every time he wished he'd brought a machete (with a gallon of bug repellent), he imagined what staffers near the stone mills would make of seeing him emerge across the way wielding a large, sharp blade.

If all went well, none of them would see him and he'd be on his way with nobody the wiser.

When he reached the creek, he peeked along the opposite shoreline and spotted the stone mill where Janie died. He splashed through the shallows of the creek until he lined up with it. Everything looked different from this perspective. As soon as he turned his back to the mill, the large tree was right where he remembered. It was uncanny how faithfully his dream had recreated the shoreline.

It didn't take long to climb the hill to the base of the tree. It was older than the surrounding slim trees. Must be over 100 years old. The sun was beginning to drop and Stuart took out the spade, now wishing he'd brought the stupid shovel he'd thought was a rake.

He shivered, though it wasn't cold out, and found the patch from the dream. Strange, most dreams drifted and scattered with consciousness. This one had grown sharper and insistent.

Stuart clung to the Janie part of the dream and began to plunge the spade into the dirt between the roots. Smaller roots spider-webbed among the thicker ones and Stuart nearly turned an ankle when he stomped on the handle to force the blade deeper.

Between the roots and the rocks caught up in the subterranean net, progress was much more difficult than he'd imagined. He glanced toward the mill. "Well? I'm digging. Happy? Or do you want me to topple the whole damn tree?" He began to laugh and for an instant worried he might not be able to stop.

A cloud passed in front of the sinking sun. The shadows swallowed the trees and he remembered how dark the stretch of town could get with no lights nearby. When the cloud moved off, the first ray of light speared right at the spot where he dug.

He bore down on the blade and sweat dripped down his face. All at once, the spade cut through a root and plunged deeper. When he yanked it out, it flung dirt and small stones into his face.

"Shit!" Stuart wiped the grime away and shoved his hand in the space he'd cleared. More dirt, more rocks, worms, grubs and anything except a damn point.

Stuart began to reach in and fling the rocks he found across the creek at the mill.

"There! Happy?" He yelled. It was after hours, so he didn't think anyone would hear. He didn't care.

His fingers found a smooth, fairly flat rock that might make a good skipping stone. As soon as he worked it loose from the soil, he knew it was something else.

Black and rectangular but bent. It was metal and, in the last of the light, Stuart realized it wasn't black at all, but tarnished. For an instant, it felt like he'd grabbed a battery as he understood what was in his hand.

A lighter.

* * *

Back home, Stuart felt lucky he hadn't crashed the car on the way. He could barely take his eyes off the lighter the whole drive back and must have been veering all over the place like a texting teen with a new driver's license.

The lighter was old and had elaborate, scrolled patterns and a diamond shape in the center. He used some Brasso to remove the tarnish and more detail emerged. He found a manufacturer's mark, Thorens.

The case looked like it had been fired from a gun or caught in an ... explosion. He felt a flash in his mind and a snapshot of a blast he knew at once was from the mill.

Or what you imagine.

Sure, probably so, but he never used to be so imaginative.

He flipped it over to polish the other side. What was this? Cleaning away the deep tarnish, he blackened several cotton balls. There was writing engraved on one of the smooth sides. He pawed through his junk drawer in the kitchen for a magnifying glass.

An old twist-tie poked into one of his cuticles, but he forgot about the pain and found the elusive lens.

He held the lighter up and studied the scratchy cursive.

"For Lucy, the only light I'll ever need again. —S."

* * *

Hagley

"I need to speak to Dave." Stuart felt weird conversing with the woman, who let him pass without a word.

"He'll be down for the tour in half an hour." She paused. "Same as always. Is it something I could help you with?" Stuart could see on her face that she hoped not.

"Actually, no. I had a question about his grandfather," Stuart lied.

"Wait a moment." She stepped from the desk and retreated to an office. Stuart hoped it wasn't to summon security. The lack of sleep was taking its toll and he'd already called in sick to work.

Dave met him and they stepped outside. "What can I do for you, Mr. Talley?"

They'd never formally met, but of course everyone knew who he was. "Your grandfather, how well did he know this guy Smokey?"

"You've heard my speech enough times you could probably give it yourself. Pretty well, I guess. Why?"

"Did he tell *you* much about Smokey? About his personal life?"

Dave frowned at that. "What do you mean by that, son?"

Stuart wasn't sure the best way to approach the question. "I found something." He dug into his pocket and held out the lighter.

Dave took it with polite interest at first. But, as he squinted and adjusted his glasses, his breathing sped up.

"Where did you find this?"

Stuart pointed toward the mill. "Across the creek. It was stuck in the dirt. I cleaned it up. It's old."

Dave stared at Stuart in disbelief. "What made you look over there? You don't look like one of those treasure hunters with the metal detectors."

Stuart smiled at the image before he realized how ridiculous the truth was. "Would you believe it was a dream? "

Dave's gaze had returned to the lighter and he glanced up. "I might." He held onto the lighter and pulled out a set of keys. "Come with me."

Dave led Stuart into a back entrance to the indoor museum section. He waited while Dave dug through some old photo albums. He held a large magnifying glass and pored over the crumbling old black and white shots.

"I'll be damned. Look at this, son." Dave waved Stuart over.

Stuart saw a vintage shot of three men posing in front of the iron gates of the Hagley Mill. The gates looked much as they did today. Stuart recognized one burly bearded figure instantly. The face was so familiar the smiling man practically winked at him.

Smokey.

When Dave passed the magnifying glass over Smokey's hand, they saw the object in his hand. A silver lighter.

"That explains how it got all dented. It must have shot across like a bullet."

"It confirms Gramps' story," Dave said.

"But it doesn't explain why he did it. It couldn't have been an accident."

"I might be able to shed some light there," Dave said. "See, I leave something out of my speech on the tour."

"What's that?" Stuart said. He turned the lighter over in his hand, feeling the smooth sides and creases where the metal had buckled.

"Seeing that name Lucy brings it back. Gramps told me there was a pretty young lady named Lucy Caldwell who dated one of the men on that crew."

"Smokey." Stuart could swear the lighter grew warmer in his hand.

"That's just it. It was Jake, the other man who died trying to stop Smokey."

"Really?"

"Yup. Seeing that now tells me old Smokey was jealous as hell, maybe even trying to arrange an accident." Dave smiled. "But for a smaller feller, Jake gave him all he could handle and the place went up before Smokey had a chance to be on the other side of that wall."

Now the lighter felt almost hot and Stuart noticed his right hand was curled into a fist. The urge to slug the old man came on so fast he nearly acted on it. Then it was gone.

What the hell was that?

"Something wrong?" Dave asked.

"No. I mean, all this time, I don't know what I was looking for out of all this. The dreams, the crazy—I don't know what you'd call them—sensations? All pointed me to do something. But what does it mean?"

"Psychiatrists make more per hour than tour guides." Dave grinned. "But just maybe part of you wanted something to make sense to balance out a terrible experience that made none."

"Shit. You might be right," Stuart said. "But I don't feel any different."

"Maybe you're crazy as Smokey." Dave laughed. "We have an article from a couple years back on descendants of the workers killed in explosions who still live in the area." Dave opened a long file drawer and began to flip through manila folders. "They had a sidebar piece on Lucy Caldwell's granddaughter."

"Why?"

Dave found the piece and handed it to Stuart. He read that Betsey Moran had told the reporter that the explosion had left her grandmother so distraught that she swore she'd never get married. Of course, she eventually changed her mind and Betsey was living proof two generations later.

"Sad story." Stuart agreed. "Think Smokey wanted the truth to come out? A 'confession is good for the soul' kind of thing?"

"Not important what I think, son. What do *you* think?" Dave held his gaze.

"You sure you weren't a psychiatrist in your old career?" Stuart said. "All right, I guess I'll have to show him we have the goods on him now."

"If you're going to do that, you might as well hit him where he lives, so to speak." Dave gave Stuart the cemetery address where Smokey was buried.

* * *

Green Hill Cemetery, Greenville, Delaware

Stuart thanked the lady at the church and added a 20-dollar donation toward the care packages she prepared for soldiers overseas. He found the old worn headstone and worried he might walk past because of the name. He felt a pull as soon as he saw it.

Leonard Parker

Corporal

U.S. Army World War I—1898-1920

It was Smokey, all right. "I don't know what else you want from me." He took the lighter out of his pocket. So much for Dave's career as a psychiatrist. Stuart felt exhaustion press down on his shoulders.

"You wanted me to find this? Here you go. Everyone knows you were nuts and here's proof. Take it and leave me alone!" Dave drew back his arm to throw the thing at the headstone and the lighter felt burning hot in his hand. He dropped it and it bounced off another marker.

And broke open.

He touched it gingerly. The metal now felt cool. He slid the top piece out the rest of the way and inside the lighter was a rusty mat of steel wool. "Weird." The stuff was where the cotton wadding would normally be in a working lighter, used to hold the fluid. Stuart picked at the wool, which crumbled at his touch. Then he felt something else. A ring.

A gold ring with a tiny diamond set just like ... "An engagement ring?"

He felt a weight come off his shoulders.

* * *

Hagley

Dave met him at the gate after Stuart's frantic call. "Bring it inside."

In the museum back-office, Stuart took out the old lighter and showed him. "The stuff is real crumbly."

"That was in there? With the ring?"

Stuart nodded.

"It's steel wool, all right."

"Was that ever used in lighters?"

Dave shook his head. "They used cotton wadding to absorb and retain the fuel."

"Then this lighter should be hollow and empty after all this time. The cotton would have decomposed," Stuart said.

"Exactly! This lighter would have never functioned in that condition."

"So, Smokey didn't set off the explosion. At least not with this lighter."

"No," Dave took a deep breath. "But he still could have smuggled in a match."

Stuart held up the ring. "Does this look like the sort of thing you buy with nothing to live for?"

"That depends."

"Rejected?" Stuart thought about the article. That made sense. He thought about the article that included Lucy's granddaughter. "Do you think the granddaughter might know?"

"We can ask," Dave said.

* * *

They found the number for Betsey Maron. When they called, she picked up right away. David identified himself and she said she recognized the museum on the caller ID.

Stuart introduced himself as well and mentioned the discovery of the lighter and a ring.

"That doesn't sound familiar," she said.

Stuart read the inscription and thought she'd hung up. "Ma'am?"

"Gram always said she would have taken him back, cigars and all, if she could."

"I thought she was with the other guy. Jake?"

"I'm not surprised. I never could get the paper to print a correction. They misquoted me and at the time I didn't figure it mattered much. My Gram was heartbroken over Smokey. She said she always was sorry to have to break it off with Jake, but Smokey was the man for her, if only he could have stopped with those awful cigars."

Stuart felt a lead weight drop onto his chest. "He was going to quit for her. That's what he meant by 'the only light he needed.' He was going to quit and propose."

"The whole thing is terribly sad, but I suppose I wouldn't be here if she hadn't moved on. Was there anything else?" she asked.

Dave began to shake his head, but Stuart held up a hand and spoke. "Just one thing. Where is Lucy, I mean your gram, buried?"

"Green Hill Cemetery, why?"

* * *

One week later

Stuart stood in the back in his old spot. He hadn't been to the mill since his discovery. But, after several nights of sleep, he felt he it was time.

Dave led a tour group and gave Stuart a quick wink, but otherwise went through his usual routine. When he got to the part about the 1920 explosion, Stuart ears perked.

"We may never know for sure what happened that day, but some think the scuffle may have been over a lovely young lady and that our friend Smokey was trying to stop a desperate man from making an awful mistake."

Stuart braced himself, then sampled the air with a deep inhale. Not a hint of cigar smoke or gunpowder. He sniffed again and nearly fell over as the scent of citrus and florals filled his head.

He glanced around and saw no one next to him. Even so, he felt fingers brush his cheek and the scent drifted away with the touch.

"Ewww, what's that stink?" A kid was pointing to him with his nose crinkled. "Smells girly."

Stuart smiled and said, "Newsprint. A whole jar of newsprint."

NEIGHBORS FROM HELL

BY GRAHAM MASTERTON

It was pretty horrible the way my grandmother died. I was working in The Blue Turtle Bar in Fort Lauderdale last summer when the phone rang and it was Mr. Szponder, the super in my grandmother's apartment building. He said in his rusty old voice that she'd tumbled into a bath of scalding water and that she was now in intensive care at St. Philomena's.

"Oh, God. How bad is it?"

"Bad. Thirty percent third-degree burns, that's what they told me. They don't expect her to make it. Not at her age."

"I'll catch the next flight, okay?"

I asked Eugene for the rest of the week off. Eugene had greasy black curls right down to the collar of his red-and-yellow Hawaiian shirt and a face like somebody had been using a pumpkin for a dartboard. He hefted his big, hairy arm around my shoulders and said, "Jimmy ... you take as long as you like."

"Thanks, Eugene."

"In fact, why don't you take forever?"

"What do you mean? You're *canning* me? This is my grandmother I'm talking about here. This is the woman who raised me."

"This is also the middle of the season, and if it's a choice between profit and compassion ... well, let's just say that there isn't a Cadillac dealership in town which takes compassion in exchange for late-model Sevilles."

I could see by the look in his pebbly little eyes that he wasn't going to give way, and it wasn't even worth saying "screw you, Eugene." It just wasn't.

I went back to the tattily furnished house I was sharing on Broward Street with three inarticulate musicians from Boise, Idaho, and a wide-eyed brunette called Wendiii who thought the capital of Florida was "F."

"Hey, you leaving us, man?" asked the lead guitarist, peering at me through curtains of straggly, sun-bleached hair.

"My grandma's had an accident. They think she's probably going to die."

"Bummer."

"Yeah. She practically raised me single-handed after my mom died."

"You coming back?"

I looked around at the bare-boarded living room with its broken blinds and its rucked-up rug and every available surface crowded with empty Coors cans. Somehow it seemed as if all the romance had gone out of the Fort Lauderdale lifestyle, as if the sun had gone behind a cloud and a chilly breeze had suddenly started to blow.

"Maybe," I said.

Wendiii came out of the john, buttoning up her tiny denim shorts. "You take care, you hear?" she told me, and gave me a long, wet, openmouthed kiss. "It's such a pity that you and me never got it on."

Now she tells me, I thought. But my taxi had drawn up outside, and it was time to go. She lifted her elbows and took a little silver crucifix from around her neck and gave it to me.

"I can't take this."

"Then borrow it, and bring it back safe."

* * *

In Chicago, the sky was dark and the rain came clattering down like bucketfuls of nails. I hurried across the sidewalk outside St. Philomena's with a copy of *Newsweek* on top of my head, but it didn't stop water from pouring down the back of my neck. The hospital lobby was lit like a migraine and the corridors were crowded with gurneys and wheelchairs and people arguing and old folks staring into space and nodding as if they absolutely definitely agreed that life wasn't worth living.

A tall, black nurse led me up to intensive care, loping along in front of me with all the loopy grace of a giraffe. My grandmother lay in greenish gloom, her head and her hands wrapped in bandages. Her face was waxy and blotched, and her cheeks had collapsed so that you could see the skull underneath. She looked as if she were dead already.

I sat down beside her. "Grandma? It's me, Jimmy."

It was a long time before her eyes flickered open, and when they did I had a chilly feeling of dread. All the blue seemed to have drained from her irises—did you ever see eyes with no color at all?—and it was obvious that she knew that death was only hours away.

"Jimmy ..."

"Mr. Szponder told me what happened, Grandma. Oh, Jesus, what can I say?"

"They're keeping me comfortable, Jimmy, don't you worry." She gave a feeble, sticky cough. "Plenty of morphine to stop me from hurting."

"Grandma ... you should have had somebody looking after you. How many times did I tell you that?"

"I never needed anybody to look after me, Jimmy. I was always the looker-afterer."

"Well, you sure looked after me good. Nobody could have raised me better."

Grandma coughed again. "Promise me one thing, Jimmy. You will promise me, won't you?"

"Anything. Just say the word."

She tried to raise her head, but the effort and the pain were too much for her. "Promise me you won't think bad of your mother."

I frowned at her and shook my head. "Why should I think bad of her? It wasn't her fault that she died."

"Try to understand, that's all I'm saying."

"Grandma, I don't get it. Try to understand *what?*"

She looked at me for a long time, but she didn't say anything else. After a while she closed her eyes, and I left her to sleep.

I met her gingery-haired doctor on the way out.

"What chances does she have?" I asked him.

He took off his eyeglasses and gave me a shrug. "There are times when I have to say that patients would be better off if they could come to some conclusion."

"*Conclusion?* She's a human being, not a fucking book."

* * *

I took a taxi over to her apartment building on the South Side, in one of the few surviving streets of narrow four-story Victorian houses, overshadowed by the Dan Ryan Expressway. It was still raining and the expressway traffic was deafening.

I opened the scabby front door and went inside, carrying a brown paper shopping sack with six cans of Heineken and a turkey sandwich. The hallway was dark, with a brown linoleum floor and an old-fashioned umbrella stand. There was a strong smell of lavender floor polish and frying garlic. Somewhere a television was playing at top volume, and a baby was crying. It was hard to believe that I used to think of this building as home.

A door opened and Mr. Szponder came out, with his rounded face and his saggy gray cardigan. His gray hair was swept back so that he looked like a porcupine.

"Jimmy ... what can I say?" He held me in his arms and slapped my back as if he were trying to bring up my wind. "I always tried to look out for your grandma, you know ... but she was such a proud lady."

"Thanks, Mr. Szponder."

"You can call me Wladislaw. What do you like? Tea? Vodka?"

"Nothing, thanks. I could use a little sleep, that's all."

"Okay, but anything you need."

He gave me a final rib-crushing squeeze and breathed onions into my face.

* * *

On the fourth floor, grandma's apartment was silent and gloomy and damp. It seemed so much more cramped than it had when I was young, but very little had changed. The sagging brown-velvet couch was still taking up too much space in front of the hearth, and the stuffed owl still stared at me from the mantelpiece as if it wanted to peck out my eyes. A framed photograph of a sad-looking 7-year-old boy stood next to the owl, and that was me. I went through to the narrow kitchen and opened the tiny icebox. I was almost brought to tears by grandma's pathetic little collection of leftovers, all on saucers and neatly covered with cling-film.

I popped open a can of beer and went back to the living room. So many memories were here. So many voices from the past. Grandpa singing at Christmas. Grandma telling me stories about children who got lost in the deep, dark forest, and could only find their way out by leaving trails of breadcrumbs. They looked after me as if I were some kind of little prince, those two, and when Grandpa died in 1989 he left me a letter which said, *"There aren't any ghosts, Jimmy. Always remember that the past can't hurt you."* To be honest, I never knew what the hell he was trying to tell me.

I tried to eat my turkey sandwich, but it tasted like brown-velvet couch and lavender polish, and after two or three bites I wrapped it up again and threw it in the trash. I switched on the huge old Zenith television and watched this movie about a woman who thinks that her children are possessed. The rain spattered against the window and the traffic streamed along the Dan Ryan Expressway with an endless swishing noise, and out on the lake a steamer sounded its horn like the saddest creature you ever heard.

* * *

I woke up with a jolt. It was dark outside, and the apartment was illuminated only by the flickering light of *Wheel of Fortune*. The audience screamed with laughter, but I was sure that I had heard somebody else screaming, too. There's a difference between a roller coaster scream of hilarity and a scream of absolute terror.

I turned the volume down and listened. Nothing at first, except the traffic and the muffled sound of a television from downstairs. I waited and waited and there was still nothing. But then I heard it again. It was a child screaming, a little boy, and when I say screaming, this was a total, freezing fear-of-death scream. I felt as if I had dropped into cold water right up to my neck.

I stood up, trying to work out where the screaming was coming from. It wasn't underneath me. It wasn't the next-door apartment, either. And this was the top story, so there was nobody living above.

Suddenly I heard it again, and this time I could make out part of what the child was screaming. *"Mommy! Mommy! No Mommy you can't! Mommy you can't, you can't, you can't!* NO MOMMY YOU CAN'T!"

I went quickly through to grandma's bedroom, where the covers were still turned neatly back, and grandma's nightdress was still lying ready on the quilt. The screaming went on and on, and I could tell now that it was coming from the top-story apartment of the house next door. I thumped on the wall with my fist and yelled out, *"What's happening? What the hell are you doing?"*

The screaming stopped for a second, but then the child let out a high, shrill shriek, almost inhuman, more like a bird than a child. I hurried out of the apartment and ran downstairs, three and four stairs at a time. When I got to the hallway I banged on Mr. Szponder's door.

"Mr. Szponder! Mr. Szponder!"

He opened his door in his vest and suspenders with a half-eaten submarine sandwich in his hand. "Jimmy? Whatsa matter?"

"Call the cops! It's next door, that side, there's some mother who's hurting a kid! Tell them to hurry, it sounds like she's practically killing him! Top floor!"

"Hunh?" said Mr. Szponder. "What do you mean, killing?"

"Just dial 911 and do it now! I'm going up there!"

"Okay, okay." Mr. Szponder dithered for a moment, uncertain of what to do with his sandwich. In the end, he put it down on the seat of a chair and went off to find his telephone.

* * *

I ran down the front steps into the rain. The house next door was different from the house in which my Grandma had lived. It was narrower, with a hooded porch and dark, rain-soaked rendering. I bounded up to the front door and pressed the top-floor bell push. Then I hammered on the knocker and shouted out, "Open up! Open up! I've called the cops! Open the fucking door!"

Nobody answered, so I pressed every single bell push, and there were at least a dozen of them. After a long while, a man's voice came over the intercom. "*Who is this?*"

"I live next door. You have to let me in. There's a kid screaming on the top floor. Can't you hear him?"

"*What do you mean, kid?*"

"There's a kid screaming for help. Sounds like his mother's hurting him. For Christ's sake, open the door, will you?"

"*I don't hear no screaming.*"

"Well, maybe he's stopped, but he was screaming before. He could be hurt."

"*So what's it got to do with me?*"

"It doesn't have to have anything to do with you. Just open the goddamned door, will you? That's all I'm asking you to do."

"*I don't even know who you are. You sound like a maniac.*"

"Listen to me—if you don't let me in and that kid dies, then it's going to be your fault. Got it?"

There was a lengthy silence.

"Hallo?" I called, and pressed every bell push all over again. "Hallo? Can anybody hear me?"

I was still pushing the bells and banging on the door when a police cruiser arrived with its lights flashing. Two cops climbed out, a man and a woman, and came up the steps. The man was tall and thin, but the woman looked as if she could have gone nine rounds with Jesse Ventura. The raindrops sparkled on their transparent plastic cap-covers.

"What's the problem?"

"I was next door—staying in my grandmother's place. I heard a kid screaming. I think it's the top-floor apartment."

The woman cop pressed all the buttons again, and eventually the same man answered. "*Look—I told you—I didn't hear no screaming, and this is nothing to do with me, so stop ringing my bell or else I'm going to call the cops.*"

"I am the cops, sir. Open the door."

Immediately, there was a dull buzz and the door swung open. The cops stepped inside, and I tried to follow them but the woman cop stopped me. "You wait here, sir. We'll deal with this."

They disappeared up the rickety stairs and I was left standing in the hallway. There was a mottled mirror on the hallstand opposite me and it made me look like a ghost. Pale face, sticking-up hair, skinny shoulders like a wire coat hanger. Just like the 7-year-old boy on Grandma's mantelpiece.

It was strange, but there was something vaguely familiar about this hallway. Maybe it was the beige-and-white diamond-patterned tiles on the floor, or the waist-high wooden paneling. There must have been tens of thousands of old townhouses that were decorated like that. Yet it wasn't just the décor. There was something about the *smell*, too. Not damp and garlicky like next door, but dry and herby, like potpourri that has almost lost its scent.

I waited for almost 10 minutes while the police officers went from floor to floor, knocking on every door. I could hear them talking and people complaining. Eventually they came back down again.

"Well?" I said.

"There's no kid in this building, sir."

"What? I heard him with my own ears."

"Nobody has a kid in this building, sir. We've been through every apartment."

"It was the top floor. I swear to God. He was screaming something like, 'Mommy, Mommy, you can't'—over and over."

"The top-floor apartment is vacant, sir. Has been for years. The landlord uses it for storage, that's all."

"You're sure?"

"Absolutely. We're going to check the two buildings either side, just to make sure, but I seriously think you must have been mistaken. Probably somebody's television turned up too loud. You know what these old folks are like. Deaf as ducks."

I followed them down the steps. Mr. Szponder stood in his open doorway watching me.

"Well, what's happening?" he asked me, as the cops started ringing bells next door.

"They looked through the house from top to bottom. No kid."

"Maybe your imagination, Jimmy."

"Yeah, maybe."

"Better your imagination than some kid *really* getting hurt. Think about it."

I nodded. I couldn't think of anything to say.

* * *

The next morning, while I was brushing my teeth, the telephone rang. It was the gingery-haired doctor from St. Philomena's.

"I'm sorry to tell you that your grandmother reached her conclusion just a few minutes ago. She didn't suffer."

"I see," I said, with a mouthful of minty foam.

* * *

I called a couple of my cousins to tell them what had happened, but none of them seemed to be very upset. Cousin Dick lived in Milwaukee and could easily have come to Chicago to meet me, but he said he had a "gonad-cruncher" of a business meeting with Wisconsin Cuneo Press. Cousin Erwin sounded, quite frankly, as if he were stoned out of his brain. He kept saying, "*There you are, Jimmy … another milestone bites the dust.*"

Cousin Frances was more sympathetic. I had always liked Cousin Frances. She's about the same age as I am and worked for Bloomingdale's in New York. When I called her, she was on her lunch break, and she was so upset that she started to cough and couldn't stop.

"Listen," she said, "when are you going back to Florida?"

"I'm not in any hurry. I was fired for taking time off."

"Why don't you stop over in New York (*cough*)? I'd love to see you again."

"I don't know. Have a drink of water."

Pause. More coughing. Then, "Just call me when you get to La Guardia."

* * *

Cousin Frances lived in a terraced brownstone on E 17th Street in the Village. The street itself was pretty crummy and rundown, but her loft was airy and beautifully decorated, as you'd expect from somebody who made a living designing window displays. Three walls were plastered and painted magnolia. The fourth wall had been stripped back to its natural brick, with all kinds of strange artifacts on it, like driftwood antlers from the Hamptons and a Native American medicine stick from Wyoming.

Cousin Frances herself was thin and highly groomed, with a shining blonde bob and a line in silky blouses and slinky pajama-like pants. She was the youngest daughter of my mother's sister Irene. In a certain light, she looked very much like my mother, or at least the two or three photographs that I still had. High forehead, wide-apart eyes, distinctive cheekbones, but a rather lipless mouth, which made her look colder than she actually was.

She poured me a cold glass of Stag's Leap Chardonnay and elegantly unfolded herself on the maroon leather couch. "It's been so long. How long has it been? But you haven't changed a bit. You don't look a day over 22."

"I don't know whether that's a compliment or not."

"Of course! Are you still working on that novel of yours?"

"Now and then. More then than now."

"Writer's block?" I could smell her perfume now, Issy Miyaki.

I shrugged. "I think you have to have a sense of direction to write a novel. A sense that you're going someplace ... developing, changing, growing up."

"And you don't feel that?"

"I don't know. I feel like everybody else got on the train, but I dropped my ticket and when I looked up the train was already leaving the station. So here I am, still standing on the platform. Suitcase all packed but not a train in sight."

She looked at me for a long time with those wide-apart eyes. In the end, she said, "She didn't suffer, did she?"

"Grandma? I hope not. The last time I saw her she was sleeping."

"I would have come to the funeral, but ... the ..."

"It doesn't matter. We had a few of her friends there. The super from her building. An Italian guy from the grocery store on the corner. It was okay. Very quiet. Very ..."

"Lonely?" she suggested.

"Yes," I said. "Lonely." But I wasn't sure who she was really talking about.

* * *

She had a date to go out later that evening to some drinks party, but all the same she made us some supper. She stood in the small designer kitchen and mixed up *conchiglie alla puttanesca* in a blue earthenware bowl. "Tomatoes, capers, black Gaeta olives, crushed red chilies, all mixed up with extra-virgin olive oil and pasta ... they call it 'harlot's sauce.'"

I forked a few pasta shells out of the bowl and tasted them. "That's good. My compliments to the harlot."

"Do you cook, Jimmy?"

"Me? No, never."

"*Never?* Not even meatballs?"

"I have a thing about ovens."

She shook her head in bewilderment. "I've heard of people being afraid of heights, or cats, or water. But *ovens?* That must be a first."

"Stove-o-phobia, I guess. Don't ask me why."

We ate together at the kitchen counter and talked about grandma and about the sisters who had been our mothers. Mine had died suddenly when I was 5. Frances' mother had contracted breast cancer at the age of 37 and died an appalling, lingering death that went on for months and months.

"So we're orphans now, you and me," said Frances and laid her hand on top of mine.

* * *

Just after 9 o'clock the doorbell rang. It was a wiry-haired guy in a black velvet coat and a black silk shirt. "Frances? You ready?" he said, eyeing me suspiciously.

"Almost, just got to put my shoes on. Nick, meet my cousin, Jimmy. Jimmy, this is Nick. He's the inspirational half of Inspirational Plaster Moldings, Inc."

"Good to know you," I said. "Glad you're not the plastered half."

"You're welcome to come along," Frances told me. "They usually have organic wine and rice cakes and all kinds of malicious gossip about dadoes and suspended ceilings."

"Think I'll pass, if it's all the same to you."

* * *

After Frances and Nick had gone, I undressed and went for a long hot shower. It had taken a lot out of me, emotionally, seeing Grandma die. When I shampooed my hair and closed my eyes I could still see her sitting on the end of my bed, her head a little tilted to one side, smiling at me.

"Grandma, why did Mommy die?"

"God wanted her back, that's all, to help in heaven."

"Didn't she love me?"

"Of course she loved you. You'll never know how much. But when God calls you, you have to go, whoever you are and no matter how much you like living on Earth."

I was still soaping myself when I thought I heard a cry. I guessed it was probably a pair of copulating cats in the yard outside, and so I didn't pay it much attention. But then I heard it again, much louder, and this time it didn't sound like cats at all. It sounded like a child, calling for help.

Immediately I shut off the faucets and listened. There was silence for almost half a minute, apart from the honking of the traffic outside and the steady dripping of water onto the shower-tray. No, I must have imagined it. I stepped out of the shower and wrapped a towel around my waist.

Then, my God, the child was screaming and screaming, and I ran into the living area and it seemed like it was all around me. *"Mommy! Mommy! You can't! Stop it Mommy you can't, you can't!* STOP IT MOMMY YOU CAN'T!"

I tugged on my jeans, my wet legs sticking to the denim. Then I dragged on my sweater and shoved my feet into my shoes, squashing the backs down because I didn't have time to loosen the laces. I opened the loft door and wedged a book into the gap so that it wouldn't swing shut behind me. On the landing, I pressed the button for the elevator and it seemed to take forever before I heard the motor click and bang, and the car come slowly whining upward.

I ran out into the street. The wind was up and it was wild, with newspapers and cardboard boxes and paper cups whirling in the air. I hurried up the steps of the next-door house and started jabbing at the doorbells. I was so frantic that it took me 16 or 17 heartbeats before I realized that these were the same doorbells that I had been pressing in Chicago.

I stopped. I took a step back. I couldn't believe what I was looking at. Not only was I pressing the same doorbells, but I was standing in front of the same house. It had the same black-painted front door, the same hooded porch, the same damp-stained rendering.

I felt a *compressed* sensation inside my head, as if the whole world was collapsing, and I was the center of gravity.

How could it be the exact same house? How could that happen? Chicago was nearly 1,000 miles away, and what were the chances that I was staying right next door to a house that looked identical to the one that was next door to Grandma's?

For a moment I didn't know what to do. Then a man's voice came over the intercom. "*Who's there?*" I couldn't tell if it was the same voice that I had heard in Chicago.

"I—ah—do you think could you open the door for me, please?"

"*Who is this?*"

"Listen, I think there's a child in trouble on the top floor."

"*What child? The top floor's empty. No children live here.*"

"Do you mind if I just take a look. I work for the ASPCC."

"*The what?*"

"Child cruelty prevention officer."

"*I told you. No children live here.*"

I was unnerved, but I didn't want to give up. Even if I couldn't work out how this building was the same building from Chicago, I still wanted to know what all that screaming was. "Just open the door, okay?"

Silence.

"Just open the fucking door, okay?"

Still silence.

I waited for a while, wondering what to do, and then I held onto the porch railing and gave the door a hefty kick. The frame cracked, so I kicked it again and again and again, and then a large piece of wood around the lock gave way and the door juddered open.

I went inside. The hallway was dark, but I managed to find the light switch. The walls were paneled in darkly varnished wood, waist-high, and the floor was patterned in beige-and-white diamonds. There was a hall stand with a blotchy mirror in it, and there was a dry, barely perceptible smell of dead roses.

I climbed the stairs. They were creaky but thickly covered in heavy-duty hessian carpet. Chinks of light shone from almost every door, and I could hear televisions and people talking and arguing and scraping dishes. A woman said, *"There should be a law against it ... haven't I always said that?"* and a man replied, *"What are you talking about? How can you have a law against body odor?"*

I reached the second story and looked up toward the third. Without warning the lights clicked off and left me in darkness, and it took me quite a few moments of fumbling before I found the time switch. When the lights came on again, there was a man standing at the top of the stairs. It was impossible to see his face because there was a bare light bulb hanging right behind him, but I could see that he was bulky and bald and wearing a thick sweater.

"Who are you?" he demanded.

"Child cruelty prevention officer."

"That was you I was talking to before?"

"That's right."

"Don't you hear good? There's no children live here. Now get out before I throw you out."

"You didn't hear any screaming? A little boy, screaming?"

He didn't answer.

"Listen," I insisted, "I'm going to call the police and if they find out you've been abusing some kid—"

"Go," he interrupted me. "Just turn around and go."

"I heard a boy screaming, I swear to God."

"*Go.* There are some things in life you don't want to go looking for."

"If you think that I'm going to—"

"Go, Jimmy. Let it lie."

I shielded my eyes with my hand, trying to see the man's face, but I couldn't. How the hell did he know my name? What was he trying to say to me? Let it lie? Let *what* lie? But he stayed where he was, guarding the top of the third-story stairs. I knew that I wasn't going to get past him, and I wasn't sure that I really wanted to.

I lowered my hand and said, "Okay. Okay," and backed off along the landing. Out in the street, I stood in the wind wondering what to do. A squad car drove slowly past me, but I didn't try to hail it. I realized by then that this wasn't a matter for the cops. This was a matter of madness, or metaphysics, or who the hell knew what.

* * *

"What do you know about your neighbors?" I asked Cousin Frances, over breakfast.

"Nothing. Why?"

"Ever give you any trouble? You know—parties, noise, that kind of thing?"

She frowned at me as she nibbled the corner of her croissant. "Never. I mean like there's nobody there. Only the picture-framing store. I think they use the upstairs as a workshop."

"No, no. I mean your neighbors that way."

"That's right."

Without a word I put down my cup of espresso, walked out of the apartment and pressed the button to summon the elevator. Cousin Frances called after me, "What? What did I say?" I didn't answer, couldn't, not until I saw for myself. But when I got out into the street I saw that she was right. The building next door housed a picture-framing gallery called A Sense of Gilt. No narrow house with a hooded porch. No peeling, black door. No doorbells.

I came back to my coffee. "I'm sorry. I think I need to go back to Florida."

* * *

There were thunderstorms all the way down the Atlantic coast from Norfolk to Savannah, and my flight was delayed for over six hours. I tried to sleep on a bench next to the benign and watchful bust of Fiorello La Guardia. But I couldn't get that screaming out of my mind, nor that narrow house with its damp-stained rendering.

What were the options? None, really, except that I was suffering from grief. Houses can't move from one city to another. My grandmother's death must have triggered some kind of breakdown which caused me to have hallucinations, or hyperrealistic dreams. But why was I hallucinating about a child screaming, and what significance did the house have? There was something faintly familiar about it, but nothing that I could put my finger on.

We were supposed to fly directly into Fort Lauderdale, but the storms were so severe that we were diverted to Charleston. We didn't get there until 1:35 a.m., and the weather was still rising, so United Airlines bussed us into the city to put us up for the night. The woman sitting next to me kept sniffing and wiping her eyes. "I was supposed to see my son today. I haven't seen my son in 15 years." Rain quivered on the windows and turned the streetlights to stars.

When we reached the Radisson Hotel on Lockwood Drive, I found more than 100 exhausted passengers crowded around the reception desk. I wearily joined the back of the line, nudging my battered old bag along with my foot. Jesus. It was nearly 2:30 in the morning, and there were still about 70 people in front of me.

It was then that a woman in a black dress came walking across the lobby. I don't know why I noticed her. She was, what, 32 or 33. Her brunette hair was cut in a kind of dated Jackie Kennedy look, and her dress came just below her knee. She was wearing gloves, too, black gloves. She came right up to me and said, "You don't want to wait here. I'll show you where to stay."

"Excuse me?"

She said, "Come on. You're tired, aren't you?"

I thought: *hallo—hooker*. But she didn't actually *look* like a hooker. She was dressed too plainly and too cheaply, and what hooker wears little pearl earrings and a little pearl brooch on her dress? She looked more like somebody's mother.

I picked up my bag and followed her out of the Radisson and onto Lockwood. Although it was stormy, the night was still warm, and I could smell the ocean and that distinctive subtropical aroma of moss and mold. In the distance, lightning was crackling like electric hair.

The woman led me quickly along the street, walking two or three steps in front of me.

"I don't know what I owe the honor of this to," I said.

She half-turned her head. "It's easy to get lost. It's not so easy to find out where you're supposed to be going. Sometimes you need somebody to help you."

"Okay," I said. I was totally baffled, but I was too damned tired to argue.

After about five minutes' walking we reached the corner of Broad Street, in the city's historic district. She pointed across the street at a row of old terraced houses, their stucco painted in faded pinks and primrose yellows and powder-blues, with the shadows of yucca trees dancing across the front of them. "That one," she said. "Mrs. Woodward's house. She takes in guests."

"That's very nice of you, thank you."

She hesitated, looking at me narrowly, as if she always wanted to remember me. Then she turned and started to walk away.

"Hey!" I called. "What can I do to thank you?"

She didn't turn around. She walked into the shadows at the end of the next block and then she wasn't there at all.

* * *

Mrs. Woodward answered the door in hairpins and no make-up and a flowery robe. I could tell that she wasn't entirely thrilled about being woken up at nearly 3 a.m. by a tired and sweaty guy wanting a bed and a shower.

"You were highly recommended," I said, trying to make her feel better.

"Oh, yes? Well, you'd better come in, I suppose. But I've only the attic room remaining."

"I need someplace comfortable to sleep, that's all."

"All right. You can sign the register in the morning."

The house dated from the 18th century and was crowded with mahogany antiques and heavy, suffocating tapestries. In the hallway hung a gloomy oil portrait of a pointy-nosed man in a Colonial Navy uniform with a telescope under his arm. Mrs. Woodward led me up three flights of tilting stairs and into a small bedroom with a sloping ceiling and a twinkling view of Charleston through the skylight.

I dropped my bag on the mat and sat down on the quilted bed. "This is great. I'd still be waiting to check into the Radisson if I hadn't found this place."

"You want a cup of hot chocolate?"

"No, no thanks. Don't go to any trouble."

"Bathroom's on the floor below. I'd appreciate it if you'd wait until the morning before you took a shower. The plumbing's a little thunderous."

I washed myself in the tiny basin under the eaves and dried myself with a towel the size of a Kleenex while I looked out over the city. Although it was clear, the wind had risen almost to hurricane force and the draft seethed in through the crevices all around my window.

Eventually, ass-weary, I climbed into bed. There was a guide to the National Maritime Museum on the nightstand, and I tried to read it but my left eye kept drooping. I switched off the light, bundled myself up in the quilt, and fell asleep.

* * *

"*Mommy, you can't! Mommy, you can't! Please, Mommy, you can't!* NO MOMMY YOU CAN'T!"

I jerked up in bed, and I was slathered in sweat. For a second, I couldn't think where I was, but then I heard the storm shuddering across the roof and the city lights of Charleston through the window. Jesus. Dreaming again. Dreaming about screaming. I eased myself out of bed and went to fill my toothbrush glass with water. Jesus.

I was filling up my glass a second time when I heard the child screaming again. "*No, Mommy, don't! No Mommy you can't!* PLEASE NO MOMMY PLEASE!"

I switched on the light. There was a small antique mirror on the bureau, so small that I could only see my eyes in it. The boy was screaming, I could hear him. This wasn't any dream. This wasn't any hallucination. I could hear him, and he was screaming from the house next door. Either this was real, or else I was suffering from schizophrenia, which is when you can genuinely hear people talking and screaming on the other side of walls. But when you're suffering from schizophrenia, you don't think, "*I could be suffering from schizophrenia.*" You believe it's real. And the difference was, I *knew* this was real.

"*Mommy no Mommy no Mommy you can't please don't please don't please.*"

I dressed, and he was still screaming and pleading while I laced up my shoes. Very carefully, I opened the door of my attic bedroom and started to creep downstairs. Those stairs sounded like the Hallelujah Chorus, every one of them creaking and squeaking in harmony. At last I reached the hall, where a long-case clock was ticking our lives away beat by beat.

Outside, on Broad Street, the wind was buffeting and blustering and there was nobody around. I made my way to the house next door, and there it was, with its hooded porch and its damp-stained rendering, narrow and dark and telling me nothing.

I stood and stared at it, my hair lifted by the wind. This time I wasn't going to try ringing the doorbells, and I wasn't going to try to force my way inside. This house had a secret, and the secret was meant especially for me, even if it didn't want me to know it.

I went back to Mrs. Woodward's, locking the street door behind me. As quickly and as quietly as I could, I climbed the stairs to my attic bedroom. I thought at first that the boy might have stopped screaming, but as I went to the window I heard a piercing shriek.

The window frame was old and rotten, and it was badly swollen with the rain and the subtropical humidity. I tried to push it open with my hand, but in the end I had to take my shoulder to it, and two of the panes snapped. All the same I managed to swing it wide open and latch it, and then I climbed up onto the bureau and carefully maneuvered myself onto the roof. Christ, not as young as I used to be. The wind was so strong that I was almost swept off, especially since it came in violent, unexpected gusts. The chimneystacks were howling and the TV antenna was having an epileptic fit.

I edged my way along the parapet to the roof of the house next door. There was no doubt that it was the same house, the hooded-porch house, because it was covered with 19th century slates, and it didn't have a colonial-style parapet. I didn't even question the logic of how it had come to be here, in the center of historic Charleston. I was too concerned with not falling 75 feet into the garden. The noise of the storm was deafening, and lightning was still crackling in the distance, over toward Charles Towne Landing, but the boy kept on screaming and begging, and now I knew that I was very close.

There was a skylight in the center of the next-door roof, and it was brightly lit. I wedged my right foot into the rain-gutter, then my left, and crawled crabwise toward it, keeping myself pressed close to the slates in case a sudden whirlwind lifted me away.

"*Mommy you can't! Please Mommy no!* NO MOMMY YOU CAN'T YOU CAN'T!"

Grunting with effort, I reached the skylight. I wiped the rain away with my hand and peered down into the room below.

It was a kitchen, with a green linoleum floor and a cream-and-green painted hutch. On the right-hand side stood a heavy 1950s-style gas range, and just below me there were tables and chairs, also painted cream and green. Two of the chairs had been knocked over, as well as a child's high chair.

At first there was nobody in sight, despite the screaming, but then a young boy suddenly appeared. He was about five or six years old, wearing faded blue pajamas, and his face was scarlet with crying and distress. A second later, a woman in a cheap pink dress came into view, her hair in wild disarray, carrying a struggling child in her arms. The child was no more than 18 months old, a girl, and she was naked and bruised.

The woman was shouting something, very harshly. The boy in the blue pajamas danced around her, still screaming and catching at her dress.

"*No, Mommy! You can't! You can't! No Mommy you can't!*"

His voice rose to a shriek, and he jumped up and tried to pull the little girl out of his mother's arms. But the woman swung her arm and slapped him so hard that he tumbled over one of the fallen chairs and knocked his head against the table.

Now the mother opened the oven door. Even from where I was clinging onto the roof, I could see the gas was lit. She knelt down in front of the oven and held the screaming, thrashing child toward it.

"*No!*" I shouted, thumping on the skylight. "*No, you can't do that! No!*"

The woman didn't hear me, or didn't want to hear me. She hesitated for a long moment, and then she forced the little girl into the oven. The little girl thrashed and screamed, but the woman crammed her arms and legs inside and slammed the door.

I was in total shock. I couldn't believe what I had seen. The woman stood up, staggered, and backed away from the range, running one hand distractedly through her hair. The boy got up, too, and stood beside her. He had stopped screaming now. He just stared at the oven door, shivering, his face as white as paper.

"*Open the oven!*" I yelled. "*Open the oven! For God's sake, open it!*"

The woman still took no notice, but the boy looked up at me as if he couldn't understand where all the shouting and thumping was coming from.

As soon as he looked up, I recognized him. He was the boy in the photograph that had stood on my grandmother's mantelpiece.

He was me.

* * *

I don't know how I managed to get down from that roof without killing myself. It took me almost five minutes of sweating and grunting, and at one point I felt the guttering start to give way. In the end, however, I managed to get back to the comparative safety of Mrs. Woodward's parapet, and climb back in through my attic window.

I limped downstairs and into the street, but I guess I knew all along what I would find there. The house next door was a flat-fronted three-story dwelling, painted yellow, with a white door and the date 1784 over the lintel. The house with the hooded porch had gone, although God alone knew where, or how.

* * *

Three weeks later, when I was back in Fort Lauderdale working at The Scorpion Lounge, I received a package of photographs and letters from my grandmother's attorneys.

"Your late grandmother's legacy will be settled within the next three months. Meanwhile we thought you would like to have her various papers."

I opened them up that evening, on the veranda of my rented cottage on Sunview Street. Most of the letters were routine—thank-you notes from children and cousins, bills from plumbers and carpet-fitters. But then I came across a letter from my dad, dated 26 years ago, and handwritten, which was very unusual for him.

Dear Margaret,

It's difficult for me to write to you this way because Ellie is your daughter and obviously you feel protective toward her. I know you don't think much of me for walking out on her and the kids, but, believe me, I didn't know what else to do.

I talked to her on the phone last night and I'm concerned about her state of mind. She's talking about little Janie being sent from hell to make her life a misery by crying and crying and never stopping and always wetting the bed. I don't think the Ellie I know would hurt her children intentionally but she doesn't sound like herself at all.

Please, can I ask you to call around and talk to her and make sure that everything's okay. I wouldn't ask you this in the normal way of things, as you know, but I am very anxious.

All the best,

Travers

Fastened to this letter by a paper clip was a yellowed cutting from the *Chicago Sun-Times*, dated 11 days later. MOTHER ROASTS BABY. Underneath the banner headline there was a photograph of the house with the hooded porch and another photograph of the woman who had pushed her child into the oven. It was the same woman who had guided me from the Radisson Hotel to Mrs. Woodward's lodging house. It was my mother.

There was also a cutting from the *Tribune*, with another photograph of my mother, with me standing beside her and a little curly headed girl sitting on her lap. "Eleanor Parker with baby Jane and 5-year-old son James, who witnessed the tragedy."

Finally, there was a neatly typed letter to my grandparents from Dr. Abraham Lowenstein, head of the Psychiatric Department at St. Vincent's Memorial Hospital. It read:

Dear Mr. and Mrs. Harman,

We have concluded our psychiatric examination of your grandson, James. All of our specialists are of the same opinion: that the shock he suffered from witnessing the death of his sister has caused him to suffer selective amnesia, which is likely to last for the rest of his life.

In lay terms, selective amnesia is a way in which the mind protects itself from experiences that are too damaging to be coped with by the usual processes of grieving and emotional closure. It is our belief that further treatment will be of little practical effect and will only expose James to unnecessary anxiety and stress.

So it was true. People *can* forget terrible experiences, totally, as if they never happened at all. But what Dr. Lowenstein couldn't explain was how the experience itself could come looking for the person who had forgotten it—trying to remind him of what had happened—as if it *needed* to be remembered.

Or why I shall never give Wendiii her crucifix back, because I still wake up in the night, hearing a young boy screaming, "*No, Mommy, you can't! No, Mommy, please, you can't!* NO MOMMY YOU CAN'T!" And I have to have something to hold on to.

FINDING RESOLUTION

BY PATRICK DERRICKSON

I tapped the display to silence the alarms in the cockpit. Blinking green and red lights lit up the control board like a Christmas tree. Look at me, said a red light. No, me, said another. Still another said look at me now, or you *will* die, stupid.

Months of Colonel Sharpe's training kicked in and I worked the problem. Going through my checklists, I quickly reduced the 13 red lights to just two. But they were pretty important.

Main engines, critical failure. Thrusters offline.

Out of the port window, the Mars Space Station grew smaller. I guess the bottle of The Knot I had promised to toast to Rogers, Buckhead, and Romano would have to wait. My com beeped.

"Phoenix, come in Phoenix," a voice called through speakers. Speak of the devil, Fred Romano to the rescue.

"Hey, Romano. Reading you loud and clear. What's up?"

"What's up? What the hell, man. I'm getting critical engine failures on the Phoenix. Are you okay?"

"Me? I'm golden. Freaking out a little. Thrusters are offline, too, so I can't turn around. Trying to get them back, but the power won't reroute. Could be a board's out. I'll have to check that next."

"We are waiting to hear from NASA, but that will take 22 minutes. How are your criticals?"

"Environmentals are green."

"Everything else okay?"

"Um, I'm floating away from Mars with no propulsion to prevent said exit vector. I'm a little concerned about that, so, yeah."

"Sorry, George. What can I do?"

"Work the problem, Romano," I told him, using my best Colonel Sharpe impression.

"Aye, sir," Romano laughed.

"Do Rogers and Buckhead know yet?"

"No, they're still planetside prepping the return flight to the MSS. I wanted a better understanding before interrupting them."

"Don't say anything until they return to the MSS. They have enough to worry about. I need to check that circuit. I'll get back to you."

Pushing away from the pilot's chair, I floated out of the cockpit, through the main cabin to the engine room. The display indicated no hull breach, and the compartment remained pressurized. The nuclear reactor containment field still held, so I wouldn't melt to death. At least not yet.

As the door cycled through the opening sequence, I braced for the worst. A slight hiss of oxygen, then the odd odor of burnt electrical equipment. Black scorch marks decorated the wall near the thruster control panel. The access panel wouldn't open easily, so I braced my foot against the wall and yanked hard. The door flew open. The lights inside the panel blinked on, showing the extent of the damage inside.

Tsk, tsk, George. You're screwed.

The entire thruster control panel had melted into some weird metal origami. If it were just a circuit board replacement, no problem. I could handle that with my eyes closed and one hand behind my back. I trained for that. But the slot I needed was now part of this warped monstrosity. I pulled my tablet from the holster at my hip and took a picture of the molten console and the scorch marks on the walls for NASA. Maybe they could figure something out. They were paid more.

I activated the com. "Romano?"

"I'm here."

"The thruster control panel is shot."

"Damn. We need to slow your exit trajectory. Any ideas?"

"I could vent the oxygen out the front port. That might stop the ship. But then I'd die of lack of oxygen. Any response from the NASA boys and girls?"

"Not yet. But nothing expected back for another 12 minutes."

"Okay. I'm going to run a full set of diagnostics. I need to know what else is broken."

"Sounds good."

Back in the cockpit, I initiated analysis of the primary and secondary systems. Most had redundancies, so the threat of failure was low. But an entire thruster control rack was not something I had stored in my parts cabinet. It would take an immense energy spike to knock out the engines *and* thrusters. The console chirped.

"Phoenix, this is Jack Parsons at NASA Control. We've received the transmissions from MSS and the Phoenix. We're still analyzing the data. We need to stop or slow your exit trajectory."

"No shit, Sherlock," I replied. Which I'm sure Jack heard on Earth. The man had ears like a bat.

"We'd like you to prep your hard and soft suits, then take stock of remaining supplies. We need to validate what you have to provide accurate estimations. We'll transmit another update within 30 minutes."

A no-nonsense guy, Jack ran his team like a well-oiled machine. I responded, indicating acknowledgment of his instructions. The diagnostics were completed and indicated an increase of carbon dioxide. The smoke from the thruster cabinet must have upset the environmental balance. A filter change should remedy that if the problem persisted. But if it was something else, I would add it to the growing list of items threatening to kill me.

After 90 minutes of analysis, hundreds of highly paid NASA engineers, with their Ph.D.s and years of technical training, told me what I sensed within 30 seconds of the alarms sounding. I couldn't stop or turn the ship, and Rogers didn't have the extra fuel to launch the Mars Lander to retrieve my ass. NASA wouldn't risk the lives of the three onboard the MSS, or future missions, for one person. I had gone all in on a pair of twos and Death had called my bluff with a mutha-effin' royal flush.

My ship had flown through the outer edges of a massive solar flare at the same time the thrusters kicked on to adjust my orbit around Mars. The Phoenix is shielded from solar flares, gamma rays, and anything else otherworldly designed to end life out here. The powerful spike in energy tripped the safety measures, and the reactor core severed its connection to the engines. The thrusters were designed to adjust output power in case of engine malfunction, which they did, but the unforeseen power surge toasted the boards and melted the rack. Everything worked as designed, and yet, here I am, adrift toward certain doom.

The humor is not lost on me.

Designed to test the psychological effects of solo spaceflight, my mission had reached its midway point. Six months to Mars, a month or two in orbit, then a four-month return flight. I complete mental assessments a couple times a day, as well as a daily video log—my vlog. Maybe one day NASA will post them on the internet and I'll become a star. Mom always said I had a face for TV.

* * *

"Phoenix, this is Commander Rogers of the Mars Space Station. Do you read me?"

"Phoenix Pizza Company, pickup or delivery?"

"Commander Canon, now is not the time for jokes."

Tight-assed Mission Commander Bill Rogers, always one for protocols.

"Hallo, Bill," I said in my best British accent.

"George, how are you?" Abby Buckhead said. I wish I could have seen her one last time. As hot as she was smart, Abby was the total package. Eyes that would melt your heart, lips that I could suck on all night long, and a mind Einstein would have bowed to when discussing astrophysics.

"Things are a little, how did the kids used to say, cray-cray?"

"Commander Canon, please follow—"

"Bill, call me George. Please."

"Fine," Bill said after moment.

"Thanks, Bill. By now, you've read the data on how I got into this mess. Romano, did the MSS sustain any damage from that solar flare?"

"No, we're shielded from that stuff. You should have been, too."

I caught the edge in Romano's voice. Back on Earth, we would have been best friends.

"I am. Was. Still am. A fluke thing, what can you do? It won't happen again, that's for sure. NASA's probably already working on a fix."

Romano laughed. "You're right about that. They sent us a software update to address the routing of our engine power. They're putting together an EVA plan to add shielding to the thruster ports."

"See? You guys got nothing to worry about. With my ad-hoc user testing out here, and NASA providing up-to-the-minute fixes, you guys should be fine for another five years out here."

"Five years?" Abby said. "We've got 30 days before we head home."

"The replacement crew still on schedule?" I asked. NASA couldn't have canceled the four-month trip to Mars even if they wanted. The new crew would bring supplies and man the MSS for the next two years, as well as complete the setup for the permanent settlement on Mars. Rogers and Buckhead would conclude testing the habitat by the end of the week. All it needed now was a paint job and some furniture.

"Yeah, they'll be here in three weeks," Romano added. "They said they brought a surprise. Maybe some beer. Or wine. I could definitely use a drink."

"I hear ya. Wait a second, I do have a bottle of something around here somewhere. Now where did I put that bottle of Knot?"

"What? You selfish bastard, did you sabotage the Phoenix on purpose to avoid having to share my favorite whiskey?"

"I know, Romano, I was going toast you as I flew by the MSS. I wasn't even supposed to talk to you guys. Because of my mission parameters. You understand."

"Hiding behind your mission parameters again? That excuse is getting old."

"When it's all you got, you milk the shit out of it."

I heard laughter through the com. Good. There was nothing they could do, and dwelling on my situation only made their own jobs harder.

"Okay, I've got to go count supplies. Ping me with any updates."

I spent the next 45 minutes counting supplies. Dull work, but it helped get me out of my head. I made a game out of it. One package of freeze-dried chicken would provide one day of life. A package of eggs, a half a day. I tried to do the math in my head but lost count. I sent NASA my data and went to change the air filter. Once I swapped out the filter, the carbon dioxide levels normalized. A filter was only designed to last a month, and I had another 12 left. So, a year's worth of clean air. Damn, that seemed like a long time to drift through space.

NASA transmitted its calculations on how long my food could last based on several rationing schedules. The longest was two years, but my air wouldn't last that long. Time for a drink.

I rummaged through my personal tote until I found the bottle of whiskey. I unscrewed the lid and popped out the sipping attachment I had added before I launched from Earth. The whiskey was a concession by my NASA medical team when we discussed the risks of spaceflight. I glanced back into the tote and noticed the box my mother had sent me before I left. I hoped to avoid opening her package until I returned to Earth. Maybe she packed me some homemade oatmeal raisin cookies. I unsnapped the lid and pulled out a cylinder wrapped in blue foam. After peeling off the foam, I held a metal container with a note from my mother. It smelled of Old Spice.

"George, your father always had a hard time expressing how proud he was of you. He understood why you couldn't see him when he was sick. At the end, he asked me to give you his ashes. He wanted to travel to the stars with you. He loved you, George. When you return, please come see me. Safe travels. Love, Mom."

"Well, shit, Mom, maybe you could have said something a little sooner. Maybe you could have come to my last press conference. Or the NASA dinner party you were too busy to attend. You're going to throw this on me now?" Since my father died, we've struggled to stay in touch.

I tossed the urn back into the box. "You didn't want anything to do with my life after Lisa and I divorced, Dad, and now you want to bond because—what?—you died? Yeah, I don't work like that. My life isn't a sitcom resolved by the end of the episode."

I heard a slight hiss behind me. I turned, expecting to see oxygen escaping from a crack in the ship. Nothing seemed out of place. On the way back to the cockpit, I realized the sound seemed more like a sigh.

I turned off the console lights and stared out the window. So many stars out here. So many lights, like lighthouses in an endless, dark sea. I had tried to get away from the hurt, from the drama, but my parents' reach is long, even out here. I'd done a good job of pruning the negative and nonsupportive people that surrounded me because life is just too goddamned short. I grabbed the bottle for another swig.

Sometime later, an incessant ping woke me from the mesmerizing view from the Phoenix. After a moment of thinking about letting the call go to voice mail, I remembered I didn't have voicemail here. Another recommendation I needed to send to Jack. One should always have voicemail. I rose and stretched cramped muscles.

"George here."

"Hey, George."

Romano, again. His voice sounded quiet and strained.

"Romano. How's it?"

"You okay? You sound a little loopy. How are the environmentals?"

"I changed the filter, so they are …" I paused and tapped the console. "Nominal."

The silence dragged on for a bit, and I looked back to where the MSS should be.

"I guess you received the update from NASA?" I asked.

"Yeah. I'm sorry man, this really blows."

I laughed. "It does. But whatcha gonna do when they come for you?"

That got a chuckle from Romano.

"Only you, man, only you."

I bowed, then added a curtsy, because why the hell not.

"In all seriousness, what can I do? Is there anyone you want me to talk to back on Earth?"

"Nah. I've said my goodbyes."

"We've talked with NASA, and we can adjust our remaining tasks so one of us can be available to talk whenever you want."

"I appreciate that. But I was thinking about doing something else."

"What?" Romano said. His voice was edged with concern.

"Don't worry, nothing like that. I'd like to continue my mission, let NASA collect data on me now that I know I'm not returning to Earth. Maybe my psych reports could benefit future missions."

"The last thing you need to do is worry about your mission."

"What else am I going to do? There's only so much space I can look at, and I've already seen all the entertainment videos.

Maybe I can learn a new language, just in case a passing Vulcan ship sees me out here."

"It's a big universe, George. You never know."

We talked for a few minutes more before I told him I had to use the little boy's room. After doing my duty, I reviewed the communication relays and signal strength. The lag between Earth and the Phoenix had grown to 34 minutes. Within the month, I'd be looking at a two-hour lag. Within six months, I'd be closer to a half a day.

I'd give the MSS crew another day, and then cut off communication. The sooner they let me go, the sooner they could get on with their own mission. I am excess baggage at this point.

Abby called a few hours later.

"Hello?"

"Hey, George."

"Abby! I was hoping I'd get to talk with you. It's late there. You on duty?"

"Duty?"

"Talk with the dying guy duty. Romano mentioned a schedule."

"I, ah, well—"

"Abby, it's fine. I'm good. There is nothing I or you can do about it. Keep your mind on your mission. Don't make me turn this runaway ship around."

"Maybe you should."

"Now you're just being mean. The prettiest girl in space can't flirt with a dying man with no way of reciprocating said flirtatious assertions."

"I'm the only woman in space, George."

"True. But if we were on Earth, I'd only go home with you."

"You're a mess."

"I am what I am."

"And funny. My mother would have liked you."

We laughed and talked for a while longer before she had to wake Rogers. She took a while to say goodbye. I helped by saying I had to go fix a hole in the wall. Abby laughed and signed off. She had an infectious laugh. I'd miss it.

I hoped she'd find someone that was just as awesome.

* * *

When you don't look at a calendar, the days fly by so fast you don't even miss them. Where had three months gone? I scratched at my face where my bushy beard tickled it. A reminder pinged, indicating it was time to complete another video log. NASA wouldn't receive my logs and assessments for hours, but at least they knew I was still alive.

"This is Commander George Stroud of the USS Phoenix. Log number 241. I'm doing okay, no physical or mental concerns. I decided not to shave to see how long I could grow my beard. You never know when you'll need to know how fast hair grows in space. I still clip my fingernails, though. In case I do meet with an advanced alien race, I don't want them to think I'm some kind of monster. Ship is nominal, supplies are what they are. George out."

I logged out and stared out the window. Smudges from greasy fingers and noses blurred the bright stars. For a second, I wondered who made those marks before I realized it was me. Cause I'm the only one here. Well, other than my dad's ashes, I'm the only living being on this ship. Are ashes still alive? I added this to the questions I needed to ask Jake. Er, Jack.

Why do I smell Old Spice? Was it time to replace the filter already?

My dad wore that aftershave. Weird.

*   *   *

I glanced at my dad's urn, perched atop the main console.

"George here, recording live for log 332. Twelve inches, longest beard I ever grew. Longest in the family, I'm sure. Another record, Pop. At this rate, I'll be the most accomplished man in the family. Cheers."

I raised my pouch of cinnamon applesauce and sucked it down in one long pull. I crumpled the container into a small ball and pushed it into an open cabinet door.

"3, 2, 1, clang! Off the rim, Team George loses! Another tally in the loss column, folks. Team George is on a record losing streak. Who will step up and end the string of bad luck?"

"I will! Put me in coach. No, put me in coach, I'll bring the rock home."

"Pull yourself together, George," said a voice behind me.

"Who's there?"

But no one answered. Dummy, you're the only one here. I pulled the water hose from the cabinet and took a long sip. The water was cold. Space cold. And what was that smell? I sniffed around the main cabin, but the acrid odor followed me. When I scratched my head and came face-to-face with my armpit, I realized the terrible funk emanated from me. Now that was funny. The skunk in the cabin was me.

Tap, tap.

I whirled around again. I glided into the cockpit, but nothing seemed out of order. Except that stupid yellow light flashing. Gotta replace something or other. I'll get to it later.

Gotta find that noise. Can't have rats on board. Not sanitary. Jake wouldn't like that.

Tap, tap.

The noise was behind me now. Back in the main cabin, my dad's urn frowned down to me. Clean yourself up, George, it seemed to say. You stink.

"Aye, aye, sir." I saluted the urn.

I turned and noticed I hadn't yet logged off the video. Tapping the save and send button, I hoped Jake was keeping score of my accomplishments. I was racking them up.

* * *

"Log 360-something. Jake, you're not going to be happy about this, but someone is here with me. He found a good hiding spot because I haven't been able to find him."

Tap, tap.

I pushed through the smog of wrinkled, gray plastics floating in the cabin. My last Christmas on Earth was foggy. Does it snow in space?

Beep, beep, beep.

I floated into the cockpit and crashed hard against the pilot's seat. A red light blinked rapidly on a display crusted with something green. Slime. Or protoplasm. Ghost snot. Who you gonna call?

"I'll find you, my little pretty, and your little doggie, too!"

The silence teased me.

"Keep hiding. Go ahead. When I find you, you're in big trouble. Big trouble."

When no one appeared, I tried a different tack.

"It's okay, I'm just joking. I'm not going to hurt you. I just want to play. Wanna play?"

I bared my teeth and slowly rotated my head, just like the doll in that old horror movie.

Still nothing.

Tap, tap.

"Forward, ho! Haul the anchor and strike the sails!"

At the edge of my vision, a shadow moved.

I pushed off the console and soared into the main cabin.

"I've got you now!"

A figure stood in the room, arms crossed and shaking his head.

"Dad?"

I passed through him and crashed into the wall.

* * *

My head felt as if it was wedged in a slowly tightening vise. I clenched my eyelids shut against the brilliant white lights of the cabin.

"Dad," I croaked. My tongue slid over the ragged edges of my lips.

"Dad," I called out.

I shielded my eyes with my hand and looked around the main cabin through small slits between my fingers. I was alone, floating face down in zero gravity. My foot brushed the wall, and I pushed off, propelling myself to the control panel. I dimmed the lights in the cabin, finally able to open my eyes enough get a clearer view of the ship. I batted used food containers past my head.

My father had disappeared.

The cockpit was empty as well. I must have imagined him standing there with the usual look of disappointment on his face. Nothing was ever good enough. I grabbed a half-empty container of a protein shake out of the air and sucked it dry before going to the water cabinet. The water tasted stale.

Displaying the water recycling log, I noticed it had been 178 days since the water filter had been changed. What else had I forgotten to do? Based on the blinking red and yellow lights, quite a lot, it seemed. My finger hovered over the display. I couldn't remember the folder path to the rest of the logs. My hand started shaking.

"Don't remember how to check the logs, dumbass?" a gruff voice said behind me.

I whirled and immediately regretted it. Even though I had stopped turning, my vision continued to spin. My stomach lurched. I grabbed the edge of the pilot's chair and pulled myself down. Once my stomach calmed, I glanced to where my father had just stood. But the archway was empty.

I must be losing my mind. Or maybe I already did. I went back into the main cabin and grabbed a packet of pain meds. I felt my face for gashes or bones sticking out and was relieved to find nothing out of place. I filled an empty container with cold water and pressed it against my head.

"What are you doing?" a voice said behind me.

I didn't turn around.

"Who are you?" I asked.

"Seriously? You don't even recognize your own father?"

"He's dead."

"Then how do you explain me?"

I twisted slowly this time. My father stood in the doorway dressed in dark-gray sweat pants spotted with white paint, and a grease-stained, light-gray sweatshirt. He sported a ragged salt-and-pepper beard, and his mostly bald head sprouted a few strands of thin hair. He looked like my father, but that wasn't possible. His ashes filled a small, bronze urn.

"I banged my head on the wall. I'm probably suffering from a concussion. Maybe I'm dreaming."

"Dreaming, huh? Do you usually feel pain in your dreams? Must have gotten that from your mother."

"Shut up. This is just some repressed memory that decided now was the time to resurface."

"Would I know that you're out here alone, waiting to die, wishing you could have spoken to me one more time?"

"Yeah you would, especially if you were a part of my subconscious. I said all I had to say to my father before he died."

"Really? Nothing? No words pushed so far deep because you were afraid to say them out loud?"

I pushed through the floating garbage and slipped under the blanket attached to the foldout bed. The blanket would keep me anchored, allowing me to get a decent amount of sleep. I rolled away from the smirking figure.

"Last chance, buddy boy. I won't be here forever."

"Why don't you jump out an air lock? I don't need you."

Laughter boomed in the cabin. I covered my ears until I drifted off to sleep.

* * *

What happened to the pretty white stars? Everything is so gray. So dull. No one to talk to, nothing to do. Just stupid yellow and red blinking lights. Maybe aliens trying to contact me, communicating through those blinking lights. At least I could talk to someone then. Or something.

"Dad?"

No answer.

The red light on the console grabbed my attention for a moment until an odor distracted me.

Man, something in here smells bad. Like rotten meat bad.

* * *

"Hi, son."

I twisted around in the chair to find my father standing in the doorway. He looked like shit. Sunken eyes, hair oily and limp, and lips curled under toothless gums. He looked like an old meth-head.

I laughed so hard I had to wipe tears from my eyes.

"How's it going, Pop? No offense, but you look like crap."

"You should look in the mirror. Not the babe magnet you once were."

"Still offering your unique parental skills, I see."

"I call it as I see it. I can't hold your hand your entire life. You need to stand on your own two feet, buddy boy."

"Not sure you ever held my hand," I muttered, and stretched my arms. Something in my elbow popped, and pain flashed a moment before receding. I looked at the gaunt arms, blue veins so vibrant against pale skin, leading down to long, yellowed nails. When did I grow talons?

"So, how can I help you, Dad?"

"I think I can help you."

"How exactly are you going to help me?"

"When it's time, you'll know."

"What the hell does that mean? I'm not on some quest."

"It's going to be okay."

"Is it? You're just going to make it all better?"

"We'll be doing it together."

"Yeah, 'cause that's not crazy."

"Not quite. You're just a little lonely. And stressed."

"I'm waiting to die out here. I don't even know where here is."

"We're almost to Jupiter."

"Jupiter? Did I already pass the Belt?"

"Yes, a few weeks ago. You took a few pictures."

I studied my father a long time. The weathered lines around his eyes. The many freckles that covered his forehead. The dimple in his chin that I inherited. We were the same height and wore the same shoe size. Hell, even our receding hairlines matched.

"Why come back now? You had years to talk to me."

"Would you have gotten here if I babied you?"

"You mean, on a collision course with Jupiter and certain death?"

"You relied on your own strength and made your own choices. Decided what was important to you. To live your own life. You made decisions based on the mistakes I made."

He was right. I hadn't wanted the same life as my father. I wanted to show people I cared, that I could love. To feel loved. As much as I could have from the unemotional childhood I experienced. Long-term relationships never work out.

"So, what do we do?" I said.

"Whatever you want. Tell me about Lisa. What happened?"

"Nothing much to tell. I wanted to go to space, she didn't want me to go. She needed a husband at home every day. I wanted to travel among the stars. Kinda all worked out. She remarried to a corporate stiff. I'm in space."

"Do you miss her?"

"I used to. I moved on. Wasn't worth spending my energy to worry about something I couldn't change."

My dad smiled.

"What's so funny?"

"That's something I would say."

"Mom said I had a little of you in me."

His face grew serious. It made me uncomfortable.

"I'm sorry about your mom. I didn't treat her very well. I apologized to her, but it was too late for us."

"Why were you so mean to her?"

"Insecurity? Jealousy? I lost my business, remember? You were young. I had a lot of stress and no good way to deal with it. Your mom was younger, pretty, and when she had to get a second job, I got worried she'd find a more successful man. A better man than me."

"So you decided to push her away instead of *maybe* being hurt by her?"

"I guess."

"You know how asinine that sounds, right?"

He shrugged. We sat in silence for a while. I studied my almost transparent skin. I couldn't remember the last time I ate. Just talking hurt my dry, cracked lips.

"Want a drink, Dad? Something to eat?"

"Nah, I'm fine. You go ahead."

"Will you be here when I get back?"

"I'll be here as long as you need me to be here."

I went to the food locker and grabbed a pouch of chicken soup. The salt burned my lips as I slurped it down. The cold liquid soothed the ache in my throat, but I felt it splash down inside my empty stomach. I tensed, waiting for a cramp that thankfully did not come. I made my way back to the table "What else do you want to talk about?"

"Tell me about how you became an astronaut."

I smiled. And for the next few hours, I told him about the best times of my life.

* * *

I shuddered to consciousness when the ship shook as if someone had decided to dribble it like a basketball. Another tremor hit the ship, followed by an even stronger one. I struggled out of my bed.

"Dad?"

"I'm here, George."

"What's happening?"

"You're in Jupiter's gravity."

"Why is the ship shaking?"

"You're the space guy. You tell me."

"Probably because the ship's not rated to withstand the force of Jupiter's gravity."

We looked at each other for a few moments.

"What do you want to do?" he asked.

"I don't want to die on this ship."

"Then don't."

"I don't really have a choice in the matter."

"There's always a choice. You just need to find it." Another tremor rocked the ship. I grabbed the wall to keep myself from pinging around the ship like a pinball. "Let's truly be astronauts. Let's go out in a blaze of glory."

"We're going to burn in the atmosphere after we're compacted like an empty beer can. We'll be a freaking ball of fire."

"Let's go extravehicular. See Jupiter with our own eyes."

I opened my mouth to ask if he was crazy but realized he had always been crazy. And for the first time in my life, we could be crazy together.

"Okay. Let's do this."

I stepped into my hard suit, and the heads-up display activated when the suit sealed itself. The oxygen level flashed red at 10 percent. Only an hour's worth left. It would be enough.

My dad waited by the door to the transition chamber with a huge smile on his face. Like he had just won the lottery. I smiled back.

I remembered I needed one last thing. I shuffled back into the room, the gravity-assist boots keeping me anchored to the floor, and grabbed the urn that still sat on the console. When I entered the chamber, my dad nodded toward the urn. "Why do you need that?"

"It's your ashes, dummy. If I'm going to be the first person on Jupiter, alive or dead, then I want to share it with you."

"Thanks, son."

I closed the door to the main cabin and vented the air. The pressure in the chamber eased.

I opened the outer door.

The bright clouds of Jupiter swirled below. We were still thousands of miles away, but the planet filled our vision.

"It's beautiful," I said.

"Ready?"

I nodded and grabbed his hand.

We jumped together as father and son, Earth's first emissaries to Jupiter.

THE FIERCE STABBING AND SUBSEQUENT POST-DEATH VENGEANCE OF SCOOTER BROWN

BY JEFF STRAND

"So, Mr. Galen, how many times did you stab Mr. Brown?"

"I don't recall."

"Really? Surely you recall such a thing."

"It's not like I was counting every single stab."

"Of course not, of course not, but I think you can at least give me a ballpark figure."

"I dunno. Twenty?"

"Try 43."

"Forty-three? Really?"

"Yes, Mr. Galen. You stabbed the victim 43 times."

"Wow. That's a lot of times to stab a person."

"It certainly is. So would you mind explaining to me why you felt it was necessary to stab him that many times?"

"Well, I was trying to kill him."

"That much is obvious, Mr. Galen."

"I thought it was obvious, too, but you're the one who asked. I wouldn't have asked, myself. Seems like common sense."

"My question was not about whether you wished for Mr. Brown to live or die. My question was about quantity. If you stab a man once, twice, or perhaps even three times, then your motive may have been murder. But when you stab him 43 times, one must surmise that there's a deeper issue."

"No, I just wanted to make sure he was dead."

"Where did your second stab occur, Mr. Galen?"

"Behind the bar."

"Do not try to turn this into a madcap comedy routine, Mr. Galen. You know perfectly well that I was asking about which part of his body received that particular stab wound."

"Oh. I forget."

"Do you, Mr. Galen? Do you?"

"His neck?"

"His *throat*. You plunged the knife directly into his throat."

"Ah, yeah, that's right. Got him right in the Adam's apple."

"Are you proud of that?"

"No, sir."

"So tell me, Mr. Galen, how many people do you think can survive having the eight-inch serrated blade of a hunting knife slam into their throat?"

"I'd think that somebody has, at some point. It's inevitable."

"Perhaps so, perhaps so. But do you agree that delivering another 41 stabbings after that could be considered excessive?"

"They weren't all in his neck."

"No, they weren't."

"I know at least one got his finger. You aren't going to die of that."

"Of the 43 stab wounds that were received by Mr. Scooter Brown, exactly two of them were on his fingers. What do you think about that?"

"He should have held up his hands more to defend himself."

"Are you taking this seriously, Mr. Galen?"

"Very much, sir."

"It doesn't sound like you are."

"I'm just saying that if somebody is stabbing you repeatedly with a hunting knife, that you should maybe put your hands up a bit more. That's all."

"Are you suggesting that Mr. Brown had suicidal tendencies?"

"No, not necessarily. All I'm saying is that if *I* were being stabbed, I'd make more of an effort to block the knife. That's all I'm saying."

"Is it possible, Mr. Galen, that once the blade entered his throat, that his mental faculties may have been compromised, making it difficult for him to determine the proper method of defending himself?"

"Yes, that's possible."

"Because I consider myself well above average in the art of self-defense. Yet, if I am truly honest with myself, I have to admit that arterial spurting would create difficulty for me in making the best judgment calls."

"I already agreed that it was possible! You don't have to keep bitching about it!"

"Why are you being antagonistic, Mr. Galen?"

"I'm not."

"Do you mean to say that you used the b-word in a non-antagonistic manner?"

"I'm just trying to explain what happened, and you keep judging me!"

"Give me an example of where I judged you."

"You accused me of saying he was suicidal just because I said that I'd put up my hands more if I were being stabbed."

"You're right. I did. And for that I apologize."

"Thank you."

"Where were we before that?"

"I forget."

"I remember now. You stabbed him 43 times but, as we've discussed, even somebody with no formal training in medicine or anatomy would know that the second stab was going to be fatal to Mr. Brown. And yet you continued to stab him over and over and over. Why?"

"I guess I have a bit of a rage problem."

"A bit?"

"Yes, a bit."

"Come now, Mr. Galen, certainly we can both agree that such a high quantity of stab wounds counts as more than 'a bit' of a rage problem?"

"Why do you keep bringing that up? Aren't one stab wound and 43 stab wounds the same amount of rage? Let it drop, for God's sake."

"No, I don't believe I will. Because you know where I'm headed with this, don't you?"

"Nope."

"I think you do."

"I really don't."

"How much time elapsed between the first stab and the final stab?"

"I don't remember."

"Interesting."

"I didn't look at the clock."

"How convenient."

"Do you always look at the clock before you start doing something and when you finish doing something? How long did it take you to shop for that pair of pants?"

"Stop trying to change the subject. My pants are irrelevant and you know it."

"I'm just saying."

"What are you just saying?"

"That you don't know the time of every single thing you do in every single day."

"Fair enough. I suppose I will accept your challenge, Mr. Galen. It took me approximately 15 minutes to shop for this pair of pants, if you count the time spent in the fitting room and the time spent in the checkout line. During that time I believe I also purchased two or three shirts. So, 15 minutes is my answer. What's yours?"

"I'm not sure."

"Really?"

"I guess it might have been about 15 minutes."

"Are you seriously trying to convince me that you believe it was 15 minutes?"

"About that."

"Please do not lie to me, Mr. Galen."

"It might have been longer."

"How about two hours and 36 minutes?"

"Was it that long?"

"It was indeed."

"Wow."

"And how long did it take him to die?"

"Fifteen minutes?"

"Two minutes, Mr. Galen."

"Oh."

"Two short minutes for Mr. Brown to bleed out. And yet you continued to stab his corpse for quite some time after that. Do you believe that's indicative of a healthy psyche?"

"I suppose not."

"Is it not, in fact, appropriate to say that you are a sick and deranged human being?"

"It depends on your definition of 'sick.'"

"Are you making light of the situation?"

"No, sir."

"Did you truly believe that I was using the definition of 'sick' used by today's youth, the one where it means 'awesome' or 'really cool?'"

"Maybe."

"Mr. Galen ..."

"Okay, no, I didn't truly believe that."

"There is nothing 'awesome' or 'really cool' or 'groovy' about your recent behavior. It was, in fact, quite disgusting. It was not admirable, nor noble, nor even particularly clever. It did not make you seem macho. If you'd killed him with your bare hands, then perhaps I'd admire it—not from a moral standpoint, of course, but purely in terms of skill. But what you did made you seem like nothing more than a drooling psychopath."

"I didn't drool."

"Still lying, Mr. Galen?"

"I only drooled a little."

"You wiped your mouth on seven different occasions."

"That doesn't mean I was drooling!"

"You also made slurping noises."

"Some blood got in my mouth!"

"One does not slurp when blood from one's victim sprays into one's mouth. One slurps when the drool of excitement spews from their salivary glands. You repulse me, Mr. Galen. You repulse me to the very core of my being. In fact, I wish that you were not in my office, because your presence causes my skin to feel like it's covered with dirt and insects."

"Should I leave?"

"No, you're already here. We might as well get this over with."

"Are you sure? You seem irritable."

"No, no, it's all right. The ability to gaze into people's memories does make me cranky, but I'll be fine. So you want me to bring Mr. Brown back to life?"

"Yes, sir."

"Why?"

"To apologize."

"Is that so?"

"Yes."

"Are you sure?"

"Yes."

"You won't stab him some more?"

"No, sir. I'm done with that. It was wrong to do it in the first place, and I've learned from my mistake."

"I'd like to believe you, Mr. Galen. I really would. But I find it rather disturbing that you didn't even know Mr. Brown before you went on your stabbing spree."

"I understand your concern."

"If he had wronged you in some way, even a minor way, like cutting you off in traffic, I might think to myself 'Well, that was a disproportionately violent reaction, but at least I can pinpoint the motive.' But when you lure a gentleman into your van under the guise of needing medical assistance for a nonexistent wife who is having a heart attack, and then proceed to stab him to death, and then continue to stab him for more than two hours after he is dead, I am forced to conclude that you are mentally ill."

"That's fair."

"I'm not trying to be rude. I simply believe, based on the information I have retrieved both from our conversation and directly from your brain, that you mean this man further harm."

"No. I just want to apologize."

"I don't believe you."

"Can't you read my mind?"

"Yes, but my psychic abilities are more about memories. Specific images. Not emotions. I know, for example, that you vigorously masturbated on Tuesday evening but not how you felt about it."

"Oh. Uh, sorry about the image."

"No need to apologize. I've seen worse. Now, I do have the ability to probe deeper with my abilities, to know if you are telling the truth, but it requires that I caress your eyeballs."

"Caress my eyeballs?"

"Yes."

"That sounds awful."

"It is."

"Okay, do it. Go ahead."

"Are you sure?"

"Yes."

"Very well, then. Keep them open wide."

"*Ow!*"

"You knew that it would hurt, right? That couldn't have been a surprise."

"I didn't know it would hurt *that* much!"

"Well, now you do. Hmmm. Okay, I now have to apologize for expressing doubts about your intentions, because I can see that you truly do wish to tell Mr. Brown that you're sorry. For some bizarre, demented, unfathomable reason, his acceptance of your apology is important to you. Very, very odd."

"I told you!"

"Don't act like my suspicion wasn't justified, Mr. Galen. You are a savage beast."

"But you can bring him back to life?"

"Yes."

"When?"

"He's already alive again. I don't care to waste time."

"Scooter ...?"

"*You!*"

"I just want to say I'm sorry."

"*Fuck you!*"

"And he's dead again. Sorry. My power to reanimate the dead is not long-lasting."

"He ... he ... he rejected my apology!"

"Yes, he certainly did. Nothing wishy-washy about his response."

"But ... I paid $5,000 so he could accept my apology!"

"You might have mentioned the expenditure while he was still alive. Personally, I would have opened with that, but since I've never stabbed a man to death, I can't honestly say that I know how I'd behave."

"That selfish bastard!"

"He was rude, but you can understand his point of view, right?"

"He was supposed to ease my conscience! Now I'm going to have sleepless nights for the rest of my life! The scorpions that live under my skin will never stop their incessant stinging! I can feel them now! Their pincers slice through my veins! I can see the blood in his eyes! So much blood! So much blood!"

"Is our business here finished, Mr. Galen?"

"So much blood!"

"Please close the door on your way out. Thank you very much."

ON THE HOUSE

BY JACOB JONES-GOLDSTEIN

"I told you we should have stopped at that burger place an hour ago," said Tom.

Lisa rolled her eyes even though it was too dark for Tom to see. It was the second time he'd brought it up. He wasn't being passive-aggressive this time, just whiny, which annoyed her less. He always got that way when they ate late. He liked to stick to a schedule whenever he could. Usually she loved that about him. Among other things, he was never late. But when he got like this, it drove her nuts.

"I'm sure we'll find something soon. That last sign said there was a town in a couple of miles." She tried to keep the irritation from her voice.

He was silent for a few moments before grumpily saying, "Everything is closed by now." Lisa rolled her eyes again and glanced at the clock on the dashboard. It was almost 10:00 p.m., so he was probably right. She had lived in New York City all her life and was used to the rhythms and patterns of the city. There was always somewhere to get a bite to eat there, regardless of the time of day. Out here in East Nowhere, as she had a habit of thinking of any place more than five miles outside the city, it would be a challenge.

Tom had talked her into the trip by appealing to all the Steinbeck she had read during college. They met in an American Folklore class at Columbia University where she had been working on an English degree. She took the course because it was taught by a professor she liked from a previous semester. Tom had taken the course because he thought it would be an easy credit. He was studying philosophy but always liked the folktales centered on the Hudson Valley where he grew up. They had been a couple since.

The trip was the first real extended vacation they had taken together in the three years they had been dating. There were a couple of weekends on the Cape and one soggy Memorial Day at Virginia Beach, but not much more than that. They were almost a cliché in how little they left the city. His parents had moved to Brooklyn the year before he started college and her Mom had passed away several years before they met. She had never known her father, whom her mother had rarely talked about. He had left when she was two, going back to his hometown somewhere in "The Flyover States" as her mother always called them. In the years following graduation, they barely had enough money to pay rent and eat each month, never mind take vacations.

Seven months ago, their situation changed. Lisa, who was working as a clerk in a bookstore and doing some tutoring on the side, had gotten a job with a midsized publisher as an editor. The next month, Tom could leave the call center, where he had been slowly losing his will to live since graduation, for a job in the mayor's office. His father had pulled some strings, but Tom and Lisa hadn't complained. After barely scraping by, they now felt like they had won the lottery. They talked about going somewhere warm with nice beaches and drinks made with sweet rum and weird-looking fruit. Lisa had even gone as far as getting some brochures from a travel agent when Tom had his brilliant idea.

She remembered his enthusiasm when he broached the idea to her with the same fondness as she did his first fumbling request for a date. "What if instead of some island where we're going to do nothing but sit on a beach and get drunk, we went looking for the real America, like *Travels with Charley*?" The idea interested her, but she wished he hadn't mentioned that particular book.

Travels with Charley was one of the last of Steinbeck's books she'd read. She remembered enjoying it, but one particular passage early in the book had always haunted her. Steinbeck arrives at a hotel in New Hampshire, looking for a place to stay the night, and there's no one there. The signs out front say *Open* and *Vacancy*, the doors are open, there are dishes in the sink of the café, but no one is there. He spends an uneasy night in his truck in the parking lot and leaves in the morning feeling disturbed. No one ever shows up. Lisa could never shake the weirdness of the scene, especially the dishes in the sink. She had nightmares for a week after reading the book.

Lisa was a city person at heart. She had rarely left New York and, when she did, it was always to popular places, usually filled with tourists. The notion of places out in the great, wide America, where people were and then suddenly weren't, filled her with an existential dread. She liked the idea of wandering and finally seeing the country. But somewhere beneath the excitement of the trip was the memory of the abandoned dishes in that lonely sink and that *Open* sign out front.

And so, instead of putting together an itinerary and making reservations, they decided to just take two weeks off, head west, and see where the road led them.

Tonight was their fourth night out of New York. The previous three days had gone without a hitch. They took turns with music, stopped and ate when they wanted to, took some random detours, and spent most of their time just driving and taking in the sights. The fourth day had been a bit rockier. They headed toward Northern Michigan to see Green Bay, but weren't going to make it tonight. They had stopped at a few tourist traps along the way and then tried to make up some time. They had gotten off an exit almost an hour ago to find something to eat. Through a combination of stubbornness and faith in how far the reach of places like Applebee's went, they'd gotten lost.

"Look, if there's nothing open in this town—I already forget the name—we'll just grab a hotel room at the first place we find." Isa said. "Gorge ourselves on vending machine snacks and then have a big breakfast in the morning."

Tom said, "That sounds like a good plan. I think the town was named Fortson."

"Great!" she replied. "Sounds like a nice place."

They drove in silence for a while before passing a sign that read *Entering Fortson, Pop. 313.* Lisa's shoulders slumped as she drove. That small a population didn't hold much promise of a restaurant or a hotel. The impenetrable darkness surrounding them didn't help matters. She was used to the constant light of a city, and the pitch-black nights of the country unnerved her. She had begun to look for the glow of distant towns against the night sky as a beacon. Several times she had commented that she now understood how the wise men and the shepherds in the Bible went so far following yonder star. Tom stopped laughing at the joke, but Lisa only partly meant it to be funny. Despite passing the sign for the town, the sky was as dark as ever.

"Maybe we should just turn around and try to find our way back to the interstate," Lisa offered glumly.

"I gue—hey, look!"

They had come around a corner and down the road was a flickering sign and a building with lights. The sign read *Happy Garden Asian Restaurant.*

"Oh, thank God," Lisa said. "They look open." She glanced at the dashboard clock again—9:55. She said a silent prayer that the place stayed open later than 10:00 or would be willing to make them a meal after hours. She would take almost anything. Steinbeck's hotel with its *Open* and *Vacancy* signs flashed through her mind before she abandoned that thought.

As they pulled into the large gravel lot, they saw an *Open* sign hanging in the door. The building looked straight out of the '50s. Lisa thought it might have gotten its start in life as an ice-cream shop or maybe a fast-food restaurant, which would explain the large parking lot. It may have once held picnic tables or simply been a place for people to park and hang out. The front of the building was a small, glassed-in area with no tables or chairs. The counter was several feet from the front door and stood high. It crossed the entire room, making it a wall between the small waiting area and the back of the restaurant. The ceiling lights were yellowing fluorescent. The building had an air of exhaustion about it, like it had given up and resigned itself to be slowly reclaimed by the surrounding woodland.

They parked directly in front of the building next to an old, banged-up Ford. As they got out of the car, they didn't see anyone through the large, plate-glass windows. Lisa grabbed the door handle, looked over at Tom with a glimmer of hope in her eyes, and pulled. It opened with a surprisingly loud chime, announcing their presence. She went in and Tom followed. The sign next to the door read *Open noon to 10:00 p.m. daily.*

They didn't see anyone, but they heard voices coming from the other side of a door that led to the back of the building, and presumably the kitchen.

"Hello?" Tom called out, loud enough that whoever was there would hear him. A large crash came from the back, making them jump. After a moment, an Asian man emerged through the doorway. He looked to be in his mid-50s, with hair that had gone almost completely gray. His face had the weathered look of someone who'd spent many years doing hard work outside. Behind him was an Asian woman of roughly the same age. Her hair was still jet-black, but the lines around her eyes gave the impression of someone who'd spent most of her time worrying. Lisa made eye contact with her and started to smile but was cut short by the haunted look in her eyes. She looked like she was seeing a ghost, and not for the first time.

"Hello," said the man. "I apologize, but we are closed."

The words struck Lisa like a blow. They were tired, hungry, and had quickly gotten fixated on the idea of Chinese food.

Tom spoke first. "Mister, we've been driving for hours, we're exhausted and starved. I know it's late, but you would be our hero forever if you would stay open a few minutes. At this point, I would be willing to pay double."

The man flicked his eyes over Tom's shoulders as he spoke. Lisa turned and saw he was looking at a clock. It showed 10:00 on the dot. The man then looked back at Tom and shook his head. "I'm sorry, but we are closed." Lisa noticed the woman looked past them through the windows toward the road.

Tom sighed and put his hands together as if he were praying. "Please, buddy, I promise we'll be out of your hair as quickly as possible. I think you're our only hope for something to eat."

"I'm sorry. You should leave," the man said.

Tom's head and shoulders slumped. The woman had yet to take her eyes off the road behind them. Tom wasn't picking up on it, but Lisa noticed the man sounded nervous rather than angry. She wondered if they were afraid of being robbed.

"I'm begging you, man, just a couple of egg rolls and some rice or something. We're starving and it doesn't look like there's anything else around." Tom sounded dejected rather than angry. One reason Lisa loved him was that he didn't have much of a temper. He could be frustratingly unreasonable, but he never got very angry. Lisa wasn't prone to anger, but she had her moments. Normally, this situation would press her buttons, but the demeanor of the other couple made her nervous.

"I am sorry, but—" Bright lights from outside suddenly shone into the restaurant. Another car had turned into the parking lot. Lisa turned to look at the car, but not before she saw the woman's jaw set as she turned from the window to look at the man. They began talking in a language Lisa recognized as Japanese.

"Sorry, but?" Tom said. The couple's behavior had not registered with him at all.

"Maybe we should go," Lisa said. She didn't want to get caught in the middle of something just because they hadn't eaten dinner. The other woman stopped talking briefly after Lisa said this, then started talking much louder to the man, still in Japanese.

The car outside stopped in the middle of the parking lot and killed its engine. After a few moments, it turned off its lights and the driver-side door opened.

The Asian man stopped arguing with his wife and looked out the window again. He swallowed hard and then said, "Okay, we will make you dinner. But please lock the door and turn sign to closed. Thank you."

"Huh?" Tom sounded a bit surprised. He then turned and looked at the car. A person emerged wearing a hoodie with the hood pulled low over the face. The person slowly walked toward the door. Through the glass, it was hard to make out any features other than a slight build.

"Please, lock door and turn sign to closed. Thank you," the man repeated, much more urgently.

"Seems rude, don't you think?" Tom responded.

"Please," the man said.

The person outside got closer.

Lisa was torn. Clearly they feared the person coming toward the building, but she still didn't want to get in the middle of something. They were a long way from home, no one knew where they were outside the ballpark of "Northern Michigan," and suddenly she wasn't that hungry.

"Uh, I don't want to intrude here. We can just go," Tom said with a nervous catch to his voice.

"NO!" the man and woman said at once. The man then followed with another plea. "Please, just lock door now."

The person outside continued walking at a leisurely pace, the hood pulled low. It was still too dark to see any features on the face.

Lisa turned slowly toward the woman. Their eyes met, and Lisa could see the raw fear in her eyes. The woman mouthed the word "please." Without turning, Lisa heard the crunch of footsteps on the gravel near to the door. She broke eye contact, spun, took a step over to the door, and turned the lock.

The figure outside froze instantly. The person stood outside the glow of the restaurant lights. Lisa guessed it was a man, based on the build. He was under six feet and skinny. She still couldn't make out a face. He stood there for a moment, then slowly turned and walked back to the car. They all watched as he got in the car, started the engine, backed out of the parking lot, and drove away. He never turned on his headlights.

All four of them stood looking at the now-empty road. The man broke the silence. "Please, come around, we will cook you dinner. Do you know what you would like?"

Tom and Lisa stood motionless while staring at him as he flipped up part of the counter and opened the door under it. The casual tone of his voice, as if nothing had just happened, confused Lisa enough that she wondered if she had imagined the whole thing. Tom, who had never gotten past being confused, was the first to respond. "Um, are you sure you wouldn't like us to just go?"

"No!" the woman said, a little too quickly thought Lisa. She then cleared her throat and composed herself. "No, please stay. We have a table in the back." She motioned for them to follow her. Tom and Lisa looked at each other, shrugged, and went through the door.

The restaurant's back room was a combination of kitchen and office. There was a small table with a TV on it and a couple of chairs in the back corner. The kitchen took up the rest of the room. There were two large refrigerators; a large flat grill; a couple of fryers. It was a small enough setup, like a home kitchen with a few extra appliances. A storage closet stood open in the corner opposite the table. It contained stacks of soda, takeout boxes, and condiments.

Lisa had never been in the back of a restaurant that she could recall, but the normalcy of it snapped her back to reality. Whatever that had been with the guy outside, it was not her concern. Probably just a crazy regular customer that they didn't want to deal with. She never would have thought that seeing soy sauce packets in bulk would have been a comfort, but it was.

"Please, sit," the man said. He motioned to the table. "We don't have much left tonight, but we can make you some sweet and sour chicken and fried rice. Would this be acceptable?"

"That would be wonderful," Tom said.

Lisa was not as ready as Tom to ignore what had happened. "Thank you, but I feel like we're imposing. Also, that was pretty weird. Why were you so worried about that guy?"

The woman answered in a manner meant to end that line of inquiry. "He was a bad customer. Would you like a Coke?"

"If you are sure it's no trouble, that would be wonderful," Tom said before Lisa could press the topic. "By the way, I'm Tom and this is Lisa. We appreciate this."

"It is no trouble," the man answered. "I am Takashi and this is my wife, Kiyoko."

Kiyoko stepped to one of the refrigerators and pulled out two glass bottles of Coke. She put them on the table and motioned for Tom and Lisa to sit. Tom pulled out a chair for Lisa and sat down opposite her. She took one more look toward the front through the door and shrugged. If this was in New York, it wouldn't seem weird, she reasoned. "It's nice to meet you. Thank you for feeding us!" She sat down.

"It would not be Christian of us to turn away lost and hungry strangers," Takashi said. Lisa could not tell if he was joking.

"Can't help but notice," said Tom, "you both have Japanese names and were speaking Japanese earlier. I might have misread the sign, but I'm pretty sure it said Chinese restaurant."

Kiyoko laughed, not entirely mirthfully, and said, "Small town, most people can't tell the difference. They have no interest in Japanese food. When in Rome, as they say."

"That's a shame," Lisa responded. "Have you lived here long?"

"It feels that way," replied Takashi.

"We came years ago," Kiyoko said. "Nice to be far away from everything."

Tom and Lisa both nodded. Tom said, "We're from New York. We decided to take a road trip to see America and get away from the city."

"Not many people come through this way that don't have a reason to be here," Takashi said. He turned on the grill and poured oil on some rice. Kiyoko poured frozen, breaded balls of chicken she had gotten from the fridge into the fryer cage. Lisa could smell the grease as it began to heat. It smelled delicious.

"Is there a hotel nearby?" Lisa asked. She noticed that Kiyoko and Takashi shared a quick look.

Takashi answered, "There's no hotel in Fortson. Even though it is late, you would be better off returning to the interstate and driving north two or three exits. There is a hotel there."

Tom groaned, and Lisa slumped her shoulders. That would be at least another hour of driving tonight. She was already exhausted. "What about a bed and breakfast?" she asked. "There must be something like that around here."

"No," Kiyoko said more sharply than Lisa would have expected. "This is not a tourist area. Nothing here to see. Better to do as Takashi suggests. There are many nice places in that direction."

Lisa was sure they did not want them to stick around or go into town. She had no idea why, but it was all surreal enough that, even though she was tired, she was okay with the drive if it meant going where people were normal. She had to admit she was curious what they were hiding. Something obviously bothered them, clearly related to the person who had been outside. But she did not see much point in badgering them. For all she knew, the whole town could be one big drug operation. She had read so much about the meth epidemic in the middle of the country that she had begun to assume any abandoned house they saw or small town they drove through was loaded to the gills with meth. Silently, she cursed Tom for making her watch *Breaking Bad.*

They were all silent. Kiyoko and Takashi focused on cooking while Tom and Lisa sat drinking their Cokes and hoping no one could hear their stomachs rumbling. After a minute or two, Kiyoko pulled the chicken from the fryer, shook it vigorously to get the grease off, and put the chicken on top of two big bowls of rice. Tom was all but drooling as she brought it to the table. Before she got there, a light from the front of the building crawled across the wall. It looked like the light from a car pulling into the parking lot. The sound of an engine revving followed immediately.

Kiyoko dropped the plates to the floor. She moved so fast toward the door that Lisa had barely registered the plates crashing before Kiyoko disappeared into the front. She shouted something in Japanese that sounded like a swear to Lisa. Takashi ran to the front after her.

Tom looked at Lisa and said, "You know what, we should just leave. I'm not that hungry." Lisa shook her head and got up. She was ready to see the back of this weird little place. She walked to the front and gasped at what she saw through the window.

A dozen cars were lined up across the parking lot and onto the grass on either side. They all had their headlights off, except for the one in the center of the line, which had its engine running and its high beams on. Standing next to each car was a person with similar build to the one who had been there earlier. They were all wearing hoodies in the same way, completely obscuring their faces.

Tom had followed Lisa and was now looking over her shoulder at the scene in front of them. "What the hell is this?" he said. No one answered him. They all stood looking out the window in silence. Eventually, Takashi sighed deeply, looked toward the ceiling for a moment, and then turned to Tom and Lisa. He had a determined look in his eye, as if he had just made a difficult decision.

"Please, come with me," he said. A crunching sound outside made him pause. The hooded people had begun to walk slowly toward the restaurant. Takashi moved toward Tom and Lisa to herd them into the back room. "Quickly now."

The serious tone in his voice got the point across, and all four of them went to the back room. Takashi closed the door behind them.

"Do you know those people?" Lisa asked. "Should we call the police?"

Once the door closed, Takashi walked to the storage closet and began removing things and tossing them into the room.

Kiyoko answered Lisa. "The police will be no help." Her voice, a mixture of fear and resignation, did more to scare Lisa than the people outside.

There was a loud bang from the front. It sounded like someone had punched the window.

"We will address the situation with the ..." Takashi paused, "people outside. It would be best if you went into the closet and did not come out until we tell you."

"I'm not hiding in the damn closet because of some punks," Lisa practically shouted. "Just call the goddamn cops."

A second bang came from the front, quickly followed by a third and the sound of glass breaking.

"They are not merely punks, and this is our problem. Please go into the closet, now. You will be safe there."

Another crash and more glass breaking came from the front.

Lisa glared at Takashi, but the look of pleading on his face got the better of her. "Fine."

"You will be safe, we promise," Kiyoko said. Tom and Lisa entered the closet. There was barely enough room for them, but they managed to squeeze in. Lisa, who was slightly bigger and in better shape than Tom, went in after him. Kiyoko shut the door. It was immediately too dark to see.

"Next time I suggest we stop at a hamburger place, we should just stop," Tom said quietly. Lisa elbowed him hard in the ribs.

Outside the closet, they heard Kiyoko and Takashi pull the table in front of the door. The sound was muffled, but Lisa thought she heard the front door open. After another moment or two, they heard Takashi shouting angrily in Japanese. No one shouted back. He would pause periodically as if he was conversing, but his angry tone never changed. Lisa wished that she had taken Japanese instead of German in school more than she had ever wished for anything in her life.

They lost all sense of time in the dark closet, but eventually the shouting stopped. The banging stopped, too. They could only hear their own breathing.

"Think we should open the door?" Tom asked.

Lisa shrugged before remembering they were in the dark and he couldn't see her. "They said to not open it until they come ba—"

A loud bang on the closet door interrupted her.

"Oh, shit!" Tom said.

Another bang on the door. Someone was pounding it.

"Fuck off!" Lisa shouted.

A third bang made them jump. It was harder than the first two.

"See if you can find anything to use as a weapon," Lisa said.

A fourth bang.

"Damn it, there isn't anything," Tom said.

A fifth bang.

"Fuck off and leave us alone!" Lisa shouted. "Tom, help me brace the door!"

The door opened inward so Lisa put her back against it, bracing her feet against the back wall. Tom pivoted so his shoulder pressed against the door as well.

The sixth bang was hard enough that they felt the door shudder.

"Just go away and leave us alone!" Tom shouted, his voice higher pitched than normal.

Neither of them had ever even been in a fight. The closest Tom had come was when a black Labrador Retriever attacked him once as a kid. He knew he would do whatever he could to protect Lisa, but he was afraid it wouldn't amount to much.

Lisa had taken some self-defense courses and had done some of the team fitness programs that were all the rage. She knew she could probably hold her own against one of the guys that had been outside, but there were at least 10 of them. She loved Tom, but she was pretty sure he could not take a punch.

"The banging's stopped," Tom said.

"What?"

"The banging's stopped. It's been like five minutes."

"Shh."

Lisa couldn't hear anything.

"Should we open the door?" Tom asked.

Lisa was about to respond when there was another bang, hard enough that they thought they heard the wood crack. Lisa yelped. Her ear had still been pressed against the door.

"Shit!" Tom yelled again. "All we wanted was some dinner, leave us alone!"

They braced themselves against the door, waiting for the next punch. Lisa didn't know how much longer it would hold. If the people outside wanted to get in, they would get in eventually.

Tom and Lisa stayed braced and tense against the door for a long time. Lisa had no idea how long. After a while, she couldn't keep pressing and relaxed a little. Eventually, Tom sat on the floor as best he could with his back pressed against the door. Lisa sat down beside him.

They stayed that way for what felt like hours. There was no more banging or shouting from outside. Before long, their adrenaline drained and they were left exhausted and scared, sitting in the dark.

"Lisa," Tom said quietly.

Lisa started at the sound of his voice. She realized she had fallen asleep. "How long have I been sleeping?"

"No idea. I think I slept for a little while, too."

"Do you hear anything?"

"Nope, it's been dead silent out there," Tom replied. She felt him gather himself. "I think we should go."

Lisa agreed, "Yeah."

They awkwardly stood. There was nothing in the closet to use as a weapon, but Lisa suggested that, as soon as the door opened, they make a break for the kitchen. There had been knives and other utensils they would be able to use if the hooded people were still there. Tom agreed.

"Ready?" he said.

"As I'll ever be."

Lisa reached over and gave him a kiss. "Let's do it."

She yanked the door open, and they were blinded by the light in the room. After spending the night in a pitch-black closet, the dim light in the room felt like a floodlight pointing directly into their eyes. Despite being temporarily blind, Tom bolted into the room and immediately tripped over the remnants of the table.

Lisa followed him, blinking her eyes rapidly to get used to the light, and made for the kitchen area. The knives she remembered being on the counter were gone and, as she realized once her eyes adjusted to the light, so was everything else.

The room was a mess. Old beer cans and broken bottles were everywhere on the floor. Graffiti covered the walls, and everything had a thick layer of dust. The table lay in pieces. The room looked like it hadn't been used in years, other than as a spot for teenagers to drink.

Lisa's eyes lingered on the sink full of broken dishes.

"What the hell?" Tom said as he got up.

Lisa had no reply. She had no frame of reference for what she was looking at. When they went into the closet, it had been a normal-looking restaurant. Now it looked abandoned.

They carefully made their way toward the front, stepping over bottles and other detritus. The door between the front and the back rooms was gone. Only a couple of broken hinges remained.

The front room looked almost as bad. All the windows were broken. The front door was still there, swaying on its hinges, but the glass was gone. Graffiti covered the counter like the walls in the back room. The register, menus, and everything else was gone.

Slowly, Tom and Lisa made their way around the counter and out the front door. Their car was the only one in the lot.

Once outside, they turned and looked at the building. The sign was half gone. It was a shell of the place they had walked into the night before. Even the parking lot was mostly overgrown with weeds and grass.

They walked to their car feeling shell-shocked. Tom saw something tucked under the front windshield wiper.

"What's that?" he asked.

Lisa pulled it free. She stared at it, and then blanched. Tom took it from her hand. It was a Chinese restaurant menu. On it was written *On the house.*

"I think I want to go home," Lisa said.

"Me, too."

He crumpled the menu and threw it through the open door into the abandoned building.

"Open," said Lisa. "Vacancy."

"Huh?"

"Nothing. Let's go," Lisa said. She shivered.

They got in the car and pulled out of the parking lot, turning left toward the interstate.

Four days later, they were on a plane leaving LaGuardia for the Bahamas.

NO GOOD DEED

BY GAIL HUSCH

Never in real life had she seen such desperation on any human face.

Twenty-five years ago, 5:30 on a cold Sunday evening early in November, already dark. Eleanor, after a day at the museums and with a train to catch, hurried down Fifth Avenue. She had already passed the public library—no time to admire the lions—and was about to cross 40th Street, when a man hurtled across the avenue, an old-fashioned hard suitcase swinging violently from one hand. The suitcase could not have weighed much, Eleanor realized. Maybe it was empty.

Although the crossing signal told her to walk, she hesitated, one foot off the curb, waiting for the man to reach the sidewalk on the opposite side of 40th Street. Keep on going, she silently urged him. Clearly, he was not right in the head, probably drunk, maybe high on something, cocaine or worse, maybe PCP, obviously disturbed. She nervously scanned the area, looking for protection, searching for someone normal, ideally a policeman.

But it was one of those strange moments when, in the middle of New York City, no other soul was in sight, not a pair of strolling passersby, not a car, not a taxi or a truck, no pigeons, nothing alive on the hushed streets but Eleanor and the man, now standing on the sidewalk on the other side of Fortieth Street and spinning crazily while the suitcase banged against his legs.

He flapped and flailed in the pooled light of a single streetlamp, a man apparently without bearings, with no conception of where he was and even less where he should be. Eleanor could just make out his face. A youngish man, she judged, 30s, maybe 40s, around her age. No sound came from his open mouth, gaping in a soundless wail.

Eleanor was about to change her route, leave the man behind, turn right onto 40th Street to head down Sixth Avenue, when he turned and saw that she watched him. Across the deserted street, he met her eyes.

Never in real life had she seen such desperation on any human face.

Eleanor raised one hand and stepped slightly forward, two small movements she hadn't meant to make. The man took them as an invitation and lurched toward her, crossing the pavement with his suitcase swinging and an arm outstretched. He was crying now, noiselessly, tears catching in the stubble on his cheeks and chin. Were the tears in gratitude for the help he thought she offered?

Eleanor fled to the right, toward Sixth Avenue. I'm sorry, she whispered. She did not look back.

What else could she do, a woman by herself? Most likely he was foreign and didn't speak English. Surely a cop would come along soon. She'd look for one on her way to the station, send him back to find that lost, lonely man with a suitcase.

* * *

When she got home, the children had eaten and were settled in the family room watching their allotted hour of Sunday night television. From her seat at the kitchen table, wineglass in hand, Eleanor could hear their laughter, Sean's staccato ha-has, Sara's upwardly running trill. No point bothering them now. They'd wave her off, an annoying fly. They'd be sweeter at bedtime, each wanting a good-night kiss.

"That stupid home video show," Paul said. He stood at the stove, spooning puttanesca sauce over a plate of reheated penne, her belated meal. "We shouldn't let them watch it."

Eleanor sipped her wine, a stringent Shiraz that Paul liked more than she did. "You're right. Someone's always falling off something or getting hit in the crotch with a ball or a bat."

"That, or a dog eats a birthday cake or a baby farts in the bathtub." Paul set the plate down in front of her. "Cheese?"

Eleanor nodded. With a glass of wine in one hand and a container of Parmesan in the other, he joined her at the table. "So what did you see?" he asked.

Two big exhibitions, too many images to comprehend and digest. Eleanor didn't like visiting art museums with a companion, not even Paul. Although he had a good eye and never asked her to explain what a painting meant or why the thing on the floor was considered art, she didn't like talking about what she'd seen after she'd seen it. Such a pointless exercise, she thought. Would you ask someone to hum the symphony they'd just heard?

"Matisse—a huge retrospective at MoMA. And Magritte at the Met."

"Which did you like better?" Paul leaned both elbows on the table, watched as she loaded penne onto her fork. A good man, Eleanor thought. I love him.

She chewed, swallowed, drank some wine. "Matisse," she said. "The colors. You can't imagine the reds and blues. I think Magritte is too literal. A slice of ham with an eye. Ugh." And that troubling picture of a man and a woman kissing, each head shrouded in white cloth, both blind, mouths not touching. That's not us, Eleanor thought, smiling at Paul.

She was hungry. She ate while Paul kept her company, undemanding, patient, sipping his wine, shaking his head in amused exasperation at the children's insistent laughter.

Maybe it was the wine. She hadn't meant to bring it up, had intended to push it out of her mind, just an odd but insignificant incident toward the end of a full and tiring day.

Still, Eleanor paused, fork in hand. "I had a strange little encounter," she said.

"Oh?"

Eleanor kept her tone light. "I was about to cross 40th Street, just below the public library, when I saw a man on the other side of Fifth Avenue." She speared two cylinders of penne with her fork. "He was carrying a suitcase, an old, boxy suitcase. He looked so upset. He was spinning around as if he didn't know where to go or what to do. There was nobody else around, just that man and me."

Eleanor laid down her fork. She looked directly at Paul, through his glasses into his soft brown eyes. "He came toward me like he was asking for help. But I didn't help him. I ran away." Absolve me, she silently begged.

"Of course you ran away. Who knows what was wrong with him. You did the right thing." Paul touched her hand. "Don't let it bother you."

Eleanor picked up her fork. "You would have helped him," she said.

* * *

Lying on her back with her eyes open, Eleanor felt the bed gently spin. They'd finished the first bottle, opened a second, and Eleanor drank more than she was used to. She'd had to watch herself at the children's bedtime, brushing her teeth so they wouldn't smell alcohol when she kissed them, struggling to keep her words clear when she wished them good night.

Paul slept, his back to her and his knees drawn up. How easily he fell asleep. Eleanor envied him that talent. Even on the best of nights, she had to force herself to stop rehearsing the next day's chores, playing out the errands she'd run, worrying if there was bread for the children's sandwiches, wondering if she should get a job, take some of the moneymaking burden from Paul's shoulders now that Sara's college was only 10 years away.

Eleanor closed her eyes, woozily willing herself asleep. But the bed spun faster. If she didn't sit up, she knew that she'd be sick.

With her head propped in one hand, she sat in darkness broken only by the faint glow of the alarm clock on her bedside table. She listened to Paul's soft breathing, tried to match hers to his steady rhythm. The effort calmed her. She leaned back against the headboard, her arms hanging loosely and her hands resting palms up on the bed, one against each thigh. She closed her eyes again. This time she felt a pleasant dizziness, a gentle drifting that promised sleep.

His face, that gaping mouth, those terrified eyes. That outstretched, pleading arm. The suitcase clutched in his hand, too big to be so light.

Eleanor snapped awake. She no longer felt drunk. She sat frozen in the night, her husband, blameless, sleeping by her side.

A man begged me for a rope, she thought, and I left him to drown.

* * *

Although she never consciously called his image to her mind, for months afterward he came to her. He showed up in her dreams, sometimes as himself, sometimes as the agonized figure in Munch's *Scream*, sometimes as a panic-stricken animal, Picasso's shrieking horse or a wild-eyed cow facing the slaughterhouse.

Sometimes when Eleanor lay awake with Paul peacefully asleep, or sat over a book she meant to read, or paused while cutting vegetables in the kitchen, he'd come to her. What tragedy had sent him running blindly through the streets? What precious things were hidden in that suitcase?

But the questions disturbed her and, since they could not be answered, she chose not to speculate. Whatever he had suffered, she told herself, he must be better now.

He came to her less and less as the years went by. Sometimes, though, she felt a twinge of ancient guilt, like the phantom pain of a limb amputated long ago.

* * *

"So you'll go with me tomorrow?" Eleanor set one mug on the coffee table by the couch and kept the other in her hand. Of course he would. He'd promised her last night. Still, he deserved one final chance to bow out. At 69, several years retired, he preferred a leisurely day of raking leaves and watching football to a trek into the city. "To the museums?" she added.

Paul looked up from the computer resting in his lap. "I said I would. But if you ask me one more time, I won't."

Eleanor heard a hint of exasperation in his good-humored tone. She didn't blame him. She annoyed herself sometimes, how anxious she'd become, how often she caught herself fishing for reassurance. A few years ago, she would have been perfectly happy—happier—to make the trip alone. Now when she thought of New York, she imagined it a claustrophobic maze. Although she'd once had friends in the city, they'd all moved away. If something happened, if she felt sick, she'd have no one to call. It comes with age, she recognized, that gnawing sense of vulnerability.

Eleanor settled in the chair beside the couch. She held the mug in both hands and raised it to her lips, felt the steam on her face and breathed its aroma. The morning sun, a sharp November light, brightened the room and fell on Paul's hair, gone from salt and pepper to gray and now to white, a clean, pure white like his mother's.

Eleanor drank her coffee slowly. Sweet Teddy, already 15, climbed into her lap and began to purr, his soft body—the living stuffed kitty, they called him—vibrating gently against her legs.

Eleanor leaned back in the chair. Why so fortunate? Aside from Sean's short, intense teenaged episode with drugs—nothing worse than marijuana—and Sara's unhappy divorce, its memory dimmed by a compatible second marriage, life had moved smoothly for the family.

And Paul. There never was a man as kind and generous as Paul.

She glanced at her husband, his head still bent over his computer. In the perfection of that moment, a terrible truth struck her.

This cannot last much longer, she thought. You haven't earned unbroken happiness.

*　*　*

Already 5:30 and the train they hoped to catch left Penn Station at 6:15. But, after 30 blocks of fast-paced walking with a museum shopping bag in one hand and her purse digging into a shoulder, Eleanor was out of breath. By the steps of the public library, she caught the sleeve of Paul's coat. "Stop," she huffed. "Let's rest for a moment."

They'd waited in vain for a bus outside the Frick. After 10 minutes shivering in the November dusk, they'd started down

Fifth Avenue. No taxi or Uber, they'd agreed. New York was best experienced on foot. They were strong enough. Besides, Paul said, it felt romantic, as if they were the young couple they once had been, too poor and too independent for taxis.

"There," Eleanor said. "Beneath the lion."

Together, they leaned against the statue's stone plinth. First Paul set his shopping bag down and then Eleanor dropped hers, heavy with a hardbound book. She folded her arms, comfortable and safe in the lion's shadow. On the other side of the avenue, two pedestrians, not together, hurried forward. A moment later, a lone black car with tinted windows whisked by.

"It's so quiet," Paul said. "You'd never expect it to be so quiet in the middle of New York City."

Yes, so quiet. Eleanor would have agreed, but an overwhelming sense of déjà vu disoriented her. I've felt this before, she realized. I've lived this moment before, in just this light, this silence, and this emptiness. Eleanor, remembering, moved closer to Paul: That strange November evening, all those years ago.

"Ready?" Paul hoisted his bag and took her arm. "Either we give in to a cab, or we get moving."

Eleanor picked up her bag and let Paul guide her forward, toward 40th Street.

The signal said DON'T WALK. Paul, a stickler, made her stop although the street was clear. "You never know," he said.

Eleanor didn't want to wait at that corner. There wasn't time to waste. "Turn," she said. "Let's turn here and then go down Sixth Avenue."

"Good thinking."

Together, they turned right, Eleanor on the side closest to the curb, Paul beside her.

As she walked, she glanced across Fortieth Street.

A man with an old-fashioned suitcase, standing alone, very still, was looking at her.

"That's him!" Eleanor meant to shout, but her throat clutched and the words were lost. She turned to face him across the empty street.

"What?" she heard Paul say. "Why are you stopping?"

The man's mouth was closed. There was no panic on his face. He contemplated her with sad disappointment, his forehead creased. Slowly, he raised his shoulders. Why? he seemed to ask.

Strange, Eleanor noticed. He looks no older than he did before.

"What are you staring at?" Paul's voice was muffled, as if he spoke from far away.

The man shook his head and pivoted on one foot. He began to walk, quickly, back toward Fifth Avenue.

"Stop!" Eleanor called. "Wait! Please!"

She stepped into the street, one arm outstretched, her shopping bag swinging against her leg. "Please wait!" she called, but the man had reached the avenue and was gone.

"Eleanor! Watch out!"

Eleanor had no time to turn. She felt a push, a frantic shove that sent her flying forward. She landed on her hands and knees, felt the sharp pain of a broken wrist.

She groaned, rolled into a seated position.

She looked right, into the headlights of a yellow cab, its driver's side door open, its engine running. She looked left. A man kneeling, another man lying face down, one leg drawn up, his arms splayed. Paul, she knew, and crawled screaming to his side.

HAUNTING THE PAST

BY JASPER BARK

I'm digging away with my bare hands. Trying to reach the light. Shifting great, wet clods, but it's never enough. There's just too much mud on top of me. I'm all closed in. Trapped in this tiny little space. Can't make it any bigger cos my fingers are too torn up and my arms are so tired they're shaking.

Then I feel something in the dirt above me. Something soft and gentle but colder than death itself. It pushes through the earth and takes hold of my hand. Tiny fingers grip mine, chilling my whole arm.

I go rigid. I can't face this. I wrench my hand free and crawl back down the tunnel. Back through the shattered window frame and into the room. Where I belong. Every time I think I'm going to make it, I just slide back down here, ready to do this again and again.

Prison chaplain once told me every man builds his own private corner of Hell. This one's mine. I ain't getting out today.

* * *

Everything stinks of mud and damp. There's broken glass all over the floor. Window shattered when the mud poured in.

All the rooms upstairs are like this. There's five of 'em. Six if you count the bathroom. There ain't no water and there ain't no light. Both were cut off 'fore I got here.

Far as I can tell I been here three days now. Hope to God it ain't longer. I got such a hunger on me. Even the mud looks tasty right about now.

Thought I was being clever robbing a bunch of deserted homes. Reckoned folk would have left too quick to take all their valuables.

All I had to do was drive up after they'd gone and help myself. Guessed I could break into at least 10 houses before the mudslide.

That's the reason they all left. Freak rainstorms hit the mountains behind the town. There'd been a forest fire earlier, and all that rain sent the mud sliding down the slopes. Local fire crews came and helped clear out the neighborhood. That's when I hit town.

Figured I'd have two, maybe three hours 'fore I had to get out. I was wrong. Mudslide hit while I was doing my second house. Dumb thing is I nearly skipped the house. Whole place was empty when I broke in. But I reckoned the owners must've left something behind.

I was going through the bedrooms when I heard it. Sounded like a cross between a rockslide and a dam bursting. Ground was shaking and everything. I looked out the window and saw this great tide of mud come charging down the hills behind the yard. Couldn't believe how fast it was moving.

Raced downstairs, but it swallowed the house by the time I got to the hall. Front door came clean off its hinges, back door as well. Mud pushed 'em in and the windows too. Was like each one of 'em had its own tiny little avalanche.

Tried to get out of the upstairs windows, but the mud was pouring through when I got there. S'pose that's a good thing. If I had've gotten out mud would've just pulled me under.

Was only later, going through the kitchen for food, that I found the Realtor's details. That's why the place was empty. That's why the lights and the faucets don't work and why I haven't eaten for so long. House was on the market. Talk about bitch-ass luck.

Only thing now is to sit tight and wait for the rescue crews. Have to feed 'em some bullshit when they dig me out. Tell 'em I'm a buyer turned up on the wrong day or something. Can't let 'em find out why I'm really here.

Shit, they'll just laugh their asses off and stick me in the can. Be my third strike too, that's me down for life.

* * *

You see that? Over there by the door.

Course you didn't. You ain't even here. You're just something I dreamed up to block out the hunger and the loneliness. Used to do the same thing in solitary. Only way to stop you going outta your mind. Start talking aloud to someone who ain't there. Telling 'em what's going on around you like you was doing some voice-over for the National Geographic Channel or some shit.

That's all you are. Some imaginary audience in my head.

Anyways, what you missed was the little gal. She's gone now. This ain't her room. She'll play with her dolls, I expect.

Tell you what though. If you had've seen her you would've shit. Hell, I did the first time.

Well, not quite the first time. I didn't see 'em properly to begin with. First thing I saw was little shimmers in the air.

Thought my eyes were playing up. I'd blink and rub my eyes, but they didn't go away.

Then I tried staring at 'em, see if I couldn't make out what they really were. Was like tuning the picture on a TV. Suddenly she was just there. The little gal I told you about. She looked like someone had sketched her out of some silver-blue light right onto the air in front of me. Could make out every detail of her face, but I could still see right through her.

She didn't see me or nothing. She moved her head like she was talking to someone. Then she walked straight at me.

I jumped back, but she kept coming. Then she walked right through me. I didn't feel nothing, but it shocked me. Hairs stood up all over my body and I started shouting that I hadn't seen what I just saw. Took me a good while to calm down. Never wanted to be more drunk in my life.

Course, once I'd seen her there was no going back. She started appearing all over the house. Then I saw the other two. Her ma first and then her pa. Way they dress is real old school. Like something out of a silent movie 100 years ago.

Now I see 'em all the time. That's why I started talking to you. To try to make sense of the situation. Or maybe I wanna avoid facing the truth.

I'm buried alive in a house full of ghosts.

* * *

You wanna see the little gal? She's in her room like I said. That's down the end of the landing. Can't get enough of this old-time furniture they use. You can't see it, but it's straight out of an antique shop.

Started seeing objects after I saw the ma and pa. Began with the stuff they were holding, then I started to see the things they put that stuff down on. Can't make out colors or nothing, just outlines in that same silvery-blue light. It's like seeing things through some crazy night-vision goggles.

Ghost vision, I call it. Make my way round better when I've got the ghost vision.

Here she is. Combing her hair. I've watched her do that for hours. Spend a lot of time with her when she's around.

Don't have nothing to do when she's not here. That's why I love watching her. She was the first ghost I saw, so I feel a special bond with her.

My own daughter would be about her age now. Never got the chance to watch her brush her hair. Doubt her mother would let me now.

Things were different in the little gal's time. No one could deny her pa his right to see her. Men were respected back then. It wasn't a household without a man at the head.

Not like nowadays, when the law don't give any rights to a man. Don't even let him work to support his family no more. Man can't be a father these days. He grows up without his pa and grows old without his children.

They had no idea back then how bad things were gonna get. Be good if there was a way to reach back and tell 'em. To affect the past from the future. To fix things so they don't change.

That's what I'd like to do. Reach into this past and be a proper pa. Be her pa. Take her in my arms. Put her on my lap. Brush her hair for her. Can't tell you how much I wanna touch her hair.

Can't though. That'd bring back the hand. The tiny, cold one from the tunnel. With its little fingers chilled by death, grasping at me. Trying to pull me back to where it comes from.

Last time I stroked her hair, it nearly got me. Couldn't stop myself. I'd been watching her so long. I was missing my own daughter so bad. Stuck in here, starving for food and company.

I knew she wasn't real, so I just reached out to where I saw her hair falling off her shoulders. And I swear I felt my palms tingle. Like the ghost of a sensation. Guess that's what you get when you touch a ghost.

But her hair moved, too. Like I'd really touched it. Like I was running my fingers through it.

She screamed, but I couldn't hear it. I was too busy looking at her hair moving through my fingers. Then I glanced at her face and saw it was all screwed up. Her eyes were terrified. She jumped up and ran down to her ma and pa.

Never meant to scare her. Couldn't believe I'd just touched a ghost. I was shocked. I backed up to the window. Wasn't looking and I fell in the mud.

The little fingers pushed through and they grabbed my collar. Back of my neck was like ice. Tried to pull away, but I was held fast. The hand was trying to pull me outside. I know it was. For a moment, I felt like I ought to just give in. Stop struggling and let it.

But I fought back. I shucked off my shirt and I ran downstairs in my vest.

When I got to the dining room, she was telling her ma and pa. She was jumping up and down and crying, and her pa was scowling. He wasn't listening. He cared more about her making a fuss than why she was upset.

He started shouting and marched her to her room. But she didn't want to go in. She was too frightened. She clung on to his leg, crying and shaking her head.

He was about to raise his hand to her when her ma came and quieted 'em both down. Her pa went downstairs and her ma took her off to wash her face and tidy up.

Afterwards I watched her ma go and talk to her pa. Don't know what she said, but he looked real sorry when she was done and he went to talk to the little gal.

She was sleeping in the spare room. Guess she didn't want to go back in her own room in case I touched her again.

I don't think he knew what to say. He might've been trying to make her feel better, maybe even say sorry, but I don't think she was listening.

Ain't gone near her since. I daren't.

* * *

Been here over five days by my reckoning. Those rescue crews better hurry up and find me or there won't be nothing left to find.

My stomach hurts. Ain't had nothing in it since I was trapped. Hasn't stopped me shitting though. Can't help myself, liquid mostly. Probably blood in it, but I ain't bothered to check. Don't even take my pants off now. Ain't much point. Gotta conserve my energy. Don't have as much as I used to.

I got rashes on my chest and my legs, too. Skin's all sore and itching like a motherfucker.

Ain't seen the little gal for about a day now. Don't know why that is. Had no idea I'd miss her this much. Got to thinking about her pa and how he treats her. Ain't sure if he don't realize how lucky he is to have her. Or if he just don't know how to tell her.

Anyways, it got me thinking about my own pa. He was a miserable son of a bitch. Deserted my ma and me when I was just a baby. Never got to know him when I was growing up.

Used to make up all kinds of stories about him. My ma would tell me things about him if I bugged her long enough. Had to be careful, though, cos she was like to fly into an awful mood if I kept at it too long.

Weren't her fault, I guess. She was still hurt and mad at him. That was something she never got over. Weren't my fault neither. I didn't have no father figure to look up to. So I had to invent one from whatever I could learn about him.

I developed early, and by the time I was 15 I had the body of a man. Was also getting a bad name around the neighborhood. Didn't see myself graduating from high school, and I didn't want any of the dead-end jobs on offer, so I up and left home.

What sparked it was meeting an old friend of my pa's. I was hungry for information about my old man, and he was happy to feed that so long as I kept buying him drinks. He fed me a line of bullshit about what a mighty fine fella my pa was. How he'd do anything for anyone. How he had a heart of gold but wouldn't let nobody cross him. Would stand up to any man alive if he had to.

And I ate it all up. Especially when he let slip that he knew where my old man was living. Over in the next county but one. I didn't let up on him 'til he told me. Then I packed my bags and went off in search of my long-lost pa.

Wasn't quite the reunion I'd planned when I found him. Slept rough for a couple of days and asked around 'til I tracked him down to a bar. Barman pointed him out to me, slumped over a table in the corner. Didn't look nothing like the two photos I had of him. He was old and gray with a mouth full of broken teeth.

Barman hoped I'd come to carry him out. Instead, I bought a bottle of bourbon, which I knew was his drink, and took it over to him.

Don't know exactly what I was expecting. But I thought he might at least react when I sat down, poured him a drink, and told him who I was. Instead he knocked back the drink without even looking at me. Then he up and left the bar and took the bottle with him.

I chased him outside and asked him if he'd heard what I said. He said he'd heard me, but he weren't interested. He didn't care about no son. Told me to run along and stop bothering him.

I wasn't done with him, though. I followed him back to his flophouse and waited 'til it got dark. Next time he went out I cornered him in the alley and started wailing on him. He didn't try and stop me neither. Just lay there and took it. Only stopped when my arms were tired and my fists were covered in blood. I was hollering questions, and both of us were crying.

That's when the whole sorry story finally came out. Seems he did send for my ma and me to come join him. Only the day before we got there he lost his job, fought with his landlord and got kicked out of his apartment.

He was feeling pretty lousy when he got to the bus station to pick us up. When he saw us both waiting for him, he just froze. He said it was seeing me what done it. I looked so much like him. He was so proud and so full of love for me that it hurt him. He knew he couldn't be the pa I deserved. Thought it better to let some other man take the job.

He didn't think he deserved the happiness that we might bring him. Thought we were better off without him. So he just turned tail and ran. He left town and never came back.

When he was done talking, I just turned my back and walked away. He was sniveling and begging me to forgive him, but I just kept on walking and never looked back. Never saw my pa again. Could be dead for all I know.

I went seriously off the rails after that. Didn't care nothing for myself or nobody. Up 'til that point I'd always made excuses for my pa. Always believed he had good reason for walking out and staying away. Always imagined he'd do anything to have me back if only he could.

Now I knew different. Didn't care what I did after that. Or what happened to me.

'Til I became a pa myself.

I'd just started a year in County when she was born. Her ma sure was pissed at me, leaving her high and dry. She came round though. Even agreed to take me back when I got out.

Didn't want her coming up to no prison gates with my daughter. So I arranged to meet 'em both at a diner in town. Saw 'em through the window when I got off the bus.

Can't describe how I felt when I saw my daughter. Her ma mailed me two pictures when I was inside. But they didn't compare to seeing her in the flesh.

Was like my guts just tumbled outta my body and hit the sidewalk. She was the most perfect thing I'd ever seen. I couldn't breathe.

That's when I realized I couldn't ruin anything that perfect. I couldn't let her down, make her cry and break her heart like I had with every other female in my life, from my own ma right through to hers.

I wasn't up to the task of raising her. So, I just turned round, walked two blocks, and caught the first bus outta town.

Course I knew just what I was doing. And I hated myself every step I took away from her. Sometimes wonder if my own pa left me cos of what I done to my daughter.

Maybe it's cos I ain't eaten in so long. Might be affecting my brain or something. But I get to wondering if every action does have a consequence. Perhaps every consequence creates its own action in order to justify it existing.

Don't know if I'm making sense here. What I mean to say is, I wonder if it's possible to affect the past by what you do in the future. Did I reach back in time somehow and make my pa walk out on us to punish myself?

Cos I oughtta be punished for walking out on my daughter, and that seems about the best way I could've done it. Prison chaplain once told me every man builds his own private corner of Hell. This one's mine. Trapped my daughter in here with me. Just like my pa trapped me.

Ain't got no way to make it up to her neither. Guess that's why I feel so close to the little ghost gal. If I can't make it up to my daughter, maybe I can make it up to her somehow.

Gets me to thinking. If I do die in here, I'm not saying I will, but if I do then that little ghost gal might be my only salvation.

* * *

Ain't feeling too good at the moment. Just spat another tooth out. Blood tastes good in my mouth. About the only thing I've tasted in over a week, 'cept for bile.

Throat's so dry it hurts to swallow. Ain't had nothing but my own piss to drink for days. Even that's dried up now.

Keep thinking I should get back to digging my way out. Don't have the energy or the urge though. Don't want to do much of anything. Even breathing's getting painful.

Saving my energy for watching the little gal. Have to make sure I don't touch nothing when I do. I've started knocking things over in the ghost world. Picking 'em up, too.

Knocked the little gal's bedside table over last time I saw her. I was just watching her sleep and I kind of stumbled and hit it. Usually go straight through things in the ghost world, but they've started to get more solid. I can almost feel 'em now.

So anyway, the table and everything on it hit the floor. The little gal woke up and cried out, so I tried to comfort her. Put my hands on her, but I don't know my strength in the ghost world. She couldn't hear me comforting her and she couldn't move neither. She started screaming and panicking, so I let go of her and she ran to her ma's and pa's room.

Her pa was mad at her for waking him up and her ma was trying to calm 'em both down. The little gal was crying and pointing to her room, but I could see they didn't believe her.

I got real mad at 'em. I wanted 'em to believe the little gal. So, I reached out and I took hold of the water jug on their dresser. Didn't think I was going to be able to at first. Had to concentrate some to get my hand round it. But then I picked it right up.

Her pa didn't see to begin with. So, I threw it at his head. Only just missed him and the jug shattered against the wall. That shut 'em all up.

The little gal ran into her ma's arms, and her ma took her back to bed. When she was done tidying, the little gal's pa came in and sat with her 'til she fell asleep. He comforted her like I wasn't able to.

I knew he was saying bad things about me. Turning her agin me. I was boiling up as I watched him.

That's when I decided I wasn't gonna lose the little gal to him. That's when I knew he had to die.

* * *

Ain't certain why I pulled this floorboard up. Curious, I guess.

Just watched the little ghost gal come in here. She has this little ritual when she thinks no one's around. She pulls up a floorboard over by the window and pulls out a chest with lotsa little keepsakes in it. I've watched her do it a few times now.

There's tiny dolls and other stuff in there, but mostly it's jewelry. She ain't allowed to wear jewelry normally, so she has to keep it hidden. When her parents ain't about she puts it on and parades up and down like a little princess.

There's one ring in particular she really loves. It's shaped like a butterfly. She slips it on her middle finger and gets this look on her face like she's lost in some cotton candy dream world.

She left a few minutes ago, and I got me a strange notion. Cleared away all the mud, found the same floorboard and pried it up. Don't know what I thought I'd find under there, but I reached in anyways. Couldn't believe it when my fingers hit something.

Pulled it up, and there it was. Same chest I'd seen the little ghost gal with. Only it wasn't a ghost object. It was real. I opened it and inside were the same china dolls and some ancient toy jewelry.

This was their house. They really lived here over 100 years ago. Until now I thought I might be imagining this. That they were just some phantoms my mind had conjured up outta the dark. But they ain't. They were real. I'm seeing real people.

That's why I can reach back into the past and move stuff. They ain't the ghosts. I am. I'm haunting them.

I'm their ... what was that movie called? Poltergeist, that's it. I'm their poltergeist.

*   *   *

Ain't moved a muscle all day. Wouldn't want to even if I had the energy. Rash on my chest has been itching like a motherfucker. Haven't even scratched it. Just been sitting here, wishing this whole stupid mess away.

Throat's so dry and cracked I don't dare swallow no more. Even breathing's gonna get too painful soon. Ain't no rescue crews gonna come dig me out. I know that now. I'm gonna die in here, trapped under all this mud.

I should die, too. After what I done. I should keep dying, over and over for all eternity.

It's her pa's fault. Wouldn't have happened if he hadn't tried to turn the little gal agin me. Wouldn't have tried to kill him if he wasn't such a bastard.

Been following him around for a couple of days. Looking for my chance.

Knew I'd found it when I saw the urn. Was a big old fancy thing, made outta marble I guess, sat atop the mantelpiece at about chest height. Probably had his ma's or pa's ashes in it.

Mantelpiece isn't there now. Must've been torn down years ago, fireplace too. Was one of those big old fancy affairs.

Every evening pa lights the fire. Don't have no bellows, so he bends really low and blows on the base of it. Reckoned if that heavy old urn were to fall on him, it was like to crush his skull.

Only thing was, it was big and I was weak from not eating. Couldn't move it more than an inch 'fore I ran out of strength, even though it was a ghost object. Had to keep resting and moving it bits at a time. Finally had it on the edge of the mantelpiece. Ready to crush the bastard next time he blew on the fire.

Must've fallen asleep or something then. Cos the next thing I remember is coming to and seeing him putting wood in the grate. I got to my feet, but I was kinda dizzy. Kept seeing blotches and things in front of my eyes.

I put my hands on the urn, but I couldn't get no traction. Fingers just kept going through it. The little gal's pa was lighting the kindling. Then he sets to blowing and I knew it was my last chance. Wouldn't be strong enough to do this tomorrow.

Focused myself and got the urn to wobbling. Strained so hard I felt something in my shoulder pop. I stumbled backward and hit the floor. That's when the little gal ran in.

She ran up to her pa, raising all kinds of hell. Pointing to the mantelpiece and trying to push him outta the way. He reared up and took to shouting at her, even raised his hand. The little gal slipped and fell on the stoop.

Then the urn finally fell forward.

I tried to pull her up or push her out of the way, but I was too weak and too slow. The urn hit her dead on and she crumpled like a paper doll.

Ashes spilled out of the urn and mixed with the pool of liquid forming under her. Can't see color in the ghost world but I knew it was dark red.

Pa got the urn off and held her to his chest. She wasn't moving. There was a big dent in the back of her head and her left arm was hanging all wrong. There on her middle finger was the little butterfly ring. She must've forgotten to take it off.

Her ma ran in and set to crying and hollering worse than her husband. Started crying myself then. Blubbering and screaming at the pa that it was all his fault. If he hadn't moved. If he hadn't been such a bastard to his daughter. If he hadn't tried to turn her agin me.

Ma looked up from crying and I swear she caught my eye. Stopped me dead on the spot. I knew who she blamed for the little gal's death.

And I knew she was right.

Got outta the room and tried to get through the front door. Was beating my fists against all the mud when the tiny fingers broke through and grasped my wrist.

Cold seemed to seep right outta the fingers and into my arm. Numbing me so I couldn't pull away. Wasn't only cold that seeped outta the fingers. I could feel sadness, too. Like an ache in my bones, begging me not to stay. To break the cycle and stop punishing us both.

I got real mad then, and that gave me the strength to wrench my hand away. I had to be punished. After what I'd just done, I had to stay. Had no right to drag me outta all of this. Always striking when I'm too weak, when it's all too painful. Had no right.

I've gotta stay here. I'm gonna be here forever.

* * *

Ever counted down your breaths 'til the last one? That's where I'm at. Surprised I can even talk. Maybe I ain't talking aloud. Maybe it's in my head now. Can't tell anymore.

Still see the ghosts from time to time. Whizzing past me like a film on fast forward.

Wait, something's happening. There's three of them now. The ma and pa and some other guy, wearing funny clothes like a ... like ... wait, he's a priest.

Funny-looking fucker with bulbous eyes and a beard. He's carrying a Bible and a big old crucifix. Keeps waving it around. Hah, they know I can't leave, so they've brought in the good book and a bad priest to evict me.

He's walking around the room saying some mumbo jumbo. Pa's following him, throwing water around. Must be holy, I reckon. Lot of good that'll do 'em.

Priest keeps changing direction, turning his head like he's trying to sniff me out. That's right, over here. To your right, down a bit. There you are.

Last thing I ever see is the ugly mug of a priest who died 100 years 'fore I was born.

Time for me to slip out. I know how this one ends. No point waiting for the credits.

* * *

Can't tell you what a relief death is. Feels like a deep, contented sigh, no more pain, no more hunger.

Don't see nothing at first. Then I find the Light. It's so bright it burns right through me. I feel purer just by looking at it. So perfect it lifts me up and drags me toward it. I can't stop myself. I wanna reach it so bad.

But the closer I get, the smaller it looks. Like it's at the entrance of a tunnel. A tunnel made out of all the bad things I ever did. I'm pulling them to me as I move toward the Light.

Like thick, black mud, every wrong move I ever made is coming down on top of me. Keeping me further from the light 'til finally it blocks it out altogether.

* * *

I'm digging away with my bare hands. Trying to reach the light. Shifting great, wet clods but it's never enough. There's just too much mud on top of me. It's too narrow. I'm all closed in. Trapped in this tiny little space. Can't make it any bigger cos my fingers are too torn up and my arms are so tired they're shaking.

Then I feel something in the dirt just above me. Something soft and gentle but colder than death itself. It pushes through the earth and takes hold of my hand. Tiny fingers grip mine, chilling my whole arm.

And there on the middle finger I feel a little butterfly ring. It's the little gal. She wants me to come with her toward the light. She knows the way. She can take me away from all this.

She's been waiting for me this whole time. I knew she'd be my salvation. She's begging me to leave with her, to break this cycle. She's trying to tell me I got a choice. I can feel it in her touch. It's pouring outta her fingers. But I can't do it.

I need to be punished. If I have a choice, then I choose to go back. Even though she can't leave without me. I've trapped her here with me.

I go rigid. I can't face this. I wrench my hand free and crawl back down the tunnel. Back through the shattered window frame and into the room. Every time I think I'm going to make it, I just slide back down here, ready to do this again and again.

Prison chaplain once told me every man builds his own private corner of Hell. This one's mine. I ain't getting out today.

TO HEART'S CONTENT

BY SHANNON CONNOR WINWARD

I wake up outside the cabin in just my pajamas and socks, but I'm not feeling the cold. I think I'm dreaming, but then I realize I can smell the pine and the wood smoke and even the snow—that crisp, elemental scent so particular this has to be real. So then why is there a stranger in a monk's habit by the outhouse, and why am I not afraid?

His face is hidden in shadow beneath his deep hood. He lifts his hands. The hood falls back. He has a tonsure of copper-blond hair coming to a point on his brow, the scalp bare and gleaming in the light of the moon, though really the light seems to be coming from within. I don't think I've ever seen his face before, but I know him. I do.

"What are you doing here?" My voice sounds so loud and coarse in this ethereal moment. Something in the underbrush thinks so, too, and skitters off into the night. The monk looks at me with sadness so intense my instinct is to run away to escape it. If I were thinking rationally, I would have done that anyway, the moment I saw him. I'm unarmed, and this is a stranger. Strangers in these times always mean danger. *But I know him.*

I try again. "What is it?"

Now I'm staring at the spot where the monk had been. There are no prints in the snow, nothing to suggest he was ever there, other than the echo of his voice in my mind speaking a language that isn't English (Gaelic, maybe) but that I understand, anyway saying, "Heart's content."

I let out breath I didn't know I was holding. It clouds in front of my face. Now I notice the biting air, the wetness seeping through my socks and up my legs. Now I notice the hollow in my stomach, and I begin to shake.

I return to the cabin and nestle up close to the wood-burning stove. Gabby wakes and comes over—she thinks my shivering is from the cold. She strips off my socks and leggings and tucks a blanket around me, casting looks from under her white-blonde lashes. The freckles above her nose are folded into constellations of worry.

She keeps her thoughts to herself lately. The last several weeks have been hard on her. Not just the physical part—although long-distance trekking is a rough life, the kid was used to the woods, the weather. She'll manage. She misses her people, though. She feels guilty for sneaking away, dodging the search parties that came looking. She refused to turn back until it was too late, so now I am her family. Not a responsibility I wanted, particularly, but the calling dreams that send people my way are strong. At 15, Gabby may be the youngest person to follow me, but she's not the first, and probably not the last.

We're trying not to disturb the others, but Howard appears in the doorway of the cabin's only bedroom. His hair is sticking up in sleepy clumps, but less so on the top (partly why he always wears a cap during the day). For a moment, it reminds me of the monk with the weird ring of hair, and I frown, which puts Howard more on edge. He looks like an old man, leaning against the doorframe, squinting at me. His hand is out of view, resting on the rifle he keeps in the corner. "What's going on, Danae? Vision?"

I shake my head. "Just a nightmare." Howard studies me for a moment, then nods and turns away. A month ago, he would have known I'm lying. But now he has Reesa.

We hear the bed creak, muffled voices, and then quiet.

"I'll be all right," I tell Gabby. "Go back to sleep."

"I don't think I can," she says, in a not-quite-whisper. "I had a nightmare, too."

"About?"

"You. Guns. Fire. The usual."

I sigh, tilt my head in invitation, and Gabby pulls her sleeping bag closer. She leans on my shoulder. We feed another log to the stove and watch the flames together until dawn.

* * *

In the morning, after going to the outhouse for the usual reason, I consider what meaning, if any, I'm meant to draw from last night's vision. The sun shines brightly through the whimsical little moon shape that Howard carved in the door. I return to the others with a decision.

"It's Brigid's Day," I announce. "The weather is clearing. It's time to move on."

Reesa glances up from the coffee she's brewing on the stove. "Brigid?"

"S'like Groundhog Day for witches," Gabby says over a mouthful of trail mix. I flinch at the word—it's not wrong, per se (I've heard worse names for what I am), but it's dangerous. Gabby chews, oblivious, happy just to show off how worldly she's becoming since leaving Trachtenberg, her homogenous little Christian mountain town.

Howard meets my eye—old habits, unspoken history—but Reesa is good people. There was a reason she was hiding out up here in the cabin, alone, when most of central Pennsylvania had either been absorbed into the fallout cities near Scranton or Cleveland, or gone on to Jesusland. Reesa and Howard are kindred spirits—loners, survivalists. Within hours of meeting at a trading outpost in State College, she invited us back to the cabin to weather the coming storm in safety. Howard, who didn't trust anyone, was the first to vote yes.

It'd still been my call, of course. I didn't have to be psychic to see what was up. Reesa's lean and strong, closer to Howard's own age, and handsome, with creamy brown skin and traces of red in her hair—a hard-to-read ethnic mix, like me. If we were on better terms about it, I'd tease Howard for having a type. We're not there yet ... but I let Howard go to her without a word of reproach. I didn't want him for myself, anyway, not anymore. Not since Trachtenberg. I figure if Reesa wasn't safe, my inner compass would have told me by now—but that doesn't mean I *like* her, or want to throw words like "witch" around until I know for sure where she stands.

"We've been cooped up here since before Christmas," I point out. Staying that extra week had been for Gabby's benefit, an attempt to stave off the homesickness with forced festivity. But Howard and Reesa, flush with new sex, weren't in any rush, and then the second storm hit, and then another. But winter isn't like it used to be. It's cold at night, but the days are not so bad if you're moving, if you've got the right gear. It's been over a month now—the smell of tension and underwashed bodies in these close quarters is starting to drive me batty. I'm guessing I'm not the only one.

Gabby gives a thumbs up. Howard nods, but he and Reesa exchange a look. He stomps outside to do rounds and scare up lunch.

Reesa slowly sips her coffee. Her dark eyes almost disappear under her furrowed brow. "Any idea yet on where you're going?" I note the emphasis on "yet."

"Still north." I pour myself a cup.

"North," she echoes. The lines in her forehead grow deeper, then disappear as she shrugs. "Want me to show you those fishing knots, Gabs?"

* * *

I know what Howard is going to ask me. Once again, it's nothing supernatural—after going on five years together, I just know how to read him.

I find him by the creek, removing a rabbit from one of his traps. It's still kicking. He finishes it off with a twist, purposefully not looking up, although I know he knows I'm here. He doesn't have to be psychic, either. He heard me crunching along the path.

Back before the world went to hell, Howard was an accountant or something, a weekend warrior. But here in the heart of darkness, he's gifted. I've gotten much better at stealth under his training, but I'll always be just a suburban girl in hiking boots compared to him.

"You want to stay," I say.

Howard slits the rabbit's belly, tosses the offal into a plastic bag for later. "We've got a good thing here. The land is good. No one around. We can get to the interstates easy enough when we have to, but—"

"Howard ..."

"No, listen." Howard puts the carcass aside. He reaches for my hands, then stops, realizing his are still covered in gore. With an exasperated noise, he grabs fistfuls of snow to clean off the worst of the mess. "I'm with you, Danae. I've always been with you. I thought it was crazy to come north after Trachtenberg—why head straight into enemy territory, after everything we've been through? But here we are. We're safe. We have Reesa. What if ... what if *this* is what we came for? What if this is where the visions were leading?"

"It isn't."

"How do you know?"

Because I haven't found him yet, but I can't say that. The letter I've been hiding next to my heart feels like it's burning a hole through my bra. "I just know," I tell him. I hate lying, but Howard would never understand. Not this.

He looks so unhappy, I'm tempted to tell him he doesn't have to come, but I bite my lip. Could I really do this without him? I survived The Chain—all the bombings, the skirmishes, the quakes, the outages, and the outbreaks—but those were different times. Gas stations that still had gas, working hospitals, ice cream. The old world took months to die. Howard had my visions to thank for leading him away from the worst disasters, but I'd been under his wing as much as he'd been under mine. The idea of leaving him behind scares me—and I have Gabby now. There's no way she'd stay with him, without me. I have to keep her safe.

So I say nothing.

It's not like I'm putting a gun to his head, I think, eyeing the rifle leaning against the tree and the AK-47 on his hip. It's always been Howard's choice. I've never forced anyone to follow me—they just do.

I flash on images, memories of dead friends—an unwelcome reminder that following me can lead to other kinds of disasters. *What am I doing, leading these people into the lion's mouth on false pretenses, for a* guy ...

I turn my head, and I see the monk standing behind Howard, morning sun glinting off the copper in the strange triangle of his hair. His eyes—a deep, aching blue—are ringed with shadows. He looks haunted, tortured. He reaches out his hands and I jump up, screaming, suddenly convinced that Howard is in danger.

"What? What is it?" Howard is on his feet, the AK in his hands. He sees nothing. He turns back to me, brow knit in concern. The monk is mouthing something—a prayer? a plea?—in that musical, archaic tongue. Then he's gone, motes of snow and forest matter sparkling undisturbed in the stream of sunlight where he'd been.

"Danae?" Howard points the gun to the sky, waiting to be told the direction of the threat. How natural, the way he balances the spiritual and the real. How easily he's adapted to my world.

As I catch my breath, Howard concludes that there's nothing to shoot at and lowers the gun. "What did you see?"

I shake my head. It's not what I saw but what I heard, again. *Heart's content.*

What does it mean, I think, touching the letter against my breast, and *why am I so sure it has to do with* him?

* * *

The last time I saw him, Gabe told me I was going to Hell.

I didn't think much of it. He said that all the time. But in retrospect, I think he really meant it that night. As in wished for it.

When we were kids—maybe eight or nine—Gabe decided he was going to marry me. He informed me of this in the park where we'd met, halfway between my house and his trailer. Never, in all the years since, did he ever say *I love you*, but he'd often talk of what it would be like when I was his wife. How I wouldn't read the tarot any more, or swear, or wear such short skirts (the kind he loved to see me in). We'd have four children, three boys and a girl, and go to church every Sunday, and do mission work in places like Haiti or Laos. He said he saw it all in one of his dreams.

I always knew he was wrong, but I went along with it because I loved the way he made me feel. Not the shame part— even back then, ever my mother's daughter, I knew what misogynist bullshit that was—but the rest of it. Having someone accept your place in his life so completely. Being wanted. The way he looked at me, the way his hands felt under my short skirts.

But he was a good boy, as boys go. He wanted to wait, so I figured it was okay not to tell him that I would never marry him, that I didn't want the life he'd imagined. But that night, the last one before I went away to school, he was so afraid of what his dreams were showing him, he was convinced that the world would end, and if I left him I wouldn't come back. He was ready to throw it all away—his principles, his plans, even God—if I would just stay with him—or, barring that, sleep with him.

In that moment, he was more beautiful and more vulnerable than ever. He reminded me of the sad and arrogant little boy I'd met in the sandbox, the one with shards of glass in his curly brown hair, telling me about the angels that hugged him in his bed while his father raged at night. I loved him so hard, so much, I had to say no. "Go home, Gabe," I told him, and he told me, "Go to hell, then," I never saw him again. Three years later, the lower half of the state, including our houses and our park and our parents, were all leveled by bombs and the power plant explosion. I thought he died, too. But then, three years after *that*, in a library in Trachtenberg, I found his letter in a Lost and Found.

Every pocket where people live has an "El and Eff," as Gabby calls them; from tiny little farming hamlets to the nasty, sprawling fallout cities of refugees, and the in-betweens like Trachtenberg, where survivors try to build new lives—much like their old ones, but leaner, and unplugged—in the wreckage of the past. As closed off as we all are to *not-us*, everyone respects the Lost and Found because everyone has lost someone. To go there, to register, town after town, to leave the names of your missing in the hope that fate, along with the diligence of strangers, might someday bring them back to you— it's a kind of religion now, no matter what god you worship.

Even though, according to his letter, Gabe belonged to Jesus now more than ever, he'd been leaving letters at the altars of the L&Fs for me—and it worked. I found one. Now I know he's alive, or at least that he was a year ago. I know where he is, more or less. For a long time after I watched my friends die ugly deaths, I'd lost all confidence in myself and my visions—I'd lost my faith—but the revelation at the L&F gave it back to me. Now my faith burns against my breast and from within my rib cage and in my gut—Gabe is alive. Gabe is waiting for me.

Gabe is north.

* * *

Maybe that's what the monk was about, I tell myself, downing a shot of whiskey to soothe my nerves. Maybe he's a symbol, a reminder that this isn't just about love for a boy I used to know. As my mom, the hippie new-age witch, used to say, everything happens for a reason. Gabe and I happened (and didn't happen) for a reason. Whatever this thing is that's been pointing me like a compass this way, that way, always toward life, it's also been pointing me toward *him*. I just have to have faith in that.

Gabby is gathering her few belongings. Howard is in the bedroom with Reesa, explaining. They're in there for a long time. I should be doing something productive, something other than staring out the window at the outhouse, trying not to interpret their voices through the wall. But I'm already packed—I've been living out of my bag since we got here—and I don't want to make decisions about what food and supplies to take without consulting Reesa. She contributed to everything we have. Also, let's be honest, I feel guilty for taking Howard back.

But when they emerge, they announce that Reesa is coming with us. That, I did not see coming.

"Look, I don't know about this prophecy stuff," Reesa tells me after Howard leaves to check on the tents. (He says he needs to make sure they're still in good shape after so many weeks in storage, but I think he thinks we need to have some kind of female summit). "I've just had enough of being lonely.

The walls don't talk back, you know? And a vibrator is a sinful waste of batteries," she adds with a wink.

Gabby turns red and busies herself with the knot on her knapsack.

"Is that what he said? That I'm a prophet?"

"Not in so many words, but that's what you seem to be, isn't it? A guide of some kind, here to save us from the evangelicals and the crazies who want to fuck everything up all over again?"

"Did he tell you about—"

"Your friends? Strung up and crucified by those racist fucks in Lutherville? Yeah, he told me."

I glance at Gabby. She wasn't swayed by that information, either, though I spared her the more gory details.

"You think it's your fault?" Reesa asks. "Howie said you warned them, but they went back anyway." She looks at me with sympathy. "Funny thing about people—they tend to have minds of their own."

"I just ... I want to you to be sure." I don't know if I'm hoping she'll change her mind or hoping she won't. Howard seems a little less gloomy with the decision. Having her along will certainly make things easier between us, if also more awkward. But I'm not ready to absolve myself for Maria and Santos, even weighed against all the others we saw to safety along the way.

Reesa grabs her coat, says something about killing the chickens. I start thinking of all the things people can do with axes, and have to shake my head to clear it.

This time we're heading into danger, not away from it.

Have faith, I remind myself. *There are reasons.*

Heart's content, intones the monk in my mind.

"What?" Gabby tosses her sack on the floor by the door and plops down, waiting for instruction.

"What what?"

"Heart's content?"

Did I say that out loud? "We can talk to our heart's content, but we've still got work to do." Nice save, I think, throwing open cupboards. Not every vision is meant to be shared.

* * *

Gabby got a little soft at the cabin. She doesn't complain, but I can tell she's struggling with the weight of the packs, the constant chill, and the snow-muddy trails that only seem to go uphill. She's slowing us down.

Howard will only go so far ahead, afraid to let us out of his sight, but he keeps throwing dark looks over his shoulder. I glare back at him—with a destination of "north" it's not like he's got a schedule to keep. But that's part of the problem, too. I think he knows I'm holding something back, being deliberately vague.

We pause at a scenic outlook to let Gabby pee and breathe. While she's behind the trees I rifle through her pack, looking for something else I can take to lighten her load. Some canned food. A bag of rice. I'm not exactly walking on air, either—my back hurts a lot—but this won't last forever. Gabby's young and healthy. She'll catch up.

When she returns to the outlook, she's fingering the necklace I made her for Christmas: bits of bone, river-smooth glass, and a chunk of white stone from our campsite outside Trachtenberg. She treats it like protection magic, even though I've told her it's just a thing I do.

We pause to check out the view. It's not inspiring—big humps of brown spotted with white and some evergreen. The mountains are coughing up mist like they're already sick of this day, this winter.

But Gabby isn't really looking at the valley. She's watching Howard and Reesa, who are standing together higher up the trail. "Do you think there will be other girls that like girls where we're going?"

I turn to look at her. It's not that I didn't know, but ... "Is that why you left home?"

"No." Gabby lifts one shoulder in a divinely adolescent gesture. "I mean, kind of? There were, like, 10 people between age 12 and 20, and three of them were related to me. I was basically betrothed to Ricky Schneider, who has a ..." she waves a finger at her face, "... a funny eye. And, like, even if they didn't care—which they *would*—it wouldn't matter. It's our duty to get married and have more kids and repopulate and all that."

I let out an exasperated breath. "Well, Christ, Gabby, you're not going to find somebody in Jesusland either. If you even tell anyone, you could get yourself killed."

"Yeah, I'm not an idiot, Danae. I mean *after*—whatever it is you're going there to do." Gabby catches something in my expression, scoffs, and rolls her eyes. "Assuming there is an after. You don't have any plan at all, do you?"

"I ... have some plans." *Find Gabe.*

"What's at Heart's Content?"

It takes a moment for her question to sink in. "What? What do you mean *at* heart's content?"

"Are we moving?" Howard shouts. Ignoring him, Gabby goes to the bench where I'd set down our packs. She unzips the front of mine and pulls out my beat-up, dog-eared, personally annotated map book. She flips back and forth a bit, then points to a dot in the northwest corner of the Allegheny National Forest. *Heart's Content Recreation Site.* I stare at it, then at her. Now I'm sure I didn't say those words aloud—and this little punk's been keeping secrets of her own.

"How do you even know this? Three months ago you thought Puerto Rico was in Mexico."

"Well, there isn't much to do besides read and talk, is there? And you've been all broody, and the only stuff Reesa had at the cabin were travel guidebooks and fashion magazines from *before*. I know all about Brangelina, and what colors are gonna be hot in the spring of 2000-and-who-cares, and I can tell you 10 reasons why I know Howard's still in love with you, but I figure geography's a lot more practical. And kinda interesting, actually," she adds, glancing back at the view. "Heart's Content is virgin forest—in the olden days they passed laws to protect it from logging and stuff." She sniffles, wipes cold snot from her nose. "They shoulda done more of that."

"Yeah, they should've," I mutter, feeling like we've sidestepped several more important issues—but this roller coaster conversation is more like the old Gabby, which is nice.

Howard comes huffing up behind me. "Ladies. We've got maybe four more hours of good light."

"We're coming," I say, trying to look casual as I snatch the map back. I catch Howard's eye before he heads back up the trail to Reesa, and my stomach gives a little twist thinking about the "10 reasons" thing. I think Gabby's right about that, too.

* * *

In a way, knowing exactly where we're going is harder than just having an impulse and a direction. The journey to Heart's Content will take us at least another three weeks—longer if winter decides to make a comeback, or if we encounter rough roads, or trouble. So every step, every moment is an agony of smallness. There's so much farther to go.

And yet I'm dragging, falling behind even Gabby. I spent the last night turning over in my sleeping bag, listening to Abby's cotton snoring and the creaking, sighing voices of the forest. Every time I started to drift off I saw the monk, but in memory, not a vision. Would he come back? If I fell asleep would I wake up outside the tent, in this unknown terrain?

He never showed—but he's left me with an echo, a feeling like I'm dragging something along with me but I can't remember what, or why. I'm having trouble placing my feet on the ground, seeing the path ahead.

On the second night, I decide to do a cleansing, a riff on the new-age smudging thing my mom taught me as a kid. I don't have any sage, but it doesn't really matter. Fragrant pine will do. It's all in the intent.

The ritual seems to help. By the third day, I'm finding my stride again. I feel lighter, focused. My inner compass keeps pounding the same point: *this way. This way.* Heart's Content is this way, and Gabe is there. He has to be, and he will feel the same way that I do, and everything—our childhood, what we were to each other and what we weren't, and everything that's happened between us and what's coming—it all must have a purpose.

Otherwise, I'm just a delusional girl leading delusional people to nothing good for the sake of a ghost.

* * *

Two weeks in, Howard wants to detour west. We're low on supplies, particularly batteries and booze, and we've heard of settlements between Pittsburgh and Punxsutawney where we might be able to trade or work for what we need without getting shot on sight. What he's saying makes sense, and any other time I'd agree, but I can't. It will tack on too much time—and honestly it might kill me to turn deliberately in the wrong direction.

I have to tell him why—not all, but enough.

His first question, of course, glancing up from my map book is, "What's in Heart's Content?"

"I don't know for sure," I say, which isn't strictly a lie. "I think ... someone. I'm not sure."

Howard considers me for a long time—and, for once, I can't tell what he's thinking. "How long have you known this is where we're going?" Gabby, to her credit, gives nothing away, but Howard glances between us and nods, clearly remembering the day at the outlook. "We're keeping things from each other now?"

I open my mouth to respond, but Howard flaps the map and stomps off, leaving the rest of us sitting around the campfire in awkward silence. Gabby busies herself with the two skimpy trout she caught for our lunch, supplemented by canned beans that are stewing in the coals. Reesa and I have nothing to do but wait—wait to eat, wait for Howard to return.

Later, as I'm blowing on a forkful of pintos, we hear gunshots—not the crack of the hunting rifle, which Howard left leaning against a maple tree, but the *chickachick* rattle of the AK-47. Gabby looks up, confused.

"What's—"

"Shh." Reesa and I are on our feet. Reesa has a Colt .45 she calls Kelly. I jump for the rifle. Without needing to talk about it, we take up positions facing the direction of the sound, between Gabby and the woods.

We wait. Three minutes, five, nothing. We're holding our collective breath, ears perked like dogs. Finally, we hear a crunching, measured step. Howard emerges from the pines, alone. He has an ugly gash across his face and an unfamiliar bag slung over his shoulder. His eyes find me first, though it's Reesa who forces him onto a stump and calls for the first aid kit.

"Arrow," Howard says, sneering as Reesa applies an antiseptic and tugs at his cheek, trying to determine if he needs stitches. No matter what, he's going to have a scar on his right cheekbone, just under the eye. It won't add any value to the real estate of his face, already nicked and crooked and lined.

"How many?" Reesa asks.

"Three, as far as I can tell. I got them all. Plus this."

"Well, I'll be damned," Reesa says, whistling, as I lay open the captured bag at Howard's feet. Canteens of water, a bottle of vodka, six packs of jerky, a porno magazine, and a gold mine of batteries.

"Heat this," Reesa says, handing Gabby a needle from the kit. Howard glances at me over Reesa's shoulder. "So, is this a sign? Listen to Danae if you want to live?"

I wince. Howard used to say exactly that—with pride, not irony. "No," I tell him. I mean, I could use it, twist it to suit my needs, maybe sting him back a little bit, but no. I didn't foresee this, and I don't think it's related—just fortunate. People are dangerous fuckers no matter which way we go.

And anyway, I can see in the way he's not looking at me anymore that he's already decided. We're heading north, not west, like I wanted. Despite his puffing and resentment, it was never really in doubt.

* * *

I wake up with words in my ear. *I love you. I love you. Love me back.*

I feel his hands over the length of me, my breasts, between my legs. My body has been awake to it longer, full of ache and longing, but my mind knows this is not right. I open my eyes.

The face above me is a pale moon, shining where no light should be, here in the belly of the tent. The eyes are hungry and haunted, deep set below a reddish gold halo. *You,* I think, and for a moment I know exactly what that means, but as I sit up, pushing against a body which is not, in fact, there, the name is gone. I know him only as the monk who set me on the path to Heart's Content.

With a rush of lilting Gaelic, the monk leans over me once more, and suddenly I am lying on stone. His mouth is on my neck, my cheeks, my hair, while above us floats an angel, gleaming snow white, sun yellow, ocean blue. The angel's wings are spread as if in benediction, as if what we do is good and right, and though I am full of guilt, sick with it, my body says *yes*, this is right, *yes*, this is love as God intended, *yes*.

There is a softness beneath my head—the cushion of my wimple and veil. The monk pulls a lock of my hair through his fingers. It is the color of turned butter and, freed from its habitual constraints, it reaches well past my waist. He traces it all the way down, brings his fingers lazily back, all the way to my lips, which he kisses with a tenderness that makes me want to weep. I don't, but I feel his tears, taste the salt of him. It is perfection and torture all at once

Love me back.

We cannot do this again, I tell him. It has to end.

It does not. I must come away with him. We will go where no one knows us, where we can live as husband and wife, where we can touch and love each other to our heart's content.

I do not disabuse him—not now. I will tell him in the morning, after Lauds, when there will be others near, and he'll dare not make a scene. For now, we speak no more, though his eyes continue with promises and pleas, a cacophony so great I have to turn away, toward the face of the angel Gabriel, a face of pale fire, bursting with all that is yet to come.

* * *

When we finally reach Heart's Content, there is no one here. And though we camp for days, doing little but watch the snow melt, no one comes.

What's worse, my head is empty, and my gut. Nothing telling me I'm too early, too late, how long to wait. Every morning I stand among the centuries-old white pines, watching birds dance over the water and the forest brighten and stretch toward the equinox, toward spring. I listen for instruction, the way I do, with handfuls of earth. I let it fall between my fingers, watch the way the wind takes it—or doesn't. Nothing. No direction, no impulse, no compass screaming *go, yes, go now.*

I have only the ancient, remarkable nothing of Heart's Content going on around me, as forests do. I have only the anxious faces of the others biding time, waiting for me to tell them I was wrong.

* * *

After almost a week at Heart's Content, Howard begins to plan. He spreads the map on a rock, discusses what we know: a pocket here, bad skirmishes there. Good hunting in upper Old New York and Canada—elk, bears. *Gods*, I think, *Canada?*

Howard's done this before. He leaves openings large enough for me to step in, take the lead, but not so large that we'll fall apart if I don't. It was like this for months after Maria and Santos—so long I'd begun to believe the gift was gone for good. So long that it was hard on Howard to step aside again when it finally returned.

Or when I said it returned, I remind myself. For the thousandth time, I touch the letter tucked into my bra. Gabe said he was "north." Maybe that's all the "vision" I ever really had. Maybe all the rest was just fantasy.

Reesa suggests a trek back to the cabin, how it'll be a faster trip now that spring is looming.

I can't take any more. I saw in the map that there's a town southeast of here, St. Sebastian's—not far. I'll scout there, see if there's anything to be seen. I don't wait to discuss it. I just go.

Gabby follows me.

* * *

I make a mental note to correct the map when I get back. There *was* a town here. There isn't anymore.

From the look of it, St. Sebastian's wasn't much to begin with—a main street with some strip malls, a gas station, a chain restaurant recognizable from the strips of striped cloth still fluttering in the rubble and the giant apple visible under the dust of the half-broken sign. We passed a couple of neighborhoods on the way in, a Walmart, and what looked to be a small medical plaza. Mostly just roads passing through on the way to somewhere else, which is where all the survivors apparently went.

The place is such an afterthought that it might be worth our while to check what's still standing for anything useful, tradable, left unplundered because no one remembered the town was even here. But I don't have the heart for it now. I didn't really come here to be useful.

Gabby and I pick our way down the main street, past hulks of old pickups, a school bus with no windows, islands of waist-high weeds growing through cracks in the blacktop. We pass a skull grinning at us from the middle of the road and, for Gabby's sake, I mutter "scavengers" and then, "dogs, maybe." Young as she is, she didn't have to see much of that kind of thing back home.

There comes a point, when the sun glints over the top of one of the looming brick walls, that I realize there's a reason we're not turning back. The main street seems to be dragging me toward a tumbledown stone structure just visible behind a wilderness of grass and the spread fingers of almost-budding trees. Mounting a slight rise in the road, I see the upward jut of a steeple—a church, missing its cross.

The building has no standing vestibule, no roof, and no western wall, but by and large the pews are in place, rising like Viking longships in a sea of dead leaves and debris. The central aisle is blocked by the cross, fallen from the steeple—a massive and disconcerting thing when seen from this angle. I suspect the ruins of the altar are crushed beneath it, but the thought flits away as I step further into the nave and catch the glint of color from the far wall.

"Oh, my Lord," Gabby breathes. "How is that not broken?"

On the right, at the back of the church sanctuary, late-morning sun creeps toward noon behind a fully intact stained-glass window, creating an orgy of color and light. My heart jumps into my throat. It is modern and gaudy, not the same as the window in my vision or dream, but near enough: an angel in white, six-foot high, at least, replete with trumpets and sunbeams. In the lower right corner, all but eclipsed by the fanfare and glory, kneels Mary, her head bent, hands piously spread, ready for the word and will of God.

Something else draws my attention—a dangling shadow. A foot. The hem of a robe. Turning back to where the altar should be, I see a different sanctuary, superimposed—narrow, dark, featuring only a rough wooden altar with a white cloth and a man, my lover, hanging from the rafters.

Love me back.

I hear myself screaming, but it's as if it's happening far away, long ago, and I can't stop. I stumble backward, my foot catching on something, a remnant of carpet, maybe. Gabby breaks my fall—she's calling my name, *Danae*, the name I have now not the one I had then. I'm trying to respond, trying to tell myself it isn't real, it isn't *him*, but I know, oh, I know, that it is. That's Gabe, hanging lifeless from a ceiling that isn't there. He's dead, he'll burn in Hell, and it's all my fault.

"Danae!" Gabby muscles me into a pew and grabs my face to make me see her. She's struggling not to cry. "Please, Danae, I don't know what to do!"

I squeeze my eyes shut—of course, I can still see him because he's not *really* here in this podunk church. I see his beloved face, bruised and bloated in silent reproach, because it's a memory—one I've carried with me over lifetimes.

With every scrap of sanity I can muster, mumbling words of power and banishment, I disperse the vision. I'm left with sunlight burning my eyelids and a headache like the world's worst hangover. I feel Gabby's fingers gouging my shoulders and open my eyes. Hers are wide, frightened, wet.

"I thought I lost you," she whimpers. "I don't know what I'm doing, Danae, please don't leave me."

"It's okay," I tell her. "I'm here. I'm okay." Then Gabby looks past me, up to where the door to the church should be. She only looks surprised, not concerned—no hint of recognition because how would she know?

But I know. Even before I turn in the pew, my hands curling around the rotting, splintered wood, I know.

He's aged since I saw him last, but that isn't surprising. A world has come and gone since then. Every one of us carries lifetimes on our shoulders. We all wear our nightmares on the outside. Still, it's a shock to see how trauma has erased the softness from his face and turned him into a young old man. He even has streaks of premature gray in his curls. It makes me wonder what I look like to him—I pat my head, feeling for frizz.

Gabe is standing at the opening to the nave, flanked by two large men with automatic rifles—one meaty and bearded, the other tattooed and bald. Their size and severity starkly contrasts with the *mildness* of him. He has a satchel slung across his shoulders, a loose-fitting Oxford shirt, slightly open, no coat, a simple wooden cross resting in the nest of tawny hair on his chest. He's thin—too thin—with a long ponytail and a shaggy beard. I want to laugh; he looks like a bohemian Jesus, probably on purpose. But I can't laugh because my heart hurts.

He stares at me as if he'd been sleepwalking and someone just shoved him awake. "Dani?" He takes a halting, rustling step forward. One of the guys with guns shifts, clicks something. Gabe's hand comes up, a gesture of command, not even looking at them because he's staring at me. A smile erupts on his face. He lets out a laugh. "*Dani?!?*"

I'm off the pew, stepping into the aisle, and then I'm in his arms. I feel his hands on either side of my face—I'd forgotten how long his fingers are. He's wiping tears away with his thumbs. He doesn't kiss me, but he brushes my lips and I can taste him, sharp and sweet.

Gabe steps back, sniffling, smiling. "Wait, wait," he says. He reaches into his shirt pocket and pulls out a pair of black-rimmed glasses. He peers at me, frowns, puts the glasses back, takes out another pair from his khaki pants. "No eye doctors in the New World Order," he mutters, his voice a hoarse rumble, and suddenly I want nothing more than to kiss his throat. I don't.

Gabe sets the second pair of glasses on his face. "Better," he says, with a self-conscious chuckle, then resumes staring at me.

"I got your letter," I whisper. I retrieve it from its place next to my heart—the paper is faded, the writing hopelessly smeared from my sweat, but that's not even the point.

"Oh, God, Dani. Praise Him, I knew I'd see you again, in my heart I knew, but I never thought ..."

He trails off. It's the references to God that remind me this is not a dream—but although the old me would teasingly ask him whose notion of God is responsible, something stops me. The men with the guns maybe. They're making Gabby nervous, too—she hovers at my elbow, not wanting to interrupt my reunion but unwilling to make a target of herself by stepping away.

My senses are consumed by two separate thoughts of equal urgency: one, whatever it is that has been guiding me all these years is real—I was meant to cross paths with the man I loved, have always loved, here in this church, at this moment. Two: I have never been in more danger.

"Gabe, this is Gabby. My friend." I squeeze her shoulder, hoping it conveys what I need it to. *Keep your mouth shut. Follow my lead.*

Gabe gives Gabby the briefest glance. "As in Gabrielle?"

"Gabriella."

"Close enough. Well met, sister of angels." Gabe gives her a wink, but he's already turned back to me. "These are Robert and Ike," he says of the men behind him, not bothering to explain which is which. Gabe's eyes are burning into mine. "Members of my flock. Dani ... What are you doing *here*, in St. Sebastian's?" He grabs my hands, folds his long fingers around my wrists.

"Praying," I tell him, which is not quite so far from the truth as to be a lie.

Gabby is a knot of tension beside me. Her voice squeaks out as if of its own volition. "What are *you* doing here, scaring girls with your big guns?"

Gabe looks at her again, as if seeing her for the first time. "We're hunting."

Gabby narrows her eyes. "Hunting what?"

"Heretics," Gabe tells her with a charming smile. He looks back at me, still smiling, but there's a flash of something there that makes my stomach turn with dread. I glance at Gabby, notice her eyes have gone wide. I follow the direction of her gaze and notice what she sees—from their waists to their boots, Robert and Ike are both spattered with what looks like blood.

Oh, Gods, Gabe. What have you done?

* * *

We leave the church at Gabe's suggestion, the armed men following close behind. They have walkie-talkies, coordinating with what sounds like several other teams combing the town for more travelers. Someone spotted us this morning, it seems, and sent word to Gabe's party, which had been passing west of here. I tell Gabe there are no others—Gabby and I are on our own.

Gabe explains it's a fluke that he's here this far down into the Allegheny. He's a speaker and a community leader in Jamestown, Old New York. With the advent of spring, there's plenty of work that should have kept him back at the colony, but he had one of his dreams, telling him to tag along with a trading convoy into Ohio, then more, spurring them to broaden diplomatic patrols along the way. There are a growing number of homesteaders in Warren County, some more resistant than others to the overtures of the New Church. Then, about a week ago, they heard rumors of false Christians, pagans, and atheists threading their way through the region.

I glance at Gabby, who's doing an admirable job of keeping quiet, but she's starting to look panicked. I can't imagine he means us. We haven't been in contact with anyone since early December—anyone living, that is. Not that it matters ...

Gabe leads us to a rise above the church, into a grove of apple trees—once decorative, now sadly diseased and overgrown. He takes my hands. "Danae." Rob and Ike linger in the jungle of the church's parking lot to talk to another group that's straggled off the main street—there are six of them in all, with more coming. "I know how things were when we were children, but after all that's happened ... finding you in the church today, I need to know. Dani, have you found God?"

In another life, I would have answered Gabe straight—he admired my mind, my ability to hold my own in debate, even if he thought I was naive and wrongheaded. But now? Rob and Ike aren't the only ones down there with weapons—and some of these sweaty, frowning faces look disappointed to be deprived good hunting. A few of them are eyeing Gabby with particular interest.

I squeeze Gabe's hands, pull him closer. "Can we go somewhere to talk, just us?"

"Let's get your things. Where are your packs? Where's your camp?"

As I try to think how to answer him, something slices the air where Gabe's head had just been. A chunk of wood flies off the nearest tree. Gabby lets out a yelp, then slaps her hand over her mouth as she realizes what's happening. Gabe takes a moment longer, looking about in slow confusion—long enough for Howard (it has to be Howard) to take another shot and take him down. Except that I don't let go of Gabe's hand or let him pull away from me.

The churchyard erupts in a storm of sound. Three people fall before the others react, diving for cover, returning fire—but it's a guerrilla assault. Reesa is hiding somewhere in the suburban rubble, pinning them down. In a lull, Ike rises from behind a dumpster and begins to stalk in that direction, when suddenly his bald head disappears in a cloud of red. That was Howard.

Gabe bellows in my ear, "Enough!" Suddenly something hard is forcing my head back. I can feel the length of him behind me, a sensation familiar but terrible in its context. He's using me as a shield. "Hold your fire!" Gabe shouts—his voice echoes through the churchyard.

My body fills with hot, indignant rage. "Did you just put a gun to my head, you little shit?"

Gabe curls his long fingers over my mouth and murmurs in my ear, very softly so only I can hear. "I would never hurt you, Dani, but he doesn't know that, whoever he is." He's right. Howard won't shoot if he thinks he might hit me. Silence falls once more. The only thing I can hear beyond my heartbeat and Gabby's ragged breathing beside me is the bubbling whimper of one of Gabe's men, not dead but dying, down in the weeds.

"Would you like to leave, Gabriella?" Gabe says into my hair.

I can't see her face, but I can imagine it, Gabby's eyes tearing between me and the tree line. It breaks my heart. "Go," I scream into Gabe's hand.

"An act of good faith!" Gabe yells. "You stop shooting my people, I'll give you one of yours." After another long moment of silence, Gabe tells Gabby to leave—when she hesitates, the mouth of his gun leaves my neck for just a moment. "I'm trying to save you, sister, don't make me shoot you." I hear quick footsteps, feel the emptiness where Gabby had been. The gun nests once more in the hollow under my chin.

A walkie-talkie squawks at Gabe's hip. "Hold that thought, will you," he says, slowly removing his hand from my mouth, but not the gun. He confers with his people—the ones down in the parking lot and the ones closing in on the church from other directions.

"Don't suppose you'll tell me how many friends you have out there?" Gabe mutters.

I snort.

"Are they willing to die for you?"

"Are you?"

"In a heartbeat," Gabe says, "though I'd prefer not today, and not with the added cost of good men's lives."

Good men. "You should just let me go, Gabe, it isn't worth this ..."

He laughs a humorless laugh, his breath hot on my ear. "Whoever that is out there has a lot to answer for, Danae. Let's take a walk."

On his word, the three remaining men break away from their hiding spot and maneuver to where we are, ready to lay down suppressing fire to cover our exit—but there's nothing from Howard or Reesa. Clouds move silently over a town of ghosts. With Gabe's arm wrapped like a lover's around my waist, we descend awkwardly down the backside of the hill and onto a narrow street. We pick our way across some derelict lots, round a corner, and slip through the side entrance of a Masonic hall that survived the quakes—a rendezvous point. But no one is here.

I hear a burst of gunfire in the distance.

"Beacon," Gabe calls into his walkie-talkie. We're leaning against the wall of a lobby that smells of mold and animal piss. Milky sunlight seeps in from the cracked glass door to my right. To the left, the hall sprawls away into shadow. Narrow windows near to the ceiling only illuminate dancing dust motes.

"Gabe ..."

"Beacon, beacon." A breath of static comes in reply, then nothing. "Hell," he growls, with a glare at the device.

"Can we put the gun away now, please?"

Gabe looks up as if surprised by the sound of my voice. He stares at me for a moment, tears welling up in his eyes. Then in one smooth motion, he stashes the gun in his waistband, grabs my face with both hands, and kisses me. The walkie-talkie clatters to the ground.

For a fraction of a second, maybe, my body responds—I can't help it—but instinct takes over. I snatch the gun and hit him with it, hard. His glasses clatter across the floor. He staggers away from me, clutching his head.

"What the hell is wrong with you, Gabriel?"

Gabe touches his head, examines the blood on his fingers. He glares at me. "Your people shot at *me!*"

"And I saved you! So you repay me by taking me hostage, pulling a gun on me?"

"I told you, I would never—"

"Never hurt me, right. What do you do when you catch a heretic, Gabe? Do you sit him down for coffee and eggs at the Eagle Diner and debate, like you used to do with me?" Gabe doesn't answer right away, and I don't allow him to. My mind is full of memories of my friends—pagans, false Christians, they called them in Lutherville, Catholic spics. "What do you do with witches in New Church, huh?"

Gabe has straightened by now, his hands up, fingers spread, trying to look the victim, though I see what's turning over in his mind, the ghosts of other heretics reflected in his eyes. I level the gun at him. "Do you suffer us? Or do they have a pyre set up right in the town square? A block party barbeque for the righteous?"

"Dani—"

"We've lost our minds, Gabe!" Tears smear my vision. It's too much, seeing him, how much he's changed and how much he hasn't. I think I was better off when I thought he was dead. "The whole damn world's lost its mind!"

"I know." He takes a step toward me, arms lowered, hands out. I'm shaking so hard, I can barely hold the gun straight. I'm so angry, but the thought of letting him hold me seems like the only thing that can make anything right.

I don't know what makes me do it. Maybe I see a shadow move, or maybe the choreography of dust in one of the windows shifts direction, reflecting chaos. Or maybe it's just my inner compass, as always, telling me where to go. I step forward, shoving Gabe back with my body, causing us both to fall. The glass door behind us explodes.

"Danae!"

Howard emerges from the dark hall, no more need for stealth—he knocks over a folding chair in his haste to get to me. He pulls me bodily off Gabe, frantic to assure himself I'm unhurt in the light from the shattered door.

"I'm fine, I'm fine," I tell him, struggling to disentangle myself from both men. "What's happening, where's Gab—"

Another gunshot goes off by my head, deafening. I duck, covering my ears, then realize Howard is on his back. I scrabble out from under someone's legs, shake off Gabe's hand as he tries to haul me up. Howard is blinking in surprise at the ceiling, blood blossoming from a hole in his chest.

I try to go to him, thinking only that if I cover the wound I can keep him from bleeding out. But suddenly Gabe is dragging me backward, and, though I'm fighting, biting, screaming like a wild thing, he's stronger than I remember. We crash through the broken door, my fingers ripped by glass in the struggle. The rest is a blur of daylight and brick, the mottled green shadows of trees. I hear more shots, somewhere. I see smoke. I feel nothing.

Then we're on the edge of a meadow, our feet sinking into the mud of a shallow creek. On the other side is the forest, thick, dark—home. But is it, really, if Howard isn't there?

Gabe lets go of my hand. I stare at it stupidly, unable to remember at what point we stopped struggling with each other and simply ran, together.

Gabe is crying. "Go."

I just blink at him, in shock, confused. I don't know where we are or where my friends are. I've had a terrible dream that Howard is dead, and Gabe is standing before me in a monk's habit, sunlight glinting off the weird triangle of his golden hair.

"Dani, go," he says. "You're right. They'll kill you, and I couldn't bear it." He grabs me again, whispers that he's sorry. I can feel the wet of his tears. "I love you," he tells me, "I've always loved you," and that's what snaps me out of it. Gabe kisses me again, shoves his gun into my hands, and pushes me toward the water. I stumble, barely feeling the cold. I lurch for the trees, and then I'm gone.

* * *

The campsite seems empty when I return, the fire burnt down to ash and ember. But I pause, listening, stretching out my senses—for the last couple of hours that's all I've been, senses without thought. I don't want to think.

I take a step to the side, duck around a shrub, and there's Gabby, still as a statue, leaning against an ancient pine with an axe in her hand. That's all we left her to protect herself with. She sees me, knows it's me, but can't release her grip. I stumble over to her, wrench away the axe, and she flies into my arms.

We can't stay this way. I hear bird call in the branches overhead, so mundane—so surreal. I tug at Gabby's coat, nudge her toward our tents, thinking: *Grab what you can, quickly.* She does as she's told.

I'm adjusting the straps on Gabby's pack when I hear something snap, back in the trees. My arms are so tired, my soul, but I lift Gabe's gun.

"Don't shoot me, for fuck's sake," Reesa says.

She lurches into view. Her face is singed, part of her lovely red hair burnt off. Her eyes are eerily calm. She looks at me, a question. I swallow thorns, shake my head.

Reesa inhales, then lets her breath out slow, adjusting to this new reality. She nods. "Ladies, we've got to go. Like, now."

* * *

Ten minutes later, we've packed up everything we can carry—it hurts to look at how much we have to leave behind. I notice the map spread out on the rock. I wipe as much blood from my hands as I can and snatch it up, fold it as small as I can get it, and stuff it into my shirt. How many miles did we mark off on this damn thing? How am I ever going to look at it again without only seeing where we've been?

But there's no time for that now. Reesa's already turning away, plowing through the trees.

Gabby hangs back. She swapped out the axe for Kelly, the .45, snug against her side in Reesa's holster.

"Okay?" I ask.

"Yeah, okay."

After a little while, Reesa slows down, then stops, waiting for us to catch up. We stand together at a fork in the trail. Reesa looks me over. For the first time she notices the cuts on my hands, but there's no time for that either. She rips the bottom off her flannel shirt, tears it in two, and wraps the strips around my palms.

"I hope you did whatever you came here for," she says, finishing off a knot, painfully tight. "I hope it was worth it."

I don't have an answer, but she isn't expecting one. Not to that, anyway. She's looking at me—they both are—waiting for me to choose a direction.

I close my eyes. For a second, I see Howard. He kisses me on the forehead. Then I see Gabe, as he was, as he is. Then, further down, past all that, I see light, straining from within, saying, *this way.*

Go this way.

TWELVE STEPS

BY JEFF MARKOWITZ

"Hi, my name is Jake and I'm an alcoholic."

"Hi, Jake," they answered from every corner of the dusty meeting room.

"It's been one day since I had a drink."

The regulars smiled and nodded their heads, grateful for his return. After all, Jake was one of them, one of the regulars. If Jake had fallen off the wagon, so could they all. Just two days earlier, they'd been there when Jake announced a full year of sobriety.

"Hi," he'd said, barely 48 hours earlier. "My name is Jake and I'm an alcoholic."

"Hi, Jake," they'd responded in unison.

"It's been 365 days since I had a drink."

And then, after a year of sobriety, on the one-year anniversary of his kid brother's funeral, Jake Newbury allowed himself a shot of peppermint schnapps. He drank a toast to his dead brother. Hell, he drank a toast *with* his dead brother. At AA, they didn't need a psychic to predict what was going to happen next. But, sitting there in the community meeting room—with the recovering lawyers and doctors, with the schoolteachers, accountants, and engineers, the butchers, the bakers, the candlestick makers—was Desdemona, the town's resident psychic. More than one recovering alcoholic in Princeton had, over the years, availed themselves of her services.

"Hi, my name is Desdemona and I'm an alcoholic." With her big hair and her costume jewelry, dressed in Liz Claiborne casual wear, Desdemona joined Jake at the lectern.

"When Jake came to see me yesterday, I knew he was troubled. Sober, but troubled. He asked me to contact his dead brother, Lenny."

"She checked the limit on my credit card," Jake shrugged, "and then she said that we could begin."

"Anyway," she continued, "the room suddenly grew dark," darker than the setting programmed into her dimmer switch. "A voice seemed to float down from the ceiling."

"Jake ... Jake, is that you?"

Jake answered. "I'm here, Lenny."

"I didn't think you'd come, Jake."

Jake shuddered. "I promised."

"You also promised to protect me, Jake."

Jake was beginning to sweat in the cool confines of Desdemona's parlor, and again in the AA meeting room. "I did protect you, Lenny. The only way I could."

Jake tried to block out the image—the terror in his kid brother's eyes as they said goodbye, his brother grabbing Jake's hand, holding on for dear life as Jake closed the lid on the simple pine box. "Jesus, Lenny. I figured it'd be over if they thought you were dead."

"Well, you were certainly convincing." Lenny's whisper filled the room, as it had once filled the pine box. "You were supposed to come back and dig me up."

Jake tried to block out the memory of the night he buried his kid brother alive. It had been a private ceremony but, just as Jake expected, the Macaluso Brothers had been there. To make sure Lenny was really dead. They were not happy about the closed casket, demanding to see the body, to pay their last respects. It took all the rabbi's Talmudic wisdom and charm to convince the Macaluso Brothers to accept the tradition of the closed casket.

"We were supposed to split everything 50-50," said Lenny. "But you got the reward and all I got were maggots." It grew silent in Desdemona's parlor, and in the AA meeting room, waiting for Lenny to continue. "Is that fair, Jake? I ask you, is that fair?"

"What do you want from me?" Jake asked.

"Have a drink with me, Jake ... for old time's sake, have a drink with me."

Suddenly Jake noticed the bottle of peppermint schnapps, Lenny's favorite. *Where'd that come from?*

"You promised to dig me up," reminded Lenny.

"But it's been a year," Jake protested.

"Dig me up," repeated Lenny. "Have a drink with me."

Desdemona frowned, remembering. "I drove with Jake to the cemetery. Under the cover of darkness, we unearthed Lenny's coffin." Desdemona shuddered. "It had been a year. The maggots had had their way with him."

Desdemona had spent many years conversing with the dead, but coming face-to-face with the decomposing body was another thing entirely. For once, she didn't know what to do. Desdemona turned away, counting the steps as she walked back to her car. Twelve steps. "I retreated to my Plymouth, where I passed the hours until morning, while Jake and his dead brother Lenny polished off the bottle of peppermint schnapps."

Jake poured two shots and sat there, in the dark, in the cemetery, talking to his dead brother Lenny. "Your plan didn't work out so well," Lenny said. "At least not for me."

Jake stared into the shot glass and mumbled, "I was trying to protect you."

"I'm sorry if I sound bitter, Jake, but could you explain just how this was supposed to protect me?"

Jake refilled his shot glass. "When mom died, I promised her I'd take care of you. You were gonna be an accountant."

"I was gonna be an accountant," repeated Lenny. "That seems so very long ago now. A lifetime ago."

While Jake hauled dirt, busting his hump for the Macalusos, he smelled of dirt and sweat and something else, something dangerous. But, to Jake and the other drivers, this was why the job paid so good. While Jake busted his hump, he got Lenny a part-time job in the office.

And it might have ended there, if only Lenny hadn't found a problem in the general ledger. Lenny couldn't let it be. He never did tell Jake exactly what he'd found, but it wasn't long before the whispers started. And the threats. Jake knew he needed to do something to protect his kid brother from the Macalusos. That's when it hit him. They couldn't hurt Lenny if he was already dead. *If they thought he was dead.*

And so they concocted a plan. *Thank God*, they agreed, *their mother was no longer alive.* 'Cause this would have killed her, for sure. They would fake Lenny's death. Jake would alert the police. And when the police picked up the Macaluso Brothers, Jake would go back and dig up his kid brother.

It might have worked. If Jake had come back that first night, the way they'd planned it.

Jake looked out on the room full of recovering alcoholics. "He thought I did it for the money. Thought I left him there, buried alive, slowly suffocating ... for the money." Jake spit out the words. "And I let him believe it. How could I tell my kid brother the real reason I left him there to die?"

In a room full of recovering alcoholics, men and women who had ruined their lives in all the usual ways, even in such a room as this, Jake's story unnerved the crowd, regulars and newcomers alike.

"I meant to dig him up," Jake paused. "Really I did. But I needed something to steady my nerves. What harm could there be, I asked myself. Just one drink."

But the harm was obvious. "By the time I climbed out of the bottle, it was too late. I left my brother there to die ..." Jake explained, "for a shot and a beer."

Jake looked for a sympathetic face in the stunned room. "I'm Jake," he said, "and I'm an alcoholic."

"Hi, Jake," they answered in unison.

"It's been one day since I had a drink."

SONG OF THE SHARK GOD

BY JM REINBOLD

Riding the swells off Rehoboth Beach near where two great whites pinged close to shore earlier in the day, Mannie thinks the chances are good that the sharks are still in the area. The sun is setting, but it's stinking hot and so humid he feels as if he's breathing water. The meager breeze drops off, and without it the sail is useless. Mannie engages the Hobie Mirage's automatic roller-furling to wind the red/yellow/orange sail and switches to the kayak's pedals to take him farther out. Weather on the water can change in an instant, but the NWS Marine Forecast has predicted fair weather and light winds for the next 24 hours.

Scanning the shoreline, Mannie tries to pick out the deck of the beach house he and his wife, Tina, rent for his annual Shark Week party. There is still enough light that he can spot the carving of Kauhuhu, the Hawaiian shark god—seven feet tall, brightly painted, baring a mouthful of jagged teeth—that Tina, an unapologetic impulse shopper, bought him at Tiki Mike's to celebrate his recent amazing discovery. Tina spends hours on the internet now looking up everything Hawaiian. Mannie loves Tina like crazy, but her enthusiasm is starting to bother him. She wouldn't be so gung ho if the "amazing discovery" had happened to her.

Mannie's amazing discovery—his Hawaiian ancestry—is the fault of a DNA kit, another gift from Tina. Certain there was a mix-up, Mannie sent in another tube of spit. His mother's family is from Bay Head on the Jersey Shore. He has blonde hair and blue eyes. How can he be Native Hawaiian? Six weeks later, his retest came back. No mix-up, just undeniable proof that, Phil, the man he hoped was his dad, the man he had convinced himself was his dad, couldn't be. Tina thinks they should go to Hawaii and search for his biological father. Still in shock, Mannie knows one thing. He is not going back to Hawaii, ever. Hawaii is where the ghosts of his mother and father are: a woman who lived like a man and the man she disguised in legends.

Mannie adjusts his life vest where it's chafing his side, then checks his supplies for the umpteenth time. His safety kit, first-aid kit, water, and protein bars are packed in a dry bag and stowed in the kayak's twist-and-seal hatch. His phone, keys, chart, and compass are zipped into the pockets of his vest. He is only a mile offshore, but he might go farther out, maybe. He has a plan, but anything could happen. The Hobie could capsize. He could get caught in a rip current and dragged out to sea. In his 16-foot kayak he is a speck on the vast back of the ocean.

Tina is sure his Hawaiian heritage explains his obsession with sharks. How many people, she points out, have a shark-tracking app installed on their phone and check it every day. Maybe, but Mannie blames his mother. She named him Mano. That's the name on his birth certificate—no father listed—and it's Hawaiian for shark. She insisted that they get shark-bite tattoos around their ankles, and that he wear a shark's tooth pendant when he swam or surfed so the *aumakua*, ancestor sharks, would recognize and protect him. It's true, he's fascinated by these apex predators, especially the great whites, but he's also terrified of them. The story he tells his Shark Week buddies is that he hasn't gone in the ocean since *Jaws*. It isn't the truth, but they get it. They laugh and don't ask questions.

Mannie hasn't always been afraid of sharks. Growing up, he and his mother lived in a surfing community on Oahu's North Shore. They and everyone they knew surfed, dived, and fished. Their property, beachfront near a line of infamous breaks, attracted surfers. His mother supplemented their income by renting out sleeping spaces on their living room floor. One of his mom's friends, a guy named Phil, hung out with them a lot, even helping with housework and babysitting to cover his "bunk" fee. Phil had unofficially adopted him, sort of. But, after Phil qualified for the world surfing circuit and started following the waves, Mannie only saw him when he came to Hawaii for tournaments.

The year Mannie turned 8, Phil flew in to surf the Eddie, an exclusive, invitation-only competition. He stayed with them just like old times. The day before the tournament, word spread that there were monster waves at the Pipeline break. Mannie, his mother, and most of their neighbors went along to watch Phil and some of the other competitors shred. Phil was showing off, racing in on a nine-foot wave, when a tiger hit his board. The board spun out of control, Phil went in the water, and the shark bit him. With help, Phil made it back to shore. His right leg gone, he bled out on the beach. Everyone said it was a fluke. Fluke or not, Mannie hasn't gone in the water since.

He still sails on bays and lakes and rivers. But the ocean is everything, it's in his blood. He feels the pull of the tides. In the middle of the city surrounded by concrete and steel, triggered by nothing he can identify, his nostrils fill with sea-smell. When he sips his coffee he tastes salt brine, and then he hears the rush of waves and the cries of seabirds. He knows what he has to do, and he focuses on that: Sail out, stay out, face the fear.

Not long after Phil died, sitting on the beach with his mother, counting stars and listening to the waves roll in, Mannie asks about his father. "One night, I was sitting on the beach, just like this," she tells him. "Your father walked out of the ocean. We made you, then he went back to the ocean." No matter how many times he asks her answer is always the same. As he grew older, he realized she told him that story because she didn't want to tell him the truth—he was the result of a one-night stand. Most likely she'd been stoned. Back in the day, his mother and her friends smoked a lot of weed. Maybe she didn't know who his father was, maybe she didn't care.

Phil looked out for Mannie, played with him, taught him cool stuff. Phil was always there for him, until he wasn't. But that didn't matter now because his biological father was Hawaiian, and the most likely suspects were the native guys his mother surfed with. He didn't want to believe that, but he couldn't un-know the truth. Damn DNA. Thanks a lot, Tina.

Then the dreams started.

In the dream, he is on the beach in Oahu watching Phil surf. The wave rises like a wall behind him, the lip curls; Phil drops through air and disappears in a shower of spray and foam as the wave runs him down. Mannie's mother is there, too. He can't see her, but he can hear her. She's chanting in old Hawaiian, a language he recognizes but doesn't understand. The words are only sounds to him, but he knows this much. She's singing the song of the shark god. She's calling him.

Phil's board shoots out of the tunnel of water, but Phil isn't on it. An enormous white shark breaches with Phil's body in its mouth. It hangs in the air for a second before plunging back into the ocean. The breeze off the water dies. In a place where the sea is always restive, it is now dead calm. Everything around him is unnaturally silent. He sees a single ripple in the water. A feeling of dread sweeps over him. Something is swimming in a straight line toward the shore. He cowers in the sand as the ripple gathers itself into the shape of a man. The man comes out of the water. He is dark; his hair is black and long. As he bends to brush seaweed from his legs, Mannie sees the fin on his back, jagged and scarred. He stares at Mannie with eyes like black holes, empty, without emotion, and the longer he stares the harder Mannie's heart pounds. He thinks this must be what it's like when relief turns to terror after a shark swims away, only to whip around for an attack run. The shark man's shadow elongates, stretches out like a hand and covers him. Mannie wakes in a panic. He has the dream every night now, and it's always the same.

The last light dissolves into darkness. Out on the water, riding the swells, Mannie thinks he might have made a serious mistake. No one knows where he is or what he's doing. He told Tina he was on a night-fishing charter. He has a fish bag stowed under the yak's seat, so he has something to show her in the morning. This quest business—when did he start calling it that?—made a lot more sense sitting in the living room of the beach house after a few artisan brews. It isn't too late to go back. He can steer toward the lights on shore. If he runs the Hobie up on the sand, he'll be okay. But even with the full moon, there are jetties, piers, and sandbars he might not see until it's too late.

The last thing he needs is to start giving in to doubt. He wishes it wasn't so dark, so quiet, so eerie. He busies himself checking anything he can check. If he starts thinking up excuses now, he'll never go through with this. Seriously, what are the odds of him encountering a shark? Sharks are rarely seen, because they don't want to be seen. The two great whites this morning, one big one and one juvenile, that pinged at the mouth of the Delaware Bay, he wouldn't even know about them if wasn't for OREACH and their tracking devices. He's been closer to a shark at the Baltimore Aquarium than he's likely to get here. He's seen videos of a woman, a shark scientist, swimming with great whites, hanging onto their dorsal fins while they tow her along, paying her no more attention than they do the remoras attached to their bellies. He knows the shark attack statistics, too. He is more likely to get hit by lighting than be attacked by a shark.

Mannie stops pedaling and lets the Hobie drift. He's not worried about that, he has a drift bag if he needs it. Light from the full moon illuminates the tips of the waves and allows him to see a short distance. When he turns toward shore there are pinpricks of light that Mannie knows come from the condos that line the beachfront. When he looks toward the horizon, there is only darkness. It's as if he's poised on the border between two worlds. Behind him is everything familiar. Ahead, a vastness that might, at any moment, become something unimaginable. A hot flash of anxiety blooms in his chest and spreads. A few times in his life, Mannie has done reckless things, things he found difficult to explain even to himself. This is one of them.

He focuses on being still, listening, paying attention to what's going on around him. What he perceives as silence is hundreds, maybe thousands, of nearly imperceptible sounds. It's like a roar of natural white noise. The drone of the breeze. The slap of the waves on the sides of the yak. The rattle of the rigging. Splashing when a fish leaps out of the water and dives back in. The soft sucking sounds that seem to come from all around. The infinite darkness is less disconcerting if he closes his eyes. Concentrating on his breath, Mannie begins to relax. He can do this.

It occurs to him that his mother told him what anyone might tell a little kid. Maybe, if she'd lived, she would have told him a different story. Maybe she couldn't tell anyone his father's name. Back then, the native and nonnative communities, especially the surfing communities, didn't get along. They clashed, sometimes violently, if the stories he's heard are true. Maybe the guy she told him came out of the ocean really did come out of the ocean. Those native surfers were hardcore, long-distance swimmers, and the ones whose ancestors were shark *aumakua* were fearless in the ocean. A cold tingling electrifies his every nerve. Memories begin to move and shuffle like a child's sliding puzzle. Mannie has an exhilarating sensation as if he's just received some alien wisdom from the Universe. He can't say what this new knowledge is. He only knows that something is different. He's different.

He has no idea what time it is. He could check his phone, but he doesn't. With the sea and sky full of stars, the boundary between them dissolved, it could be any time or no time at all. He hears the bellow of a ship's horn. The moon-path ripples. A swell lifts the yak and Mannie scans for lights. Unless he's drifted, he isn't far enough out to be in the shipping lanes. If the swell that lifted the yak is from another boat, it isn't one with an engine. He turns on the battery-powered LEDs attached to the mast. There should be another wave, and possibly another after that, but there isn't. If it isn't the wake of another boat that caused the yak to rise, then something disturbed the water underneath. Could be the fluctuation of a deep current or maybe he's drifted over a trench.

Mannie shines his flashlight in the water. The beam reflects off the scales of thousands of small fish. Suddenly, the school wheels as one and sweeps away. Seconds later, something else swims into the tunnel of light. It looks like a big fish. At least, he thinks it's a fish. It doesn't reflect the light. It's more of a shadow. As the shadow passes through the beam, he sees the tail fin flip. Mannie douses the light. He waits minutes, long minutes, before he looks over the side again. Moonlight illuminates something just below the surface, round, about the size of a baseball. It takes him a minute to grasp that it's an eye. He's looking a shark in the eye and it's looking back. Mannie's whole body is shaking. He's no Kahua. He's an idiot.

The dorsal fin of a white shark breaks the surface of the water and glides past the Hobie. Mannie is glad he has the amas, the outriggers, extended. They give him extra stability. A second fin emerges. Two sharks! Mannie thinks they will dive, but they don't dive. One of the sharks bumps the Hobie with its snout. Then there's another bump from behind. The Hobie starts to spin. The sharks are on both sides now, bumping the yak. He can see the back of one of them, could reach out and touch it. Then they're gone. Mannie holds his breath. If he's lucky, the sharks have checked him out, decided the Hobie's not a whale carcass or other carrion, and moved on.

Mannie sees a fin surface again, slicing through the water, coming straight at the yak, then disappearing below the surface. If the shark rams the boat or comes up underneath, he's done. The image of a great white biting his boat in half flashes across his mind. He feels the yak rise. The fin comes up on the other side a distance away and turns. A second later, the shark hits the end of the ama. The Hobie shudders. He hears the shriek of rending plastic as the port side flies up. Mannie registers that the kayak is capsizing seconds before he hits the water headfirst.

Mannie flails underwater. He must keep his wits about him. He feels rather than sees something above him. For an instant, he thinks it's a shark. He needs to keep his eyes open, but it's near impossible and it doesn't matter anyway, there's only blackness underwater. Then he sees the lights. The LEDs on the Hobie's mast are still glowing. He comes up under the yak and feels his way to the side. As he grasps an ama, Mannie feels the body of the shark slide past him. Its skin feels like sandpaper. Sure he is going to die, he heaves the yak with every bit of strength he can muster. For a moment, he thinks it's not enough, then the yak flips and Mannie scrambles in. He feels a tug on the boat and thinks the sharks are back until he realizes the cooler is floating at the end of its tether. He grabs the rope and starts to pull it in. As he drags it closer to the yak, a shark's head breaks the surface, mouth open, ready to make a meal of it. Mannie jerks hard on the rope. As the cooler bounces across the water toward the yak, the shark lunges.

Mannie hauls the cooler on board, afraid the shark will come after it. His chest is so tight he can hardly breathe. A hot trickle of urine spills down his leg. He reaches for his shark-tooth pendant. He runs his finger along its serrated edge. He hears his mother's voice as clearly as if she's sitting next to him. "Every Hawaiian has an *aumakua* that protects them." Then she begins to sing. Mannie knows that song. It's the song she sings in his dream. The song of the shark god. He listens intently, trying to remember the words, and then he tries to sing along, awkwardly at first, then stronger with more confidence as she repeats the chant. He doesn't know what the words mean, but he guesses it doesn't matter.

His mother stops singing. The night becomes preternaturally silent. Mannie is afraid she's left him. Then he sees her, a glimmering luminescence in the water. A smile flickers across her face as she fades away. Through the tears running down his face Mannie sees a light in the distance. The ocean is deadly calm, like in his dream. Mannie should be pedaling, but instead he's praying, watching that ripple swimming straight at him like a sliver of ghost light from out of the dark ocean. Briefly, he sees a dorsal fin emerge, and then disappear as the glowing ripple increases its speed.

The white shark's head breaches the surface only a foot or two from Mannie. The shark is looking right at him. Looking him in the eyes. Mannie has seen sharks' eyes before on documentaries and at aquariums. Their eyes are cold, lifeless black holes. This shark's eyes look like that, too, but Mannie sees something else: recognition. He has the disconcerting realization that this shark knows him. The shark-bite tattoo on his ankle burns as if it has just been seared into his flesh. The shark holds Mannie's gaze for seconds that seem like an eternity, and then sinks back into the sea.

He remembers the fish bag, amazed it wasn't lost when he capsized. He has to feed the shark, his *aumakua* ... his father. He pulls out a fish, tosses it in the water, followed by another and another until he's emptied the bag. A shaky laugh escapes him. There is a breeze now, so light, though, it won't do him any good. Mannie begins to pedal, resigned to a long trip back to shore.

A big fin rises between the body of the yak and the ama. The Hobie turns and begins moving forward. Mannie, stunned, forgets to pedal, not that he needs to. He recognizes that fin and reaches out, touches the jagged notch, traces the lines of scars, holds on tight. When they are about fifty feet from shore the fin drops away. The sun is coming up, staining the water red. He's been out all night. He sees another kayaker not far off, paddling parallel to shore. A few minutes later, the long, slim craft crosses in front of him.

"I saw a shark," Mannie shouts. "Watch yourself."

The kid grins at him. "For real? What kind?" he shouts back.

"A white."

"Awesome!" The boy waves and paddles away.

Mannie beaches the Hobie and drags it above the tide line. The sand has never felt so good between his toes. He sees Tina on their deck, a small figure, hand shielding her eyes against the rising sun. She is still in her pajamas. Mannie chokes up. Tears prick his eyes. Tina turns in his direction, spots him, and waves. He waves back. The party is today. He knows what his gift to her will be. They are going to Hawaii.

DOLLHOUSE

BY JENNIFER LORING

Abigail examined the doll with almost scientific curiosity. She lifted the leather arms one by one, sifted the brown, corn-silk hair through her fingers, and straightened the dress until it met her standards of perfection.

"It's Vinnie," she said.

"I know how lonely you've been since ..." Still difficult to believe, let alone talk about. Michael swallowed a fresh wave of tears and looked away. "Now she'll always be with you."

Abigail hooked her arm around the two-and-a-half-foot-tall doll's waist. "Thank you, Daddy," she said, and offered him the closest thing to a smile he'd seen in months.

* * *

First Rebecca's death in a car wreck—the drunken bastard who'd run her off the road unscathed, and Michael in the courtroom, repressing with the barest of control the rage that whispered in his ear to throttle the son of a bitch with his bare hands. Then Vinnie's accident. Guilt gnawed at him with termite insistence, the scene replaying in his mind each night as he stared at the ceiling.

The streetlights outside cast a soft glow on Rebecca's forest-green paint. She had fallen in love with the 160-year-old house before they'd even set foot inside. The steep, patterned, many-gabled roof and asymmetrical window arrangement gave the house a distinct sense of animation, as though it moved every time you looked away. But it was the porch, with its whimsical gingerbread detailing, which had really sold her. The interior—a characteristically unconventional Victorian floor plan, textured walls, and complex shapes such as curves, arches, and hexagons—was icing on the cake. The house projected personality, as much as an inanimate object could. Rebecca had said all the men and women who had passed through in its boardinghouse days probably left some of their energy behind.

A muted voice carried from Abigail's room through the thin walls. She was talking to the doll again. Whenever she suspected he could hear her, she dropped her voice. Telling the doll whatever she couldn't share with her own father.

Their mutual pain had brought them closer together after Rebecca's death. The girls had consoled him often, when grief consumed him so that he functioned as a human being, let alone a father, only superficially. But something fundamental had changed in Abigail with her sister's death. Such was the nature of twins. She needed an objective outlet for her pain, not a man who couldn't keep his own emotions in check. After therapy had failed—four sessions and she'd refused to utter a word—he didn't know what else to do.

* * *

Abigail flung her backpack onto the floor and shed her coat. Daddy didn't hear her come in over the sewing machine's clacking. Thus far, the third grade and multiplication tables in particular bored her to death. But today she'd received a more exciting assignment to research and write a report on a game played in another part of the world. The school year might not be a total loss after all, though she'd never quite adjust to seeing someone not Vinnie in the seat behind her.

Daddy kept the computer in the formal dining room because it was next to the workshop, easy access for printing out doll clothing patterns and tracking orders. They never used that room except for holiday dinners; it was one of the many extra, unnecessary rooms. Mom had repainted the outside something called "softened green" because the color "spoke to her." She'd thought it was pretty, but the only thing it reminded Abigail of was baby food.

Abigail opened the browser and googled "games around the world," and then scrolled down. "Boring. Boring." She refused to lower herself to reporting on some silly baby game. Another click brought her to a website designed in a sinister tandem of black and red. A cheap plastic doll that looked as if it had endured a fire glared at her from the top right corner.

"*Hitori Kakurenbo*," she sounded out, her tongue tripping over the second word. She presumed it was Japanese because it resembled the names in the credits for *Naruto*. "Hide and Seek by Yourself." How convenient, since by herself was the sole option now.

Abigail printed out the page and rushed upstairs. She dumped her backpack and coat onto the bed and waved the paper around. "Guess what, Vinnie? I found a game we can play. I have to do it for school, but I bet it's gonna be fun." She grasped the doll's shoulders and pulled her close. "Maybe you'll finally talk to me. I'm so lonely since ..."

Best she left that train of thought alone.

"Abigail?"

"Yes, Daddy," she called.

"Come downstairs for a snack. I'm taking a break."

Abigail shoved the printout under her pillow before cinching her arm around Vinnie's waist and carrying her downstairs.

* * *

"Can you clip my fingernails, Daddy?" Abigail was dressed for bed in fleecy red pajamas, her skin soft and fruit-scented from her bubble bath. The soporific warmth of the fleece and the bathroom tugged at her eyelids, but she must stay awake.

"They don't look very long, but sure." He snipped at the tiny, white half-moons. "I've got a few more hours of work to do. Can you read yourself a story tonight?"

"Yes."

"I'll make it up to you, I promise." He dumped the clippings into the trashcan and kissed the top of her head. "Get to bed."

Once his steps faded, she fished a few fingernails from the trash. Cupping them like a caught insect, she crossed the hall to her room and set them on the nightstand. The rest had to wait until Daddy went to bed, and she'd need to complete her assignment downstairs so he couldn't hear her.

Time dragged by. She memorized the game instructions instead of reading a story. They didn't make much sense for a hide-and-seek game, but she supposed it was natural that people played games differently in Japan. Then she dozed off for a couple hours, until the sewing machine ceased its clattering and Daddy's weary footfalls ascended the stairs. Her digital Barbie clock read 1:03 a.m., but she could kill some time preparing the doll. Abigail let 10 more minutes pass, Daddy's gentle snores issuing through the wall, before she grasped Vinnie's arm in one hand, the fingernails in the other, and tiptoed down the stairs.

She brought the doll into the bathroom and laid her on the tile floor, then searched the kitchen cabinets and the pantry for a box of rice. Two would be better; Vinnie was big. Abigail hugged the boxes to her chest as she entered Daddy's workshop and scanned the tables for a needle, red thread, and scissors. He owned many of each.

She shut the bathroom door behind her and closed the toilet lid. With Vinnie laid across her lap, she opened a seam in the crotch and pulled out every shred of stuffing, then poured in the rice until Vinnie's limbs and body plumped up again. She sprinkled in her fingernail clippings and sewed up the opening. The crimson gash between Vinnie's legs bothered her, though she could not articulate why. Maybe some half-remembered, terrible secret Vinnie had told her long ago, which she had shoved out of her mind. She unwound the spool of thread and wrapped it around the doll.

Abigail glanced at the clock over the toilet. Two a.m. She started the water in the porcelain claw-foot bathtub Mom had begged Daddy for, in the interest of keeping as much of the house's Victorian charm as possible. Mom said that was why she gave them Victorian names, too. Vinnie argued that hers was a boy's name, and even after Mom explained it as a diminutive of "Lavinia," Vinnie muttered about her "boy's name."

At 3:00, Abigail scooped up the doll and said, "Abigail is the first it" three times. She set the doll in the cold bathwater and turned out all the lights. Hiding in her room was too obvious, and anyway, the hiding place must have a television. Daddy hadn't yet allowed one in her room.

With scissors in hand, Abigail pattered into the living room, switched on the flat-screen, and wedged herself behind the couch. She closed her eyes and counted to 10, then ran back to the bathroom and gazed down at the submerged doll. "I've found you, Vinnie." Abigail plunged the scissors into Vinnie's chest, tearing through the thread-web, the network of doll blood vessels crisscrossed over her pliant leather body. She set the scissors aside. "You're the next it, Vinnie." She dashed back to the living room and her hiding place behind the couch.

I forgot the salt water. That's supposed to end the game.

Abigail crinkled her nose. It was just a stupid game, and she didn't intend to follow it to completion anyway. Not if, as the instructions insisted, she had to burn Vinnie and throw her away.

She waited. The clock on the wall ticked in time with the pulse in her ears. Shadows clawed their way across the room, searching for something. She yawned and rubbed her eyes. The TV picture shattered into dozens of pixels, then blackness. Abigail hadn't turned on the receiver, but a sound like someone screaming into the wind pierced the house's silence. She shot a glance at the stairs, strained to hear Daddy's footsteps.

Nothing.

Abigail crawled out and returned to the bathroom. Her steps toward the tub grew smaller, more hesitant, until with her eyes squinted and her hands over her face she forced herself to look into it.

Vinnie's serene gaze penetrated her from beneath the water. Abigail giggled and retrieved her, heavy with water and rice, so she could dry out. "Stupid game." She set Vinnie in the sink, crimson threads flowing from her like blood. Then she crept up the stairs and into her room, burrowing under the covers as if she'd never left her bed at all.

As she dangled over the precipice of sleep, she felt someone crawl into bed beside her.

* * *

"Abigail!" Michael gusted into the kitchen, scissors in one hand and discarded rice boxes in the other. "What the hell is going on?"

She sat in the breakfast nook and stared across the room, her eyes focused on nothing in particular.

"What is that mess in the bathroom?" He examined each limp hand and arm for what would have to be a life-threatening injury, given the vivid color in the tub. It couldn't be blood, of course; dye or paint must be the culprit. Still, it had shocked him enough that a wave of nausea had struck like a storm at sea. She and his mother were all that remained of his family. To lose her ...

He slumped beside her on the banquette. Insomnia had carved deep purple recesses into the skin beneath her eyes. Michael imagined if he prodded her pallid flesh, he would leave an indentation as in soft wax. "What's wrong, baby? You know you can tell Daddy anything, right?"

Many minutes passed in silence. Then, with great effort: "She kept me up last night."

"Who?"

She dropped her gaze to the table and her uneaten, mushy bowl of Cheerios. "Vinnie."

A product of her grief, a longing for the dead so acute she visualized their presences. It broke what was left of his heart. "Sweetie ... you know she's gone."

A tiny shake of her head.

"I know how hard it is, how lonely you've been. I have, too. But we still have each other, right? And Grandma."

Above them, thumps like feet or fists pummeled the floor. Abigail offered a drained, disinterested sigh. The sound too closely resembled someone falling—too much like that day ...

"I'll see what it is. Maybe a pipe or something. Old houses make a lot of noise sometimes." Michael took the stairs two at a time. The noise had stopped but was easy enough to pinpoint; Abigail's room lay above the kitchen. He peered inside. The window closed against the cold, nothing could have blown over. The floor was spotless anyway. Abigail, always Vinnie's opposite. Even her room's chosen colors—pinks and purples—contrasted Vinnie's red and dark brown palette. Such mature colors for a child, and Michael fought the urge to unlock her room, just once. Maybe he'd have the contractor swing by just in case.

The doll lying on Abigail's bed drew his attention as he turned to leave. A sense of foreboding hung thick in the air, one more thing he'd attribute to Abigail's grief, and even to his own, were it not for the expression he didn't remember sculpting. He'd been half-present at best in his own life for a year now, but he would not have carved that kind of vague malevolence.

You're imagining it. The business, raising a kid on your own ... Might be time to bite the bullet and have Mom move in.

When he returned to the kitchen, Abigail hadn't budged, nor had her vacant stare located anything of interest to which it might affix. Michael gathered her flaccid body into his arms. "I'm putting you back to bed. And if you're not better by tomorrow, I'm calling Dr. Peterson. Okay?"

"Yes," she whispered. But she wrenched herself out of Michael's embrace, scrambled over his lap, and shuffled zombielike out of the kitchen.

* * *

The thumping. Abigail pressed a pillow over her head and rolled over, away from the closet, but the noise intensified. Daddy was right. Old houses did make a lot of noise, and Vinnie had often complained about strange ones in her room. Abigail hurled the pillow aside and stood before the closet. She glanced back at the spot on the bed where Vinnie should be but wasn't. "We're not playing anymore. Stop it!"

Abigail yanked open the closet door. A blast of fetid air crashed over her, and horrible thoughts leaped into her brain—

—This is what Vinnie smells like now; this is what dead bodies smell like—

—and somewhere in the darkness behind her clothes arose the malicious tinkle of a little girl's laughter.

The strength rushed out of her body like a deflating balloon. She pitched toward the floor and landed on her hands and knees. She tried to scream for Daddy but found her voice, like her energy, depleted. Abigail hauled herself back to bed. Curled into a shivering ball, she waited out the night, fearing what she would see if she opened her eyes.

* * *

Michael had received several new orders before the approaching holiday season. Grateful for the work, he nevertheless battled a fresh wave of guilt for leaving Abigail alone much of the time. He couldn't afford a marketing person or web administrator, so every aspect of running the business fell to him. He'd started sending Abigail to his mother's on the weekends.

As he stitched a cloth arm onto a body, Abigail's footsteps sounded on the stairs. *She must be up for a glass of water.* But the main bathroom was just across the hall from her room.

Her silhouette passed the doorway to his workshop, the floorboards creaking beneath her. Michael set down his needle.

"Sweetheart? Do you need something?"

No response. He approached the doorway and reached into the hall to flip on the light. Rubbed his eyes. She looked so small. Abigail took no notice of the sudden illumination, merely kept walking with a bizarre, stiff gait as if her legs were made of ...

Leather.

He backed away in silence so as not to draw her attention, then ran up the staircase and locked the door to his room.

The stairs groaned. A shadow darkened the ribbon of light beneath his door. Michael held his breath.

She's your daughter, for God's sake. What is wrong with you?

The footsteps resumed, then ceased with the opening and closing of Abigail's door.

You're imagining things. You're overworked. She's sleepwalking.

Outside, snow fell onto the quiet street. He longed for something to break the tension—a teenager's laugh, the putter of a scooter, anything.

Michael turned off the light and lay with his clothes atop the covers. Sleep refused him.

* * *

"You scared Daddy," Abigail whispered to her sister. The glass eyes opened and closed in a lethargic blink. "You shouldn't have let him see you."

Don't be angry, Abigail. I'm the one who should be angry after what you did.

"I was only playing. It was an accident." Abigail picked at the hem of her nightgown. She'd said those words 100 times at least.

So you keep telling Daddy. But now you listen to me. Now you do what I say. You wanted me back, so here I am.

"I'm sorry, Vinnie."

Tomorrow we'll play a new game.

Abigail crawled under the blankets. Beside her, Vinnie lay rigid, hiding herself within the doll's body. Abigail linked her fingers with Vinnie's leather ones. She would not question this; her sister's miraculous return was a gift to be treasured. A chance for atonement on both their parts. Together forever, as they were meant to be.

* * *

The dead grass had disappeared beneath a blanket of fresh snow. Abigail stood at her window. It would be soft to land on, like a pillow or a cloud. Fun.

Vinnie waited below. *Come on*, she urged. *You want to be with me, don't you? Come out the window.*

The scent of bacon wafted through the floorboards. Abigail's stomach rumbled, but the fluffy white snow was too inviting to resist. And so was Vinnie's voice, her niggling whisper a rat gnawing on the circuitry of Abigail's brain. Abigail pushed the window up, then climbed onto the ledge. Cold winter air blasted her face and bare arms and prickled her lungs when she inhaled. The sky was New England gray, full of menace. The sugar maple's barren branches furled like fingers in a summoning gesture. It occurred to her, briefly, that birds never nested there.

"Abigail, breakfast is—Abigail!"

Daddy cinched his arms around her waist and dragged her from the window. A ragged splinter caught on her knee and peeled the skin away like tape from a package. Howling, she beat her fists against his shoulders.

"Abigail, what the hell are you doing?"

"We were playing!"

He plunked her onto her bed, where the doll sat in perfect stillness.

"We'll discuss this later." Michael gripped her hand, too tightly. "Come downstairs and eat breakfast."

He'll try to separate us. What are you willing to do about it?

"Whatever I have to."

"Abigail?"

She opened her mouth to explain, but she could not hear her own thoughts over the din of Vinnie's voice in her head.

She tried to form other words, to make her mouth obey, but the syllables forced themselves out like vomit: "I'll do whatever I have to." Tears streamed down her cheeks. Her voice was not hers, though it sounded like her. They were twins, and not even she could tell the difference. "I'll do whatever I have to."

"Go downstairs." Michael ushered Abigail out of the room and closed the door behind them.

* * *

Michael had sent Abigail to his mother's house for the day to bake cookies and watch cartoons, and with any luck Abigail would feel like herself again. But she had insisted on taking the damned doll with her. Had thrown herself on the ground like a child half her age when he refused to allow it, until he relented to spare himself the possible allegations of child abuse from the neighbors and his eardrums from her shrieking. Now he was glad, in a way, after all he'd seen over the past two weeks. His skin crawled at the thought of being alone in the house with it.

It was just Abigail.

Leather limbs creaking like a new pair of shoes ...

She's sick from losing her mother and sister. You've seen the way she acts lately.

Michael drove the last nail into the windowsill. She'd been an empty vessel all these months, but whatever had come over her was worse.

He spotted a white scrap sticking out from beneath Abigail's pillow. He yanked it out and scanned its contents.

Hitori Kakurenbo. *Hide and Seek by Yourself.*

This is a ritual for contacting the dead.

"Jesus Christ." He crumpled the printout into a ball.

He walked down the hall to his room and, sighing, sat down on the bed. He wasn't ready to admit defeat, that he'd all but abandoned her—and Vinnie—as a father.

He stared at the vanity, at Rebecca's cosmetics and perfumes strewn about as if she'd just used them that morning. Strands of her dark hair twined around the brush's bristles. If she and Vinnie had found each other in the afterlife, were there such a thing, they must be watching in dismay for what he had done or failed to do, mired in his own misery, to wrench Abigail from hers. A doll could never replace her sister. And on the wings of grief, he had invited in some sort of madness to Abigail's life, as if she needed more.

His mother's asthmatic car grumbled to a stop outside. Michael peered out from behind the curtain, past the porch that spanned the width of the house. Abigail climbed out, the doll in tow, then waved as the Toyota pulled away. She glanced around. Assured no one was watching, she cupped a hand around the doll's ear. Michael shook his head.

He met her in the foyer. "Did you have fun with Grandma?"

Abigail nodded. "She bought me a new book, and we played LEGOs. And she sent over some cookies for you." She held out a Tupperware container redolent with brown sugar and stuffed to the lid with chocolate chip cookies.

"That was nice of her. We'll have to do something nice in return. Come into the living room, sweetheart. I'd like to talk to you."

Abigail set the container on a side table and followed him. "What's wrong, Daddy?" She sat on the sofa, one arm protectively curled around the doll.

"Abigail, ever since I gave you the doll, you've been acting ... strange. Do you feel all right, sweetie? Is everything okay?"

"Did I do something, Daddy?"

"No, no. I'm just worried about you. Would you let me have the doll back for a little while?"

Her round, blue eyes shimmered with incipient tears. "But I love her. I hoped and hoped she would come back, and she finally did."

"Abigail, that isn't Vinnie and you know it. It's just a doll I made to look like her. And maybe it wasn't such a good idea."

"Please let me keep her." Abigail hugged the doll and, snuffling, buried her face in its hair. "I'll be good, I promise." The corn silk muffled her words.

Michael hoped his expression didn't betray his intentions. "All right. Go upstairs and get ready for dinner."

"Yes, Daddy." Abigail gave him a hesitant embrace before mounting the stairs, dragging the doll behind her.

* * *

I told you.

"I won't do it."

He'll steal me when you aren't looking. He'll smash my face and tear off my limbs. Is that what you want?

"I can take you apart and hide the pieces so he can't find you."

But then I'll need a new home.

"What do you mean?"

The doll's porcelain eyelids fluttered over her glimmering glass eyes. *We lived together inside Mommy. We can live together again, inside you. You will be my dollhouse, and I'll be safe.*

"I'm scared."

Don't be. Besides, you owe me for what you did.

"I know." Abigail let out her breath. With a pair of craft scissors stolen from Daddy's workshop, she began snipping the doll's stitches.

* * *

Michael gazed at the ceiling. Now and then, his attention drifted to the vanity. So little of his family remained, and Abigail was slipping away from him every day. So he clung to Rebecca's things, to the memories they invoked, like her hairs in that brush.

You.

He sat up. He'd locked the door but for once, no noises emanated from Abigail's room.

You.

The whisper permeated his brain, within and without, from everywhere at once. He pressed his hands to his ears. Abigail was doing this somehow. Psychokinesis. Some kind of poltergeist.

A shadow materialized in the mirror. Michael's teeth clacked, and he rubbed his arms. His breath condensed with each exhalation, the air so icy the very act of breathing might shatter it. The mirror glass no longer reflected the room, and the shadow flickered in and out of view like images on an old movie reel.

You watched while she did it. You did nothing.

It happened too fast. He couldn't react in time. He rationalized it to himself in those exact words often enough. Maybe this was his punishment. He was finally going crazy. Like Abigail.

She's not crazy. How could you even think that?

But Dr. Peterson had run all the tests and found nothing physically wrong with her. Nothing else fit.

Though he could not see its eyes, the glare of the thing in the mirror crawled over him. Vinnie? Or Rebecca, who always haunted the edges of his thoughts, who lurked just beyond the periphery of his vision. If he turned fast enough, he might catch one last glimpse of her—

The overhead light burst, sparked, and rained glass shards onto the carpet, onto Michael's hair and shoulders as he flinched away.

He had to get rid of it.

* * *

Daddy's gone crazy.

What do you mean? Abigail no longer spoke to her aloud. Vinnie's presence in her mind was as tangible as her own thoughts. At times, the crowding was so profound she could hardly breathe.

He will tell you lies. Don't listen to him. You must protect us.

I won't hurt him.

Then I'll do it myself.

The voice was not Vinnie's. Not even human. Everything Abigail ever feared coalesced in the demonic growl clanging through her head. She tried not to think of anything that might anger it further. Her heart thundered in her chest, and her stomach bubbled with nausea.

I can't. Please. He's all I have left.

What about me?

Abigail's breath hitched. Darkness flowed over her, binding her with invisible tethers over a bottomless chasm. Pictures flitted across her brain. Hands pushing into Vinnie's stomach. Her sister stumbling backward, one heel slipping over the first stair. She rocked forward once, counting on momentum to fling her back into the hall as Abigail reached for her. Mom had always warned them not to play by the stairs.

But Mom was dead.

Vinnie toppled backward. Abigail squeezed her eyes shut against the sickening *thud-thud-thud*. Daddy screamed from the bottom of the stairs, and when Abigail peeked over them, he was kneeling beside Vinnie. Her neck was twisted at a horrifying angle, a baby bird fallen from its nest.

The worst, though, was her accusing, angry eyes. Even dead, they glared up at Abigail with pure hatred for cutting her life so short.

Abigail tried to scream, but her mouth refused to open. Vinnie had locked her away in a dark place, a room with no doors, her eyes the only windows. Few things were crueler than a child's vengeance, nothing purer than a child's rage.

"Daddy, can we play a game? I want to play hide and seek."

He appeared at the workshop door. Bits of wool adhered to his shirt and pants. "All right, sweetheart. But not for very long."

Abigail ducked around the corner, closed her eyes, and counted to 10. The basement door creaked open.

Please don't—

She could no longer hear her own thoughts. Abigail emerged from the hallway to find Daddy on the first basement step, treading slowly to conceal the footsteps toward his intended hiding place. She stretched her arms out, pressed her hands into his back.

And shoved.

He tumbled headfirst down the stairs, his body meeting each step with a grotesque thump. A sharp crack silenced his cries. He stared up at her, lips still struggling to form words, to vocalize his pain. Blood trickled from his mouth, his ears, his nose.

Abigail stepped around the body and retrieved the doll parts from the boxes containing Vinnie's belongings, then carried them to the workshop and sewed the pieces back together. With each suture, a fragment of her slipped away. Sometimes, no matter how hard a family tried, something went wrong. Maybe it had been there before they were even born. Something had gotten into Vinnie—adults always said that about children, but they didn't really understand. It had been here for a long time, in this house. Waiting for someone like her sister, who had told her the vicious and cruel story that Mom had driven off the road on purpose. That it had commanded her to, and she had obeyed because she would do anything for her beloved old house. Abigail had tried to spare Daddy the future suffering Vinnie would cause, and it so resembled an accident that even she believed it after a time.

I don't need your body anymore. It will age, sicken, and die. This one never will.

Lightness overwhelmed her, a burden lifted, but the thing had stolen some vital component. The weightlessness became a consuming desolation, and the doll's otherwise impassive face mirrored what she once saw in her own reflection, what made her human.

* * *

She opened her eyes onto a blur of white walls and hazy light. A needle in the crook of her elbow fed her from a plastic bag. Abigail blinked. Grandma sat at her bedside, tears streaming down her cheeks.

"Thank God." She clasped her hands over her heart. "Don't say anything, honey. Just rest. You must have fainted when your father ..." She gulped. "We'll talk later."

Abigail didn't want to talk, anyway. So cold, so empty inside.

Don't worry. We'll finish it once and for all, and then we'll be together forever.

The doll lay beside her, its soft sculpted lips bowed in a slight smile Daddy had not fashioned.

You let me live.

I couldn't have done this without you, Abigail.

Abigail looked at Grandma again, and her lips bowed in a slight smile.

THE BLACK DOG OF CABRA

BY J. PATRICK CONLON

*Dublin City Police. £100 REWARD! MISSING,
Since the 1st of July last, from the personal stock of
the right honorable Lord Norbury, a ceremonial
sword. Steel blade, with a ruby embedded in the
gold-embossed pommel. An additional £50 reward
for any information leading to the apprehension of
any accomplices of the thief. The individual in
custody was not detained with the sword.*

The wanted poster might as well have had his friend John's name on it. It was just the sort of reckless heist that made Thom grateful he was usually the one who planned their schemes.

"John, what have you gotten yourself into this time? If you weren't my oldest friend, I swear I'd let you rot," Thom muttered under his breath. He walked into the streets of Dublin and grabbed the first urchin he could find.

"Lemme go, I ain't done nothing!"

Thom held up a gold florin. The boy's eyes grew wide, and he stopped struggling.

"Can you take me to the tavern the jail guards favor?" The child smiled and nodded. Thom dropped the coin into the boy's hand, then released his grip and followed him through the crowds into the city.

* * *

Thom sat at the corner of the table, watching as a young man, whose name he'd learned was Michael, massaged the dice in his hands. He closed his eyes and let the dice fly across the table.

"Snake eyes again, I'm afraid," the man running the table said as he smiled wickedly.

"Double or nothing?" Michael wrung his hands.

"I think the bill has come due. We are not prepared to extend any further credit."

"But, Andy, I don't have 50 florins!"

"You should have thought of that before rolling the dice. I'm afraid we are unforgiving to patrons who cannot settle their tabs." Andy snapped his fingers and several large men began to approach, cracking their knuckles.

Thom waited until the brutes had almost reached the table before holding up a heavy coin purse. "I am willing to square this man's debt."

Andy raised an eyebrow. "Really now? And who are you to offer such charity?"

"Seems to me a man of your standing need not concern himself with anything other than the coin at hand." Thom turned to Michael. "Unless, of course, you'd rather square this yourself?"

"No! Please! I accept your generous offer!"

Thom smiled pleasantly and tossed the purse to Andy. Andy opened it slowly, then grinned. "He's square with me. How you settle up with him now is your affair."

Thom rose from his chair and gestured to Michael. "I think we should get out of here, don't you?"

"Yes," Michael rose and moved through the room toward the exit, with Thom following close behind.

Once they were outside the bustle of the tavern, Michael turned to Thom. "Thank you for rescuing me. How can I repay you?"

"Go to your post in Kilmainham and cause a distraction at exactly 10 o'clock this evening. Once you distract the guards, lead me to the cell that contains the man who was captured in connection with the stolen jeweled sword."

Thom watched as Michael's eyes grew wide.

"What if I refuse?"

"You don't want to do that, Michael. You may have settled your debt with Andy, but your debt to me is far from square."

Michael's shoulders slumped. Thom held out his hand. Michael hesitated, and then shook it.

"Don't be late, Michael. I'll look for you at 10:00."

* * *

Thom pulled out his pocket watch. It was 10:05 and still no sign of Michael. He swore, moving from his spot crouched by the rusty metal door. The door opened with a slow creak. He snapped around to see Michael peeking around the door.

"Michael, making me wait was not your best idea."

"I couldn't get away!"

"You're lucky to be here now, and I know you would not want to disappoint me."

"No! I'm here, and the guards are all busy with the shift change. You'll have at least 10 minutes to get to the thief."

"The plan has changed, Michael. Your delay has caused me to lose valuable time. I'm going to need another favor."

"I can't do anything else!"

"I'm afraid you don't have a choice. You are already an accessory to a jailbreak. Or did you think I wouldn't take you down with me?"

Michael's face fell. "What do you need?"

"Take me to your armory. I'll need a lot of gunpowder."

Thom watched Michael's eyes widen. He patted him on the shoulder.

"Relax, this is going to be fun."

* * *

The dream was always the same. The smell of peat and bubbling stew filled the old cottage. John sat on a rickety chair while his father poked at the small pot.

"Tell me again about Captain Gallagher," John heard himself say.

His father smiled, his eyes gleaming. "He was the last and greatest of the Rapparees, and I ran with him when I was not much older than you are now. We robbed from the nobility, sharing some of our spoils with the farmers. He was a great man."

"Tell me about the treasure again!"

A woman's voice answered this time, "George, stop filling his head with your nonsense! It's bad enough you being a disgrace."

"It's not nonsense, woman!" The shout made John flinch. His father turned to him, speaking lower. "The treasure is real! The only thing they found was his sword, but they didn't know what they had! I'm the only one left who hasn't forgotten! Get that sword, boy, and it will lead you to the treasure!"

His father then grabbed him roughly and shook him. "Find the treasure, boy. Prove me right. But beware the Hanging Judge. Only the sword can protect you from him." A thunderous roar filled John's ears and the cottage shattered before him.

The explosion shook the walls and ripped John from sleep. He sat up and looked toward the cell door. He could hear the screams and stomping of boots.

John banged his fist on the door. "Hey, get me out of this cell!"

"Quiet in there!" The guard said. "You aren't going anywhere."

"What's going on? What was that explosion? You can't keep me locked up while the jail collapses."

"I said quiet in ..." John heard a grunt and then something hit the door.

"Hey, hey!" John pounded on the door.

"Would you please shut up!"

"Thom?"

"Yes, I'm here to save your sorry skin!"

"How did you find me?"

"I'd love to discuss this in detail, but that explosion will keep them distracted for only a few minutes. Now let me get this door unlocked, unless you'd prefer to stay."

John smiled despite himself. "No, I think I've seen enough of Kilmainham for this trip. But we can come back sometime, right?"

A click and the door swung open, revealing Thom kneeling by the lock. John rushed out, grabbing his friend in a hug.

"Yes, yes, it's good to see you, too." Thom struggled to get free of John's grip. "But let's have this touching reunion beyond these walls. I'm eager to get free of this place."

They ran down the corridor, away from the sounds of fire and shouting.

"First, we get the sword," John said.

"We don't have time for this," Thom panted. "We need to get out of Dublin."

"If we leave without the sword, then we lose out on the treasure it hides." John glanced over at Thom as they ran.

After a moment, Thom said, "Fine."

John clapped his hands together. "I knew you'd see it my way."

They turned the corner to find several guards waiting for them with pistols drawn.

"Stop right there, by order of Queen Victoria!"

"Sorry about this," John said as he kicked Thom's legs out from underneath him. Thom fell forward and crashed into the guards. All four men tumbled across the floor. John plucked the keys off one of the downed soldiers as Thom slammed his elbows into the bridges of their noses. The guards stopped moving. He finally picked his rescuer up and lightly brushed Thom's shoulder.

"Thanks for the warning." Thom slapped John's hand away. "Now let's get this bloody sword."

* * *

"Just give me a second, I've almost got it." John pulled another brick from the chimney. He then reached his hand into the opening and withdrew a leather backpack and a long object wrapped in cloth. He slung the pack over his shoulder and slid the bundle through the straps.

Thom narrowed his eyes. "Is that the sword?"

"Yes," John replied tersely. "It'll fetch quite a price back in London."

"Take it out. I want to see it."

"There's no time for that now. We're exposed out here."

"John, please tell me this isn't about Captain Gallagher."

"Of course not! I told you, I've given up on that."

"Fine. Then, now that we have the blade, we can get out of here." Thom moved to the edge of the roof and looked down. The street lamps were being lit, and the shouts of police filled the air.

"You think we have any hope of making the docks tonight?"

"Well, we can't stay on the rooftops. They'll capture us for certain."

"Don't worry. I have a place we can lay low tonight and make our way out of town tomorrow."

John started to rise, but Thom grabbed his shoulder.

"You've been in this town for three days, where on earth did you find a safe house?"

"I heard several prisoners talking about it. They say the place is cursed."

"Cursed? Will the Irish ever stop being so superstitious? What is this curse supposed to be?"

"They say the Hanging Judge's spirit haunts it."

"Judge? You want us to hide out in a judge's house? We may as well go back to jail!"

"Relax, he's been dead for years. And this place is perfect. They say no one has been inside since he died. If there are any treasures, they'll be ours for the taking."

Another shout rang out, and they fell silent.

"I suppose we don't have a choice," Thom said after a few minutes.

"Come on, Thom. This could be fun."

John got to his feet and ran across the rooftops, with Thom grumbling but following close behind.

"This looks more like a mansion!" Thom said.

"It's Cabra House, the home of a Lord who also happened to be the Chief Justice of Ireland. What did you expect?"

"I thought you said this place belonged to John Toler."

"John Toler was Lord Norbury."

"And you're sure this place is abandoned?"

"Do you see anyone around?"

"It's almost midnight. Of course I don't see anyone around!"

Thom moved from the alley across from the large estate to crouch in the doorway. He pulled a set of lock picks from inside his coat and began working on the door.

"Why are you doing that?"

"Because, I know that you would prefer to go swinging in through a window like Robin Hood. But our safe house wouldn't be very safe if a shattered window let every constable in Dublin know where we are."

John's brow furrowed. "That's a good point." He shrugged. "But Robin Hood had a lot more fun."

Thom sighed. "Just keep a lookout for the police while I get this open."

After several minutes, John heard a click and turned as Thom pushed the door open. "Let's go."

John and Thom slipped into the building. Thom pulled the door closed behind them. John lit a nearby lantern as Thom crouched and began working on the lock again.

"Thom, what are you doing?"

"I'm making sure that when the police come by, they will find this house locked and still abandoned."

"I didn't think of that. Good idea."

Another click and Thom stood. "You know, John, I was wrong. This place is the perfect safe house."

"I told you so." John smiled, and then furrowed his brow. "Wait a minute, why?"

"Because this place is so decrepit, I'm inclined to believe that it *is* cursed."

"It's not that bad."

Thom pointed to the dust-covered floor, then gestured around the room. Tattered curtains covered every window, moonlight trickling in through the rents in the fabric. Overhead hung a large chandelier, darkened but for the occasional bit of light that caught and splintered the shadows with the sparkle of burnished silver. "This place is not a mansion. It's a tomb."

"Well, I wasn't lying about the place being left alone, right?" John shrugged. "Besides, this is the last place they would look for us."

"I would think the police would search this abandoned place first."

"The superstitious ones steer clear, and the practical ones know that criminals avoid this place. It's perfect." John moved toward the stairs. "We might as well get the lay of this place if we're going to be holed up here for the night."

"Fine, you look around up there while I take a look around down here," Thom said. "Don't go making a racket, though.

Even if everyone avoids this place, we don't want to give them a reason to come snooping."

* * *

John ran his hand along the oak railing at the top of the stairs. The stories of the Hanging Judge raced through his mind. How the judge would fall asleep during trials, then awaken to sentence some poor thief to death. How death had made his hatred grow. The appearance of the spectral black dog shortly after he died. None of those stories mattered. All that mattered was the last story his father told him. The fateful day when he escaped the noose. The watch that was left behind. The watch that Toler had taken. He knew it was here. He tightened his grip on the railing.

With a gasp, John drew his hand back. Looking down, he saw a splinter embedded in his palm. He pulled out his short knife and worked it free. A small drop of bright red blood welled in the center of his hand. He stared at it a moment, and then wiped his hand on his trousers. He moved to the closest door and opened it.

Dust and cobwebs swirled as he entered. He covered his face and doubled over, coughing. Once he regained his composure, he took in the room. The same signs of neglect and disuse as in the rest of the house. A substantial four-poster bed, tattered damask curtains swaying gently, dominated the far wall. Beside it was a large dresser on which sat a rusted metal bowl and a large pitcher. A sheet hung loosely from the wall above, covering an oval shape.

John moved over to the dresser and pulled at the sheet. It fell to the floor, revealing an ornate mirror. He glanced at his reflection and stroked his stubble.

"If I were Toler, where would I hide that watch?"

"You will never find it." John leaped back at the sound of a strange voice.

"Who's there? Show yourself!"

Smoke poured from the edges of the mirror and formed into a large black dog.

"You know the watch doesn't exist, don't you, John?" The dog's maw moved in time with the words.

John felt his throat tighten. He exhaled, and a cloud of mist burst into the air before him. Could this be the entity haunting this place? The Hanging Judge, Lord Norbury?

"Your father was a crazy old fool. His stories of the treasure were fantasies."

"You lie!" John said. "The treasure is real."

"Then why did your father never go to find it?" The dog smiled broadly, teeth glistening. "He was mad, and you are following in his footsteps."

"Shut up!" John slammed his hands down on the dresser. "The treasure is real!"

"You must face the truth, John. Behold your father's legacy." The mirror shimmered.

The cottage from John's dream replaced the black dog. This time though, it smelled of filth and whiskey. John looked at his younger self, seated at the table. His father sat crumpled in a heap in another of the rickety chairs, a bottle grasped tightly in a fist. He tilted the container, and the last remains of brownish liquid poured onto his face, the smallest amount making it into his mouth.

"This is not real." The words felt like ash in John's mouth.

"Did I ever tell you how I was a great highwayman?" his father slurred.

"You have, but tell me again." The child cringed away, and John felt a stirring of recognition. The large man moved with sudden speed, backhanding the child. The small form spun from the chair and landed roughly on the floor.

"Don't sass me!" his father raged. "I was great!"

"Leave him alone." A woman's voice, but this time there was fear, not anger, in the tone.

John watched in horror as his father picked up the carving knife from the table. The small child flung his arms around the legs of the larger man, tears streaming down his face.

"This is a lie. None of this is true." John closed his eyes but still heard the thump of the kick, the air leaving his younger self in a rush.

"Your father killed your mother that night. There was no Captain Gallagher. Your father was a drunk. His life in service to the Rapparees no more than the desperate lies of a broken child."

John opened his eyes to see that the mirror again showed a black dog. Tendrils of smoke reached out and enveloped him once more as he fell to his knees. The cloth-wrapped sword shook free from his pack and clattered to the floor. The fabric parted and the jeweled hilt gleamed with an unnatural light. The smoke enveloping him vanished, a howl shattering the silence.

* * *

Thom was poking at the dust and ash in the disused fireplace when the howl came out from the second floor. He moved toward the stairway and pulled his pistol. As he ran toward the noise the far window exploded. A large black dog landed in the middle of the room. Thom swung the pistol to bear and fired. The bullet passed through the dog with no effect. Snarling, the dog took a step toward him. Thom turned and ran for the stairway at top speed, the beast following close behind.

He reached the top of the stairs and scrambled through the only open door. The wooden floor behind him splintered as the full weight of the dog landed where he had just been.

"John, we're in trouble."

John wiped at his eyes, and the hilt of the sword came into focus. He grabbed it and pulled it free of its wrapping. Getting his knees underneath him, he spun toward the door. Thom slammed into the bed, falling forward onto the mattress. The monstrous dog appeared in the doorway and locked eyes with John. The dog leaped at him with a gaping maw. John brought the sword up to meet the charge. The dog crashed into John, the momentum carrying them both into the mirror. It shattered, and they flew through the revealed hole into darkness.

John groaned as he rolled to a stop. Holding a hand to his side, he scanned the room. The dust that covered the rest of the house was absent here. Paintings adorned the walls and the outer edges were lined with small cases.

Before John could take a closer look, the massive pile of fur stirred next to him. The sword lay just out of reach. John rolled away, the dog's jaws snapping shut in the space he'd just occupied. He snatched the sword as he got to his feet. The memory of his father drunkenly attacking his mother was fresh in his mind. What if his father was just a drunk? What if the treasure didn't exist? His grip on the sword loosened.

The dog jumped forward. One of its paws swiped John's leg. The claws cut deep. John staggered back, barely managing to get the sword up into guard. The tip passed through the beast's flank, forcing John to fall back to avoid the teeth meant for his throat. He scrambled back to his feet, staring at the sword in disbelief. His father had said the sword would protect him from the judge. His entire life to this point was a lie.

"What's the matter, John?" The voice dripped with glee. "Is your father being a total failure finally setting in?" Another swipe almost knocked the sword from his hand.

"You are out of time, son of a failed thief." A claw batted his blade aside, and then John was slashed across the chest. He toppled backward before one of the pedestals. He started to pull himself up when a plaque filled his vision. **Cpt. Gallagher 1818**. John looked atop the stand to see a small, tarnished pocket watch resting in the middle of a cushion. He wrapped his hand around it. He immediately felt stronger and lighter.

"I think it's time for you to die a failure. Like father, like son," the dog said.

John brought the sword around just in time to meet the dog's next lunge. This time the sword connected, throwing the dog back. John regained his feet, swinging the sword between him and the dog. The black mass sprang to its feet.

John regained his footing and spun the sword. He waggled the sword tip at his opponent.

"We played the first round of this game in your realm, but now—" A smile spread across John's face. "—it's my turn."

"What trickery is this?" the dog growled. "I am proof against you."

"But not against this," John opened his hand and let the watch dangle from its iron chain.

The black dog sneered, and its front paws dug into the wood. The two began to circle each other, searching for an opening. Each time the dog swiped or lunged forward, John brought the sword up to parry it and counter.

"What's wrong, Lord?" John's smile sharpened. He flicked the tip of the sword out, forcing the dog to skitter back and away from reach.

"You figured out the secret of the blade, but no matter. This ends now." The dog leaped at John's throat.

John quickly dodged to the right and thrust the blade into the dog's side. The sword struck true, to the heart, and the dog yelped and burst into a cloud of smoke. John fell to a knee, his breath coming hard. He had the watch and the blade. He could finally prove his father was right.

Thom poked his head through the hole. "What are you doing? Where is that dog?"

"Gone. I fought it off." John got to his feet and let Thom help him out of the small room.

"That's good, but we have other problems," Thom said. A loud boom came from downstairs. "My gunshot seems to have alerted the police to our presence. I think we have to leave now."

"Then let's take to the rooftops and get out of here."

Thom went to the bedroom's single window and opened it just as the sound of the front door splintering could be heard from downstairs. Thom helped John out the window and then passed the backpack to him. Thom was handing up the sword when a burly policeman stepped into the doorway.

"Stop, thief!" the man bellowed as he rushed Thom.

"I would love to stay, but I'm afraid I've worn out my welcome. But thank you for your hospitality." Thom flourished a short bow, then grasped the top of the window and flipped his legs over the edge and onto the roof. He winked and saluted the watchman, and then disappeared into the darkness of the Dublin night.

* * *

The campfire flared higher as John's and Thom's bodies slumped together. The frantic flight across the rooftops had left them exhausted. Thom stood with a groan. John remained seated by the fire and drew the jeweled sword. He laid it across his lap and reached into his pocket. He pulled out the small tarnished pocket watch.

"Where did you get that?" Thom stared as the watch spun slowly on the end of its chain. The campfire's light caught a bit of untarnished metal, and the watch gleamed bright silver.

"This watch used to belong to my father." John stopped the watch from spinning and turned it over slowly in his hand. "I never told you the end of the story about my father and Captain Gallagher."

"Not this again," Thom began. But an icy stare from John stopped him dead.

"My father was the youngest of the group at the time, and Gallagher entrusted the watch to him. But he lost it as he fled from the King's army. He told me that he saw Gallagher pick it up. When I found out the sword was with the current Lord Norbury, I figured he would have the watch as well."

"So, Toler hid the watch, but not the sword. Why?" said Thom.

"You saw that trophy room. The Hanging Judge kept small mementos of all his cases. The watch could be hidden away while the sword would have been missed."

"Well," said Thom, climbing to his feet. "Now that you have both the watch and sword, we can finally put this business to rest."

"Not yet. There is still the treasure to find."

"And how exactly is this sword going to lead to any treasure? Isn't it enough that we have defied the odds against the entire police force of Dublin, as well as that beast of a dog?"

"Without the treasure, this will never be over for me, Thom." John grasped the ruby embedded in the hilt of the sword and wrenched it back and forth until the gem broke from the pommel. He then produced a knife, using it to pop the back off the watch in one swift motion. The inner workings consisted of a single small gear, which he removed and fit into place in the sword's pommel.

"Would you care to wind it?" John offered the sword hilt to Thom, who took it carefully and began winding. After the fifth turn, there was a loud click, and the grip came off in his hand. Thom reached into the hollow and pulled out a small scrap of paper.

"This will lead to Captain Gallagher's treasure, and I will finally clear my father's name." John's voice had grown steady and determined at the sight of the wrinkled paper. Thom unrolled the paper to reveal a bearded, red-robed man seated with a book in his lap. Beneath him were 10 sets of letter and number combinations.

"This isn't a map." John's face fell. "This isn't right."

"That is John the Baptist," Thom remarked. "And those are chapter and verse combinations."

"How do you know that?" John looked at Thom. "You're not exactly the church type."

"Yes, but I am the rare and expensive type," retorted Thom as he tapped the scrap with his hand. "And that is copied from the Book of Kells. And you know what that means."

John's smile returned, with a familiar gleam in his eye. "It means we get to break into Trinity Church with the entire watch hunting us already. This is going to be fun."

THE ANGEL'S GRAVE

BY CHANTAL NOORDELOOS

Duff McGaffrey slaved away for years at the Pemberton Mill until its sudden collapse in January of 1860. Since his father's death, the responsibility to take care of his mother and feed seven hungry mouths was his to bear, and the loss of his income was a blow to his family. There was not a lot of work for a former textile factory worker—especially not one who was linked to a scandal such as that of the Pemberton Mill collapse—and each day he went out in search of a new occupation. It was as if the mill had left him cursed, for each night he returned home to face his mother's scornful looks. One night, after a terrible row, Duff fled to the pub to spend his last shillings on ale.

At The Warren Tavern, the oldest pub in Massachusetts, Duff saw a lot of familiar faces. Some of the workers found new work, some moved away, but many suffered the same fate as he. There were those who had jobs but had lost their wives or children in the collapse. The pain still hung thickly in the air, and the pub lacked its usual mirth from days past, and most men looked at their drinks in silence.

"This seat taken?"

Duff heard a dark, throaty voice. He looked up and shook his head. A large, middle-aged man smiled and showed a mouthful of rotting teeth. With a grace hardly expected from a man of his size, the stranger slid into the seat next to Duff.

"Bill O'Grady." The man with the rotting smile held out a shovel-size hand, which engulfed Duff's as they shook.

"Duff McGaffrey."

Suspicious of strangers, Duff sized up the man. As he sipped his ale, he took in the watery blue eyes and bulbous, cratered nose, set in a wrinkled, scarred face. "What brings you here?"

"Family," the man said simply, with a thick accent.

"Irish, eh?" Duff wondered if he spoke the truth. Something about this man struck him as dishonest, but he couldn't quite put his finger on it. The tone of voice, or perhaps that cunning smile, and he didn't feel much love for the Irish.

"Aye, and you seem like a fine, strong lad." Bill slapped his big hand on Duff's shoulders.

"Strong enough." Duff's back tingled with the impact of the slap, and he leaned away in annoyance.

Bill poured a gulp of ale down his throat and continued. "What sort of work do you do?"

Wary of this prying stranger, Duff offered only the basic facts, just to be polite. "I am ... I *was* a factory worker, until the disaster over at Pemberton Mill. I'm looking for a new line of work."

"There are other mills."

Duff shook his head. "I've had my fill of mills, and I don't care much to travel back and forth between home and someplace new." The ale, plus a sympathetic ear, loosened Duff's tongue. "I don't much like the idea of uprooting my family. I'd only resort to that if there really is no other way to provide for them. But then, a new house would cost money we don't have."

"Or you could try a more lucrative job." The man rubbed his chin but kept his expression innocent and aloof.

Duff saw him smile slightly and realized that his face must have betrayed his interest.

"Barkeep, two more pints, here."

His new friend treated him to a few more drinks, and then Bill told him of his plan. At first, he was reluctant to see the merits of such a thing, but several drinks later young Duff warmed up to the idea. The more he drank, the more opportunities he saw, and, before he had time to really think things through, Duff made a pact with his new partner. They shook hands and, with that, Duff changed his career. He went home that very night to inform his mother he was leaving.

"Will you leave tonight?" His mother's voice shook, and she shot Bill a disagreeable look.

"Yes Ma, I want to earn money as soon as I can."

"But what about us?" ·

"I'll send you money every week." He patted his mother's hand, and she looked at him with weary eyes.

Duff's heart ached as he looked at his mother. Her dark red hair was tied in a bundle and escaped in feathery wisps that defied gravity, making it look like she wore a crown of flames.

"But I need you here," she said stubbornly, shaking her head.

"I'll be no good here if I ain't earning no money, Ma," he pleaded. "You need food on the table. And I will be back for Christmas."

Her reservations were unspoken, but Duff saw them on her face. "It's only until they get the mill rebuilt, and then I'll be back," he lied. "It's good money, Ma. Bill promised me good money."

Finally, she nodded and took his big, round face in her hands. "You go, lad," his mother said. "Make your old mother proud. Be back for Christmas, though, and don't forget about us now. We won't get by without you!"

His strong arms gathered around her thin frame, and he squeezed until he heard her gasp for air.

* * *

Duff McGaffrey was a free man, and he whistled a merry tune as he carried his few belongings in a knapsack down Brewer's Lane. At the end of the street, Bill waited for him to start their new future together.

When they first met, back at the pub, Bill told him what he did for a living. He was a grave robber. At first the information shocked Duff, and for a moment he wondered if he wanted to continue a conversation with a man of such dubious character. What God-fearing man would stoop to robbing graves? However, Bill's story of riches was sweet and alluring to young Duff. Poverty was the only life he knew, and he was so tired of it.

Duff disagreed to begin with, naturally. He argued it was illegal, immoral even, but Bill said to him, "There is nuthin' immoral about grave robbin'. What's immoral is to bury yer dead with jewelry that could be used to feed starvin' children, that's what!" His words reminded Duff of his poor mother and five siblings. How their bones could be seen through their skin, and how hollow their eyes were.

"They just lay there in the ground, rottin', me boyo," Bill continued. "Just feedin' the worms with those lovely gold rings, pearl necklaces, gold-fob watches. The dead dunnae mind that you takes from them, they're dead. They feel nuthin', they miss nuthin'. If ye ken what I'm saying?" Bill winked with his watery eyes.

Duff considered his words and believed he couldn't fault them. Who would miss the items they stole? Not the dead. And the living wouldn't know the belongings were gone. Duff explored the thought. He could buy good food and nice clothes for his family, and there would be plenty of money for rent, and coal in winter. The money would make all the difference for them, his *living* family, and he only had to rob dead people. It would be different if he stole from people who were alive; they would suffer from the loss of their possessions. If the families of the deceased needed those jewels, they shouldn't have buried them in the first place. Duff didn't need a lot of effort to change his mind about the morality of stealing from the dead. In hindsight, it only took six pints and a few hours' worth of talk to convince Duff McGaffrey to become a grave robber.

* * *

The first grave was Duff's worst. The digging held little challenge for young McGaffrey; he was strong and used to hard work. The darkness that surrounded them while they worked held no obstacle; he had worked long days in gloomy conditions before. But while he worked, Duff imagined that God's eyes peered down at him in discontent. A small prayer ran through his mind as he forced the shovel into the loose earth of the grave of one J. K. Harling, born July 18, 1837, died December 22, 1859, only a month and a half ago.

"Hurry up, slowpoke." Bill hissed between his teeth and waved the shovel at him. "We want to fill this grave up before dawn, leave as little tracks as we can, as to avoid suspicion. Then we can open another grave on this same graveyard tomorrow night without alerting the authorities."

Duff sighed and focused on his work opening the casket. J. K. Harling was a young woman when she died, but now her skin blistered, and Duff looked at the swollen abdomen of the corpse with some disgust. The pungent smell that emanated from the dead woman turned his stomach.

"She were pregnant when she died," Bill said bluntly as he held the lantern over the woman's body. He pointed to something slimy between her legs and added, "Coffin birth." When Duff realized that the clammy substance was a dead baby, he lost his breakfast, right there next to the coffin in the hole they dug. The thought of having to touch the woman was too much for him, and he scrambled out of the grave in a panic, his own vomit running down the front of his shirt.

"Come back here, ye fool." Bill hissed loud enough that Duff stopped his climb.

Duff sat down next to the grave, blood drained from his face and smelling sour. "I ain't touching her," he said, and the sick feeling stirred in his stomach again.

"Ye don't have to, not at first," Bill assured him. "I'll do the pickings, and you just help me dig for now."

Duff nodded gratefully.

"Ye hold the light so I has me hands free," Bill said, handing him the lantern.

Obediently, Duff shone the lantern on the corpse. Her skin was an unpleasant dark hue, and she looked like she was slowly melting. For a moment, he felt his stomach heave again, but he swallowed it back.

"Good pickings," Bill said from the depth of the grave. His voice sounded no more than a whisper, but loud enough for Duff to hear. "Gold earrings, and a pearl necklace ..."

He pulled at the necklace to get the clasp to the front. The body moved a little, and Duff jerked away, startled. Bill's large hands easily undid the tiny clasp of the necklace as if he had done nothing else in his life. Then he removed the small, golden hoops from her ears, and grabbed the girl's wrists.

"Two gold bracelets and a pearl one, some rings too." With another quick movement, he undid the bracelets, but when Bill tried to take her rings off, he found them stuck.

"I need the pliers," he said, holding out his hand to Duff.

"What for?" Duff asked suspiciously.

"The rings are stuck. I need to cut off her fingers."

"You can't do that!" the younger man exclaimed, horrified.

An amused look appeared on the older man's face. "Ye have a better idea to get them loose?" He held up the girl's hand. "Ye are welcome to try yerself."

"No," Duff said. "Can't we just leave them?"

"And leave all this good money?" Bill spat. "I don' think so, son, this here's hard work and I'll get what I came for, all of it!" He looked at Duff for a moment. "Gimme the pliers," he said again, and Duff handed them over. The younger man looked away, but the dull cracking sound resonated throughout his whole body, making his stomach flip once more.

* * *

Grave robbing became easier after that first time. Bill and Duff settled into a good routine for their nightly act, and only a month later, Duff dared to touch the dead and strip them of their fineries. He was not prepared to cut off fingers or other limbs for their treasure hunt, but he no longer vomited when Bill asked for the pliers. It was all part of the job. They made a reasonable living, as Bill knew some gents that gladly took the goods off their hands, although they only paid a third of the real value. But such was the way of their world.

One night, in a pub called the King's Crown, Bill raised a pint to Duff. "Here's to many more fine pickings."

Duff raised his own glass and touched it to the older man's pint. A faint clinking noise chimed. Bill took a sip, which left a foam moustache on his scarred upper lip. The older man remained a mystery to Duff after working together for seven months, despite their constant companionship.

They travelled the roads for days at a time. The two men spent no more than five nights at any cemetery, sometimes less. To stay in one place was too risky. It could make the authorities suspicious.

During the day, Duff scoured the papers for information about rich funerals, and at night, Bill bought drinks in the local pubs for chatty folk who knew all about the people who lived and died in the area.

"So far we've had fair pickins, but nuthin' too big yet." Bill smacked his lips. "What we wants is real old graves. The kind where they buried the most prized possessions with the deceased. Now if we can find a grave like that, we'll be rich, me boyo, bloomin' rich." He burped and patted his stomach. "Tomorrow we are goin' to a graveyard right outside Bedford. There are rumors some rich count was buried in one of the mausoleums." He shot Duff a meaningful look. "Perhaps this is the one, boyo." Bill's grin was big, and his eyes misted over as he glanced away. "Perhaps this is the one."

* * *

Despite the good money, the job gave Duff nightmares. In his dreams, the dead visited, and they pleaded for their lost heirlooms. His most common visitor was J. K. Harling, who haunted his dreams almost every night. Sometimes she would appear as a young woman with dark red hair, just like his own ma. In her arms she would carry a plump, pink babe who suckled at a naked breast. In those dreams she always tried to kiss him and asked him to warm her cold flesh. Once he did kiss her, only to find that her skin came loose at the touch, and she was the same slimy corpse which lay in the coffin that first night.

Sometimes she appeared to him as a spirit, while other times she came to him as a corpse begging for his company, her legs spread wide while the clammy, sticky babe lay between them. The babe reached out a rotting little hand to him, accusing Duff of disturbing its rest.

The nightmares caused Duff to sit up in bed, sweat dripping down his forehead. In his dreams, he promised to put things right; he would give them their rest. Come daytime, the dreams were nearly forgotten. He only thought of the coins he sent to his mother and siblings, and thoughts of the dead lingered in the back of his mind. Duff promised himself that if they found a grave full of treasures, he would buy himself a nice shop and live off that. But until that time came, he would continue to take money from the dead.

Duff knew he could go back home and find work in a factory there, but he no longer wanted that life. He felt no love for his current life either, but here there was money, and a potential future somewhere. At least he could hope for one.

* * *

The road to Bedford was not long, and they rested in a pleasant little inn near the edge of town. Bill and Duff stored their shovels and other equipment under the beds of their room, to keep them from sight, because people sometimes asked the two strangers questions about their tools. Bill would explain they were in the business of digging wells on farms and the like, and that was the end of the conversation, but both men preferred to keep the conversations about shovels to a minimum.

Dressed in mourning clothes, the men went to the Northern Cemetery during the day, where they explored their dig for that night. Bill owned a little notebook in which he drew a map and wrote down the names of the graves with potential interest. This night, the grave of Sir Henry Tolton was their mark, a rich man known for being frugal. While they strolled through the graveyard, Bill grabbed Duff's arm quite unexpectedly. The younger man looked at what his colleague pointed out.

A large gravestone in the form of a worn angel stood in the shadows of a weeping willow at the south end. It looked lavish but weathered. The writing was no longer legible, which made the grave and its owner anonymous and very old.

"Ancient and, judgin' by the angel, rich," Bill said. "Very likely someone might have buried some possessions in there with the corpse."

"Dunno, could be a duster." Duff shrugged. Dusters were coffins in which no items of value were buried. They found a few of them, but usually Bill's research brought them items of some worth.

"Could be." Bill spat a bit of chewing tobacco on the ground. "But it could be a gold mine." He crouched down by the grave and laid his thick hand on the marble. "What are ye, me beauty, a duster or a gold mine?" For a moment he stared at the grave, and then he stood up, wiping his hands on his black trousers. "Tonight, we shall see. Sir Henry Tolton will wait for us one more night." Bill clapped his hands together, and a smile broadened on his ugly face. "He'll be just as dead tomorrow."

Something about the grave unnerved Duff, and he found the whole thing eerie. *Then again,* he told himself, *grave robbing itself is eerie. Why be frightened of a grave of which the name had faded away?* It was childish to be afraid of stone, and of the long dead.

* * *

That night they snuck across the cemetery. A shiver ran up Duff's spine as they reached the old grave. The eyes of the angel seemed to follow him whenever he looked at it.

"What is wrong with ye, boyo?" Bill asked.

Duff's face paled, but he shook his head. "Nothing. Think I might be coming down with something, that's all." The young man straightened his shoulders, reluctant to tell Bill of his fears. Hidden between the branches of a tree an owl hooted and startled Duff.

"Ye are as skittish as a maiden fair, boyo." Bill laughed softly and slapped the younger man on his back, as he often did.

Without much ado, old Bill began to dig. The ground was compact and hard, no shovel had touched this earth in a long time. They dug deep, like pirates digging for their treasure, until their shovels hit the hard top of the casket.

To Duff's surprise, the casket looked unspoiled, not like an old casket weathered with age, but like a shiny, new one. Nothing about this coffin indicated that it belonged to a rich person. To Duff's eye it resembled a pauper's casket. "It'll be a duster." His mood sank, and he wanted to go home, to get away from this unnamed grave with the creepy angel. Nonetheless, he helped Bill open the damned thing. When the lid flew open, the casket revealed the corpse of a man dressed in a black suit. By the look of it, he died no more than a day or two ago. The body did not yet show signs of decomposing, but the smell was there.

The corpse disgusted Duff. The body belonged to a young man, tall and broad. Its face lay frozen in the twisted scowl of a man hanged, and the skin had a black and blue tint. The thick tongue poked out between swollen lips, and the eyes bulged.

In the light of Bill's lantern, Duff saw the noose that still hung around the man's neck. There was something familiar about the corpse, and Duff shuddered again. He squinted his eyes and leaned forward.

The dead man had thick, black hair and a round face and ... then he saw it ... he saw what was so familiar about it ... the dead man was wearing *his* suit.

A photograph stuck out of the front pocket, and with trembling fingers, Duff picked it up and looked at it. In the lantern light he saw himself, his mother, and his five siblings, each staring, dignified, at the camera. His siblings looked a little older than he had last seen them, but there was no mistake about whom they were. He gasped and dropped the portrait on the ground, then looked at the man's face. This wasn't just any face, it was his own face, contorted by death, and with a noose around his neck. The world spun around him. He took a step back, and fell flat on his backside.

Bill lifted his lantern to see the spot Duff looked at. The lantern illuminated the writing on the headstone:

Here lies Duff McGaffrey, grave robber and criminal, who broke his mother's heart, and was hanged on April 2nd of 1864.
May his soul rot in hell, and may all of his possessions be stolen by greedy men.

The angel above looked down with resentful, shadowy eyes.

"Oh, God-All-Mighty!" Duff sobbed. He knew this couldn't be his own grave. He *knew* his eyes were betraying him, and yet ... and yet this was a sign from above. Or from below!

The corpse grabbed his leg with a sodden, rotting hand, and Duff stared down into the gaping maw that was once his mouth. Panic overcame him, and he scrambled out of the grave. Dirt slipped under his fingers and feet, and he struggled to get away from the rotting image of his future self. Finally, he managed to find his footing and fled the grave, tears streaming down his face. Bill's gruff voice called after him, but Duff refused to listen. He ran.

* * *

He never did see old Bill again. Not alive anyway.

Duff returned to Lawrence, Massachusetts, to his mother and siblings. He found a right, regular job. It wasn't great work, but the wages were just enough to get them by. Fortune favored him, and soon Duff became overseer, which gave him more financial stability. He lived his life in quiet and did not dare to step foot on a graveyard again.

With more than his usual interest, he read the papers of April 1864 until he found what he was looking for. On April the 2nd of 1864, it said, Bill O'Grady and Seamus Flannigan were hanged by the neck for committing the crime of grave robbing. A photograph of old Bill O'Grady and, to him, a younger man that Duff did not recognize stared at him. An extensive article detailed their exploits and subsequent arrest by the local constabulary.

Duff felt a shiver run up his spine, and he remembered the dark, shadowy, resentful eyes of the stone angel in the Northern Cemetery of Bedford.

VINDICTIVE

BY WELDON BURGE

"You see, this is a pistol-grip mini-crossbow with an 80-pound pull," Flash Conwright said. He turned the weapon over in his hand, admiring it. "Great for intimate work, if you know what I mean. I'm getting bored with guns. No sport, no challenge. Too messy, if you think about it."

The naked woman sitting cross-legged on the floor whimpered. Conwright had forced the woman into that position to keep her from standing and running. They were in an abandoned warehouse in a desolate section of Chicago, near the river. The building was strewn with refuse and abandoned furniture, and he could smell the mildew and wet-dog odor that permeated the place. To Conwright, there was a certain comfort in the musty air, in the closeness of the atmosphere, like a blanket. And, of course, the darkness hid so much. There was a comfort in that, too.

She would scream. They always scream. The men, not so much. They often seemed resolute to their fate, some even welcoming it. But he knew she would scream. No one would hear her from outside the warehouse, however. Other than a few homeless people sleeping down by the docks, nobody else. So her screaming would be meaningless. More irritating than anything. Maybe he should duct tape a sock in her mouth. Nah. What's the fun in that?

An attractive brunette with short-cropped hair, her copious makeup ran with her tears. A slim figure. Large, artificial breasts. Of course, Conwright understood everything about her was artificial. *Not bad looking, but not my type. And I'm definitely not hers.* He could, however, understand why she attracted the boys.

"Please don't kill me," she said.

"Don't get me wrong. I love guns. A sweet Italian Bernadelli. One of my favorites. A few Berettas. Glocks. Tauruses. I even own an AK-47. Talk about messy. I'd never use that thing on the job, but it's a beautiful weapon. I have a large gun collection, all purchased legally. Not by me, of course. Background checks? What the hell are those? I'm so far off the grid, none of those guns can be traced to me."

"Please don't kill me," the woman repeated. She began to sob.

"But I love the crossbow, especially in my line of work. Like this right here, just you and me, conversing. I like to get close to my work. Far more fun, don't you think?"

"Why are you doing this?"

"Well, you and I know you're a pedophile. A murderer of young boys. I know, I know. Female pedophiles are rare, right? Probably why you got off. Of course, having money and a powerful defense attorney didn't hurt. Victoria Wainscott, one rich bitch."

"I'm innocent. I never did anything to those boys."

"Short of seducing and killing them. What was the oldest? Fourteen? Barely into puberty. Pathetic. How many did you kill? Even the cops don't know."

"Please," she begged. Tears welled in her eyes.

"See, that one boy, Billy McPatrick? He was the grandson of someone you really don't want to mess with. You probably didn't know that, did you? His grandfather hired me, an old friend of mine. Frankie Culbert. The old guy still has balls, even though he's no longer active in the Irish mob. Anyway, he's fronting the money. I think he hoped you'd get off, because prison would be too easy on you."

"You don't understand."

"I understand plenty."

"It's a sickness," she said. She sniffed, wiped away tears with the back of her hand. "I couldn't help it. It's a sickness. I need help."

"I've got the help you need right here," Conwright said. He patted the crossbow and winked at her. "We're going to have some fun."

She sobbed. "I don't want to die. It's not fair. I never meant to be this way. It's a disease. You don't need to kill me. I can disappear. No one will see me again."

"Well, lady, you're right about disappearing. I'll take care of that for you."

"Look, I have money. What do you want? Whatever he's paying you, I can double it. Triple it. Whatever you want."

Conwright shook his head. "It's not about the money, lady. It's about a scumbag rich woman who tortured and killed little boys."

He shot a bolt into her groin.

The woman howled, doubling over in instant, searing agony.

"Nothing like a perforated uterus to ground you in reality," Conwright said. He loaded another bolt into the crossbow. "I know, cliché. Poetic justice. Eye for an eye, yada yada."

Her demeanor abruptly changed, as if someone threw a switch in her head. Her eyes turned to him, and he could sense the pure evil lurking behind them, her true self finally revealed.

It was nothing new to Conwright. He'd seen so many similar transformations in the past. Evil had a familiar face, despite the mask it wore.

"I swear to God," she snarled. "You kill me now, I swear, I'll haunt you the rest of your life. You'll never be rid of me."

"How cliche." Conwright grinned. "You can't do better than that?"

"You'll never be rid of me," she repeated.

"I'm rid of you now, you sick bitch."

And shot a bolt into her right eye.

* * *

Conwright met with Solly Ventura at Arturo's in downtown Philadelphia, in a back-corner booth. Solly had linguini. Conwright had chicken parm. Solomon Ventura was Conwright's liaison, the guy who handled the transactions and set up all the jobs. The man was smart, had the connections, and knew how to deal. And he kept his best hit man under the radar. Conwright relished the relationship.

"Arturo outdid himself this time," Conwright said. "This parmigiana is the best I've ever eaten."

"You should taste his gnocchi. Made fresh every day. Blow your balls off."

Solly sipped his Chianti. Conwright was a Merlot man— well, if he didn't have a bourbon straight up. He swirled the wine in his glass. "So, how are the wife and kids?"

"All in good health. Thanks for askin'. Janie wants to go to Italy. One of those cruise deals. I don't know. I ain't much for boats."

"It'd do you good, Solly. Fresh sea air. Purge those sinuses. Get some relaxation."

"Screw the sea air. And I ain't got time to relax. You know this business, Flash. If you ain't on your toes, you're in the ground."

Solly sipped his wine again and then leaned forward over the table. "So, how did it go in Chicago?"

"It was fun, as usual."

"No problems?"

"Nope. In and out, done and clean. The client should be satisfied."

"Maybe even elated," Solly said. "I already have the next job lined up. Senator Fulbright."

"You're kidding."

"Nope. And, in this case, you don't need to know who hired the hit. You know, political ramifications. Big money, though. Big, big money. You can take a real vacation afterward. You've always wanted to go to Oahu, sip some pineapple shit."

"Hula girls. You bet."

After his arrest for "mishandling" government funds and embezzlement, Senator Fulbright was indicted and forced to resign from office—only to run again six years later. The idiots in the state re-elected him. Conwright would have taken the job pro bono, he hated the man so much. First there were criminals. Further up the food chain, politicians. Conwright despised politicians.

"I honestly look forward to it," he said.

Solly nodded. "I'll get ya the details, get the ball rollin'. You know, you really should try the gnocchi next time we're in here. Magnifico!"

* * *

Fulbright slept in a recliner in his den, snoring like a freight train, illuminated by a television facing the chair. Conwright had checked—Fulbright's wife slept in an upstairs bedroom. No children. Just the two of them in the house.

The large-screen TV was tuned to CNN, a report on a terrorist attack that had occurred in San Francisco earlier that day. Fifty-two dead in a pipe-bomb attack at a megaplex movie theater. All three terrorists were killed at the scene. Conwright watched for a moment, shaking his head. If Homeland Security would hire him, he could take out terrorists, with the proper intel, before these attacks occurred. Above the law, of course, but he could use his considerable skills for a patriotic purpose, a higher purpose. He would be far more effective than law enforcement castrated by political correctness. *Pipe bombs*, Conwright thought. *Maybe the government needs stricter plumbing laws. Better background checks at Home Depot.*

He glanced at the old man in the chair and then turned to the massive bookcase set in the wall to his right. Shelves of Hemingway, Fitzgerald, Steinbeck, Salinger, Faulkner, and other names he recognized, surely classics. Conwright pulled down a copy of *A Farewell to Arms*, opened it. A signed first edition. What, worth thousands? He replaced it on the shelf and took down *The Great Gatsby*. Another signed first edition. He put it back on the shelf and then noticed there were five other copies of the same edition. Probably all signed first editions. He didn't doubt that *all* the books in the library were first editions, likely worth millions. *All paid for with tax dollars*, he thought. *Or rich lobbyists.* He looked back at Fulbright snoring in the recliner. Conwright shook his head.

He approached Fulbright from behind, pulling from his sleeve a thin stiletto secreted there. He preferred using a garrote, to watch the man thrash, unable to breathe as the wire bit into his neck. But, aware the man's wife slept upstairs, Conwright decided to dispatch the man quietly. A quick insertion of the blade through Fulbright's temple and a twist of the knife through the frontal and temporal lobes would do the trick.

He then noticed a pinpoint of light to the left of the TV, in the darkness of the corner. The light seemed at first a reflection, maybe caused by a passing car on the street outside. But the room was in the basement with no windows. He stared at the light. It seemed at great distance, like the headlight of an approaching train. Yet the pinpoint of light, now slowly expanding, also seemed to be in the room. Were his eyes playing a trick on him?

What the hell ...

The light gradually became a gray, luminous form. Little more than a blob about the size of a basketball, hovering in the corner, stretching and bulging until nondescript arms and legs formed, followed by what could only be a head.

It was a little boy, Conwright realized. Eight or nine years old. But not quite a boy. The eyes were a dark blue, rimmed with violet. No, violet rimmed with blue, he couldn't be sure. The eyes had no pupils. The facial features seemed to shift and slide, to be in constant flux.

Conwright stood stock-still, more out of uncertainty than fear.

Is that the McPatrick kid?

The thing, translucent and somehow incomplete, moved unhurriedly, gliding above the hardwood floor. He could see the bookcase behind the specter, could see the Hemingways and Fitzgeralds through its center. There was something grotesque, something ... off ... about the boy.

Of course it's off, numbnuts. Whatever it is, it just appeared out of nowhere. And it's clearly not human.

Conwright didn't believe in ghosts. Didn't believe in anything paranormal. All bunk, the product of feeble or diseased minds.

Yet, here it was in front of him. And he was of sound mind. At least, he always assumed he was.

"You're not real," he whispered.

The face rippled, shifted. Changed. Barely human at all, the face gradually became more distinct, more recognizable. The thing tilted its head and smiled, revealing reptilian teeth.

Conwright stepped back.

The face of Victoria Wainscott. Distorted, emaciated, and gray, but her.

The face of a pedophile on a child.

"You're not real," he repeated, this time aloud.

Conwright backed away from the chair as the entity floated toward him. He didn't know what this was, and he didn't like unknowns. Unknowns could always fuck you over.

The thing seemed to be laughing, but there was no sound from its bloodless lips.

He backed out of the room, closing the door behind him, fully expecting the specter to materialize in the hallway next to him. But nothing happened. He could only hear the soft snore of Fulbright's wife on the next floor.

* * *

Conwright did indeed enjoy the gnocchi at Arturo's. He did, however, retain his balls.

"I can get one of the other boys to take out Fulbright, no sweat," Solly said. "So, what the hell happened? I think this was the first time you missed a mark."

He didn't know how to answer him. Tell Solly he'd seen a ghost? The ghost of a woman he'd snuffed and now haunted him? No, he couldn't do that. But he couldn't explain it otherwise.

Conwright shook his head. "I had a bad vibe in there, in that room. Fulbright was sleeping in the chair and I was ready to take him out. But something was off."

"Such as?"

Conwright sighed, shook his head again. "I don't know. I have to follow my intuition, and I just knew I had to get out of that room."

A lame excuse, but the best he could do.

Solly stared at him for a moment and then leaned across the table. "Look, I get the intuition thing."

"Yeah."

"But a job is a job."

* * *

A week later, Solly offered Conwright a low-profile job, a typical case of pissed-off husband and cheating wife, Jack and Maureen Madison. Usually, with these jobs, Conwright wanted to off both parties, just for spite, just because they were so irritating. But, of course, there was no money in that.

He watched the Madison house for a week, watched Maureen's boyfriend come and go while her husband was on a job assignment in Pasadena. He'd seen the woman several times outside the house, grabbing the newspaper at the end of the driveway, a frumpy homemaker that he thought would have no appeal at all for her latest lothario. But it takes all kinds.

When he was ready to finish the job, Conwright waited one night until the boyfriend left from his latest rendezvous. He then immediately approached the house, pulled on a ski mask and latex gloves, and quietly entered the house through a back window using a glass cutter. Her husband had the perfect alibi in California, and she likely had her lover's semen plastered in her vagina—the boyfriend would be the most likely suspect. The police would never even consider a hit man. At worst, they would think it was a home invasion gone bad after he tossed the place.

When he entered the living room, she stood looking out the window. She wore a sheer nightgown, hiding nothing. She must have heard him.

"Phil, didn't have enough?"

She turned around, and her smile dissolved.

Conwright unsheathed his Schrade Guthook Skinner knife. He had no intention of gutting her, although the thought had occurred to him. Unfortunately, it would have been too much fun and would throw suspicion off the boyfriend. He would merely slit her throat.

He thought she would scream. But no.

"Oh my God," she whispered, taking a step backward.

As he approached her, twirling the knife, she slipped and fell to the floor on her back, scrambling away from him like a crab. Her eyes bulged with horror. She then screamed and pointed at him.

But not at him.

He gradually turned.

Behind him was a massive, limbless figure, sluglike and bloated, yet tall and reaching just below the ceiling. The thing's mottled flesh—if it could be called flesh—was leprous and moist. A face, a misshapen skull, floated in the goo, eyeless with cavernous sockets. But the mouth ... the mouth swarmed with an undulating mass of tentacles, a Lovecraftian nightmare.

Conwright then felt the frigid air emanating from the specter, could feel the almost palpable hatred. He instinctively slashed at the figure with the knife, but the blade slid through the vaporous entity with no effect.

Maureen Madison managed to stand and ran screaming from the room.

"You don't scare me," Conwright said. "You can put on any costume you want. A pissed-off leprechaun. A ravenous unicorn. My ex-wife. Even the Devil himself. I don't care. You can't scare me."

The skull then melted like candle wax, the tentacles dripping and dissolving in air. He could then smell the stench, the overwhelming essence of putrid death.

And the melting skull became Victoria Wainscott.

"What do you want?" Conwright said to the specter. He stood in front of it, looking directly into its transparent face. "Are you going to ruin all of my jobs? That the idea? Is that all this is?"

The ghost reached for him, and he backed away.

"You don't scare me."

He heard sirens in the distance. Maureen had probably gone to a neighbor and called 911.

Conwright turned away from the specter, intending to slip out the back door before the police arrived.

He looked back over his shoulder.

The ghost was silently laughing but did not follow him.

* * *

"Flash, it's a total fuckup! The woman gave a full report to the police, gave them a pretty good description of you. Thank God you wore the mask."

Solly was angry. Angrier than Conwright had ever seen his old friend.

"The husband is super pissed off," Solly continued. "And what was that shit she said about some monster in the room?"

"No idea." Anyway, no idea that he wanted to express. "I didn't see anything. Just her running from the room."

"Well, we can forget about getting the fee. How could you screw up a simple domestic contract?"

Conwright shrugged. "Sorry. That intuition thing again." No way was he going to say anything about ghosts.

"Look, I'm worried about you, Flash. If you're arrested ... well, you have ties to the organization. We'd have to take *you* out. C'mon, what's goin' on with you? This isn't like you at all."

"What can I say, Solly? When something seems wrong ..."

Solly sighed, shook his head. "How 'bout you take some time off 'til you sort things out."

* * *

This has to end, Conwright thought. He had no idea why, but it became clear to him that he had to return to Chicago, to the warehouse where he ended Victoria Wainscott's miserable life. Back to where it began. Back to where she placed the curse on him. None of this boogety boogety stuff. He had no real religious beliefs at all. You're dead, then you're dead. That simple. You're here, then you're not.

This was different.

He stood alone in the rundown warehouse. His flashlight illuminated the stains of her blood that had soaked into the concrete floor. Victoria's body—at least what remained of her—was at the bottom of Lake Michigan, tethered to cinder blocks. He imagined her covered with lampreys.

"Where are you, you vindictive bitch?" he said to the silence. "Show yourself. I know you're here."

Nothing. Just the sound of dripping water echoing from somewhere in the dark, dank building.

He sat on the floor. Waited. Maybe this was a mistake, he thought. What did he expect to do if she confronted him again? He truly had no idea. There was no plan, no strategy. Maybe he was wrong. What did she want from him? Was she cursed to follow him forever, to foil every aspect of his life? Was she following him everywhere, only manifesting when he was on the job? Was she here *now*? Perhaps she wasn't here at all. Could she just be in his mind? No, that couldn't be it.

Why did she never speak to him? Were there regulations and policies for the dead? Restrictions? A rulebook somewhere? *Protocol for the Dead.* Was she not permitted to speak? Who knew? None of it made sense.

How do you do a hit on a ghost?

Conwright must have fallen asleep, for he suddenly awoke, aware of the frigid air around him, aware of slight movement nearby. No sound, but something shifting in the darkness, something low to the floor.

Victoria Wainscott congealed from the concrete, taking shape as if unfolding and developing from the floor itself. At first, the specter seemed embryonic, taking form as if in some monstrous womb. The arms appeared on an expanding torso, the legs extended, and a bulbous head grew on the stump of a neck. The thing stretched its invisible spine, becoming erect. The fiery-violet eyes snapped open. The full figure then floated before him, grinning. She manifested as herself this time. No more games, he assumed. No more costumes.

"Good to see you again, Victoria," he said.

The face showed confusion, hesitation.

"I keep telling you I'm not afraid of you," Conwright said. "By the way, I would have done you for free, just for the satisfaction. I'd put you down again. Gladly. Maybe even with a little more inventiveness this time. Have a little more fun. Fun for me, anyway. Not so much fun for you. I can think of several power tools that would make things interesting."

The ghost tilted its head, as if inquisitive. It smiled, grotesquely wider than humanly possible and with far more teeth.

Conwright wanted to hear the thing speak, just once. What did she have to say?

She floated closer to him, radiating hatred now.

"You have no power over me. You can't harm me. You never could. I realize that now. You're just an amusement park, ghost-house spook. A cheap carny apparition. A sheet on a string to scare the little kids."

Victoria Wainscott's smile became a silent growl, the eyes a pulsating, ice-cold blue. She reached for him, as if to strangle him.

Conwright smiled, nodded. "Come on, then. Do your worst."

Wainscott rushed toward him, arms outstretched, emanating a cold like Conwright had never felt before. But he did not flinch. The specter passed straight through him, a mere vapor, not harming him at all.

He turned. The Wainscott entity stared at him, as if waiting for something. Bewildered.

"Are we done here?" he said.

Wainscott rushed him again, with the same result. She stood in the shadows, staring at him for a moment, seemingly confused. She started to move toward him. Hesitated. Backed away this time, shaking her head. Was that fear in her eyes?

Conwright laughed.

Wainscott vanished.

* * *

Senator Fulbright was appropriately dead this time. A screwdriver protruded from his temple, a trickle of blood down his cheek. His eyes were wide in terror.

Solly had given Conwright the Fulbright contract again, to make amends. He did not fail this time.

The ghost swayed in a corner of the living room, looking bored out of whatever mind it had. If it could twiddle its thumbs, it probably would.

"Thanks for the help," Conwright said. "Always a pleasure to work with you, Victoria."

He chuckled. Tipped an imaginary hat in her direction.

"You know, now that we're best of pals—and you're clearly my Number One Fan—I think I'll start calling you Vicky. What do you think?"

The ghost rolled its eyes, and the face transformed into one of utter disgust. Then she blinked and promptly vanished.

Victoria had become his unwitting—certainly unwilling—accomplice. The ghost could do nothing to frighten or deter Conwright. If anything, her appearance had made his work easier. Senator Fulbright had pissed his pants when the ghost came swirling into the room. The man didn't even see Conwright behind him until it was too late.

Perhaps her damnation was indeed to follow him around, perpetually frustrated, as he continued his business uninterrupted. He liked to think this was her hell—and well-deserved. Several times, she didn't even attempt to be frightening, just manifested in the rooms as Conwright finished the jobs. Ho hum.

He supposed you couldn't bore a ghost to death.

But it was fun trying.

A HANGER IN THE WORLD OF DANCE

BY STEPHANIE M. WYTOVICH

It's cold amongst these corpses
I don't belong here, not with them,
The life-takers, the body-huskers

> *Why won't they stop staring?*
> *Their swollen eyes like skies of gibbous moons ...*

My spirit screams
They stuff leaves in my mouth,
Shove twigs under my nails

> *They lick lips with swollen, rubbery tongues,*
> *Their broken spines like knives ...*

I didn't ask for this death
Sometimes I can still hear father weeping,
Feel his fingertips in my hair

Their breath smells like crying
Such stale, stagnant air ...

There was rope, chaffing
They spun me in circles,
Clapped as I choked

Their teeth like cracked pearls,
Their mouths twisted in stitched-on smiles ...

At night, I hear the suicides moan,
They sing hymns about release
I cry songs about life

They celebrate this welcoming,
Strip me naked, teach me how to dance ...

THE WRITERS

JASPER BARK _____

Jasper Bark is infectious—and there's no known cure. If you're reading this then you're already at risk of contamination. The symptoms will begin to manifest any moment now. There's nothing you can do about it. There's no itching or unfortunate rashes. But you'll become obsessed with his books, from the award-winning collections *Dead Air* and *Stuck on You and Other Prime Cuts*, to cult novels like *The Final Cut* and acclaimed graphic novels such as *Bloodfellas* and *Beyond Lovecraft*.

Soon you'll want to tweet, post, and blog about his work until thousands of others fall under its viral spell. We're afraid there's no way to avoid this—these words contain a power you are hopeless to resist. You're already in their thrall and have from the moment you read this bio. Even now you find yourself itching to read the rest of his work. Don't fight it, embrace the urge, and wear your obsession with pride!

CARSON BUCKINGHAM

Carson Buckingham has been and is a professional paranormal suspense writer, proofreader, editor, reporter, copywriter, technical writer, and comedy writer. Besides writing, she loves to read and garden, though not at the same time. She lives in Kentucky with her wonderful husband and a house full of books and pets, and wishes to take this opportunity to humbly thank you, from the bottom of her heart, for spending your hard-earned money on this book. And if you like her story in this anthology, you might want to try her books *Noble Rot* and *Gothic Revival.*

WELDON BURGE

The founder of Smart Rhino Publications, Weldon is a full-time editor, freelance writer, and publisher. His fiction has appeared in *Suspense Magazine, Futures Mysterious Anthology Magazine, Grim Graffiti, The Edge: Tales of Suspense, Alienskin, Glassfire Magazine*, and other magazines. His stories have also been adapted for podcast presentation by Drabblecast, and have appeared in various anthologies including *Pellucid Lunacy: An Anthology of Psychological Horror, Don't Tread on Me: Tales of Revenge and Retribution, Ghosts and Demons,* and *Something Dark in the Doorway: A Haunted Anthology.* He also often writes author interviews for *Suspense Magazine.*

J. PATRICK CONLON

Patrick is an author and member of the Written Remains Writers Guild. He writes speculative historical fiction as well as contributing to the *All Out Monster Revolt* magazine. While not writing, he spends time with his lovely wife planning the return trip to Dublin that inspired his piece, *The Black Dog of Cabra.*

PATRICK DERRICKSON

A member of the Written Remains Writer's Guild, Patrick has finally found the outlet for the bizarre thoughts chasing one another inside his head. His publishing credits include "The Next King," published in the anthology, *Someone Wicked*; "The Repo Girl," published in *Insidious Assassins*; and "The True Enemy," published in the *All-Out Monster Revolt Magazine*.

PHIL GIUNTA

Phil Giunta's novels include the paranormal mysteries *Testing the Prisoner* and *By Your Side* published by Firebringer Press. His third novel in the same genre is *Like Mother, Like Daughters*. Phil's short stories appear in such anthologies as *Beach Nights* from Cat and Mouse Press, the *ReDeus* mythology series from Crazy 8 Press, and the *Middle of Eternity* speculative fiction series, which he created and edited for Firebringer Press.

As a member of the Greater Lehigh Valley Writers Group (GLVWG), Phil also penned stories and essays for *Write Here, Write Now* and *The Write Connections*, two of the group's annual anthologies. He also served as chairman of the 2015 Write Stuff writers conference in Bethlehem, PA.

GAIL HUSCH

Retired from teaching art history at Goucher College, Gail has written about aspects of American art, including the book *Something Coming: Apocalyptic Expectation and Mid-Nineteenth-Century American Painting*, published by the University Press of New England. In recent years, Gail has turned to fiction, completing *The Button Field*, a novel set in the late nineteenth century based on the real-life disappearance of a student from Mount Holyoke College. Gail's story, "Reckonings," was published in *Someone Wicked: A Written Remains Anthology*.

JACOB JONES-GOLDSTEIN _____

Jacob Jones-Goldstein is a fiction writer and sports blogger. His short story "What Time We Have" was published in *Lovecraftiana Magazine*, and he covers the Philadelphia 76ers for RoundballRev.com. He lives in Delaware with his wife, cats, and maybe a ghost or two. He Trusts the Process.

JENNIFER LORING _____

Jennifer Loring's short fiction has been published widely both online and in print, including the anthologies *Tales from the Lake vol. 1* and *vol. 4* and *Nightscript vol. 4*. Longer work includes the novel *Those of My Kind*, published by Omnium Gatherum, and the novella *Conduits* from Lycan Valley Press. Jenn is a member of the International Thriller Writers (ITW) and the Horror Writers Association (HWA). She holds an MFA in Writing Popular Fiction from Seton Hill University with a concentration in horror fiction and teaches online in SNHU's College of Continuing Education. Jenn lives with her husband in Philadelphia, PA, where they are owned by a turtle and two basset hounds.

JEFF MARKOWITZ _____

Jeff is the author of four mysteries, including three books in the Cassie O'Malley Mystery Series. His most recent novel, the standalone *Death and White Diamonds*, won the Lovey Award for Best Thriller and the David Award for Best Mystery. Jeff spent 40 years creating community-based programs and services for children and adults with autism before retiring to devote more time to writing. Jeff is the President of the New York Chapter of the Mystery Writers of America.

MARIA MASINGTON _____

Maria is a poet, essayist, and short story writer from Wilmington, Delaware. Her poetry has been published in *The News Journal, The Red River Review, Damozel Literary Journal, The Survivor's Review, Wanderings, Currents, The Fox Chase Review, Van Gogh's Ear*, and by the University of Colorado. Her short story "Impresario" appeared in the anthology *Someone Wicked* and her short story "The Triple Mary" is in the anthology *Beach Nights*.

GRAHAM MASTERTON _____

Graham Masterton made his horror debut in 1975 with *The Manitou*, the story of a 300-year-old Native American shaman who is reborn in the present day to take his revenge on the white man. A huge best seller, it was made into a classic movie starring Tony Curtis.

Since then, Graham has written more than 100 novels—horror, thrillers, and historical romances—as well as numerous short stories. Before he took up writing novels, he was editor of *Penthouse* magazine. It was there that he met his late wife Wiescka, who became his agent and sold *The Manitou* in her native Poland even before the collapse of Communism—the first Western horror novel to be published in Poland since the war.

Apart from five *Manitou* novels, Graham has also published the *Rook* series, about a remedial English teacher who recruits his slacker class to fight ill-intentioned ghosts and demons; the *Night Warriors* series, about ordinary people who battle against apocalyptic terrors in their dreams; as well as many other supernatural thrillers, including *Family Portrait, The Pariah*, and *Mirror*.

JANE MILLER

Jane Miller's poetry has appeared in the *Iron Horse Literary Review*, *Summerset Review*, *cahoodaloodaling*, *Mojave River Review*, and *Pittsburgh Poetry Review*, among others. A nominee for Best New Poets and Best of the Net, she received a 2014 grant from the DE Division of the Arts and was a finalist in the 2017 *Red Wheelbarrow* Poetry Contest.

BILLIE SUE MOSIMAN

Billie Sue Mosiman's *Night Cruise* was nominated for the Edgar Award and her novel, *Widow*, was nominated for the Bram Stoker Award for Superior Novel. She's the author of 14 novels and has published more than 160 short stories in various magazines and anthologies. A suspense thriller novelist, she often writes horror short stories. Her latest works include *Frankenstein: Return from the Wastelands*, continuing the saga of Robert Morton from Mary Shelley's classic; *Prison Planet*, a near-future dystopian novella; and the suspense novel *The Grey Matter*. She's been a columnist, reviewer, and writing instructor. She lives in Texas where the sun is too hot for humankind. All of her available works are at Amazon.com.

Her story, "Second Amendment Solution," was published in *Uncommon Assassins*. Billie's story, "The Flenser," appears in *Someone Wicked: A Written Remains Anthology*.

CHANTAL NOORDELOOS

Chantal Noordeloos always wanted to be a mermaid or bard when she was younger, and since she could be neither, writer was the closest thing. She shares her real-life adventures with many of her loved ones, among which are her wacky husband and her daughter, who will one day grow up to be a charismatic supervillain (she already has the mad cackle down).

You wouldn't expect someone who is scared of the dark and who everyone calls 'Noodles' to be a horror writer, yet Chantal has written things that made people want to keep their night-lights on at bedtime. She also dabbles in other genres but is most known for her darker work. At heart, she will always be a storyteller—she enjoys creating new worlds for people to escape to and creating new characters for readers to meet.

JM REINBOLD

Joanne is the author of the DCI Rylan Crowe mystery series, the Director of the Written Remains Writers Guild and the editor of the Written Remains Writers Guild anthologies, *The Cicada's Cry: A Micro Zine of Haiku Poetry*, and the *All-Out Monster Revolt Magazine*. Her short fiction has appeared in *Stories from the Ink Slingers, Zippered Flesh 2, Wanderings, Someone Wicked*, and *Insidious Assassins*. Her poetry has appeared in *Red Fez Magazine, A Haiku Miscellany*, the Haiku Society of America Members' Anthologies, *All-Out Monster Revolt Magazine*, and various other venues.

J. GREGORY SMITH

Best-selling author of the thrillers *A Noble Cause, The Flamekeepers*, and the Paul Chang Mystery series including *Final Price, Legacy of the Dragon*, and *Send in the Clowns*. In addition, he has released a young adult fantasy, *The Crystal Mountain*, and the thriller, *Darwin's Pause* under his own imprint, RedAcre Press. Before writing fiction full time, Greg worked in public relations in Washington, DC; Philadelphia; and Wilmington, Delaware.

JEFF STRAND

Jeff Strand is the four-time Bram Stoker Award-nominated author of such novels as PRESSURE, DWELLER, WOLF HUNT, and SICK HOUSE. Publishers Weekly calls his work "wickedly funny" and Cemetery Dance magazine said, "No author working today comes close to Jeff Strand's perfect mixture of comedy and terror."

SHANNON CONNOR WINWARD

Shannon Connor Winward is the author of the Elgin-Award winning chapbook *Undoing Winter* and winner of the Delaware Division of the Arts 2018 Individual Artist Fellowship in Fiction. Her work has appeared in *Fantasy & Science Fiction, Analog, Pseudopod's Artemis Rising, Pedestal Magazine, Eye to the Telescope, Strange Horizons, Star*Line, Literary Mama* and elsewhere. In between parenting, writing, and other madness, Shannon is also a poetry editor for *Devilfish Review* and founding editor of *Riddled with Arrows*, an online journal dedicated to metafiction, ars poetica, and writing that celebrates the process and product of writing as art.

STEPHANIE M. WYTOVICH

Stephanie M. Wytovich is an American poet, novelist, and essayist. Her work has been showcased in numerous anthologies such as *Gutted: Beautiful Horror Stories, Shadows Over Main Street: An Anthology of Small-Town Lovecraftian Terror, Year's Best Hardcore Horror: Volume 2, The Best Horror of the Year: Volume 8*, as well as many others.

Wytovich is the Poetry Editor for Raw Dog Screaming Press, an adjunct at Western Connecticut State University and Point Park University, and a mentor with Crystal Lake Publishing. She is a member of the Science Fiction Poetry Association, an active member of the Horror Writers Association, and a graduate of Seton Hill University's MFA program for Writing Popular Fiction. Her Bram Stoker Award-winning poetry collection, *Brothel*, earned a home with Raw Dog Screaming Press alongside *Hysteria: A Collection of Madness*, *Mourning Jewelry*, *An Exorcism of Angels*, and *Sheet Music to My Acoustic Nightmare*. Her debut novel, *The Eighth*, is published with Dark Regions Press.

THE COVER ILLUSTRATOR

TOMOKI HAYASAKI _____

Tomoki Hayasaka is a self-taught artist and designer from Sendai Japan. He makes surreal-conceptual art and design.

Tomoki saw the art of Zdzisław Beksiński on the internet in 2009, and got great inspiration from Beksiński's art. Although interested in art, he did not know of surreal artists until this time. His textbook was only the internet, but it sparked his own ambition to create art. Tomoki has been influenced by deviantART artists in particular.

He experienced earthquakes and tsunami in Japan 2011, and saw much death and grief. When experiencing his recent art, think about the theme of "Life and Death."

Tomoki has been involved with many commissioned works from all over the world since 2012, mainly cover and album designs for music, plus logos, posters, and Web art. If interested in his commission work, visit his website at http://www.sheerheart.jp/.

SPECIAL THANKS

We'd like to thank all the wonderful supporters of Smart Rhino Publications. We'd especially like to thank those kind folks who supported us during our Kickstarter campaign for the book, including (in alphabetical order):

Chris Basler
Chris Bauer
Dan Bogart
Austin S. Camacho
Kevin Davis
Eric Dellinger
Tim Eichman
Susan Frey
Stephen Goldstein
Jeremiah Jones-Goldstein
Sharon Lee Harte
Benjamin Hausman
Ashley Hayward
Nadia Heller
Joshua W. Hill
Jennifer Marang
Steve Myers
Christopher Ochs
Anne-Marie Pleau
Mayer Rubin
Robin Smith
Nancie Vuono
Keith Walls

ZIPPERED FLESH:
Tales of Body Enhancements Gone Bad!

In this dark anthology of demented stories, bizarre body enhancements play pivotal roles in the plots—and things are never pretty or pain-free. The 20 stories in this collection are not for those who are faint of heart or squeamish, or who are easily offended by disturbing imagery, bloody violence, and freakish body augmentations. Love chilling tales? You'll savor this anthology!

Michael Bailey * Michael Laimo * Adrienne Jones
Charles Colyott * Christopher Nadeau * Scott Nicholson
J. Gregory Smith * John Shirley * L.L. Soares * Aaron J. French
Graham Masterton * Michael Louis Calvillo * Jezzy Wolfe
Elliott Capon * Armand Rosamilia * Lisa Mannetti
P.I. Barrington * Jonathan Templar * Rob M. Miller
Weldon Burge

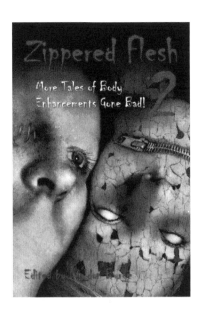

ZIPPERED FLESH 2:
More Tales of Body Enhancements Gone Bad!

So, you loved the first **Zippered Flesh** anthology? Well, here are yet more tales of body enhancements that have gone horribly wrong! Chilling tales by some of the best horror writers today, determined to keep you fearful all night (and maybe even a little skittish during the day).

Bryan Hall * Shaun Meeks * Lisa Mannetti
Carson Buckingham * Christine Morgan
Kate Monroe * Daniel I. Russell * M.L. Roos
Rick Hudson * J.M. Reinbold * E.A. Black
L.L. Soares * Doug Blakeslee * Kealan Patrick Burke
A.P. Sessler * David Benton & W.D. Gagliani
Jonathan Templar * Christian A. Larsen
Shaun Jeffrey * Jezzy Wolfe * Charles Colyott
Michael Bailey

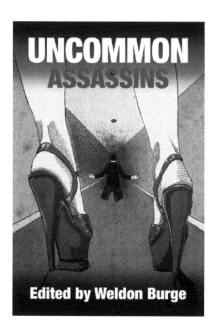

UNCOMMON ASSASSINS

Hired killers. Vigilantes. Executioners. Paid killers or assassins working from a moral or political motivation. You'll find them all in this thrilling anthology. But these are not ordinary killers, not your run-of-the-mill hit men. The emphasis is on the "uncommon" here—unusual characters, unusual situations, and especially unusual means of killing. Here are 23 tales by some of the best suspense/thriller writers today.

Stephen England * J. Gregory Smith * Lisa Mannetti
Ken Goldman * Christine Morgan * Matt Hilton
Billie Sue Mosiman * Ken Bruen * Rob M. Miller
Monica J. O'Rourke * F. Paul Wilson * Joseph Badal
Doug Blakeslee * Elliott Capon * Laura DiSilverio
Michael Bailey * Jame S. Dorr * Jonathan Templar
J. Carson Black * Weldon Burge * Al Boudreau
Charles Coyott * Lynn Mann

INSIDIOUS ASSASSINS

There is a peculiar allure of insidious characters—and especially assassins, hit men, and their ilk. With this fascination with evil characters in mind, Smart Rhino Publications decided to publish this anthology, **Insidious Assassins**, a sequel to **Uncommon Assassins**.

Jack Ketchum * Joe Lansdale * Lisa Mannetti
Carson Buckingham * Christine Morgan *DB Corey
Billie Sue Mosiman * Meghan Arcuri
Austin S. Camacho * J.M. Reinbold
Ernestus Jiminy Chald * L.L. Soares * Doug Blakeslee
Shaun Meeks * Martin Zeigler * James S. Dorr
Adrian Ludens * Joseph Badal * J. Gregory Smith
Patrick Derrickson * Jezzy Wolfe * Doug Rinaldi
Martin Rose * Dennis Lawson

SOMEONE WICKED:
A Written Remains Anthology

Avaricious, cruel, depraved, envious, mean-spirited, vengeful—the wicked have been with us since the beginnings of humankind. You might recognize them and you might not. But make no mistake. When the wicked cross your path, your life will never be the same. Do you know someone wicked? **You will.** The 21 stories in the Someone Wicked anthology were written by the members of the Written Remains Writers Guild and its friends, and was edited by JM Reinbold and Weldon Burge.

Gail Husch * Billie Sue Mosiman * Mike Dunne
Christine Morgan * Ramona DeFelice Long * Russell Reece
* Carson Buckingham * Chantal Noordeloos
Patrick Derrickson * Barbara Ross * JM Reinbold
Shaun Meeks * Liz DeJesus * Doug Blakeslee
Justynn Tyme * Ernestus Jiminy Chald * Weldon Burge
Joseph Badal * Maria Masington * L.L. Soares
Shannon Connor Winward

Made in the USA
Middletown, DE
15 September 2018